Journeys across Niagara

Also by Author D K LeVick
"Bridges—a Tale of Niagara
(2011 Readers Favorites YA General Fiction Silver Award winner)
"Potatoes"
"The Butterfly"
"The Man in the Painting"

Journeys across Niagara

The Flute, the Feather, and the Drum

D. K. LeVick

WestBow
PRESS
A DIVISION OF THOMAS NELSON

WestBow Press books may be ordered through booksellers or by contacting:

WestBow Press
A Division of Thomas Nelson
1663 Liberty Drive
Bloomington, IN 47403
www.westbowpress.com
1-(866) 928-1240

ISBN: 978-1-4497-3239-4 (sc)
ISBN: 978-1-4497-3238-7 (e)

Library of Congress Control Number: 2011961257

Printed in the United States of America

WestBow Press rev. date: 12/28/2011

"... He leadeth me besides the still waters, He restoreth my soul: . . . Yea, though I walk through the valley of the shadow of death, I will fear no evil: for thou art with me . . ." Psalms 23: 2-4 (KJV)

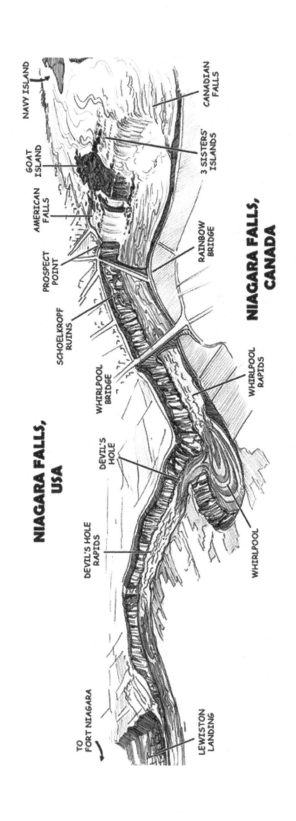

NAVY ISLAND

GOAT ISLAND

CANADIAN FALLS

3 SISTERS' ISLANDS

AMERICAN FALLS

PROSPECT POINT

RAINBOW BRIDGE

NIAGARA FALLS, CANADA

SCHOELKROPF RUINS

WHIRLPOOL BRIDGE

WHIRLPOOL RAPIDS

DEVIL'S HOLE

NIAGARA FALLS, USA

DEVIL'S HOLE RAPIDS

WHIRLPOOL

TO FORT NIAGARA

LEWISTON LANDING

TABLE OF CONTENTS

Prologue   ix

Volume 1 – the Flute   1

The Hermit's Story   28

Henry's Story   53

Volume 2 – Niagara!   101

Volume 3 – the Feather   147

Lizzie's Story   170

Volume 4 – the Drum   247

The Drummer Boy's Story   265

Epilogue   335

Acknowledgement   337

PROLOGUE

Niagara Falls
February 18, 1962

Niagara roared its contempt at the man. Only feet away, the roar of its power spewed over the abyss, pelting his yellow slicker with sheets of stinging ice. Ken ignored it—as much as anything alive could ignore Niagara—remaining focused on rappelling the 180 feet down the face of the gorge. Kicking out from the pillars of ice and twisting around and over jagged stalagmites, he finally touched bottom and stood amid the chaos of millions of gallons of water, crashing into the mountains of rock and ice fused below.

Sheathed in a layer of ice, crackling and crunching with each movement, Ken anchored the rope for the other firefighters' descent down the gorge. *"Fire"-fighters, indeed. What fire? No fire down here mister— only bitter, brutal ice.* Ken thought it ironic that their adversary was ice— frozen water—usually their strongest ally. He thought it even more ironic the ice had fused solid at the bottom of Niagara Falls, spanning the entire river from shore to shore. An "ice bridge," they called it. Weird—and some crazy fools had to go out on this thing and now got themselves stranded out there. *Never fails,* he thought. *There's one in every batch.* Far above him, tourists and residents alike strained against the railings, leaning over and pointing, gesturing in fascination at this unexpected show. The members of the rescue team were professionals who gave no outward attention to the excited faces gaping at them in awe, although deep inside, Ken secretly relished the glory of the moment.

As the rest of the team descended and assembled at the base, Ken forged ahead, picking up the trail. He wasn't sure how many of them there were—three for sure, maybe more. As was to be expected with tourists, witness reports varied, and the tracks in the snow were confusing, going in both directions. Some spectators had said they had seen the violators run off, away from Niagara, disappearing into that maze of ice columns and overhangs off to his right. But did they all run? Needing to be sure, Ken followed the trail away from the maze—toward the maelstrom.

Just ahead, half buried in the ice, something dark stuck out. Pulling it out and turning it over—a glove. There was a hole in the thumb. Running his finger over the frayed ends, a cold chill, not related to the ice around him, spread upwards from his groin as a sense of familiarity worked through his memory. *Kevin's? Naw, it couldn't be, he don't have the guts.* Ken stashed the glove in his coat.

A staccato of popping and cracking noises, sounding like gunshots, broke through the thunder of the Falls. *What was that? Are we being shot at?* He turned, looking back at the team gathered together behind him. They were waving and shouting at him, to no avail; he couldn't hear above the roar of the cataracts.

POW! CRA-A-A-CK! He heard that! The ice trembled under his feet. He felt that! It heaved, buckling upwards, pitching him backwards. Wide, jagged cracks opened, running in directions away from all around him. The ice began sheering off in slabs, rising up from around his feet, like oversized tombstones—five—six—seven feet over his head. Turning to run, he was tossed off balance and fell down hard, his face scraping along the surface, leaving a trail of bright red, defiling the whiteness of the ice.

"Ken! Get back! It's breaking up!" The others were shouting; their voices swallowed by the anger of Niagara. All but one turned, running to the safety of the ropes.

Ken was caught between slabs of shifting ice, shooting him back and forth from one side to the other like a yellow hockey puck. Chunks of ice broke off and rained down on him, hitting his back, cascading off his firefighter's hat, while he ricocheted between splinters of jagged ice peeling off in ribbons around him. A block the size of a car shot straight up behind him and came crashing down, catching his legs, dragging him backwards. Cold, wet fingers reached inside his boots, chilling his spine—the river! The solid world of the ice bridge was being reduced to islands, churning and spinning, breaking into ever smaller pieces. Ice water roiled up behind him, and he slowly was sliding into its cold embrace. He would have been swallowed by the river, if not for a sudden shift in the ice closing the gap, crushing his legs. His screams were swallowed by Niagara as the grinding islands of ice slowly pulled him farther into the murky secrets of Niagara's depths.

"Hang on, Ken! I got ya!" Hands grabbed at him from above as the river pulled at him from below. The last thing Ken remembered before losing consciousness was staring into the determined face of Thomas, shouting words that he couldn't hear, while his strong, black hands pulled him to the light, away from the darkness.

Volume One

the Flute

Chapter 1

The day we decided to go down into the gorge, to walk on the ice bridge of Niagara Falls, started out on an enjoyable note when school was cancelled and a 'snow' day declared. It quickly showed itself as anything but enjoyable, with the ice ball I took square in the face from Chuck during the snowball fight.

The snow had lost its magic. The marvel of the year's first snowfall, transforming our everyday world into a strange and mystical place, had given way to the daily assault from factories, combustion engines, and people changing the pure snow into a sloppy, dirty slush. But I was almost-seventeen, and when you're almost-seventeen, even dirty snow makes good packing. Unfortunately, "good packing" didn't help my aim any, while I was on the receiving end of several well-placed shots.

"Gotcha, Kevin!" Lenny yelled as his snowball grazed my arm.

"Did not! You missed," I shot back, hurling a misdirected missile of dirty snow at him. "That just grazed my coat, didn't touch me . . ." My words were stripped from my throat as the largest, slushiest ice ball ever thrown in Niagara County slammed squarely into my face.

"That touched you, spaz, and didn't just graze your dumb coat, neither!" A savage laugh followed Chuck's declaration of victory.

Searing pain shot through me as icy slivers merged with my flesh, plugging my open mouth and nose, cutting off air flow. The shock of the impact jumbled my senses together in a heap. No longer was I standing in the middle of Eighteenth Street on a cold February morning. Instead, I swirled inside a kaleidoscope of flashing explosions and colors while I faded against a smoldering blackness. My legs became wisps of smoke giving way as I tumbled to the ground. The world flickered in and out between light and darkness, substance and shadows; while the voices around me became the distant drone of insects buzzing a street lamp.

Slowly, the flashing lights and cascading colors began to subside. Along the edges of reason, shapes merged into faces, and the insect buzzing formed bits and pieces of words. Billy's whining voice tethered at the edge of my consciousness. ". . . eez, Chuck, you hit him pretty hard." Billy was the smallest and youngest of our group, having just turned sixteen this month, and he was always whining. I didn't know if he did because he was small or because he had no brothers or sisters, being smothered by his mother. Or maybe he just liked to whine.

"You jerk! We said no faces!" Wayne cursed at Chuck.

"It ain't my fault. How I'd know it'd hit him in the face anyway?"

"You think he's dying?" Billy whimpered.

"He ain't dying, spaz!" yelled Chuck. "It's just a snowball, for crying out loud! He's a candy-ass faker that's all."

"You okay, Kev?" Wayne unbuttoned the front of my heavy coat, apparently to see if a heart beat underneath. The flashing lights and blackness crept away, back to the lair from where they'd come, and my senses returned—all in one gigantic rush. The pounding in my head added to the searing heat slicing through my body. Somewhere, the pain switch got flipped to 'on', and thousands of red-hot needles stabbed into every nerve in my face, lips, nose, even my teeth—each competing for the seat of honor in the chamber of torture. Slowly, my eyes focused through the pain and I saw Wayne's oversized, round head bobbing up and down in front of me, his eyes wide and white, like my Mom's Sunday dinner plates. His hat had fallen off, and the big tuft of hair on the good half of his head stuck out like a patch of briars. The jingle of an ice-cream truck played in my head.

A few years back, Wayne and I had been racing our Schwinns down Porter Avenue when an ice-cream truck came around the corner, playing that annoying jingle it plays over and over. Wayne was knocked clean off his bike. It left him with permanent tire tracks on one side of his head—and that was the "good" side and no hair grew where he'd skidded on the other side. Every time I looked at Wayne's hairless, one-sided head with the Goodyear tattoo poking out, I'd hear that stupid jingle playing in my head over and over.

Now, Wayne's lips were moving, and I heard a muffled droning noise coming from the hole in his mouth. "Kev, hey Kev, you okay? You . . . hey, look guys—his eyes are open!" He had opened the front of my coat and was pressing my rib-cage as he had seen Doctor Kildare do on TV. If he didn't stop, my ribs were going to burst through my back and end up somewhere in China.

"Yeah, they are open!" Billy said. "Hey, Kev, how're you doing? You're not dead, huh?" Even when Billy wasn't whining, he sounded like he was. Lenny kneeled over me and began buttoning my coat back up, while Wayne continued doing his Dr. Kildare imitation.

Wayne, Lenny, and I hung around together all the time. Billy tagged along whenever his mother would let him. He was an okay guy—or he would be if he'd just stop that stinking whining of his all the time. His mom called mine on a regular basis complaining about something or another that happened to Billy that day, and I'd usually end up in the crapper without knowing what for. I visualized Billy, sitting under a bare light bulb at the end of each day, being interrogated by his mother, or maybe he was required to write out a detailed report of the day's events for her to critique and from which she'd mount her phone attack

"I told you he was just faking it." Chuck's accusing words didn't match his nervous tone. His angular, sharp features took shape at the edge of my vision. I couldn't make out his body or any appendages, but his face, hovering like a square helium balloon had "bad-ass" written all over it. A perpetual sneer kept his tight lips from ever being mistaken as a smile. His nose was slightly bent to one side, having been broken at least once in his hard eighteen-going-on-thirty years of living, but for the first time since I'd known this wise-cracking tough guy—he looked worried.

Chuck lived in the projects with his mom and two older brothers. He didn't get along with his brothers very well. His dad was a full-blooded Indian from the Tuscarora Reservation on the escarpment. He'd been sent upriver to Attica a couple of years ago for swiping cars and stripping them down for parts. It was a real sore spot with Chuck. Before he'd left, he had given Chuck a purple arrowhead on a chain, telling him to wear it always, because it was made from the quahog shell, the gift of the "Great Spirit" to *the people* and it would bring him good fortune. Both his brothers had dropped out of school to work and felt Chuck should do the same. Neither Chuck nor his mom agreed.

I think Chuck's mom had her hands full with three rough and tough boys and a husband in prison, but you'd never know it from meeting her. She worked at DiCamillo's bakery over on Pine Avenue and was one of the nicest ladies I've ever met. Whenever I'd go there, she'd always smile and ask me how I was, how my mom was doing, and would sneak me a couple of day-old peanut sticks.

Chuck hung around with us off and on. He was tough for sure, but he was smart too, although he tried to hide that part of himself, almost as if he was ashamed of it. I didn't know why he couldn't be both, a tough-smart guy, but apparently, in his world the two didn't go together.

When he wasn't chumming with us, Chuck hung around with a bunch of punk hoodlums who were always in trouble with the cops. I didn't know what Chuck wanted, but then, neither did he. He never said much and kept himself sealed behind a wall, but now, laying in a pool of icy slush and staring into his green eyes, I saw something behind that wall. What it was, I didn't know—but it was there. I could see it and I could feel it, angry and fuming, like an embarrassing relative locked up in secret, straining to get out.

"Whaa . . . t . . . hap . . . pen . . . ed?" The words slowly scratched from my mouth like one of those old 78 records.

"You candy-asses got creamed, that's what happened!" Chuck lost no time in covering up before anyone saw what I had seen. His quick glance away didn't stop our eyes from locking, and in that fraction of a second time was suspended, and like striking a wooden match in the middle of a dark room, I had visibility. From the fogginess of my mind came crystal clarity and I knew what I didn't know just seconds earlier. The secret inhabitant lurking behind Chuck's wall, who lived and moved in a swirling mist of dark confusion and anger—was fear. A different kind of fear, to be sure; different from the kind I was familiar with. Not the kind where you're afraid to descend into a dark cellar alone at night or afraid of getting your butt kicked by that creep, Mike Wassick. No, those things didn't frighten Chuck. This fear was different. I didn't know how I knew that, but no matter how hard Chuck tried to disguise or hide it, it was as real as Wayne was, kneeling on Eighteenth Street, pushing my rib-cage into China.

Chuck's look told me something else too; he knew that I'd seen what he kept locked up. He knew I saw his fear. Chuck wouldn't like knowing that.

Everyone gathered around, jabbering at the same time. Slowly, I began putting myself together. Spitting grimy ice and gritty water out of my mouth, I got my legs under me and shakily rose to my feet feeling a surge of wooziness as fresh blood rushed through my veins.

As the others argued about hits and misses, Chuck stood off by himself, staring into the snow. Slowly, he turned his head and looked directly at me, and again our eyes locked. This time, there were no secrets; his eyes were hard and mean. "This is a drag," he said. "Let's beat feet and hang over at Ol' Gordy's. Maybe there're some chicks over there."

"Yeah, outta sight! That's what I wanna do, too," Billy said.

Rambling down the street, Wayne and Billy couldn't refrain from firing snowballs at each other. Out of some unspoken truce after my 'incident', they didn't throw any at me. None were thrown at Chuck either, which was out of self-preservation. They had their own traveling snowball fight, knowing that when Chuck or I threw a snowball, it would be okay to throw back—and not until.

Neither of us threw back.

Chapter 2

While most colored folks lived over in Packard Court, Lenny's family moved into our neighborhood—right on our street in fact—just a block down from me. Lenny's a cool guy with a funny way of talking sometimes. We'd laugh at his saying 'heh' all the time, but it didn't seem to bother him, and he knew all the hip groups and songs better than any of us did. He talked a lot about this place called Motown (somewhere near Detroit), where some hot groups called the Miracles and the Supremes and other names like that, were coming from and who were going to be big.

Although we hung around together, I couldn't bring him home because my old man didn't like Lenny (or as he would say, "his kind"). He'd go off on a rant about colored people, calling them awful names. He especially didn't like Lenny and his family, because they had moved right on our street, and he blew a gasket over that.

"What the hell are those people thinking, anyway? Moving here on my street, as if they were decent folks and all. Just 'cause he's some kinda hotshot at the power station don't mean crap to me! Only there 'cause he's black anyway, taking a good job away from decent white folks what he's doing. And a Canadian on top of it! They belong over at Packard Court with the rest of their kind or better yet, back across the river in Canada."

When they had first moved in, I brought Lenny over to the house. Looking at our family photographs, he picked up an old picture frame that had a family heirloom inside—and that's when my old man came home. I introduced Lenny to him, but he wouldn't shake his hand or even say hello. He snatched the frame out of Lenny's hands and began wiping it off as if Lenny's touching it would leave a stain on the glass. I was ashamed and embarrassed for Lenny. He was no sooner out the door when the old man started in on me.

"Why'd you bring that kid here?" he snapped.

"He's my friend, that's why," my anger made me bold.

"Not in my house, he ain't!" his voice boomed. "That little black brat ain't *my* 'friend' and that means he ain't welcome in *my* house; you got that?"

I don't know why he'd get so angry about things. He could be okay when he wanted to, but most times he was stewing over something or another. He'd been in the war from start to finish and had done a lot of dangerous things, like being a paratrooper and getting a bunch of medals for fighting the Japs on some islands called the Negros (maybe that's why he didn't like black people). He was in the first plane of paratroopers who jumped on that island, Corregidor, that MacArthur said he'd return to and he'd gotten wounded a bunch of times. These were neat stories and got him into the Fire Department, where he did exciting things there, too. Once, a house was on fire on the next street over from us, and he was one of the firefighters putting it out. It was cool watching him in his bright yellow raincoat, with that nifty black helmet looking like an oversized baseball cap on backwards. I was proud that he was my old man that day. He was at his best when he was fighting things. It just seemed when there was nothing to fight; he was at his worst.

Silence descended on the house quicker than flipping a switch. The TV boomed out a tinny noise of meaningless chatter. My mom sat in her chair, immersed in watching Lucy doing something on her head with pizza dough that made her look like Casper the Ghost. My mom wasn't laughing. Out of the corner of my eye, I saw my two sisters sneaking upstairs to their room. I glanced at Frank, sitting at the kitchen table staring at the old man with open hostility. No love was lost between my brother and the old man. Frank was a year and a half older than me, and a dozen years madder. He was part of that other gang Chuck hung around with, and he and the old man really got into it at times. I feared something awful was gonna happen one day. Frank carried a switchblade the old man didn't know about, and while I couldn't believe he'd ever pull it, I worried that someday—he just might. Together, they were tinder waiting for a spark.

"Who the hell do you think you are, bringing a nigger into my house?" I stood in silence, staring at him. "You'd better answer me!"

"No one," I mumbled.

"That's right, *no one!* Long as you're in my house, you're a *no one*. You got that, fella? *I* pay the bills around here, mister and the day you pay the bills is the day you can bring your trash in. 'Til then, you do as I say or you get your butt outta here. You got that, *Mr. No One?*"

In all fairness, my old man wasn't a racist. He didn't discriminate in his hatred–he didn't like anybody. In addition to colored people, he didn't like Orientals, Jews, Irish, or Indians. Throw in Catholics and Democrats and just to be fair, he didn't care much for Baptists or Republicans, either. The Pope topped his "Don't Like" hit list, since he considered the Pope to be the anti-Christ. President Kennedy ran a close second because he was Irish, Catholic and a Democrat, all rolled into one, not to mention being from Massachusetts. He didn't even like Ike, who had been the commanding general in the war, saying that MacArthur was the real hero who got screwed over by Ike so that he could be a 'do nothing' president.

Our relatives were on the hit list too; aunts, uncles, grandparents, you name 'em, they're there. And I guess they didn't like him much either, because we didn't see much of them. We had lots of relatives in the area due to our family going back for generations in the Niagara region, although you'd never know it. When I was younger, they used to visit my mom and us all the time, but now, no one ever came over, and we never visited anyone. A couple of years ago, they had a whopping family reunion, right here in Niagara Falls and people came from all over the country. Except us, we didn't go. It was weird, seeing the tent set up over in Hyde Park with our name across the banner and all our relatives from everywhere out there playing games, eating and having a fantastic time, and there we were, sitting at home watching Milton Berle.

I don't know of anyone my old man liked, except for that preacher guy over at the Lazarus Revival Temple in Tonawanda, where he dragged us three times a week. He had some pretty weird ideas about religion and the Bible, always talking about Armageddon and these 'four horsemen' riding around. I didn't like going to the Temple cause they didn't talk a lot about God being good and liking us very much, but were always yelling and shouting about God not liking us and sending everyone to hell to burn forever. I didn't understand it because I thought the Bible was supposed to make you like people more, but it only seemed to make the old man dislike people more. He was always sending someone or another to hell. He believed he was one of the "chosen few" who would be taken up in the clouds any day now in something they called the "rapture." He'd yell and holler at me that if I didn't change my ways I would miss the rapture' and burn in hell too. I didn't know what 'ways' I needed to change. Once, I swiped a candy bar from Ol' Gordy's and that night I couldn't sleep worried about burning in hell for it. The next day I left a nickel on the counter without telling Ol' Gordy. Whatever this rapture' thing was if there was something in it to fight, he'd fit right in. But if not, then I think he was in for a tough time of it. Somehow, I couldn't imagine the old man sitting around in a white robe and a halo, playing the harp. Any white robe he'd wear would have a large red X on the front, and the halo would be covered over by a pointed, white hood.

"I don't ever want to see that kid in this house again, you hear me, fella?" I had turned to leave and was walking up the stairs. "Where you going?" he shouted.

"To my room, I thought you were done."

"I'm done when I say I'm done, not you! You don't walk . . ."

"For crying out loud, Ken, let it go," my mom spoke up from her chair. "He's not going to bring the kid over anymore." I didn't know if she was trying to spare me or was just tired of listening to him, but whatever her motive, it got the same results.

The old man wheeled about in mid-stride, turning on her and waving his arms in agitation. "There you go again! Interrupting me when I'm correcting these brats of yours! That's why they got no respect for me, 'cause you're always butting in, taking their . . ." The picture frame he had snatched from Lenny slipped out of his hands, flew across the room, hitting the floor making a loud cracking noise.

"Son of a bitch! Now look what you've done!" He picked the frame up carefully, cradling it in his hands. A long crack ran across the length of the glass from corner to corner. "This has been in my family for generations, and the first time a nigger touches it, he breaks it!" He turned to me, red and mean looking, "Never again, fella! You hear me? Never again!" Carrying the frame into his bedroom, he slammed the door behind him. I looked over at my mom, who kept her eyes riveted on the TV and wouldn't look at me. I climbed the stairs to my room.

Chapter 3

"Ol' Gordy's" was actually Marty's Market, over in LaSalle. I didn't understand why it was named Marty's instead of Gordy's, but it was a neat place to hang out at all the same. In addition to the *chicks* Chuck was looking for, there were lots of neat things there.

Located on the corner of Niagara Falls Boulevard and Sixty-Ninth Street, it wasn't a large store, but Ol' Gordy had it so jammed full of stuff, it always looked as if it was on the verge of exploding into the streets. On one side, a small meat cooler was set up next to a deli, where he cut lunch meats and cheeses on this super sharp saw. A while back, he had this drop-dead gorgeous chick working there, and one day she wasn't paying attention while slicing salami—she was all excited talking to her girl friend about some "groovy" guy named Eddie—and the tips of two fingers got sliced right off, slick as butter. I hoped "groovy Eddie" was worth it.

In the middle of the store were shelves, packed with dry goods and cans of food stuff. Tucked between the boxes of Arm & Hammer and 20-Mule Team Borax were the latest Topps baseball cards, where I'd been on a hunt for the 'Mick's MVP card.

At the end of an aisle, stacked with boxes of Nabisco Shredded Wheat ("Niagara Falls' own cereal, *ya know*") the tall rack of comic books resided and was where I spent too much time (according to my mom) "studying" Superman and Jughead. It's a two-sided rack, and the back side received the most of my attention. It contained the Classics Illustrated series. These were works of literature made into comic-book form. I liked them a lot and was collecting them all. They also were the source of some decent grades I got in English lit.

Up front, under a row of tall glass jars filled with licorice pipes, Snaps, Mary Janes, and Fire Balls, walled up behind a thick glass case, was a treasure trove of cool things and gadgets. I can't remember a time when I wasn't coveting and saving for something or another inside Ol' Gordy's glass case. Currently, my efforts were focused on the Swiss army knife that had twelve different blades, including a magnifying glass and a pair of fold-out scissors. Sitting next to the knife was a pair of "x-ray see-through glasses." On the package cover was a drawing of a guy wearing them and seeing through the dress of some chick. They're probably phony, but I'd like to give them a try on Janet just the same.

On the same side, down from the glass case, Ol' Gordy somehow had found enough space to squeeze in a counter and bolt some stools to the wooden floor. There, he served coffee and soda pop, along with sandwiches and pie. That's where we were headed.

"Well, now, how are you fellas doing today?" Ol' Gordy asked while we jostled and elbowed one another at the counter. Our bulky winter coats and the spinning of the tattered vinyl stools caused considerable bumping and shoving as we all attempted to get into the same seat at the same time. "Looks like you've gotten into it some, huh? Snowball fight, if I had to guess. Well, now, how about some nice, hot chocolate? Warm you up good after a hard snowball fight, ya know?"

Ol' Gordy had a large round face to go with his large round belly. A crazy mass of hair in various shades of gray and white, stuck out in different directions from his head, like a large cotton candy on a paper cone. Huge blue eyes bulged from behind a pair of thick glasses set in heavy black frames. His face sprouted a colossal, white mustache that trespassed up into his bulbous, red nose and down over his lips. Massive tufts of white hair protruded from both ears, like the stuffing coming out of the scarecrow in *The Wizard of Oz*.

"I'll have a Coke," Chuck blurted out.

"Yeah, me, too," said Billy, "with lots of ice in it."

"Man, what do you want with lots of ice? It's only freezing out, heh?" Lenny asked, scrunching his face.

"I can get what I want, candy ass. What's it to you, anyway?"

"Ain't no candy-ass, man. We kicked your butts, heh?" Lenny retorted, then turning to Ol' Gordy. "I'll have a Coke, too, Mr. Gordy and with a shot of cherry in it, please."

"Yeah, me, too!" cut in Billy. "I meant to say with cherry, too." Cherry Coke was the latest "in" thing (along with French fries swimming in globs of gravy), and Billy regretted missing his chance to show the group how hip he was.

"Got it. Kevin, what'll you have?" Ol' Gordy asked.

That hot chocolate really sounded good, but I heard my mouth saying, "I'll have a cherry Coke, too, with no ice, please." Ice was the last thing I wanted right now. I looked over at Wayne, who hadn't ordered yet. "What are you gonna have, Wayne?"

"Nothing," Wayne answered, too quickly. "I don't want nothing."

"C'mon," chirped Billy, "you gotta have something. You can't just sit there."

"I said I don't want nothing. What's your problem? You can't hear?"

"What's the matter? Mommy didn't give you your allowance today?" sniped Chuck.

"I got money. I just don't want anything that's all. Is that okay with you candy-asses?"

While none of our folks were rolling in money, we all knew that Wayne's dad didn't work much and stood in line for government handouts, so Wayne didn't have much money—or much of anything, for that matter—except second-hand leftovers. Wayne had six brothers and sisters, and he was right in the middle—number four. With three older brothers and three younger sisters, he was at the end of the line for hand-me-downs. I don't think he ever had a new, store-bought piece of clothing in his entire life. He'd joke with me that he should have been born the first girl instead of the last boy, and then he'd have new clothes. Money and clothes were a constant source of embarrassment for him. Any "allowance" he had was either found or a "five-finger discount."

Wayne and I were best buddies, having grown up together. I couldn't remember a time when I didn't know him. He'd had a twin brother named Clarence, who, one Saturday morning—the same summer that Wayne got his head tattooed by the ice-cream truck playing the jingle from hell—got into their old man's booze and drank a whole fifth of Jack Daniel's. I remember watching the priest kneeling beside Clarence on the front lawn, waving a crucifix and beads over him, chanting something called the "last rites" to usher him into the afterlife. At the same time, a medic knelt on the other side of Clarence, attaching tubes and needles and pumping out his stomach, to keep him in this life.

The priest won, and I'll never forget the way my own stomach turned upside down as I watched them put Clarence on a stretcher and pull that white sheet over his gray face, with his eyes all dull like and staring into nothing. Sometimes I wake up at night, sweating, and see Clarence's lifeless eyes staring at me from his gray, pallid face. Wayne was never the same after that. It was a crummy year for Wayne.

Well, you don't leave your best buddy alone in the waters when the sharks are circling. "Hey, Wayne, I still owe you from the last time, don't I?" I asked.

"I said I don't want nothing," Wayne snapped at me. "So don't have a cow about it."

"I know ya did, but I don't want to look like I'm welshing. So do me a favor and have a Coke, even though you don't want one, just so I can even up, okay?"

"C'mon, son," Ol' Gordy said. "I don't have all day, ya know. You having something or not?" Knowingly or unknowingly, Ol' Gordy's timing was perfect.

"Well, okay, but just to even up with Kevin, that's all, and I don't want no cherry Coke." Looking at Ol' Gordy, who was leaning against the counter, taking this all in, Wayne said, "I'll have one of those hot chocolates you talked about Mr. Gordy."

"Okie-dokie! Four cherry Cokes and one hot chocolate, coming right up," Ol' Gordy turned to fill the orders.

"I don't want no cherry Coke, just Coke," Chuck corrected Ol' Gordy.

"Yeah, me, too, I don't want cherry either," Billy blurted.

"All right, then, two regular Cokes, two cherry Cokes, and one hot chocolate. We got it right now, fellas?" He moved down the counter, shaking his head.

"Hot chocolate—what a spaz!" Chuck couldn't control himself while he elbowed Billy, and they both snickered.

Wayne snorted, "An' I suppose a cold Coke in the middle of winter is the 'manly' thing to do. Yeah, right!" Wayne didn't get perturbed by Chuck.

Chapter 4

Whenever we hung out at Ol' Gordy's and weren't debating whether Roger Maris was a better hitter than the Babe had been (n*o argument there, he beat the Babe's home-run record, didn't he?*) Or is a better hitter than the Mick (big argument there) or guessing which chicks were stacked for real and which ones stuffed their bras with socks (*could use those x-ray glasses now*), we argued about Ol' Gordy's wall of pictures.

Behind the counter, above the glasses, cups and coffee urns, in long, straight rows with frame almost touching frame was the neatest collection of Niagara Falls pictures in the whole world. The entire wall was covered with them, except for one spot in the middle, where a polished wooden case with a glass cover was mounted. Inside the case was an old, corroded clarinet. A brass plaque was mounted on the bottom of the case with an engraving that read:

"Eureka—I Have Found It!
SWB I JN 5 6 7 8 FA"

Ol' Gordy didn't play the clarinet, and when we asked him about it, he said he'd gotten it from the same guy who'd sold him Marty's Market years ago. He had told Ol' Gordy he'd found it somewhere when he was only a kid himself, a long time ago.

"Why's it on the wall?" we asked.

"It belongs there, that's why. It's old, don't ya know, part of the history, part of the Falls, it is."

"Why's that? Where'd it come from?"

"The old guy said he found it over on Goat Island someplace."

"What's that saying on the plague for?"

Ol' Gordy pointed to the bell of the old clarinet, "Ya see here? That phrase is carved into the metal right there. Kinda dim and corroded away some, but you can read it for sure."

"What's it mean? Found what? And what do those letters and numbers mean?"

"Don't know, been trying to figure that one out myself now all these years. Most folks think it's a secret code for buried treasure on the Island. Figure out the code and 'Eureka! You found the treasure!' Lots of people have looked for it, too. Just one more mystery of the Falls. Niagara has lots of mysteries ya know." Ol' Gordy liked mysteries about the Falls.

"That's bull, ain't no treasure buried on that old island. Probably some guy's prison number more like it." Chuck ended any speculation while we all laughed.

Most of the pictures were black-and-white or this creepy shade of reddish-brown. A few were in colors, but not normal colors. They were weird, as if someone had gone over them with old paint or colored pencils. There must be a minimum age to qualify for "wall" honors, as there weren't any pictures from our lifetime hanging up there. Most of them weren't like any kind of pictures we knew but were what Ol' Gordy called lithographs and daguerreotypes.

They were in different shapes and sizes, ranging from a few inches to one panoramic shot of both the American and the Horseshoe Falls that was over two feet long. There were square ones, round ones, small ones and tall ones, but regardless of the shape or size, each was inside a rectangular frame made of thin strips of black-painted wood and covered in glass that Ol' Gordy regularly wiped off with his bar towel.

Ol' Gordy was obsessed with Niagara and talked about it with anyone who would listen—and with those who wouldn't, too. He knew everything there was to know about the Falls, especially from back in those "old days," and he steered every discussion back to the times represented by those old, dusty pictures. I enjoyed these talks a lot because even though my dad's family went back for generations in the area, he knew little about it. I didn't know how old Ol' Gordy was (and he was old—past forty for sure), but I knew most of the "old days" in those pictures were long before he walked on the planet, but to listen to him, you'd think he'd taken each picture himself.

Some of them weren't pictures at all but were yellowed newspaper clippings or posters. In one frame, there was a giant five-dollar bill with a picture of the Niagara Suspension Bridge printed on it. I used to think it must have been hard to carry all that giant money around, until one day, Ol' Gordy gave me that "you're dumber than a cold Coke on a winter's day" look and said it wasn't real money, but was a souvenir from the 'old days'.

Next to the phony five-dollar bill was a picture of the real Suspension Bridge with one of those old steam-engine trains chugging across and those old-time people standing at the edge of the gorge. It was a cool picture with this huge plume of smoke and steam billowing out, leaving a long trail behind the powerful engine. You could almost hear the roar.

While the train seemed real, people in those old pictures didn't look real. They looked weird, like my sister's dolls, dressed up in costumes but not actually alive. They were miserable and bored looking. They always wore dark, stuffy-looking clothes, making me wonder if they ever had any fun at all. They stood around, all stiff and doing nothing, waiting for something to happen. I thought it would have been pretty crummy living back in those days and was glad I wasn't born then. I'll bet they never had snowball fights.

Of course, most of the pictures were of the Falls, taken from both the Canadian and the American sides at different angles and views. Some were right at the brink, as if you were there, going over the edge, while others were from behind the Falls, like in the Cave of the Winds. A few were from the deck of the *Maid of the Mist* boat, looking up at the Falls or from someplace high above, looking down on the *Maid of the Mist*, appearing like a speck on the water. We knew the *Maid of the Mist* well. It was always packed full of people in those shiny blue slickers, and it'd ride right up to the very edge of the wall of water coming down. But none of us had ever gone on it; in fact, I didn't know anyone who ever had gone on it. I guess only tourists did. Well, someday I'm gonna go on it and wear one of those shiny blue slickers too.

Chapter 5

The pictures we liked the best (meaning those we argued the most about) were of those daredevils who'd done those bad-ass tricks and stunts over the Falls. While those pictures were exciting, they made us feel cheated because the cops didn't let anyone do cool things like that anymore. All the neat stuff in life has happened before our time and everything's already been invented and done, with nothing left for us to invent or do. I was born in a generation that had nothing to achieve and no mark to leave.

Some of those pictures were of men and women who had gone over the Falls in contraptions they called "barrels" but which usually didn't look anything like a barrel. Just some old fart standing next to some piece of crap he called a barrel, staring at the camera with bug eyes, like a zombie. Big deal—bo-r-ring.

The good ones were of those guys who walked across the gorge on tightropes. Of course, they weren't ropes at all, but were wires (*why didn't they call them "tightwires"?*) And everyone always said those guys walked across Niagara Falls, but I'd never seen a picture of anyone doing that. It was always the gorge they walked across, away from the Falls. No matter, these guys were amazing. They did everything out there on those wires, suspended high over the middle of the gorge with that wild river below them. One guy took a washtub and washed clothes out there. Of course, the king was the famous Blondin, who did tricks no one could ever do. In one picture, he carried a stove across the wire and cooked breakfast, lowering it to people on the *Maid of the Mist* below. In another really cool shot, he carried a guy on his back while walking across the gorge. We could never say enough about that picture, and we argued about it a lot, more about the guy on his back than about Blondin.

"Man, I'd never do that, heh?" Lenny said.

"No crap! Who'd be so dumb as to let some guy carry your butt across the gorge on a rope?" Chuck added with a sneer.

Right on cue, Billy followed Chuck. "Yeah, that'd be nuts. What an idiot!"

"Yeah, you think so? Well, I'd do it." Wayne sometimes said peculiar things that I didn't understand.

"Would not!" barked Chuck. "You'd be so scared you'd piss your pants like a girl, right down Blondin's back."

Wayne didn't respond and only stared ahead at the picture with a distant look in his eyes. The jingle of an ice-cream truck played loud in my mind, and I wondered if there was a tire track on the inside of his head to match the one on the outside.

Ol' Gordy broke the tension by telling us that the guy on Blondin's back was Blondin's manager, and by the time they reached the other side, his hair had turned white. I wondered if he had pissed down Blondin's back.

There was one picture that Chuck didn't like at all. It was a picture of another daredevil walking on a tightrope, just like the others, but that's where the similarities ended. Two things made this picture different from the others. First, each of the daredevil's feet was inside a wooden bucket. As unbelievable as this was, it was the second difference that outraged Chuck to no end—the daredevil was a girl. She wore this funny-looking ballerina skirt, and she had this weird, flat hat on her head, with long curly hair showing underneath it—and each foot was in a wooden bucket.

"Ain't no way any girl could do that!" Chuck snarled every time he looked at it.

"Well, she did," Lenny defended her. "Ol' Gordy said she did it a couple of times, once even with handcuffs on her feet."

"Handcuffs on her feet? How do you put handcuffs on your feet, spaz?" Laughter erupted as Chuck bent over, pretending to put handcuffs over his boots.

"You know what I mean," Lenny muttered, "manacles."

"You can't believe everything that old man says. I don't believe anyone could have done that, not even Blondin. For sure, no sissy-face girl could. That picture's nothing but a fake," Chuck said. "Who knows? Maybe it's really Blondin, dressed up like a girl."

"Well, if that's Blondin, then he sure had some nice legs," Wayne said, and we laughed at that. When Billy realized Chuck wasn't laughing, he quickly stopped.

In truth, some of the pictures were fake. There was one that showed some guy falling off the wire in midair, with his long pole in space below him. We liked that picture a lot and we'd argue at length about what happened when he hit bottom with a heated debate on whether he drowned, got busted up by the river, or was crushed to smithereens on the rocks. Ol' Gordy attempted to kill our enthusiasm by telling us the picture was a lithograph that someone had faked by putting the figure of the guy falling on the "plate" first, then taking the picture with the Falls in the background. But we weren't about to let Ol' Gordy spoil our fun.

Another picture we thought was fake—but which Ol' Gordy swore was real—was of a drawing made in the 1800s. It wasn't a good drawing, being a simple sketch of the Falls, and there wasn't anything in the picture except a tiny figure of a person, right on the brink, suspended in all the water rushing around him. We thought it was a drawing of someone going over the Falls, but Ol' Gordy said the guy was suspended from some boards that were out there. According to Ol' Gordy, the guy used to walk back and forth on those boards, scaring the daylights out of everyone who saw him.

"You think that guy was real, Mr. Gordy?"

"Oh yeah, he was real enough for sure. It's all recorded ya know? Got his grave here."

Chuck didn't buy that line. "Yeah, I'd like to dig it up and see if anyone's in it. Whole thing's bull crap, ya ask me. If it's true, then how'd those boards get there, right at the edge of the Falls anyway without going over? Ain't no boards out there now." I actually agreed with Chuck on this.

"They were part of the old Terrapin walkway back in the 1800's. Not there anymore," Ol' Gordy said as he started brewing a fresh pot of coffee. "He was real enough, fellas—an A-1 nut case for sure, but real all the same he was. Lived on Goat Island all by himself, ya know. Didn't talk to no one, and he died there, too. The Hermit of Niagara is what they called him. Committed suicide, he did. Guess he just finally gave in to the water at the end. Not the first one to do that, ya know. Won't be the last, neither. Falls takes its share of people it does. Kind of spell comes over people when they look into that water for too long. Felt it myself, ya know, more than once, too." Ol' Gordy paused with a full scoop of coffee in mid-air and narrowing his large, bushy eyes, he stared hard at us while issuing a dire warning. "You fellas ever get that feeling ya look away real quick, ya hear? Break that spell, don't let the water take you—it will, if you let it."

*I wondered often abo*ut that strange man Ol' Gordy called the Hermit of Niagara and how he lived alone on Goat Island. Whenever I'd be on the island after that, I'd think about his living there. What had he been looking for, or what was he running away from? Why did he live alone and not like people?

I wondered a lot, too, about what demons drove someone to commit suicide . . .

Chapter 6

The Hermit's Story

Upper Niagara River

1831

Francis Abbott sat in the river, the strong current cutting across his wiry frame like a windstorm shearing a tree. The water was bone-chilling cold, as the last visages of ice flushed out of Lake Erie to ride the swift river. Periodically, a chunk of the frozen lake would slam into him and spin around his torso before continuing its journey to the vast abyss ahead.

Anyone who saw Francis would wonder at his pale upper body, which was in striking contrast to his lower half, where the water sucked the heat from his flesh. They'd wonder more at this strange spectacle of a bearded, nude man sitting in the frigid, turbulent rapids of the Upper Niagara River, only yards away from the brink of the greatest waterfall in the world—calmly playing a clarinet.

He liked sitting above where the water fell off the face of the earth, feeling the surging power beat and pound his body. It was both massaging and punishing, and he relished in both.

There were special spots around the island's shore where he'd bathe, and he'd bathe more than once a day—some days, as many as four and five times. Although, calling it "bathing" was misleading, as cleanliness was not his motivation; he had given up soap and shunned shaving a long time ago. He wasn't sure what the motivation was. He only knew he had to absorb the energy of Niagara, and immersing himself in the bone-chilling water, as close to the brink as possible, gave him the highest absorption.

Reaching these spots was dangerous. One misstep or the slightest slip on the greasy moss-laden stones would cost him his life. He harbored no secret wish to die, and he wasn't challenging death. One occasion was vivid in his memory. It was during a full moon on a cold, windy night the winter before. He had carefully traversed half-way across the turbulent rapids to his special sitting place when a submerged tree branch, shot under his raised foot, slamming into the ankle of his other foot. His leg flew out from under him, putting him at the mercy of the river—a river having no mercy. If not for his extraordinary reflexes and uncanny sense of balance, his life would have ended that night. Tumbling through the rapids, he'd grasped one of the large boulders of the riverbed, and strained with every iota of strength in his sinewy arms, to slowly work himself around and back up into a standing position. Finally, able to relax, with the current pressing him against the boulder, he recovered his composure—before calmly proceeding to his chosen spot in the river.

He sat now in his favorite place, a cascade that lay between the shore of the Isle of Goats and its diminutive neighbor, Moss Island. It was a shallow spot, being only eighteen inches deep, with a flat, stone bottom. In the beginning, it had been slippery and strange-feeling on his bare bottom from the slimy moss growing on it. Over time, the slippery substance had rubbed off, leaving the surface clean and smooth—although his arse had taken on a distinctive shade of green. He'd sit facing the crown, feet wedged firm against a large rock imbedded in the river, providing a solid brace against the crushing tendons of water hammering his back. On those days, when the river carried ice or debris, he'd shift slightly sideways, affording himself a view upriver being vigilant to avoid dangerous collisions. But never could he turn and face full upriver, as without bracing himself, he would be easily swept away into the abyss. Today, with the lake ice breaking up, there was an excessive amount of ice and debris in the river.

Much to his dismay, his sittings had become a spectacle, adding to the circus of distractions that surrounded Niagara. Preferring total nudity, he could do so only under cover of darkness or in secret places, away from curious onlookers. He didn't understand why people were interested in him; he had no interest in them. He wanted only solitude, to be alone with the river and his music. He despised the hoopla and glitz that dirtied the mighty Niagara no different than the ugly, gritty smoke that dirtied his hometown of London, England.

Francis had come to America as a seeker, not as a visitor or a tourist, but as a seeker. Yearning for solitude, he didn't seek solitude, for solitude can be found in many places. Solitude was but the landscape in which to seek. Francis searched for the highest order of truth. He sought the answer to the question that had plagued people for all ages. Francis wanted to know why he existed.

He knew his music held the answer but spoke it in a different language, one he didn't understand. While he heard the messenger, he couldn't grasp the message. He sought to learn the language and thereby understand the message. To do so, he needed peace, to be away from all distractions, unburdened, free to seek and learn.

In England, there had been no peace for Francis. As a child prodigy, hailed at the age of sixteen as the greatest flutist ever, the sounds flowing from his clarinet were the sounds sent down from heaven itself. His clarinet drew them, like honeybees drawn to the flower, drinking the nectar flowing from his horn and nourishing their souls with it. Hundreds jammed into his concerts, elbow rubbing elbow, wall to wall, a sea of humanity, yet in his music each was an island. There, the promise of the Garden was reclaimed, and they reunited with their gods. The deep, soothing notes resonated in the souls of all who heard. He was surrounded by throngs of people from the first waking minutes of every day to the final seconds of every night—agents, directors, musicians, fans, family—a never-ending multitude of people. His soul was swallowed.

There was no solace for Francis; the price was high to give so much to so many and in giving, he could not receive. His was the sacrifice demanded. His soul was offered on the altar of public consumption. Others were filled; he was emptied. Others grew stronger; he grew weaker. Others shed tears of joy; his tears were ones of emptiness. They fed on him, filling their void, finding tranquility, opening their hearts to inner peace and understanding. As they appeased their own starvations, they consumed his joy and Francis withered.

Upon reaching his thirty-first year, Francis was drained and empty. He didn't understand why he played his music and his music suffered for not knowing.

Immediately following his last scheduled performance at the Palais de Garnier in Paris, he made a vow: until he found what he sought, he would never again play his clarinet for people. He'd play only for those who gave as he gave—the trees and the birds would hear his music; the flowers would listen to his soft notes and, in exchange, would open their petals to the world—offerings, given in silent reverence one to the other.

He left the cities and the crowds, who expressed their shock and dismay. Those having a financial interest in Francis quickly turned to anger and resentment. How could he walk out on them? He had no right. How would he survive without them? He needed them. He owed them. Initially hurt by the intensity of their feelings, their betrayals soon served to reinforce his decision to leave.

Stopping in Niagara, Francis had planned on staying only a day to see the mighty cataracts all of Europe was talking about, before moving west to the majestic mountains he'd heard about. That was where he would seek his answers, on the peaks and snow covered pinnacles reaching into the clouds, away from all distractions. But, upon gazing into the mighty cauldron of Niagara, he was enraptured by the water and he stared for hours into the swirling shapes and colors, breathing in the mist, as a monk breathed in the incense of a holy shrine.

He stayed an extra day, then two, feeling the power of the river. He knew to stay for less was to be but a tourist. After a week, he knew what he sought lay secreted within the depths of the water. He would stay to commune with the water and to understand that secret.

Francis was appalled at how quickly the "takers" had converged on the Falls since its discovery. Taverns, hotels, and souvenirs shops had sprouted up on both sides of the river, vying for the best view and location for their own personal greed. They didn't understand that the marvel of the water belonged to no man to take for his own private profit. We are visitors only—and only for a time.

He needed to be away from the peddlers hawking their wares; the self-appointed guides who claimed to know of secret caverns with unique views and worse of all—those wandering visitors who "ooh'ed" and "ahh'ed," and then turned their backs on the very answers they sought. He needed to be away from those who put themselves above the wonder of creation for their own petty gains, trivializing the beauty of life in exchange for a pocketful of silver. Francis wanted to be far from human interaction, far from the blasphemy that intruded on the beauty of the water. He wanted only to play his music for the river and listen to the voice of the water.

That large island in the middle of the river—the one they called the Isle of Goats, sitting right on the brink as part of the precipice itself—knew the secret of the water. The water flowed and surged around it, absorbing the island into its mystery as it slowly eats it away. Shrouded in a veil of fog and spray, that island would be his cathedral and the mist of Niagara would be his holy water as he sought his answers, even if it meant sleeping on the ground.

A narrow, rickety foot bridge crossed the treacherous rapids separating the island from the mainland. Few dared cross it—so unstable was the bridge and so violent were the rapids beneath—mere yards from the cataract's brink. Francis crossed the bridge without hesitation and reveled in the beauty of the island, an untarnished wildness in the middle of this exploited carnival, surrounded by people, yet untouched by people.

Exploring the island, he was amazed to discover a cabin that, other than being waterlogged from the constant mist and overgrown with fauna, was in decent condition and equipped with a table, two chairs and a bed, as if awaiting his arrival. The cabin convinced Francis that it was his destiny to seek his answers in the bosom of Niagara and he would not sleep on the ground.

He settled into the cabin with his belongings. Although a man of means, they were meager. He needed little and wanted less. He had sparse clothing, his long chocolate-colored cloak, a blanket, basic kitchen utensils and toilet articles, writing tablets and pen and ink. He brought no reading materials, as he desired no discourse with humans, either verbal or written. His discourse would be with nature, his music and the water. Of course, Francis brought his clarinet.

He left the island rarely. A spring bubbled up within yards of the cabin, providing clean water, and he also drank of the river itself. On those rare occasions when he ventured into the village for supplies, he spoke to no one, and when others spoke to him, Francis only nodded and quickly moved on. He communicated for the supplies he needed by writing on a chalk slate he hung from around his neck.

During one trip, Francis spied a violin in a shop window. Going inside, he inspected and tested it. He didn't play the violin, but he felt disposed to have it. Perhaps it would reveal the language of music to him. Then again, he wanted no distraction from his purpose.

While pondering this, he noticed a pamphlet perched on a shelf and on its cover was a picture of a clarinet. Examining the pamphlet closely, he read, "The Psalms of David". He tossed it aside having little interest in David's Psalms, when he became aware that a worn black book had been obscured by the pamphlet. Picking it up and looking it over, he realized it was a tattered, old Bible. Francis felt an inclination, like an outside nudge, to purchase the book. He didn't want to. It would only be a distraction from his quest. He harbored no desire to read what others had written, especially some ancient ramblings of secular history and religion that meant nothing to him. The Bible had been extensively used and upon thumbing through the pages, it opened at the book of 1st John.

He left the shop with the violin in one hand and a paper sack in the other.

He soon became the subject of the townspeople's gossip. Who was he? Where had he come from? Why was he here? What was he doing on the island? Why didn't he speak? Was it true he sat in the river above the Falls? As was typical of gossipy people who have many questions and few answers, rumors became perceptions, and perceptions became reality.

"He's a spy from Canada, seeking to turn America back to the Crown."

"He's a victim of betrayed love, seeking his death in the Falls."

"He's a political outcast in hiding, seeking asylum."

"He's a gentleman, seeking investment."

"He's a criminal, seeking refuge."

"He's insane—don't ya know?"

Because he isolated himself on the island and shunned human society, they spoke of him as the Hermit of Niagara.

There was one person with whom Francis conversed, and quite fluently at that—a botanist. He had explored the island extensively. He told Francis the island was unlike any place on earth; it was a natural nursery. Due to its location on the brink of the Falls, it was constantly being bathed with a luxuriant, mineral-enriched mist that caused the native flora to flourish. And the rapids, being of such a treacherous nature, keeping man and beast away for centuries, had kept the island pristine and undefiled. The botanist had been to many lands around the world and nowhere had he seen a greater variety of species in one concentrated area as on the Isle of Goats. The two men would walk and talk for hours about ferns and bushes; orchids and snapdragons; marshland and swampland grasses.

One day, the botanist spied Francis's clarinet on the bed and asked if Francis played the instrument well.

"I do sir."

"Would you be so generous then as to play for me, Francis?" the botanist asked.

"My dear friend, please accept my most humble apologies, as much as it would give me pleasure to play for you, it is with great regret that I cannot for I have taken a vow not to play the clarinet again for man or woman until I have obtained the object of my quest." Then, reaching for his violin, he added, "But I would be honored to play for you on my violin."

"Do you play the violin well also, Francis?"

"I do not, sir."

"Then, you shall not be insulted if I decline your generous offer."

"I shall not be sir."

A stray, but brave, dog followed Francis across the narrow, rickety bridge one day and befriended him, accompanying him on his treks around the island. The first time the dog saw Francis immerse himself into the river, he jumped in after him, landing square on

Francis's back, knocking them both into the swift current. They were almost carried away before Francis wrestled him around and scraping and digging together, they clawed their way out. Back on the shore, crouching on all fours, Francis looked at the dog that had a sheepish look on his face, "You better be sorry dog. You need to grow longer legs and gain a few pounds before you try baptizing me again," he laughed. "I think we're both better off if you stay here next time, ok?"

He called the dog 'John' after that.

The Porter family, who owned the island and had built the cabin and the rickety bridge many years earlier, had also cut a path around the island. Francis and John came to know this path by heart and many times they traveled it together in total darkness. Forging their own trails, they could cross the island to all quarters, easily and quickly, without the aid of light.

From his botanist friend, Francis came to know each specie of tree—hickory, beech, walnut, oak and willow—that grew on the island. He could identify the differences between maidenhair and spleenwort ferns; wild lobelia and meadow rue as well as all the species of flora that flourished on this cherished ground. He knew when the flocks of robins traveled, bringing the first hint of spring, and he reveled in the songs of the red-winged blackbird, the blue jay and the night owl. He welcomed the hammering of the woodpecker, the arrival of the greater and lesser herons, the mallard, the wood duck, and of course, the migration of the Canada Goose.

But it was the water that called to Francis. He found every wading and bathing spot around the island's shores, as well as those of the smaller Moss and Three Sisters islands to the west, where he could stand, sit, or even lie down in the water as it washed over him. He knew each inlet and cascade where the back eddies and currents swirled against the river's flow. He learned where the deep holes hid that could trap him, and where the sharp stones lay in wait to trip him.

He learned the rhythm of the river; its breathing and pulsing. The constant thunder of the Falls, roaring and bellowing its dominance over the land was his orchestra. Always in contact with the water, either through the mist and spray or from emerging himself in the raging river itself, Francis followed his quest.

Playing his clarinet for the river, the notes rose and mixed with the music of the water. He'd play on the far side of the island during the day, sitting in the powerful current, obscured to prying eyes, and he'd play to the mainland side, near the raging rapids, under the cover of darkness. He most enjoyed playing as close to the rim as possible, before it plummeted to the rocks far below.

Sometimes he stayed in the cabin for days on end, writing. He wrote in Latin, and he wrote in music. He wrote all he had learned from the water. He'd play the music that he wrote on his violin. It screeched and squealed, and was painful to the ear—but to Francis it was as pure and beautiful as the notes that flowed from the bell of his clarinet.

When he'd finished writing, no matter the hour, he'd tie his clarinet around his neck and carry his writings to the river. There, removing his clothing and placing them neatly on a rock, he'd enter the water, traverse the powerful current and sit in his favorite spot, the holy of holies. Then, facing the crest of the great Falls, he'd take the sheets he had labored over so diligently and, one by one, tear them into quarters before placing them on the altar of the swift river, giving back to the water that which it had given to him. Following his offering, he'd play his music for the water. The sweetest, purest notes and chords flowed from him. The river took him to a level of creativity that he alone did not possess. The water listened, and the water spoke to Francis.

Off the western side of the island, a long wooden walkway led to the Terrapin Rocks situated like miniature islands at the very edge of the precipice. The walkway had somehow held up to the ice, debris, and force of the river. Only the ultra-brave or a mindless fool would give even a fleeting thought to stepping onto this walkway. One slip on the buttery boards under the racing river was certain death.

Tying his clarinet around his neck, Francis made the journey regularly, Jumping from board to rock and back again. Then standing directly over the brink of the torrent, he'd play his music for the water. People would point to him in amazement—looking like an angel, hovering on the brim of Niagara Falls. They could see that he played his clarinet, but none could hear above the roar of the Falls, and so he did not break his vow.

The walkway ended in a single twelve-foot beam, a scant ten inches wide, extending out through the brink like an accusing finger. Francis walked the length of the beam as if on a Sunday stroll down a country road. Spectators were shocked, often breaking into hysterics. He'd sit on the end of the beam, dangling his legs over the edge, and on occasion, he'd suspend himself off the beam, hanging by his arms and kicking his feet into the roaring maelstrom that spewed and tumbled down past him. Women swooned and fainted while brave men trembled, their knees buckling as they watched Francis casually pull himself back onto the beam with no more concern than if he were rising from his dinner table.

One day, the sheriff was sent to question him about this strange and reckless behavior. As he approached the cabin, he heard music coming from within. He didn't move. Stunned by such sounds, he stood outside and listened. They were sad and sorrowful, yet so sweet and soothing. They flowed into him, opening the deepest corners of a heart that had seen too much ugliness, flooding it with something he had never felt before. He could not remember the last time a tear had run down his hard, leathery face—as one did now.

When the music stopped, he didn't enter the soggy cabin but turned and walked away. When later questioned by the townspeople as to what the hermit had to say about his behavior the sheriff told them that they must be mistaken, the man who lived on the Isle of Goats couldn't be the same man they had seen on the Terrapin rocks.

Francis's one-day visit had stretched into two years, and he now sat in his favorite spot, in the bone-chilling water, for the final time. From the solitude of the island, he had bridged the language of his music and found what few men ever find. He knew why he existed. He would be leaving immediately, returning to London to play for the people.

The water had fulfilled its promise and, in exchange for his music and absolution of body and soul, had shared its secrets with him. He now knew his focus had been wrong, living in response to those around him, had made his life one of living by accident. He had been seeking outside for those things that were not to be found outside. The water had taught him that his peace came from within, not from without. He could control only one person in the entire world, the one person he had known the least about—himself. Once he understood his inner being; he would find peace with himself regardless of the outside. The well that refills is found within. But, the secret to refilling is that it can't be done alone it needs another. There is more to the inner man's purpose than just the inner man. The water and an old, tattered book had shown him the secret to filling that well.

His music had known the answer all along, and he had not understood. While he and the world had listened to the notes and the melody, they had missed the words and the lesson. He was now ready to go back and play his music and share with the world the secrets the water had shared with him. Taking his sharp pen knife, he deeply etched his message of joy into the bell of his clarinet:

"Eureka, I have found it!
SWB I JN 5:6,7,8 FA"

Facing the crest, his feet securely braced against the powerful current, he raised his clarinet to his lips and began playing his goodbye to the water. He thanked it for listening. He thanked it for sharing. He thanked it for showing him the way to peace. He played the sweetest and softest he'd ever played. He played with his heart and his newfound awareness of the inner man. Body, mind, and soul all merged into one vibrant song surpassing any music that had ever flowed from his clarinet. Through the roar of the river, he could not hear his own notes, so he played without feedback and, therefore, without constraint or reservation. He lost himself in the music and merged with the resonance of the river. Their song rose above being music alone and became the essence of life.

Francis bid his farewell to the river.

The large ice floe slammed into his back without warning, driving the clarinet deep into his throat, tearing it open. Instinctively the instrument jerked from his mouth and flew out of his hands, high into the air over his head. He watched in horror as it tumbled down toward the powerful river. Choking on the mixture of the river's water and his own blood, he spun to the side reaching for his clarinet as it struck the surface. Ignoring his burning throat and bleeding mouth, he focused entirely on the clarinet, watching it sink below the surface as the current began carrying it toward the brink. He turned further, facing fully upriver, and as the clarinet sped by, he made one final lunge for it. His fingers brushed the metal and at the same instant the river pushed hard against his midriff, a liquid fist lifting him off his seat, slowly rolling him over. Upside down, his head scraping bottom, he struggled to gain a handhold and found none, clawing desperately at the rocks to halt the forward rush. The water rolled him again and his head broke the surface. Gulping for air, he saw the edge of the precipice directly ahead. He knew now that he could not get out, and so he stopped struggling and let the river have him. His final thought, as he hurled into the abyss below, was how sad it made him never again to play for the people and share with them the water's message. There was a price to be paid, and the river extracted that price.

There would be no farewell.

After a few days of no one seeing the hermit and the townsfolk wondering about him, the sheriff again went to the island to investigate. This time as he approached the cabin, he heard no music—and the door was ajar. Inside, soggy bread sat on the table next to a writing tablet and an open Bible. An old violin with a worn bow stood silently in the corner.

Leafing through the tablet, the sheriff saw many pages were missing, and the remainder of the pages were blank. Glancing at the Bible, he noticed it was open to the book of 1 John Chapter 5. The page looked well worn and smudged. Parts of Verses 6 through 8 had been underlined:

"This is he that came by water and blood . . . not by water only, but by water and blood. And it is the Spirit that beareth witness, because the Spirit is truth . . . . And there are three that bear witness in earth, the Spirit, and the water, and the blood: and these three agree in one."

In the margin, next to verse 8 someone had written:

"Eureka—I have found it!"

Hearing a dog barking in the distance, the sheriff headed toward the sound. Following a worn path that led to the shore, he found the dog at the water's edge next to a pile of clothes neatly folded and stacked on a rock. They were wet and appeared to have been there for some time. The dog stood staring into the river, barking at the water. There was no sign of the hermit.

Francis's body surfaced seven days later at Fort Niagara. They buried him in a grave in Oakwood Cemetery. It was a simple ceremony without fanfare, although the vast number of people who turned out surprised the undertaker. They knew his name from his brief stay at Ebenezer Kelly's Inn, but none knew from where he had come or whom to contact about his death. He was now part of the lore of Niagara, and as such, he had become what he had abhorred, an attraction. He was and would forever be, "the Hermit of Niagara."

Later, alone at the grave site, the sheriff remembered the pure, sweet notes, he had heard when standing outside the soggy cabin, and how they had touched his heart. He was the last person to have heard Francis play his clarinet, and he alone wept for the man who could make the music of the angels.

Chapter 7

"Pretty cold out there today, huh, fellas?" Ol' Gordy chuckled, placing four icy Cokes on the counter. Old folks were always complaining about being cold. Then he set one steaming cup of hot chocolate with a single large, white marshmallow floating on top in front of Wayne. I watched the steam rising and swirling up from Wayne's cup and smelled the rich aroma, so strong I could taste chocolate and I regretted getting the cold cherry Coke. I wished I'd the guts Wayne had to order what I wanted. Glancing at the other faces at the counter who were mesmerized by Wayne's fragrant, steaming cup as well, it was clear I wasn't alone.

"Nah, it's nice out today," Chuck said, "great day for a snowball fight." He sneered at me, hot chocolate not on his mind.

"Humph, I remember when I was a young fella," Ol' Gordy said. "Use' ta go all day, morning ta night, we did—running, sliding, chucking snowballs at anything that moved."

Geez, maybe they did have snowball fights in the old days. I visualized a young Gordy pitching snowballs at a Model T, but no matter how young I made him in my mind, he still had a bushy, white mustache and gigantic tufts of hair protruding from his ears,

"Nowadays I stay indoors and turn up the heat," he went on. "Yup, things change, ya know. Enjoy your winters boys, while the cold is still warm to ya. It won't be that way forever ya know." Ol' Gordy had a faraway look in his eyes and seemed sad, as if he wished he could get into a snowball fight or two.

"Hey, Mr. Gordy, what are all those people doing in that picture there?" I asked.

"Huh? Which one, Kevin?"

"That one there, with all that ice and snow in it—that double picture." I gestured at one of those real old pictures, an odd one that was actually two pictures of the same thing inside of one frame. Each had a rounded top and flat bottom, and they were connected together. It was a picture of a steep hill covered in snow and with those old-time people scattered around. It didn't belong up there on the wall with all those pictures of the Falls.

It reminded me of Chestnut Ridge, where my dad took me sledding one time on my old beat-up American Flyer. They had this tall, green slide there, and for twenty-five cents, you could rent a toboggan and carry it up this steep stairway. Once on the top, you'd set it down in front of this gate, and a guy would get you and your friends all set in it, making sure everyone had their feet tucked in and were holding onto each other real tight. Then he'd pull a lever, and the gate would drop and *zoom!* You'd blast down the slide like a rocket, flying all the way to the bottom of the hill. I stood a long time watching the toboggans shoot out one after another, wishing I could carry a toboggan up that green stairway just one time, but my dad wouldn't pay. I'd like to go there again sometime—with a quarter.

"This one here, Kevin?" Ol' Gordy touched the picture in question.

"Yeah, that's the one, Mr. Gordy. What is that?"

"Why, that's the ice bridge, that's what."

"Ice bridge? What's an ice bridge?" I asked.

"I know what the ice bridge is." Chuck didn't miss a chance. "Everyone knows what the ice bridge is, spaz-o."

"Yeah smart ass, so what's the ice bridge?" I challenged.

"It's a bridge made of ice, that's what, so ice trains can drive over it!" Chuck roared back, and everyone started laughing.

"Yeah, and so snowmen can walk across, too," Billy piled on.

"To go to their ice houses to get warm." Even Lenny got into the fun.

"Not houses—igloos and, not warm or else they'd melt," Chuck added.

There was more laughter as everyone found this new "ice world" entertaining.

"Humph, well here, let's take a look." Ol' Gordy lifted the picture, exposing a faded rectangle on the wall where it had resided, embarrassed by this sudden invasion of privacy. "Well now, this here picture is what's called a stereograph," Ol' Gordy began. "That was a new type of photography back before the turn of the century. Real popular then, ya know. This one here was taken by Mister George Barker somewhere in the 1880's. He was a right popular photographer around these parts then, ya know."

"Why are there two pictures of the same thing?" Lenny asked.

"They're not actually the same, ya know. Look closely, and you can tell they're a little different from each other. Ya see, what you do is to put the stereograph into this special hand viewer they had, and looking through it, it would look like that 3-D stuff. They called it 'stereo' back in the old days."

"That's cool, heh. Can we do that?" Lenny asked.

"Well, sure, but not now. Need one of those viewers, ya do. Don't have one in the store here, but got one back at the house, with a bunch of those stereograph pictures, too. I can bring them in for you fellas to look at."

D. K. LeVick

"That'd be cool. Thanks, Mr. Gordy," Lenny said.

Ol' Gordy laid the picture on the counter. "Now, back when this here picture was taken, it was still legal for people to go out on the ice bridge. Was big business back then. People used to pay to do that, ya know. Came from all over the world to go out on the ice bridge, they did, ya know."

"But what *is* the ice bridge, Mr. Gordy?" I asked again. Ol' Gordy didn't rush things.

"Yeah and why is that picture on the wall? It ain't the Falls," Wayne added.

Ol' Gordy bristled, offended by the insinuation that an infiltrator would be on his wall. "Oh, that most certainly *is* the Falls, fella."

"Where? I don't see it?" Chuck challenged. "I see that ice mountain and those hills with people all over them, but where's the Falls?"

"Oh, it's there right in front of your eyes, it is." Ol' Gordy said. "That 'mountain,' as you call it, why that's Niagara Falls. It's frozen, mostly. That's why they call it an ice bridge ya know." Ol' Gordy was in his element now, enjoying himself as we gathered around the picture, jostling for position to see it better.

"Where are all those people standing then?" I asked.

"On the river, of course," Ol' Gordy answered.

My mouth dropped open, "On the river? How can they be on the river?"

"Cause it's frozen, that's how. It's an ice bridge like I told ya." Ol' Gordy snickered. "Ya see fellas, the ice bridge forms when it's a long, cold winter, and the water freezes out from the shores. The river, swirling around like it does, breaks that ice loose. Then all the ice from Lake Erie coming over the Falls all winter, crashing into each other and piling up down there, the whole mess starts jamming up at the bottom, ya know. With the mist and spray coating everything, sealing

48

it all together, like glue, after a while, there's no river between any of that ice anymore, and there ya go—it's a bridge made of ice, going across the whole river."

"Man, that's cool!" Lenny chimed.

"Not cool—cold! It's an ice bridge, *like I told ya, don't ya know,*" Chuck said mockingly. While Billy laughed and the others stared in shock, I looked at Chuck with disgust for the insult.

Ol' Gordy gave him a long, hard look, but he was more interested in telling us about the ice bridge than in chastising Chuck, so he allowed the offense to pass. He pulled the picture back, wiping off our fingerprints. "In early times, the ice bridge was the only way people could get across, ya know. Some would wait all year for the ice bridge to form, and then do their whole years' business right then and there. Horses, with wagons of goods, went back and forth, just like on a real bridge."

Some guy called to Ol' Gordy then; wanting a halve-pound of salami (I hoped it wasn't "groovy Eddie"). "Course, never knew when it was gonna be gone now, did they?" Ol' Gordy chuckled, moving down to slice salami.

Chapter 8

"Doesn't all that ice stop the river?" Lenny asked when Ol' Gordy returned, wiping salami from his fingers onto his apron. I didn't see any blood or missing finger parts.

"Noooooo, can't stop the river now, can we? Keeps on flowing, sure enough. Ice bridge never stop the river. No bridge gonna stop the river, for sure. Matter of fact, only one time ever, river stopped I know of."

"Really? The river *stopped*?" I asked. "When did that happen?"

"Was back in the 1800s, don't recall the exact year, but it was before the Civil War even, I know that."

"How'd that happen, Mr. Gordy? How'd the river stop? What happened to the Falls?"

"Ice." Ol' Gordy replied absently as he continued wiping the picture. "Happened up at the other end—not down here, ya know. Up by the Buffalo side it was, where Lake Erie empties into the river." He leaned on the counter, getting into his story, "Now Lake Erie's right shallow like, ya know, so it freezes over easy and makes lots of ice all winter. Well, with the water moving and the wind blowing like it does, that ice is always breaking up and moving into the river, ya know. Jams up there—four, five times a winter, it does, no big deal usually." Ol'

Gordy paused to pour himself a cup of steaming coffee that gave off a strong, thick smell, like hot mud. Setting the cup on the counter, he resumed. "Well, this one time a foul wind came along and didn't let that ice move out. Stacked it up tight, making one heck of a dam right across the entire mouth of the river, it did. Shut off all that water from going into the river, sure as turning off a spigot." He took a long swallow of black coffee. I didn't know why old folks liked coffee so much. It didn't have the pizzazz that Coke had and tasted like a mouth full of dirty dishwater, yet they'd drink it all day long. Maybe a shot of cherry would make it drinkable. "Well now, if'n no water coming out of Lake Erie, then ain't no water in the river. An, if'n ain't no water in the river, then there surely ain't no Falls, now is there?" He paused, chuckling, allowing the picture to form in our minds.

"What happened to all the fish in the river?" Lenny asked. Lenny and his father were fond of going behind the old Bedell House on Grand Island to catch bullheads and sheep heads. His question took Ol' Gordy by surprise.

"Why, I don't rightly know, but I guess it must of been okay, 'cause lots of fish out there now, ain't there?"

"How long was it stopped?" I asked.

"Oh, not long, day or so, they couldn't let it go on, ya know. Caused all kinds of trouble, what with flooding and shutting the mills down. No, they had to bust that dam up, quick like."

"How'd they do that?" Wayne asked.

"Dynamite. Few sticks, here and there to blow a couple of holes in it, and then the wind shifted. Wind kept it in—wind let it out. And just like that—instant river again." His large, bushy eyebrows danced at Lenny. "And instant fish again, too, huh, Lenny?" Ol' Gordy laughed, enjoying himself the way only old folks could. "Yup, dynamite opened up that ice jam like a new broom on New Year's Day. River came roaring back. Must have been something to see, ya think, all that water built up in Lake Erie, just a-waiting to rush back down the river?"

How I wish I'd been there to see that. "Could that ever happen again?" I asked hopefully.

"Oh, no, they watch that close now, got those ice-breaker boats up there to keep it busted up all the time now. No, never happen again, it won't. Be a real mess that ever happened today with the power plants and all, ya know."

Geez, everything happened long ago. I wasn't ever gonna see anything in my life. Those old folks got to see everything. No Niagara Falls! Hard to think of 'Niagara' without the 'Falls'. Like having 'Howdy' without 'Doody'. No water? No roar? No mist? An event the world would never see again—the Niagara River without water. What would people think today if that happened now?

I wondered what people thought when it happened then . . .

Chapter 9

Henry's Story

Niagara Falls
1848

"Come on, Henry! Hurry up, or all the good treasures will be taken!" Lawrence yelled. He was already on the riverbed, working his way around the rocks and chunks of ice, poking into and through the crevices and crannies of the river bottom—areas never before exposed to human eyes. It was amazing—the large number of people who had come to the river on this cold winter day. Never had such an outpouring of humanity stood on the Niagara riverbed. But then, never had there been a Niagara riverbed—without a river either.

The strange affair had started the evening before. Lawrence and Henry, being both from Boston, were on "honey-lunacy" with their beautiful brides. "Honey-lunacy" was becoming quite popular and was a far cry from the "wedding night walk" their parents had taken. That tradition ruined many a wedding night, going from one local drinking establishment to another, with the entire entourage of family and friends in tow throughout the evening. By the time the bride and groom were finally alone, if they weren't already incoherent, they were useless. Honey-lunacy put intimacy into the wedding night—after a brief celebration, the couple would wave good-bye to family and friends, and leave together for some secret destination, thus being alone together for that first momentous night and the next few days to follow, without being sick or hung-over. Made perfect sense to Henry, he certainly didn't want his mother-in-law with him and Sam on their wedding night.

Niagara Falls, as the most famous natural wonder in the world, located right in America, coupled with the overnight advances in travel, found itself in the right place at the right time to take advantage of this new craze. It was only a few short years earlier that a trip to Niagara was difficult and dangerous, reachable only by the hardy. Access was over land, traveling through dark forests, across steep ravines and fording numerous rivers by carriage, horseback, or on foot. It made for a long and dangerous journey. Routes were few; roads were bone-jarring and treacherous, and it took days to cover a few miles. Once arrived, the visitor found Niagara offered little in the way of accommodations.

With the opening of the Erie Canal in 1825, all that changed. The advent of the horse-drawn canal boat provided a smooth ride in an eighty-foot yacht, equipped with full ceremony to include food and bar services. The steam locomotive quickly followed, and these advances made Niagara accessible from all corners of the continent. It was a comfortable, catered journey from most of the major travel centers in America to see the greatest wonder of the New World.

Upon arrival, comfortable—even luxurious—accommodations were available and catered to for the tourist. Eateries offered a variety of dishes and specialties; sundry shops had souvenirs, gifts and the arts.

It all came together to make Niagara Falls the number-one destination for newlyweds in North America—and for those in many parts of Europe, as well. Niagara Falls was on its way to becoming the "honey-lunacy" capital of the world.

Lawrence and his bride-to-be, Lizabeth, had originally planned on a June wedding, but unwittingly, Henry and Sam ruined those plans. Recently accepting a commission in the army and receiving orders to be deployed in April to the western frontier, Henry planned to marry his fiancée, Samantha, in March, before heading out west. Once settled, he would send for her to join him. Lawrence, Henry's friend since childhood, had changed his own wedding plans from June to March to have a double-wedding ceremony with Henry and Samantha, followed by combined honey-lunacy at the famous Niagara Falls.

Beth wasn't pleased with Lawrence's changing plans without his consulting her, and she protested vehemently, but Lawrence wouldn't budge. It made Henry feel uncomfortable, and he suggested that Lawrence reconsider. Henry did not want their friendship to stand in the way of Lawrence's wedded bliss.

Rather than this suggestion relieving Lawrence, it seemed to agitate him further and he began twirling his thick mustache. Although Henry didn't follow the common proclivity towards noticeable facial hair and instead was of a clean-shaven disposition, Lawrence made up for both of them. He sported long, bushy sidebars that widened and thickened where they joined a heavy mustache above the corners of his mouth. Not satisfied with that, Lawrence took it to yet another level. On top of this formidable mustache, sat a heavily waxed, fully curved set of perfectly manicured "handlebars"—in effect, a mustache on a mustache. When annoyed or agitated, Lawrence twirled and twisted those handlebars viciously, and at times, it seemed he would pluck the whole thing right off his face.

Now, stroking those exquisite horns, Lawrence bristled at Henry's suggestion. "Do not be alarmed, my dear Henry, this has nothing to do with you and need not be a distraction to your marital happiness. It is nothing more than the opening salvo of the game between man and wife. I shall be the head of this household, and that shall be established early on with Beth."

"My dear Lawrence, it is not my place to advise you or to interfere in your most private relationship with your bride to be, but I hadn't realized you viewed your marriage as a game."

"All of life is a game, Henry, you should know that by now," Lawrence replied and giving the horns one last mighty twist, he added, "and I always play to win."

Knowing Lawrence as he did, Henry had no doubt that Lawrence did indeed play to win, but Henry had his doubts as to whether his friend would win or even if he won, would be a happy player in that game. Then again, with Lawrence it didn't matter if he were happy or not—as winning, not playing, was his pleasure.

After arriving at Niagara, the two couples visited a variety of establishments, touring the shops and crafts that plied their diverse goods and wares. The brides shopped and purchased while the grooms paid and carried. By the end of the day, when they finally arrived back at their hotel, their coach was bursting with packages and parcels.

Henry found it amusing comparing purchases. Beth had acquired a considerable collection of costly jewelry and clothing; in addition to a large number of souvenirs and trinkets. Clearly, she knew how to play her game, too.

Sam, on the other hand, had purchased only a single souvenir plate, and she'd chosen no jewelry, clothing, or trinkets but instead had an assortment of artworks and books. In addition to her being most beautiful, Henry felt his lovely bride was exceptionally intelligent and wisely frugal.

Of course, the artwork was of Niagara Falls, representing various views and perspectives. Some were paintings, while others were black-and-white sketches. Overall, it made for an impressive collection, although there was one that Henry didn't understand—it was overly modest and quite odd.

"What is this, Sam?" He asked, holding up the print.

"Why, that's the 'Hermit of Niagara', Henry."

"The 'Hermit of Niagara'? What's that?"

"Not 'what,' Henry, but 'who.'" Taking the sketch out of his hands, she pointed to a little speck in the center of the drawing at the crest of Niagara. "That's him, right there."

"What's he doing?" Henry asked. "Committing suicide?"

"No, believe it or not, he's hanging there from some timbers! Apparently, he did this quite often. The shopkeeper told me the entire strange story. This fellow was here not many years ago, and no one knows why he was here. He was a recluse on that big island on the Great Falls and, in fact, he did end up committing suicide. He was the talk of the town then and still is today, in many circles. It's quite a story. Would you like to hear it?"

"Why, yes, darling, I would love to," Henry responded as he circled his arms around her lovely, slim waist and nibbled on her earlobe. "I'm all ears."

"Well, you best leave mine alone then, or we'll never get to that story."

"Well, then, maybe 'that' story should wait," Henry replied, pulling her tighter.

"Oh, yes, Henry! 'That' story most definitely should wait." She turned in his arms, bringing her lips to meet with his.

That story waited.

Following dinner, Henry and Sam, in the company of Lawrence and Beth, clutched one another in wonder and awe as they watched the dynamic display of water ripping and roaring through the rapids, plummeting over the periphery and crashing on the monstrous rocks below. They stood at a spectacular vantage point provided by a tip of land protruding right to the very edge of the abyss—called, appropriately, Prospect Point where they could reach down and touch the water just prior to its disappearing over the edge.

As they "oohed" and "ahhed" along with the other tourists, the deafening roar began to mysteriously subside—unnoticeably at first, then predominately—and the flow of water began dwindling. Blocks of ice, which moments before had hurled over the abyss with force and vigor, began bumping and bouncing along the riverbed like tumbleweeds in a desert wind. They got caught and hung up as the river's flow deteriorated, until finally stopping altogether, settling down into a river-less riverbed. The water pouring over the precipice slowed to a stream; then dwindled to a few isolated trickles and the always-present spray that hung like a permanent cloud over Niagara grew smaller and smaller, until it dissipated into nothingness. The water had disappeared.

Niagara Falls . . . was no more!

Sam squeezed Henry's arm in fear. "Henry, what's happened?"

"I don't know" was all he could weakly and ignorantly offer. Around them, people shrieked and screamed. Some dropped to their knees, praying loudly for God to save them. Others wept. Most, being in total confusion, were silent.

And the silence was deafening. Coming so suddenly after the continuous, head-pounding roar of millions of gallons of water each minute, rushing through the shallow rapids, falling hundreds of feet to crash on mountains of stone, the abrupt and total silence that descended on the region was every bit as stunning as the detonation of a thousand cannons. It was painful—as if their ears were caught in a vacuum, being sucked out of their heads. Residents of the area sat up in their beds, awakened from their sleep by the sudden, ominous silence. Many thought the end of the world had come. Indeed, maybe it had.

Throughout the night, they came; first, the sightseers, not sure if this was a trick of some sort. Followed by those who profited from the business of the Great Falls, who knew this was not a trick. Lastly, came the people who lived with Niagara—who knew the rhythms and moods of the river as they knew their own families. They were the most fearful, for this had never occurred before, and they knew not what it meant. They had been awakened, either by the unearthly, eerie silence or by their neighbors in panic, frantically banging on their doors.

They brought lanterns and torches and lined the shores of America and Canada alike, for this was truly an international horror. The omnipotent voice of the river was replaced by the low murmur of voices up and down the waterless riverbed bridging two countries and many peoples, together in fear and confusion.

Time moved slowly as history unfolded, and Lawrence's bride soon grew weary and wished to retire.

Lawrence played his move in the game. "Beth, how can you possibly wish to leave when such an amazing event is unfolding before our eyes?"

"I grow weary of this, Lawrence," she insisted, "and I see not any amazement in this awful thing. I wish to retire and refresh myself for the evening. These dreadful people are frightening me, and I choose not to be here any longer. This is all quite unnatural, and I fear it shall make me indisposed, should I remain further." Beth also played to win.

"Very well then, Lizabeth, you shall retire, and I shall remain to ascertain what has occurred here and to bear witness to what is yet to transpire. Go, if that is your wish. By all means, do not be 'indisposed,'" Lawrence proclaimed, turning his back on his bride as his fingers feverishly worked the large handlebars. "And do not bother to wait up for me, neither."

Beth, not in a forgiving mood, welcomed neither Lawrence's mandate nor his back. The price would be high for the public snub.

"Come Beth, I will travel back with you," Sam offered. "Henry, my love, kiss me good night. Stay and keep company with Lawrence. I shall accompany Beth back for now and will be waiting for you, when you have finished here."

Henry hailed a hack driver, loaded the two brides on board, and gave the driver their destination. While paying the fee, he asked the driver if he had ever borne witness to such an event as was unfolding before their eyes.

"No, m'lord, never have, for sure. Been here since '36 I have, an' I have never seen such a thing. River's never stopped afore, what I know, sir. Don't rightly know what's happening, but I can tell you this, it don't bother me none to be leaving from here and taking your two ladies away from this awfulness."

As the first rays of the sun blazed across the horizon and spread its illumination over the riverbed, a bizarre scene slowly emerged. It was a part cast from a gothic horror novel. The riverbed, devoid of moving water, was alive and moving in a strange and unnatural manner. Chunks of ice were scattered about like giant cotton bolls and pools of water, captured between protruding rocks, spotted the landscape, looking like so many tiny lakes. On the surfaces of these pools, fish jumped and rippled. They were the lucky ones. Outside of the pools, a bounty of fish that had the misfortune of being stranded flopped and jumped in their death throes. There were giant fish, the likes of which Henry had never seen before, looking as if they'd come from some forgotten, prehistoric age. Others lay still, having already succumbed to their unexpected and sudden fate. Huge turtles strode about, not knowing what to do.

With the rising sun giving light to see upriver, the brave began venturing forth onto the river bottom. As spectators saw them walking about, more followed, to walk on ground never before trod upon by a human foot.

People began filling baskets with smaller fish; others carried off the giant turtles and monster fish, some over ten feet in length, with strange bumpy ridges running down their backs. Lawrence's blood ran hot with excitement as they watched someone poking into an exposed crevice and hold up what appeared to be a sword. He realized this was, literally, a once-in-a-lifetime opportunity that had been handed to them, by either the Lord above or the Fates below. Yelling out his invitation for Henry to join him, he ran onto the riverbed in search of treasures. Cautiously, Henry followed, stepping onto the riverbed and began carefully prying and poking around in the rocks and crannies.

But finding treasures was not an easy task. The wet rocks and stones, having been exposed to the cold winter air all night, had quickly frozen over with a combination of slushy mud and slimy moss that filled crevice and cranny. The river's current would have carried most objects over the brink, so what artifacts remained were wedged in rocks and openings where they had been held fast against the swift river. Now, they were buried under the slushy goo, coated with silt, mud, and scale. Henry thought that farther up the riverbed, where the river was deeper, and the current less fierce, would be a better opportunity for treasures.

"Henry! Look what I found!" Lawrence held up a stick that was wide at one end.

"What is it Lawrence?" Henry called back.

"It's a tomahawk, Henry, from Indians." Lawrence shouted, rubbing off the goo.

An old man, not more than a few feet away from Henry, who had been struggling with a horrid-looking fish over four feet long, having rows of sharp, nasty teeth lining its enormous mouth, gave a cry of joy as he dropped the fish, reached down, and pulled on a long rod sticking out of the rocks. As it came loose, Henry saw that one end was flat. The old man wiped it off, "Well, lookie har. This'n be a rifle now, won't it? Fr'm that thar war some yers back; wid them there Brits, I'd say, hey Sonny?"

Henry cursed under his breath, knowing he would have found the rifle if that old man hadn't been messing with that ugly fish right there. He continued probing and prying, coming up empty each time. Finally, Henry spied a smooth rod lying in a dormant pool. Hoping for a rifle too, he eagerly reached in and grabbed it in anticipation. A shrieking scream exploded from his lips as the "rifle barrel" became a living, slithering eel. He dropped the slimy creature in terror and revulsion, feeling both angry and foolish. The old man bellowed an obscene laugh and trotted off with both his prizes.

"Henry! Look what I found now!" Lawrence called, holding up what looked like an old bayonet.

Rather than risk grabbing another unwelcome surprise, Henry picked up a tree branch to use for probing, and he continued his treasure hunt throughout the morning, searching for something to take back to Sam. He found nothing.

While Henry had not found treasures to bring back to his lovely bride, he had witnessed the most incredible sights. First, a man drove a team of horses onto the riverbed, right up to the very edge of the barren Horseshoe Falls. He cut up some timbers that were embedded there and casually loaded them onto his wagon. Henry watched in disbelief while the man went about this business as if it were his daily routine, instead of something that couldn't have been in his wildest dreams when he'd lain down to bed last night. Henry recalled the sketch that Sam had purchased of that hermit fellow and wondered if these were the timbers he was supposed to have played on. He couldn't wait to tell Sam.

Next, a squadron of horse soldiers came riding down the middle of the slushy riverbed. Everyone scurried out of the soldiers path as they trotted around the riverbed rocks and crannies. Henry watched in awe as they made the turn to ride back to wherever they had come from. Were they protecting the border, or were they simply out having a joy ride? He knew not, but he felt an immense pride, knowing soon he would lead such a command himself on the western frontier.

Church bells tolled all day from the City of the Falls and communities and settlements around the area. Were they tolling to mark the event—or to warn of it? The tolling should have instilled a sense of calmness into this suddenly upside-down world, but instead, the bells sounded lost and furlong, adding to the desperation in the air.

In the afternoon, a large group of the faithful, believing this was a sign from above that the world is on the brink of destruction, assembled on the shore, singing hymns and praying loudly. A tall man, wearing a long black frock and a flat black hat with a wide, straight brim, stood and preached in a sharp, accusing voice. The end of creation had arrived he shrieked, and all needed to repent, begging for forgiveness and mercy; while they still had the chance to do so. Soon hellfire and brimstone would rain down from above on the ungodly. Many fell to their knees, raising their arms and crying out to the heavens to save them.

Henry wasn't sure from what.

Henry didn't venture too far from the large island just off the mainland. Called Goat Island, it earlier had been accessible only by a narrow, rickety bridge that crossed those same wild rapids they had oohed and ahhed about during the night. Now, there were no rapids and no need for a bridge. While others wandered across the entire width of the riverbed, Henry moved more toward the edge of the wide canyon. This was probably why he didn't find any treasures, as anything that had made it this far in the racing waters would certainly have been swept over the brink to the pit below. At the base of the Falls, an encyclopedia of history would be found.

He explored the edge of the famed precipice extensively and looked down at the massive boulders and jagged rocks protruding out of the deep, still waters below. Henry could only imagine what would have happened to anyone, like that hermit fellow, who had suffered going over the crest. Viewing the base of the ridge from above, Henry felt like the mythological gods looking down from Mount Olympus upon the tops of the mountains and oceans of the earth.

He was standing thus, at the very edge, when he felt a slight quivering under his feet. Turning to look upriver, he saw people running and scrambling toward the shorelines. A cry went up as people panicked, shouting to one another to run quickly. The vibration did not pass but continued and grew stronger. It was now a tremor that moved upwards from his legs into his torso. Henry began running back to Goat Island and away from the edge of the canyon, with its sheer drop to certain death. Approaching the island, he looked upriver again and saw a sight that made his blood freeze. On the horizon of the barren riverbed was a living wall of water and ice, moving with considerable speed and force, headed directly at the abyss—and him. He ran as hard and as fast as his legs would carry him.

He was within a mere ten feet or so of the island; when his tightly laced boot caught under a stout, thick stick wedged between two rocks. Going down hard on his side, his foot firmly snagged underneath; an involuntary scream escaped his lips for the second time that day. This time from the pain shooting through his ankle as it twisted in a way his ankle was not designed to twist in. Sitting in a puddle of slushy cold water, Henry tried to pull his foot out from under the stick. It wouldn't budge with only his top hat becoming dislodged, landing in a pool of rippling water. He could now feel the whole riverbed shaking and trembling, and it sent shivers throughout his body. Water flooded over his foot, soaking his pants. The trickling streams around him grew in intensity and size as the surge of ice and water sped closer, pushing latent pools ahead of it. His hat floated off toward the canyon.

In desperation, Henry grabbed at the stick, jerking on it with both hands. The water rose, covering his hands, moving rapidly across them. He looked up and saw that the massive wall of water had progressed with frightening speed and was now a mere hundred feet in front of him. It came at him with a fierce viciousness and determination, led by a host of icebergs.

"Dear God help me!" He yelled and with a final desperate pull on the wedged stick, it broke loose from the rocks, freeing his foot. Immediately, he struggled to his feet. Splashing through the water, he reached out his arm toward an overhanging tree limb. Swinging his arm across the limb, like a hook, the stick flew from his hand, landing on the shore of the island, just as the first surge of ice and water hit him with full force. The impact threw his body hard to the side as chunks of ice bounced off his swinging torso. But Henry held fast to the limb; the limb held fast to the tree; and the tree held fast to the island; as water and ice surged over and punished him. After the frontal wave passed over him, the intensity and volume lessened, allowing him to pull himself along the length of the tree limb, hand over hand, until his foot touched the edge of the island and he was on solid ground.

Lying exhausted and bruised, Henry watched as the surge shot out into the open air over the abyss before dropping off and plunging to the boulders below—boulders that, just seconds before, he had been admiring as if he were Zeus.

Niagara had returned! And it had taken mere seconds.

What happened? He didn't know. Maybe the repentant congregation had indeed prayed the water back. It was clear from the way they were praising God and rejoicing over on the mainland that they certainly believed they'd done exactly that, although now the river's voice had reclaimed its dominance, making it impossible to hear them. The man in the black frock and flat black hat was standing with arms spread wide, raised to the heavens, a Bible in one hand, a cross in the other and a self-serving smile on his face, while his flock surrounded him on their knees. Whether he had prayed the waters back or not, his church coffers would surely benefit.

Knowing, in his heart, that God had answered his cry for help on the riverbed, Henry felt contempt for that use of God for such self-serving purposes.

As Henry slowly stood, testing his wobbling legs, he spied the stick that had tripped him. He picked it up, as his only relic of the extraordinary events he had witnessed and his near-death encounter with the mighty Niagara. He began limping around the tip of the island toward the mainland, even as other people wandered and milled about in all directions. Both on the island and the mainland, they shouted at one another amid the confusion. Some were wet, some were dry—all were in shock.

Approaching the rickety bridge connecting the island to the mainland, the rapids underneath once again boiled and surged as they did when he and Sam had stood admiring the water hours earlier. Only now, Henry was on the other side of those rapids. People were lined up to cross over the frightening bridge, expressing much fear, having no choice but to confront it. They moved slowly across, one person at a time, their worst nightmare now a reality.

Henry finally crossed to the mainland, where Lawrence waited for him. He expressed relief that Henry was safe, but he also was concerned about Henry's injured ankle and muddied, wet clothing. Together, they reviewed the remarkable escapade and the events that had unfolded.

"What do you think happened, Henry? Why did the water stop, and why did it start again?"

"I don't know. Perhaps, as so many are saying, it was a sign from God."

"A sign? From God? For what purpose, Henry? No, I am not inclined to believe that, with the whole universe to manage, God has nothing better to do than to play tricks on us mortals, turning rivers on and off like so many spigots. There is indeed a plausible explanation, for this strange occurrence we have witnessed and which you have had the excellent fortune to survive. We just do not know what it is at this time. I do not believe that every act of nature we don't understand is a divine intervention of God. That is nothing more than an easy way to avoid thinking about things we don't comprehend, Henry."

"Yes, I'm sure you are right, Lawrence. There is a logical explanation for this event, but I am mystified as to where the water went during all that time. It had to have gone somewhere, had it not?"

"I think you seen where it went, when it came charging down upon you, Henry!"

Lawrence had considerable success on the riverbed, acquiring a respectable collection of treasures. In addition to the tomahawk and bayonet, he had found a long trident spearhead that had five barbed points on it; a knife that was in remarkable condition; and, most impressive of all, the remnants of an Indian breastplate that was resplendent with colored beads and medallions, once the frozen moss was wiped away. "What did you find, Henry?" Lawrence asked.

"Nothing," Henry replied with a mixture of embarrassment and indifference, holding up the mud—and scale—encrusted stick. "I have only this stick that almost cost me my life."

"I wouldn't keep it if I were you, Henry. Almost killed you, bad luck to hang on to that thing."

"I should keep it as a remembrance of God's mercy in saving me."

"God's mercy didn't put the stick there, Henry. If you believe God saved you, that's fine, but that stick has no mercy or anything else of good in it; it's cursed, get rid of it, Henry." Lawrence said and grabbing the stick out of Henry's hand, he flung it away.

"Lawrence! You have no right!" Henry watched the thick, scale-encrusted stick fall into a large crevice between two rocks lining the shore of the Island. Giving Lawrence a disgusted look, he turned to go and retrieve the stick, but his ankle gave out under him and he went down hard.

"Henry! Here, let me help you. See, I told you it's cursed, now let it go. We need to get you to a doctor for that ankle."

"I don't know about it being cursed, Lawrence, but you're probably right there's no reason to hang onto it. I'm going to find that man who cut up those boards out there and buy a piece of that wood to make Sam a frame for that picture she has of that hermit fellow. Be special for her to have the actual wood he played on to go with the picture."

"What hermit fellow is that, Henry?"

"Oh, just some silly tale Sam picked up in town is all."

Chapter 10

1883

It was many years later, that two young boys, exploring along the shoreline of Goat Island, were tossing sticks into the river and watching them hurl out over the brink. One of them pried a thick stick from between two rocks and was about to fling it into the river, when a piece of the brittle outer crust broke off in his hand. He felt a touch of metal underneath.

"Hey, Teddy, look it here. This stick is metal." He began breaking off the hardened crust, uncovering holes that ran along one side and corroded knobs of metal, which had felt like knots on the wood when it was covered with the crust. "Gee, I think it's some kind of music thing."

"Yeah? Let me see, Marty." Taking the stick, Teddy continued breaking off the rest of the crust, revealing the wide end. "Yeah, look here! It's a flute or something like that! And it's an old one, too." He continued to rub the hard coating off. "It's really corroded in some parts, but some of it ain't too bad. This area here is pretty good, where the bell end is. I think that hard coating on it might have protected it. Gee, I wonder how long it's been here and where it came from?"

Marty took it back from Teddy and continued cleaning and polishing the instrument, rinsing it in the river and rubbing it with his shirttail. What were left of the levers were just corroded lumps and the holes had enlarged over time, but on the bottom side of the bell, under a hard shell of scale, was some etching in the metal. "Look, Teddy, there's writing on this side."

"Yeah? Can you tell what it says?"

"I don't know, it's faded, but I they're letters and numbers for sure. This could be an 'E' . . . or an 'F,' and this one here could be anything, maybe a 'B.' Yeah, I think that's it—'B, E, or 'F A', and there's a '5' and this one, I think is an '8'."

"What's it say? Can you tell?" Teddy said.

"I don't know yet, there's more. Hold your horses, let me clean it some more." Marty said as he continued rubbing and polishing the corroded writing in the water. "It's two lines and some kind of saying."

After rubbing and studying the script for some time, Marty finally said, "Some of the letters I have to guess at, but I think it says 'Eureka! I have found it!'."

"Gee, what does that mean?" Teddy asked. "What did he find?"

"I don't know what he found, but he lost this flute looking for it."

"What's the other line say?"

"It's some kind of code, I think. 8 maybe, W, E, I, T ? N, 5, 6, 7, 3, E or F A'.

"Maybe he found hidden treasure on the Island, and that's a secret code to where it's hid."

"Yeah! Maybe it's still there!"

"But, is that where he found it or buried it?"

"Gee, it must be a valuable treasure to crave it in his flute like this."

Chapter 11

"No, nothing gonna stop that river, boys. Ice bridge surely won't. River just keeps on flowing as if that ice weren't even there. Flowing underneath, ya know. Ain't no different than any other bridge." Ol' Gordy looked at us, his bushy eyebrows exploding out from behind his black eyeglasses frames. "Rainbow Bridge doesn't stop that river now, does it? Well, be the same with the ice bridge. Whether be steel or ice, they're both bridges, and the river keeps right on flowing underneath them, surely does."

"Man!" Lenny exclaimed. "All those people are standing on the river, and they don't fall through the ice?"

"No, ice be plenty thick and strong, ya know? Like I say, they used to take horses and wagons back and forth all day." He paused and chuckled, "Well, until it broke up, that is."

"So you're saying that mountain is the Falls?" Chuck questioned.

"Not what I'm *saying*—what *is*. That's the Falls right there in the middle, and off to the side is the gorge, all iced over. Picture don't lie ya know."

Looking at the picture from this new perspective, our awe and respect for the ice bridge increased. It was taken from the bottom of the Falls, where the river should be, looking up to the brink of the Falls.

And now that we knew what it was, we could see the mountain was indeed Niagara Falls. To the left was the side of the gorge; completely encased in rings of giant icicles with columns of dark, rippled ice lined up like frozen sentries, guarding the waterfall. This ice didn't look like any ice I knew—it was mean-looking, hard, and unapproachable. We could easily have been looking at a picture of the North Pole from the *National Geographic* magazine. Along the top edge of this ice fortress were tiny black specks that we realized, when we looked at it carefully, were people lined up along the brink of the Falls.

Unlike all the other pictures showing the Falls plummeting into the river below, in these pictures—there was no river below. Knolls and ridges of snow appeared where the river should have been. Directly in front of the 'mountain' was that massive hill, reminding me of Chestnut Ridge. Scattered about all these hills, in groups or by themselves, were hundreds of people; those old-time people—dark and stiff. Even as silhouettes you could see that they were dressed up in top hats, overcoats, and gowns. They appeared to be frozen, more like black ice than people, as they stood around, doing nothing, waiting for something to happen.

Ol' Gordy leaned on the counter top, talking in that grown-up voice the old folks used whenever they thought they were spewing out wisdom. "Good for business during the winter months, it was, with not much else happening here. Had special trains running from all over bringing folks to Niagara, just to go on the ice bridge. They couldn't get out on the ice everyday cause of the weather and all, so they might wait a week before they'd get to go out. The hotel owners hired locals to create paths and build bridges going down into the gorge for the people staying in their hotels. Then, when the weather was balmy, they'd come out in droves. Hawkers would set up their shops right out in the middle of the ice. Weren't much more than shacks with tar-paper roofs, but they did a right, good business and avoided paying taxes, ya know. They'd sell all kinds of trinkets and things out there on the ice. Some time there were over ten thousand people on the ice."

"Ten thousand people! Out on the river at one time? You're kidding, right?" I asked.

"No, I'm not kidding." Ol' Gordy riled at the idea that he'd joke about the Falls. "Like I've been trying to tell ya, this was big business with people coming from all over the world. It was a prized trophy to have your picture taken while standing out there on the ice, ya know." His face contorted into his 'I don't kid about the Falls' scowl, as he hefted his coffee cup. "Funny thing is, most pictures of them folks being on the ice were taken in the hotels with a phony background and not out on the ice at all."

"Yeah? Why's that?" Chuck asked.

"Too cold out on the ice for the gentile folks, ya know." Ol' Gordy chuckled.

Chapter 12

"Have you ever seen the ice bridge, Mr. Gordy?"

"Oh sure, ain't unusual, ya know. Happens most years unless it's a mild winter, and we don't get many of them around here now, do we?" He paused and thought for a second, then said, "Although they don't seem to get as big as they did back in those old days. Probably cause of the power stations and all, sucking the water off like they do. But nature still does what it does now, ya know. Can't stop Mother Nature now, can we?"

So, those pictures were 'the old days' to Mr. Gordy, too.

"Matter of fact, got one down there right now, ya know. Good one, too. Biggest one we've had in years, it is." As he nodded his shaggy head, I couldn't help but stare at the tufts of hair sticking out of Ol' Gordy's ears as they bobbed up and down. He paused and seemed to be deep in thought and then said, "Ya know, it was the bootleggers who had the best thing going with the ice bridge, though."

"Bootleggers? What's a bootlegger?" Billy asked

"Whiskey runners," Ol' Gordy quickly answered. "You know— smugglers." Ol' Gordy shook his head in that adult way. "This was back in those days it was against the law to drink."

"It was against the law to drink? How come?" Lenny asked.

"Nothing new about that, fella, been lots of laws against drinking, ya know," Ol' Gordy said with an edge to his voice that I hadn't heard before. Looking at us, he must have seen the veil of confusion on our faces. "I'm talking about liquor guys—booze—whiskey. You know—drinking. Most womenfolk didn't like a man to drink a'tall back then. When I was a lad, they called it Prohibition. Totally against the law, it was then, ya know. Caused all kinds of trouble, it did, too. Speakeasies, gangsters running around and more popular than movie stars they were. Crazy times, ya know. Makes good movies and all, but doesn't work worth a hill of beans, makes a man be outside the law just to have a drink at the end of a hard day. Now you tell me, what kinda sense does that make. Even before the Prohibition, there were laws against it. Cops raiding one place or another, making all sorts of trouble for a man, just to have himself a little taste." He shook his head back and forth, and his lips tightened into a thin, hard line under the overgrown mustache. "Don't know why folks just can't let other folks be. Always gotta be trying to tell everyone else how to live."

Wow! Ol' Gordy thought that, too? We thought we were the only ones who knew that. We nodded our heads up and down in support of this sage wisdom.

"Well, lots of folks still wanted to have themselves a drink, every now and then, whether the law said a fella could or not, ya know. And, as is the case always gonna be, if'n someone wants something, there's gonna be them that'll provide for it. Well, those days they called those folks whiskey runners and bootleggers."

"Yeah, we know all about that, but what does it have to do with this ice bridge thing anyway?" Chuck didn't see the connection, neither did I.

"Hold your horses, fella, I'm getting to it." Ol' Gordy wasn't about to be hurried when he had the floor. "Now, each winter when the ice started setting up down there, the whiskey runners built up their stock of booze, getting ready for the run, ya know. Well, soon as the bridge was formed, they'd drag out their shanties right smack in the middle of the river and just like that—the run was on." He finished his coffee and a forlorn look came over his face, reliving some secret from years past. "Oh, yeah, it was. People come a-running from both sides of the river they did." Ol' Gordy poured himself another cup of the black smelly stuff, and I wondered if, in his mind, he was pouring himself a cup of bootleg whiskey.

"I don't get it." Billy said. "What were they running for?"

"Well, for the whiskey, of course—cause of the border," snapped Ol' Gordy. Our blank looks and scrunched-up faces showed we didn't have the foggiest idea of what he was talking about. "You know—the border. Runs smack down the middle of the river, 'tween the U. S. of A. and Canada."

Oh, *that* border. "Yeah, I know, the dividing line between us and Canada." The words blurted out of my mouth before I could stop myself.

Chuck snickered at me. "What a spaz," he mumbled.

"Yup, that's the border all right Kevin, and the booze flowed across the ice bridge faster than the water flowed over the Falls—and nobody could touch 'em. That were the beauty of it ya see."

"Touch who?" This story wasn't getting any clearer.

"Well, the bootleggers, of course." His frustration showed as we stared at him with vacant faces. "Listen I told ya, it was against the law to be selling the drink. Even when it was legal, there were so many licenses, fees, and taxes, it just made it impossible for a man to get himself a little sip and the Federals went after anyone who didn't play by their rules, see? So the bootleggers would set up shop on the ice, right smack in the middle of the river. When the cops came to arrest them—if'n they were the American police, the bootleggers would say they were in Canada, and if they were the Mounties, then they'd say they were in America." Ol' Gordy chuckled. "Cops didn't know what to do. Who knew where the border was out there?" He relished another deep swallow of his coffee-whiskey with a smile at the corner of his mouth. It was strange to hear one of the old folks enjoying getting the better of the cops. Old folks and cops usually went together, like cherry and Coke.

"Even if they arrested them, their lawyers tied up the case in the courts until the ice bridge broke up and disappeared. Then, for sure, no one knew which side of the border they'd been on. The courts got all balled up as to whom had jurisdiction, so the cases got dismissed and they be off clean as a whistle." He chuckled, revealing an Ol' Gordy, we'd never seen before.

"It was a beautiful thing, don't ya know." He had a twinkle in his eye as he took another swig of his coffee-whiskey, revealing how much he liked the "beautiful thing" or how much he liked having a *taste* now and then—or maybe both.

He looked at Kevin and added, "Kinda like finding a nickel on the candy counter it was." He moved down the counter chuckling to himself.

Chapter 13

"Why doesn't anyone go on it now?" I asked. "I've lived here all my live and I've never even heard of the ice bridge."

Ol' Gordy shook his head. "*Can't*, that's why. Oooh, no. Can't do that. Against the law to go out on the ice, don't ya know?" Ol' Gordy paused and baited his hook by adding, "Ever since that time it all broke up and those people got trapped out there."

Lenny nibbled at the bait. "People got trapped on the ice? What happened to them?"

Ol' Gordy took a long pull on his coffee and jiggled the bait in front of us. "They died of course. Got killed out there they surely did."

"Holy cow! People got murdered out there?" It figured that Billy would be the one to swallow the bait—hook, line, and sinker.

"Not murdered, just died. Lots of people died on the ice over the years. Ain't safe, ya know." Ol' Gordy set the hook and waited.

"What happened to those people, Mr. Gordy?" Lenny asked. Fish on.

"Ain't no margin with that river, ya know. Just keeps on pouring over the top and rolling on out to Lake Ontario, and there ain't nothing gonna get in its way. Don't give a hoot 'bout no shacks, walkways, or people for that matter. Just a few more things to gobble up along the way and carry out to the lake, ya know." Ol' Gordy slowly reeled us in, enjoying the action. "Oh, yeah, that ice bridge may look big and safe, but it ain't. River's always moving, working underneath—never stops; whirlpools opening and closing all the time, churning and breaking up that ice, it is. Always will, ya know. Not a matter of *if* ya know, only *when*. Ice ain't forever—river is." I was mesmerized, watching the tufts of ear hair bobble up and down again.

"What happened to those people, Mr. Gordy?" Lenny asked again.

"Don't remember exactly what year it was, but somewhere around 1913 or so . . . Well; the ice just broke up that time all of a sudden like, no warning a'tall. Everything came crashing down—walkways, bridges, shanties, supplies—all washed away. Didn't take long neither. Once the ice started breaking up it shattered like a crystal bowl, ya know? Ice one minute—river next minute. Seen it myself a few years ago, I did." He straightened up and sucked his stomach in a little. "Yup, was standing on top, watching the Falls like I do, ya know, and right then it happened. Jets of water started shooting straight up and the ice just started cracking and breaking apart everywhere. An ice earthquake, what it was. Matter of minutes and the whole thing was all broken up and gone. Something to see, it was."

"But what happened to those people, Mr. Gordy?" Straight answers were hard to come by with Ol' Gordy sometimes.

Taking another chug of coffee, he resumed at his own pace. "Now, on that day I was telling ya about, back when the bridge broke up, well lots of folks got caught out there, ya know. People were running every which way, trying to get off the ice and back up the gorge. Some folks just couldn't get off in time. Got stranded out there, they did, with everything turning topsy-turvy, giant chunks of ice and the river rushing in all around them. Well, they ended up on a couple of large ice slabs, headed down the river. Some people hung a rope off the bridge for them to grab as they floated by. One fella did manage to grab it and climbed part way up before losing his grip and falling into the river. The rest? Well, they just disappeared."

We sat in silence.

"Didn't fish the bodies out for months. Got caught in the whirlpool downriver and just kept going round and round for the longest time. Well, that was the end of going out on the ice. Against the law from then on, ya know."

"Holy crap!" Billy said, speaking for all of us.

Chapter 14

"How big can the ice bridge get, Mr. Gordy?" Wayne wondered.

"Oh, depends, ya know. Usually stays right around the Falls area, but not unusual for it to go down past the Rainbow Bridge." He thought about it for a moment and then said, "Not like it was in the times before all the water was taken away by those big power plants, ya know. Back in those old days, they used ta be a lot bigger, like in that picture you've been looking at."

He perked up, his eyes seeming to take on a new life. "Although biggest one I know'd of, I actually seen myself." He gave us a knowing look. "Went all the way down to Lake Ontario, it did."

"No way! That's over ten miles away!" I blurted.

"Further than that, and it sure did go there." Looking at us, he reflected on something. "Ya know, that's what kept me here in Niagara all these years." We were all ears—again. "Remember it well, I do. 1938, it was. Never forget it. I was in my early thirties then and there wasn't much work around these parts, coming out of the Depression and all. Was getting myself all set to go out West; to find a new life. Was all ready to leave in the spring. Well, that winter, the ice bridge got so big; it backed up the whole bottom of the gorge. Yes sir, all the way out to Lake Ontario it went. Ice built up on the side of the gorge over sixty feet high in spots. Grew so high it took out all the power stations. No power anywhere. Everything shut down. Kinda spooky, ya know."

Missed it again, I thought. *I'm never gonna see anything in my life.*

"But that was nothing compared to what was to come." He paused, allowing the seconds to tick by while we waited. "After the power stations went down—the ice brought down the Falls View Bridge." He looked at us, waiting for our reaction. We sat there, a row of blank faces staring at him. What was the Falls View Bridge?

"They called it the Honeymoon Bridge," he said.

"Holy cow! The Honeymoon? The ice took that out?" I knew it had crashed into the river, but I never knew why. I also never knew it had been called the Falls View Bridge.

"Yup, sure did, brought it down flat as a pancake." He scanned his wall. "Pretty sure I got a picture of it up here somewhere."

"How many people died that time?" Billy asked.

"No one died; there'd been plenty of warning. It'd been twisting and bending about in the ice for days. That's why I was there, why I seen it. Was all the news, ya know. Everyone was there, watching it sway and wobble, popping rivets like firecrackers, waiting for it to fall. Never forget it, I won't. Didn't have a camera of my own or I'd of gotten some pictures of it. Didn't think about those things back then. Didn't know history was happening right there before my eyes." He gave us a knowing look. "Had other things on my mind around that time, ya know what I mean, fellas?" Ol' Gordy gave us a sly wink, as if to say those words were "for men only" and we nodded back, accepting membership in that elusive club. I pictured Ol' Gordy chasing girls around the ice bridge, with his bushy mustache and hairy ears bobbing up and down.

"But here's a picture of it right here." He plucked another picture off the far end of the wall and laid it on the counter in front of us. It was a black-and-white, showing the bottom of the gorge as a solid mass of ice. Lying on top of the ice, spanning the width of the river and looking, just like he'd said, *flat as a pancake,* was the collapsed Honeymoon Bridge.

"What happened to it, Mr. Gordy?" I asked.

"Oh, it sat on the ice all winter, right on into spring. They had to use dynamite to break it up, and piece by piece, it sunk into the river. Took right into April, it did. I remember seeing the last piece of it floating down the river on a large island of ice until it rolled off and disappeared."

"You saw the whole thing?" Our respect for Ol' Gordy had just gone up a couple of notches. He had seen things we could only imagine, things that were actually on the wall. *For sure, everything's already happened. I missed it all.* What was my generation going to do, since everything had been invented and done already? Just hide in the basement and wait for the A-bombs to start falling I guess.

"Yup, sure did. Was cause of that bridge coming down I stayed and never left."

"How come? Why'd you stay just 'cause the bridge fell down?" I asked.

"Well, when the bridge collapsed, they had to build a new one, ya know, and that bridge is the Rainbow Bridge that's there right now. Took a few years to build the 'bow, it did, and a lot of good-paying work it was too. Worked on it myself, ya know?"

"You built the Rainbow Bridge?" Wayne asked. Ol' Gordy just went up a couple more notches.

"Well, that's a bit of a stretch now, to say I 'built it' and all." He chuckled to himself. "But I surely did work on it. Was honest work and darn good pay. After the Falls View collapsed, I got hired on to work construction. Well, it wasn't long before I ended up getting hitched, and then the missus goes and gets herself in the family way and all. Then you got real responsibility, ya know, and what you want to do takes a backseat to what you have to do. That's how it happens ya know."

"Hey, Mr. Gordy," Wayne asked, right on cue, "where'd you go on your honeymoon?"

Everyone answered in unison, "*Niagara Falls!*"

"Never had no official honeymoon. Too busy working on the 'bow, ya know? But we did stay in a hotel right here that first weekend." He chuckled. "So I guess you can rightfully say we had our honeymoon in Niagara Falls." He paused, and his eyes took on that faraway look again. "Never did take the missus on a proper honeymoon before she passed. One thing I've always regretted." Ol' Gordy went to refill his coffee cup, although it looked pretty full already. After what seemed a long time, he turned back to us and continued. "Well, one project led to another, and I ended up working construction until I bought this place here from Ol' Marty in '47. He'd gotten pretty old and sick by then and had other people running it for him for a while. I got myself a pretty decent deal. Never did get to go out West."

Holy cow, there had been a "Marty" for Marty's Market.

"Have you ever been on the ice bridge, Mr. Gordy?" Wayne asked.

"No, not me—against the law, ya know. Went into effect when I was just a lad myself. No, never been out on it. Never wanted to—never did. Be a dumb thing to wanna go out there now, wouldn't it? Nice to look at from up above and all. Take pictures of maybe. Kinda wild and appealing in its own right, but to go out on? No, thank you. Too dangerous." He shook his head in exaggerated animation and then sagely said, "Besides, *against the law*, ya know."

Ol' Gordy placed both his hands on the counter and spoke to us in his most serious tone. "That river never stops, I'm telling ya. Always moving, always working and pushing things around. Like I say, ice ain't forever. Only here a short time and never telling when it's gonna be taking its leave. Ice will break apart without warning, and it'd be right easy to get caught out there now. Once those people got themselves killed out there, that was the end of it. No more going on the ice. Against the law, from then on." He stood up and made himself as tall as possible. "Don't need no law for me. No sir, not me. I'll keep my feet planted on God's solid earth, thank you kindly. Nothing good about going out on that ice, far as I'm concerned. Not for anyone with half a brain, anyway." Ol' Gordy tapped the side of Lenny's Coke glass with his fingernail. "Only ice I want is inside a glass like this one here, with some Coke on it, thank you kindly."

Or maybe a little whiskey, I thought.

"Besides," he added, "just looking at it from up on top, don't see how anyone could get down there, if'n they wanted to."

"All those people in the picture got down there. How'd they do that?" Wayne asked.

"Well, like I told ya, the big hotel owners hired people to make pathways down the gorge and build walkways out on the bridge, so people would come and stay at their hotels. All about money, ya know. Can't do that now. Against the law."

"What about the trails going down? You know, the Maid of the Mist or the Whirlpool trail? Couldn't someone get down that way?" Wayne asked. He seemed too interested.

"No, of course not, couldn't do the Maid of the Mist, too close to the Falls. Becomes a sheer block of ice early on in the winter. Totally impassable." Ol' Gordy wiped off the countertop with his bar towel as he continued lecturing us. "An' the Whirlpool path gets all iced up, too. Even if passable, it'd be dangerous going down, and then don't know if a person could walk the bottom to the Falls." He paused, reflecting.

"Course, the real trick's getting out. Getting down the gorge in winter is one thing; getting back out is a whole new ballgame." He continued wiping the counter while he thought it over. "No, too dangerous. Be suicide for some dumb fool to do. And what for? Just to stand on some ice? Can do that right here at Marty's Market now, can't we?"

He picked up the pictures from the counter and looked at them reverently. "Although, people still sneak out there, usually from over on the Canadian side, where it's easier to get down the gorge. Every now and then the *Gazette* has something in it about some fool who got down there and couldn't get back out, needing to be rescued. Wouldn't want to be him. Police not happy about that. Against the law, ya know."

Ol' Gordy carefully returned both pictures to their perches on the wall, adjusting them carefully, so they covered the exposed nakedness, reestablishing the wall's former state of tranquility. As he resumed wiping down the counter, he gave us that hard, stern look old folks do when they think they're bestowing those gems of adult knowledge on us that we should write down in our sacred "Wisdom from Old Folks" books inside our heads. "Now don't you fellas ever forget, ya hear? That ice is scary, unsafe. There one minute, then—gone the next. Nope, those bridge days are over and gone now. And thank the good Lord for it too. No one's going out on the ice bridge anymore, and we're all the better off for it. Too dangerous." He stopped wiping down the counter and issued his final proclamation. "Besides, it's against the law, ya know."

Ol' Gordy moved away to wait on a lady wearing a shiny pink vinyl jacket and having large blue rollers in her hair, under a red polka dotted scarp. She looked like an alien from outer space as she stood at the checkout register, sending Ol' Gordy gestures and signals she didn't appreciate his making her wait while he talked to us.

Chapter 15

We sat in an unusual silence, digesting this unexpected information and adventure that was right here in our own backyard, under our noses all these years, and we never had an inkling it existed.

It was Wayne who finally put into words what had run through each of our minds a dozen times during the past thirty minutes. "Man, wouldn't it be cool to go out on that ice bridge and look at the Falls from the bottom up?"

"Yeah, that'd be far-out, heh," Lenny said.

"But what if the ice breaks up, like Ol' Gordy said it did before?" Billy whined.

"It ain't gonna break up with just us on it. Look at that picture and all those people on it. There are dozens of them, and it didn't break up then, did it? There's only five of us. Ol' Gordy said thousands used to go out on it." Wayne paused, "He was just trying to scare us that's all."

Wayne's enthusiasm about this worried me. "That's a picture from a long time ago, Wayne," I said, "when the ice bridges were bigger and thicker. How do we know what it's like now? Or how safe it is? I think it'd be smarter to walk over and look at it from up on top." That seemed the right thing to do.

"What for?" Wayne persisted, "Everything looks the same from up here. Let's just go down and see for ourselves," Wayne pushed.

"But Ol' Gordy said it's against the law," Billy protested.

"Who's gonna know? We just go down and come right back. No one will know we did it. Even, if they found out, they'd just yell at us. We're just punks to them anyway."

"Well, how do you propose we get down there?" I asked.

"We can go down at the Whirlpool, just like Ol' Gordy said," Wayne replied.

"That's not what he said!" I shot back. "He said he didn't know if the Whirlpool would be blocked with ice or not and, he said if it wasn't blocked, it'd be a dangerous walk to the Falls."

"Well, we won't know 'til we try, will we? I say we go down at the Whirlpool or maybe at the Maid of the Mist. Maybe it's not all iced up, like Ol' Gordy thinks. If it is, then we just come back, that's all." Wayne dismissed facts as if they didn't exist.

For the first time, Chuck spoke up. "We can't go down the Maid of the Mist cause it's a solid block of ice, and Ol' Gordy's right about the Whirlpool, might be blocked and it'd be a tough walk to the Falls if we got down it."

A nervous chill crept up my spine. I didn't like the confident tone of Chuck's voice. I had the feeling there was more to come. Wayne asked, "How do you know that?"

"It's that way every winter and besides, I've seen it." Chuck looked away from us and spoke to the wall. "But I know how we can go down and come back up the same way with no problem."

"You do?" asked Wayne. "How?"

Chuck paused a long time before answering, milking it for all it was worth, knowing he had center stage. "I know a secret trail to the bottom that won't be all iced up."

"Where?" I challenged. "I've been up and down every trail there is in the gorge, and I don't know of any secret trails that wouldn't be iced over."

Chuck smirked. "Well, Mr. Smart-Ass, it looks like you don't know everything you think you do. Get your head out of those stupid comic books for a change and maybe you'd know what's right under your nose." He continued talking to the group. "There's a trail at the old Schoellkopf that goes to the bottom of the gorge. I went down it this summer, and it's partially covered like a tunnel, so it should keep the ice out. We can go down that way, and it's not that far to the Falls once on the bottom from there."

The Schoellkopf was a neat place where we hung out sometimes. It had been a large power generation facility built right on the side of the gorge, all the way from the top to the bottom. A few years ago, the whole thing came crashing down into the gorge. Some guys were killed, and it was a big deal around here for a long time. They started building the new power station downriver at Lewiston right after the crash. That's where Lenny's dad worked bringing him and his family to our side of the river.

"All right, Chuck knows a way down!" Now, that Chuck's position was known, Billy quickly jumped on board. "Let's do it, and we'll be famous! We can walk around out there like Blondin did." With Chuck driving the engine, this train was firing up.

"You're not going to be famous unless you want to go to jail," I shot back. "And Blondin was never on the ice bridge. He didn't walk *on* the river; he walked over it."

"For cripes sake, Kev, chill out, will ya? On it, over it—what's the difference?" Wayne had a cutting edge to his voice that he seldom used with me. "Who cares a rat's ass what Blondin did, anyway? There's a way down, that's all that matters. What's your problem, man? Don't you want to do something for a change?"

"We could be trapped down there," I said. "That's my problem. The gorge is nothing to mess with, especially in winter. We don't know anything about this 'secret' trail' of Chuck's." With both Wayne and Chuck aligned against me, I knew there wasn't a snowball's chance in hell of stopping this train. But I had to try. "C'mon, guys, think about it. Who's ever been in the gorge in winter before? Have you seen the ice that's down there? That's some dangerous stuff man. What if we slip on the way down? What if we go out there and the ice breaks up, like happened to those people before? What if we can't get back up? I don't want to be stuck down there at night! You're talking some serious crap, guys. What if this 'secret' trail doesn't work?" I wasn't so sure this was going to be as easy as Chuck made it sound. The gorge was dangerous—and no place to be in the winter.

"What's the matter, Kevie; a little ice has you scared?" Chuck snarled. "That snowball in the face knock your guts out?" This was too good of a thing for Chuck to let go of. It was payback time. Even, if he never wanted to go down into the gorge in winter before, he wasn't going to let this pass. "The trail is a good one. What's the big deal, anyway?" he added. "We've been in the gorge before. Just a little ice this time, that's all. And, it ain't gonna break up neither. There are mountains of it out there. It's sturdy and thick, just like Ol' Gordy said it was. I'll bet it was spring when that thing happened Ol' Gordy was talking about, and not winter. This is February, the middle of winter. Nothing's gonna happen now. How do you even know that story's true anyway?"

I couldn't believe it. Chuck was using Ol' Gordy to support his argument in one breath and then insinuating he's a liar in the next.

Either way, Wayne was ready to go. "Let's do it. Let's have a real adventure, huh?"

Chuck looked at me. "If Mr. Know-It-All Kevie is too scared to go, then so what, we won't miss him. We'll go without him, and he can stay here with Ol' Gordy and look at pictures on the wall and read his stupid comic books."

"Ol' Gordy's never lied to us about anything," I shot back. "Probably been a lot of people killed out there we don't know about. And that's more than just a little ice! That's like nothing we've ever seen before. What if we go down there and someone slips into the river?"

"Come on, Kevin, what's with all the 'what ifs' anyway?" Wayne jumped in before Chuck could say anything. "What if the Russians drop the A-bomb, for crying out loud? Look, we'll take a rope with us and tie ourselves together, okay? Then, if anyone slips, the rest of us will keep him up." Wayne's eyes were pleading for me to let it go. "Let's just go and look at the trail Chuck knows about, and if we can't get down it, then we just turn around and come back, that's all. It's no different than going down in the summer."

"It's a heck of a lot different than going down in the summer," I argued. "Climbing the gorge in summer is tough enough. We don't know what it's like in the winter, but with all that ice, it can't be easy." Ol' Gordy was down at the other end of the counter, stocking cigarettes. I called to him, "Hey, Mr. Gordy."

He turned. "Yup, what is it, Kevin?"

"When the ice bridge broke up that time you told us about, and those people were *killed*, (I emphasized the word for effect) do you know what time of year it was?"

Ol' Gordy walked down our way while he thought it over.

Please, dear God, make it not in the spring.

"Yup, sure do. It was wintertime, of course."

Thank you, God.

He leaned on the counter. "Matter of fact, it was about the same time it is now, February, I'm sure."

Yes, God, send that rapture thing now, I'll go!

"That's why all those people were out there that day, don't ya know. Never expected it, they didn't. No one expected it. Big surprise, it was. Just came out of nowhere, all of a sudden like. You just can't figure that river. Has its own mind, ya know. Does what it wants to, for sure."

Chapter 16

Once again we sat in silence, waiting for Ol' Gordy to move out of hearing range.

"Bull crap!" Chuck finally said. "That ice ain't going nowhere."

"Let's take a vote," I suggested. "If we go, then we all go together." I was grabbing at straws and knew it, but it was all I had left. It was now or never; after what Ol' Gordy said I wouldn't have a better chance to stop this train before it left the station. I could persuade Lenny and scare Billy. "At least that way if we die we . . ."

Chuck cut me off fast and hard. "You want a vote, candy-ass? Okay, lets vote. I vote yes, let's go and look, ain't gonna hurt anything to look. If any of you candy-asses are too chicken-crap to go, then just vote no, that's all, and sit here like a girl with Old man Gordy." Chuck slammed the counter with his hand. "What do you say, Billy, you with me?"

Chuck and I both knew that, putting it that way, there was no way Billy would go against Chuck, so I didn't hold my breath waiting for his reply and as expected, Billy jumped on the train. "Yeah, I'm in. I vote yes. That's what I wanna do too." Then his eyes lit up. "Hey, I know, I'll bring my dad's camera, and we can take a picture of us on the ice bridge, and hang it on Ol' Gordy's wall, up there with all them other famous guys."

Oh, crap, I didn't expect that. I glanced at Chuck. He sat there with a big smirk on his face. He'd won now—and he knew it.

"Yeah, that'd be righteous, man!" Wayne said. "We'd be on the wall. I'm in, too. I vote yes. What do ya say, Lenny? You wanna be famous and hang on Ol' Gordy's wall like that girl up there?"

"Yeah, sure, that's what I wanna do—be up on the wall."

All aboard, this train's ready to pull out. I wondered if Lenny knew what he was saying. Probably not, but it didn't matter—Chuck had stoked the engine well and the train was leaving the station.

Time seemed to stop, and the silence became overwhelming as everyone waited for my answer. I was the only one who hadn't voted. What vote? It was four to zero already. A no vote on my part would only play into Chuck's hands. I glanced at Wayne, and he was nodding his head up and down, pleading with his eyes, for me to vote yes. Chuck just sat there, staring ahead, hoping I'd say no, so he could pounce on it like a lion on a wounded Zebra. What choice did I have? That lousy snowball to the face was going to cost me dearly. For the second time, that day, I wished I had the courage Wayne had to say no.

"Okay, I'm in, let's go down into the gorge," My mouth moved on its own, and I could hear the words being uttered, as if coming from someone other than myself. "and we'll all be famous and hang on Ol' Gordy's wall."

Chuck was right—that snowball to my face had, in fact, knocked my guts out, along with my brains. *Well, Kevin, how'd the vote go inside? Let's see: heart—no; brain—no; nerve—no; mouth—yes. Three no's, one yes. Yes, wins.* I was more upset with my vote than I was about going down into the gorge in the middle of winter.

"How about we do it next Saturday?" I suggested. That would be a whole week for them to back out, or maybe we'd have some nasty weather. "Give everyone time to get ready."

Chuck wasn't about to let me get away with that. "No, like Ol' Gordy said, we have to have decent weather to go down there. It's decent now, and we don't know what it will be like next weekend. Gotta go when we have the chance to go, *ya know*," he mimicked Ol' Gordy again.

"Well, we can't go today," I shot back. "It's too late, and we need dry clothes and time to get ready." *Maybe I could buy some time for them to think about it and change their minds.*

"Yeah, my gloves and boots are still soaked," Billy said. "Let's go Sunday."

"My clothes need drying, too, heh," Lenny added. "But I can't go on Sunday. That's when we go to church."

"Church? Give me a break. You're kidding, right?" Chuck smirked.

"No, we go to church all morning, every Sunday, and then in the afternoon, we help at the Mission."

"What are you, one of those holy roller wackos shouting and yelling all over about Jesus and dancing to a crucifix?" Chuck laughed. "Helping at the Mission, geez, bunch of losers."

Lenny bristled, not knowing if Chuck was calling his family or the Mission people 'losers'. "I don't know what a 'holy roller wacko' is, and I don't dance to a crucifix. I only know that Jesus died for me so that I could have a life and going to church to thank Him and then helping out at the Mission isn't too much to give back in return." Lenny surprised me in the strength of his response to Chuck. 'Church' was a subject I always avoided talking about, Lenny seemed proud of it.

Chuck looked at him without saying anything for a long moment. It was strange that he didn't jump all over Lenny; that wasn't like him, but something held him back. Finally, he spoke to the rest of us, "What about you girls? Sunday, 'church' day for you too?"

"Nah, my mom don't go to church. Sunday's good for me, let's go." Billy said, and I almost laughed out loud. Billy didn't want to be considered a 'girl' while riding his mom's coattails.

Chuck looked at Wayne, who shrugged and just shook his head. Wayne hadn't gone to Mass ever since that priest had 'won' the battle over Clarence.

"How about you Kevie? You gotta go to church on Sunday too, don't you? With your daddy to that temple place?"

"I don't want to, but unless I want a beating, I have to."

"Well, I guess that leaves tomorrow then, doesn't it?" Chuck said. "No problem, sooner the better, before you candy asses chicken out. We'll go tomorrow and then you two holy rollers can go to church and play with the homeless on Sunday."

"I don't go to any Mission," I fired back. "And I only go to church and that's because my old man makes me. Tomorrow's fine with me, let's go."

"Yeah, tomorrow's ok with me too." Lenny tried to calm things back down. "We should probably pack a lunch, maybe bring a thermos of hot choco—"

"What the hell you think this is a Girl Scout hike?" Chuck barked, finally having enough of Lenny. "We don't need a lot of junk. We're not going on a picnic. You want a lunch, then bring a candy bar, and if you're thirsty, then eat snow. By the time you girls are done, we'll be wearing dresses down there." Although Chuck was bitching at Lenny, he stared at me, wanting to even the score.

"Just don't eat yellow snow!" Wayne set off a round of laughter, breaking the tension.

"Tomorrow it is." Chuck resumed, glancing back and forth between me and that now infamous picture hanging on the wall that I wished to God I'd never asked about. "We'll start out first thing in the morning.

Anyone opposed?" When there were no responses, Chuck continued, "Okay, it's settled. We go tomorrow morning—at least those of us who aren't chicken will." Chuck closed the caboose with that challenge. "Let's meet at eight at the corner of Pine and Falls Street. Bring a rope, just to make Kevie here, happy." He looked directly at me. "Don't anyone be late. If you're not there, on time, we go without you, and you're nothing but candy-ass chicken—no excuses."

I felt the sting, knowing that shot was directed at me. "Going down the gorge isn't something we should take for granted," I said. Despite Chuck's minimizing of the trip, we needed to be prepared. "Even in summer time, it's a big trip. If we go down early in the morning and come right back up, it's going to take all morning. We should pack some lunch, like Lenny said, and bring extra gloves and things too." Maybe we'd get lucky, and this secret trail of Chuck's would be closed off, and we'd just have another snowball fight instead.

"I have a knapsack from the Army Surplus I'll bring," Wayne said.

"My dad has a brand new rope in the garage I can get," Lenny added, "and I'll see if I can get some sandwiches from my mom."

"Don't go telling your mom where we're going." Wayne blurted out.

"I'm not stupid, man!"

There was lots of chatter after this, talking about what to bring and wear. The mood was of excitement and anticipation. From this moment on, we were committed to this quest.

Chuck just sat there, smirking and looking at the picture on the wall.

Who knows? Maybe with any luck, there'll be a blizzard tonight, I thought.

Volume Two

Niagara!

Chapter 17

There was no blizzard during the night, and the day broke bright and clear.

We all met at the rendezvous point, and no one was late. At this early hour, being a cold Sunday in February, no one was around, and we had, not only the street, but the whole city to ourselves. Everyone was dressed warmly and wearing heavy boots, thick gloves, and insulated hats with furry earflaps hanging on them. Extra gloves protruded out of pockets. Lenny was loaded down carrying a large paper sack, a thermos, and a coil of rope slung over his shoulder. Billy carried his father's camera inside a sealed leather case. He was serious about hanging a picture on Ol' Gordy's wall.

Wayne carried a green army knapsack on his back and said he had an extra pair of gloves, some bottles of Dr. Pepper, and a coil of rope inside. He was wearing the biggest boots I'd ever seen. Wayne had enormous feet to begin with, but these looked to have at least another three sizes tacked on. He looked like that clown at the circus. I wondered how many pairs of socks he wore underneath, and if he had the toes stuffed with newspaper inside.

An abundance of candy bars were evident, some already half-eaten. I'd brought an ample supply myself, with a Hersey bar and a Baby Ruth in one pocket and a box of Milk Duds and Good 'N Plenty in the other. I also had a Coke and two packages of Twinkies I swiped when my mom wasn't looking. The pair of gloves I was wearing had a hole in one thumb where the stitching had come out. I had an extra pair stuffed inside my coat pocket.

I also brought my hatchet housed in a leather sheath that snaps over my belt. It had been the coveted thing from inside Ol' Gordy's glass case, that I had saved for last year. I didn't know why I'd brought it. When I was getting everything ready, last night, something inside me said to take the hatchet. I dismissed it as a dumb thought; after all, what was I going to chop—ice? But, then this morning as I was loading my pockets up, that feeling came back again saying to take the hatchet. To make a long story short, I brought it. And to be honest, it felt kind of cool having it strapped on, kind of like an explorer. Anyway, it's under my coat, so no one will see it and think I'm dumb.

"Here—put your stuff in my knapsack," Wayne offered. "There's plenty of room." Billy's camera went in, along with Lenny's rope, paper sack and thermos, our extra gloves, and sodas. Soon, it was filled and strapped back on Wayne's back.

"Is it too heavy, Wayne?" I asked. "We can take some things out; we don't need two coils of rope."

"Nah, it's okay. Let's beat feet," Wayne said.

I noticed Chuck hadn't put anything in it.

As we set off to the old Schoellkopf ruins, we bantered back and forth about the important things that made up our life. How would the Yankees do, after winning the World Series last year, and would Mickey Mantle hit sixty home runs and be MVP again? On a serious note, we argued about whether a world-wide plague would break out, mutating life on the planet from an alien disease that Alan Sheppard brought back from his being in outer space? We reviewed the current story from

Gunsmoke, about a fight between Doc and Chester, and argued whether Miss Kitty and Marshal Dillon were getting it on.

"Well, they don't make out or anything like that." Billy said.

"They can't show that stuff on TV, spaz, but you know they're doing it," Chuck said. "You're supposed to read between the lines."

"Not everyone reads between the lines the same as you do, Chuck." Lenny said. "There's more to life than one side of things, heh?" Strangely, Chuck didn't say anything but instead only looked at Lenny and made a face.

We talked about lots of things, and we avoided talking about one thing—the thing we were doing—going into the gorge—in the middle of winter—to walk on a bridge made of ice—over a frozen river—directly in front of Niagara Falls.

Chapter 18

The Schoellkopf ruin wasn't much of a ruin any longer, having been reduced to a series of vacant lots strung together across the top of the gorge. No buildings or structures remained. Following the disaster of '56, when the power plant had collapsed into the gorge, the structures left standing had been demolished and hauled off. We'd hung out there a lot when the wrecking crews were tearing it all down. It was pretty cool, watching the cranes swing those huge wrecking balls, smashing into buildings and knocking down entire walls and floors. There were all kinds of neat stuff lying around when they finished each day. Chuck was excited when we had found a bag full of tiny comic books showing our favorite comic characters, like Popeye, Dick Tracy, and Dagwood, doing things never seen in the Sunday comic strips, for sure. He called them 'Tijuana Comics' and said he could sell them. If he did, he never split with us.

Now, years after the clean-up, the vacant site had evolved into a colony of piles. There were piles of old bricks, piles of broken concrete, piles of debris, along with piles of dirt, piles of branches, and piles of roofing. Then there were piles of other people's piles. One moonless night, when no one was looking, someone had dumped a pile of household junk on the site. This caught on, and soon the area was littered with piles of people's rubbish. Much of it was remodeling and repair type debris; broken-up plaster, wooden slates, torn-out plumbing, chunks of sidewalks, and busted up wood. Mixed in with these were piles of broken furniture, old mattresses, busted-up appliances, toys, and other former treasures now turned into junk.

Over these piles had settled a blanket of crusty snow, laced with dirt and ice; resulting in a moonscape of grimy, irregular hills that showcased human progress by displaying its discarded trash like exhibits in an art museum.

It was a cool place.

Approaching the ruin, we glanced up and down the street, making sure no cops were cruising by, and quickly snuck around the "Keep Out! No Trespassing!" sign. Darting from one pile to another, we crossed the moonscape in short order and found ourselves at the backside of the site, close to the edge of the gorge.

Chuck took the lead, searching for something among the bushes and dense foliage that lined the edge of the gorge. The previous day's bravado had given way to anticipation, with a strong element of fear mixed in. I felt as I had when I had gone on the Comet roller coaster at Crystal Beach last summer, as it slowly clawed its way to the top, clicking and clacking along the worn, wooden tracks and rails, my heart racing and my nerves exploding. On one hand, I was all balled up inside, with cold terror and panic, at what lay ahead and prayed that it would stop so I could get off, but I knew it was too late. On the other hand, I was excited—eager for it to reach the top and start the exhilarating run down and already planning ahead to get back in line to do it again. All I could do was to grasp the car's handle with a death grip and hang on for the ride.

Chuck stopped in front of some tall bushes that were blanketed in ice and stuffed with heavy snow packed in around all the branches.

A weather-worn wooden sawhorse layered in ice, and almost entirely buried in the drifting snow, protruded in front of the bushes. Fastened to the crossbeam was a sign, also encased in a thick layer of ice:

DANGER—KEEP OUT
NO TRESPASSING
Under penalty of law
NFPD

"Gee, you think we'll get in trouble?" Billy whined.

"Nah, who's gonna know? That's only to cover their backsides for insurance anyway." Chuck walked around the icy barricades and gave the bushes a vigorous shake. A detonation of snow exploded into the air like a mini blizzard. As the artificial snow storm dissipated, an opening in the bushes revealed itself, appearing like a magical door. Chuck looked over his shoulder at us and smiled, then turned and stepped through the opening. Wayne, in his oversized boots, went next, followed by Billy and Lenny. I brought up the rear. In single file, we stepped through the magical portal to ride the Niagara gorge Comet to destinations unknown. I was scared to death to go down into that gorge, but eager to begin. All I could do was to hang on for the ride.

The thick branches, encased in sleeves of ice, heralded our progress with a musical flourish as we trampled through them, rattling together like a thousand chimes blowing in the wind. The man-made snowstorm followed our invasion through the tangle of branches. Abruptly, the bushes ended and gave way to an array of sculptures created by snow and freezing mist that had layered and coated the small trees and boulders scattered along the edge. We came out from behind a large boulder to what I knew should be the leading edge of the gorge.

I didn't see what I expected to see.

I expected to see the gorge dropping down 200 feet or so to the river below. Instead, I saw an enclosed walkway that disappeared over the side of the gorge. The rusted remains of steel beams, with fastened metal sheets across them, protruded from the ground and across the remnants of a roof. Both were in poor condition, eaten away by the assault of the elements over time, with many of the metal sheets blown away. But to us, it looked like the yellow brick road leading to Oz. Chuck turned to us with a big grin on his face. "See? What'd I tell ya? Told you this was a terrific way down, didn't I?"

"Wow, this is really cool!" Billy agreed.

"What is this? How'd it get here?" Wayne asked.

"Don't know if it was part of a walkway inside the old powerhouse or was set up by the salvage crews. Either way doesn't matter; it's here. I discovered it this summer, and it's in pretty decent shape all the way down."

I began to think I was wrong, and maybe this wasn't going to be what I had feared. As Chuck proudly showed off his secret trail, he looked at me with a smirk that cut deeply. "Guess you don't know everything you think you do, huh, Kevie boy?" He sounded like my dad.

Gaps in the structure had filled in with ice and snow, like putty shot from a giant caulking gun. Where overhead sheets were missing, the ice was a solid mass coming across from the side of the gorge or up from the ground through the openings, like large stalagmites. The result was an enclosed tunnel that blocked out the world outside laced with columns of ice inside.

Chuck led, and we began the journey downward.

Chapter 19

The tightly packed snow crunched under our boots, providing good traction for walking and making us sound like Hannibal's elephants crossing the Alps. We couldn't see the river, but we felt its power, even this far away. A tremor vibrated in the wall of the gorge in rhythm with the river below. Enclosed in this man—and nature-made tunnel, we were protected from the wind, blowing snow and any mist from the Falls. When we first walked through the 'magic' doorway, the wind was gusting—whistling and singing—around the edges of the gorge and the tunnel. Progressing downward, further into the gorge, the whistles and tunes faded, replaced by the low, steady growl of the river. Traveling down the side of the gorge, we climbed over and around the layers of ice and used the crystalline pillars as handholds. Moving carefully, one foot at a time, progress was slow but steady. Despite Chuck's cutting jab, I put my misgivings aside, being excited about the adventure.

We had traveled far down the passageway and were close to the bottom, when we came to an abrupt stop. The tunnel should have ended in a rocky shoreline leading to the river's edge, with the brisk wind slicing off the water and the bright, morning sunshine greeting us. Instead, there was a solid wall of ice.

We stood, staring at it in awe. It rose up from the ground and merged with the ice canopy over our heads. Smooth and shiny, it was layered in rows of crystalline columns, each a prism reflecting a kaleidoscope of flashing colors, and light beams. Across the top, giant icicles hung, like points on a crown which themselves were ringed with sharp, jagged daggers of sparkling ice around their bottoms. From the ground, stalagmites rose and encircled the base of the ice wall like an altar. Multiple layers of snow, looking like the rings on a tree, deep and dark at the bottom, pure and unsullied at the top, capped off the crown. It was a tremendous, mysterious formation, the likes of which we had never seen before.

But it was what lurked inside the ice that made our mouths unhinge and our eyes bulge from our heads. Something moved inside, dancing in a whirl of swirling lights, colors, and shapes, shooting out rainbows in all directions. It spun, twirled, jumped, and leaped. It was a being composed of light and color. Reddish-orange beams shot out from its eyes, and its breath was a stream of golden fire, interspersed with bolts of green and blue lightning spewing forth. Bright rivulets of radiant power ricocheted around us while we trembled in the presence of the being incarcerated inside the ice. Was it a demon? Or was it an angel?

We were speechless—frozen in wonder. Only Wayne didn't take notice as he moved along the wall, looking for an opening. After staring at it for a minute, Billy followed Wayne, glancing back in awe. Lenny stayed behind, running his hand over the smooth surface of the wall, watching the colors reflect and light up his hand. He turned to look at me, nodded his head and followed Wayne and Billy.

Chuck remained motionless, arms hanging limp at his sides as he stared into the power within the ice. He was mesmerized by the magic and the energy that whirled, pulsed, and danced in front of him. Removing his glove, he slowly raised his arm and reached out to the ice.

With hand cocked back, palm stretched out, and fingers wide apart, he touched the ice—joining with the demon or the angel.

Seeing Chuck, his hand joined with the ice, I turned and stared into the power swirling within the wall. As if detached from my body, my own arm rose of its own accord and inches away from Chuck's hand, my ungloved hand also touched the ice. A jolt of electric energy exploded from the tips of my fingers to the ends of my toes flooding me with a strange warmth. The extreme coldness burned fire in my hand, sending a molten river surging through my veins, cruising throughout my body and pumping into every molecule of my being. Something strange and exotic flooded my thoughts and overloaded my senses. Awareness overtook me, not awareness of me and ego, but of things outside of me, of the river, the gorge, of Chuck and the light inside the ice. My senses became acute. I could hear the minute spider cracks as they slowly spread through the massive column. I felt the spirit and power of the light inside. It wasn't evil, and a strong sense of peace came over me as my spirit merged and became one with it.

"Hey, guys, come on this way. There's an opening over here I think we can squeeze through." Wayne called above the power of the ice.

Trying to lower my hand, I couldn't break contact with the presence in the ice. It held on to me and would not let go. In a panic, I grabbed my arm, pulling back hard, wrenching it free. It came away, leaving behind small patches of frozen skin with the ice. The molten river of fire that had flowed through my veins and ignited my senses just seconds earlier, immediately ceased, and I felt the coldness of the world descend on me.

"Come on Chuck, let's go," I said. He continued staring into the ice, frozen in place, making no effort to break away from the grip of the presence inside.

"Chuck! Come on!" Either unable or unwilling to leave the ice, Chuck remained motionless. Grabbing his arm and jerking back hard, I broke his hand away from the wall.

Examining my hand, I saw where the skin had been torn away from the fingertips and the palm. Around the ragged, frayed edges, crystals of ice, given to me by the ice being in exchange for my flesh, sparkled like diamonds. I felt no pain, only the smoldering residue of the fire that had burned there. Chuck stared at his own tattered hand. We had exchanged a part of ourselves, as an offering to the being inside the ice. Turning his head, looking at me, our eyes locked once again, this time, there wasn't any anger or malice. Something had happened that neither of us understood, but I knew it wasn't bad and somehow I knew we would never be the same again.

Chapter 20

The narrow opening Wayne had found in the wall was just large enough for us to fit into. The others had already gone through by the time Chuck and I squeezed in. Moving sideways, we shuffled our feet along the length of the opening toward the crack of blue sky that beckoned us forward. Emerging from behind the wall of color, we found ourselves on a ledge, looking down on a scene that none of us had ever imagined, and we stood in awe of the view spread below us.

"Outta sight!" Lenny exclaimed.

"Holy crap!" Billy proclaimed.

"Ain't nothing like this on Ol' Gordy's wall," Wayne said.

Below us, a world of ice glistened and sparkled, blinding our vision, causing us to squint and shield our eyes. Living in Western New York all our lives we knew winter and we knew ice, but never had we seen ice like this. This was like nothing we'd ever seen. It was everywhere around us, in front of us, over us, behind us, under us. Colossal columns, thick pillars, and massive, brilliant overhangs filled every opening. Ribbed icicles the size of trees grew from the columns and pillars, hung down from the overhangs, and sprouted up from the bottom. It was a world devoid of color, consisting rather of a hundred shades of white. We could hear the rumble of the river rushing under and through the ice, but we could not see it. Vision, beyond our immediate surroundings, was obstructed by the columns and overhangs of ice. The sun flooded through the openings, and the perfectly straight beams of light lit up the pillars and columns like torches, contrasting starkly with the irregular jaggedness of the ice sculptures.

"Man, have you ever seen anything like this?" Lenny asked.

"Not in my lifetime!" I answered.

Our amazement was broken, once again by Wayne. "Hey, guys, how do we get down from here?"

Looking down, I realized that was a really good question. We were thirty to forty feet above what looked to be the bottom of the gorge, standing on a ledge that was almost a straight drop down and which was either all ice or layers of ice over unseen rock. It was all smooth crystal, rippled in rows, looking like giant fire hoses strung from top to bottom.

"I don't see a way down," Billy answered for all of us. We moved around gingerly, being careful not to slip and go flying down.

Wayne offered a solution to his own question. "It looks the best over here. It's not quite as steep as the rest of it. We could use the rope to lower ourselves down one at a time." The side Wayne was referring to looked a little less rippled than the rest, and it did have an outward slope at the bottom like a slide. I thought his idea would work. Besides, I didn't see any other way down.

After looking it over, Chuck nodded his head. "Yeah, okay. Turn around Wayne and let's get a rope out of your knapsack. C'mon, Billy, you go first."

"Me? Why me? Let someone else go first."

"You're the lightest guy here, that's why."

"Oh, crap! You think it'll be okay?" Billy whined.

"Yeah, of course it will be. Why not? You'll be tied on a rope we're all holding, and if there's any problem we just pull you back up. What can happen?"

"What about the bottom? You think it's safe to walk on?"

"Are you kidding? Take a look down there. Why wouldn't it be safe? That's the bottom of the gorge. You know—ground! Mother Earth! Look at it. It's solid down there—a lot safer than up here on this ledge. There's nothing to worry about."

"Why don't Lenny go first? He's light, too," Billy persisted.

"Look, when you get down, leave the rope tied on and walk around to make yourself feel okay. Jump up and down! Knock yourself out! Whatever! Just come on and quit your whimpering. Let's tie this rope on." Chuck was actually being patient in his own way.

"Well, okay, but you guys hold on tight. Don't let go, and if I yell, you pull me up right away, all right?"

Chuck waved away Billy's concern. "Yeah, sure, don't sweat it."

"Promise? Swear to God?"

"Yeah, yeah, we swear. Now stop having a cow about it. Here, let me tie it around your coat." As Chuck jerked Billy's coat hard, it was clear there was also a limit to just how far his patience went. Chuck wrapped the rope around Billy's waist, tied it into a tight knot, and gave it a couple of hard jerks. We lined up, passing the rope one to the other. It was a fifty-foot coil, so there was plenty of rope. The way we gripped it, you'd think Billy was going down the side of Mt. Everest.

"Okay, we're ready." Chuck said. "You ready, Billy?"

"I guess so. Hold it tight. Don't let go, and pull me up right away if I say."

"We got it. Now quit spazzing out and stand right there." Chuck pointed at the edge that looked the smoothest and Billy moved to the side, facing away from us. "Not that way, Billy, turn and face us. You're gonna walk down the side while we keep you upright." Billy cautiously turned around, wrapping the rope around him. "No, that's the wrong way. Turn around the other way, Billy," Chuck said.

"Clockwise, Billy! The other way!" I yelled at him.

"You're doing it all wrong!" Wayne screamed at him.

"Turn in a circle the other way, Billy!" Lenny shouted at him.

Everyone was shouting and yelling directions at Billy, who promptly got confused and flustered and turned in both directions at once, not knowing what to do.

"Shut up!" Chuck shouted at us, waving his hands and arms. "Shut up, I said! I'll do the talking. You all just clam up you hear?" We meekly shut up while Chuck turned to Billy, who was on the verge of tears.

"What's wrong? Why's everyone yelling at me?" Billy cried.

"Just ignore those yo-yos and listen to me. It's all right. The rope just needs to be straight that's all. You have it twisted around on your body. Now, turn around clockwise, nice and easy." Billy slowly shuffled his feet to the left.

"Not that way, Billy, the other way," Chuck told him. Billy turned in a full circle as instructed. "Good, that's good. Now keep turning that same way around one more time. That's it—good." After a second turn around, the knot was straight back to us, without wrapping around Billy. "Good, Billy. Now, grab hold of the rope with both hands and start walking backwards slowly, and take small steps."

"Backwards! Are you crazy? How am I gonna see? I'll fall!"

"You can't fall, Billy. We all got you. We're holding you up with the rope. Just move your feet backwards until you feel the edge and then slowly walk over it. Lean away and let the rope hold you!" Chuck called to him.

"Oh, man, this is scary! I can't see where I'm going! What if I fall? Don't let go!"

"Just watch where your feet are and take small steps."

Billy squeezed his end of the rope with a death grip as he took the tiniest of steps backward and kept turning his head around like an owl, trying to see behind him.

"Stop looking behind you, Billy. Trust us. Let the rope hold you while your feet walk down. Just keep your balance. We'll let the rope out as you move," Chuck instructed.

Billy's feet went over the ledge, and he started the descent down, whimpering. "Oh God, I can't see. Oh, help me. Oh, I feel like I'm hanging."

"That's good, Billy. You're doing fine! Just keep walking backwards. You're doing terrific! Take your time, and keep your feet on the ice."

We slowly let the rope out through our hands as Billy went over the ledge. When his head disappeared below the edge of the ledge, Chuck continued calmly to talk him down. I heard Billy mumble "Oh, crap" a couple of times when, without warning, the rope went slack.

"Hey, guys, I made it! I'm down! I'm on the bottom. That was easy—nothing to it." Rushing over to the edge we all looked down.

Billy was jumping up and down and untying the rope. "Come on, guys, it's easy. Man, it's neat down here." Billy was a hero.

Chuck quickly hauled the rope back up and grabbed Wayne. "You're next, Wayne." He tied the rope around Wayne's waist, and Wayne started down the side of the ledge—too fast. As he went over the lip, he took too large a step backwards, and his foot slid out from under him, causing him to crash into the ledge, smashing his head into the ice.

"*Yeowllll!*" Wayne was kicking and clawing at the side of the ice, trying to get a hold. The sudden jolt and added weight on the rope jerked us all forward, causing Wayne's head to bounce along the side of the ledge like the ball on one of those rubber-band paddles. "*Takes a licking and keeps on ticking*" jumped into my mind, and I immediately felt guilty, mocking Wayne with a commercial while his head beat a drum roll against the ledge.

Wayne couldn't get himself back into position. He grappled to find a grip on the smooth surface with his feet and his hands looking like a hamster on a treadmill, running and clawing like the dickens but going nowhere.

"Wayne, stop! Stop! Just hang loose. We'll lower you down. Don't move!" Chuck kept yelling until Wayne finally stopped kicking and hung onto the rope. We slowly lowered him down until Billy was able to grab his feet and guide him to the bottom.

"Okay, Kevin, you're next, then Lenny," Chuck said.

"Wait a minute Chuck; I don't see how this will work. If me and Lenny go, how are you going to get down? There won't be anyone left to hold the rope for you."

Chuck smiled. "I'll manage." He gave the rope a final tug around my waist. "Let's go."

"But I don't—"

Chuck gently pushed me to the edge, and before I knew it, I was working my way down, standing on the bottom.

When Lenny was ready, Chuck walked over and shouted down to us. "You guys grab Lenny as soon as you can to take the weight off of me, okay?" Chuck wrapped the rope around his own middle, sat down on the ledge, and dug his heels into the ice as best he could. "Don't slip, Lenny. If you mess up, as Wayne did, I may not be able to hold you by myself on this slippery ice."

Lenny nodded. "Got it. Slow and easy does it. You ready?"

"All set."

Lenny began the descent. He didn't slip or skid and Chuck slowly let out the rope until we were able to reach Lenny's feet and guide him down. Before Lenny could even untie the rope, we heard Chuck scream, "Here I come, catch me!" He followed this with a savage war chant: "Geronimooooooo!"

Jerking our heads up in disbelief, we saw Chuck slip over the edge of the slippery slope feet first, sitting on his butt, come sliding down the slope. He crashed into Lenny and me, bowling us over as we reached out catching him and breaking his almost vertical slide. We stared at him, our mouths hanging open.

"I knew you guys would catch me." He split a gut, laughing at us.

Chapter 21

Standing on the bottom of the gorge, out from under the protection of the tunnel, everything changed again, as if someone cranked the lever on one of those 3-D View-Masters. The pillars and columns now towered over us, covered by layer upon layer of rippling permafrost. We couldn't see over the tops, and our vision was limited to the immediate vicinity. Anything further, was obstructed by the mountains, pillars and columns of ice everywhere.

It was not only a change from how it looked from when we were on top of the ledge, it also was a change from the gorge I'd known and traveled many times before. That gorge had consisted of trees and bushes, rocks and river, creating vibrant, bursting pictures of green, brown, and blue. This gorge didn't have trees or bushes; all was covered in thick layers of ice and snow, creating a striking picture of white and gray. Contoured pillars of ice rose from the bottom, reaching many times our height over our heads. What once had been large rock formations scattered along the walls of the gorge had grown into massive overhangs of opaque ice extending outward twenty to thirty feet from the walls, supported only by their own bulk. Icicles, in all shapes and designs, from a few inches to a few feet in diameter, grew, hung and laid everywhere, including on top of one another, layer upon layer, like bunches of giant white carrots.

It was a primitive landscape belonging to thousands of years ago, when massive hairy beasts roamed the earth. I couldn't be more surprised if a wooly mammoth came trotting out from behind the next pillar. We were in complete awe of this strange landscape, looking more like a lost world that, amazingly, it had been here all along, literally under our noses, down a few hundred feet below our homes.

Being out from under the canopy of the tunnel, the brilliance of the sun burst upon us. It flooded the area in a dazzling radiance of various-sized light beams that danced and bounced off thousands of prisms growing on the walls and bottom. They reflected back and forth between the pillars and columns of ice, filling the air with brilliant color and illumination. If not for the snow absorbing the light, we would have been blinded by its onslaught. I thought the being I had touched inside the ice wall was the guardian to this world.

Chuck took the lead again as we set out, in single file, toward where we knew Niagara to be. While we didn't see it, there was no mistaking the constant reverberations of the plunging, tumbling water that was not far ahead. The columns, overhangs, and protrusions of ice and snow kept our line of sight limited to the small areas around us at each turn and bend.

We didn't see the river either and couldn't tell where it began or where the shore ended although we could feel it racing around us, or under us. Not knowing was unsettling.

The weather was ideal. When looking straight up, beyond the confines of the ice world, the sky was blue with a few puffs of clouds drifting in it. A slight breeze above the gorge thankfully blew away from us, providing protection from the mist and spray of the Falls ahead. The floor of the gorge was encased in layers of ice and snow intermixed with one another. The upper layer, we walked through varied in depth between three to eight inches of granular snow, providing solid traction under our crunching boots. But, even with the good footing, travel was slow due to the constant climbing and crawling over and around numerous obstructions in all shapes and forms. It was a massive ice maze, littered with frozen obstacles throughout. As we moved, we left a clearly defined trail behind us, ensuring finding our way back would not be a problem.

Our clothing soon became coated with a crusty layer of frozen moisture and chunks of ice stuck in the fibers of our coats and pants. A heavy cold descended on our shoulders, like a mantle of frozen lead, wrapping itself around us although underneath, our bodies remained warm due to the efforts of traversing this rugged terrain and by the adrenaline of anticipation.

Ahead of us, high above the overhangs and mountains of ice, the Rainbow Bridge stretched across two countries. Massive and imposing, the man-made structure of steel was out of place in this world of ice. I watched the cars flashing between the flags that flapped across the length of the bridge and had a newfound respect for Ol' Gordy, knowing he'd been part of building this bridge. Not only had he left a mark on the world but, if not for this bridge, he would have left Niagara to follow his dream out West. Where would I be now if that had happened? I didn't know where I'd be, but I knew where I wouldn't be—here. If Ol' Gordy had gone out west, then there wouldn't have been a "wall of pictures" at Ol' Gordy's. Then, I never would have asked about *that picture*, and I wouldn't be here then, on this insane journey to the bottom of Niagara Falls. It was strange how, without much notice, little things happen that lead to things that have lots of significance. It also made me realize how things happen in one place and time create other things to happen in other places and time, having no connection to each other. Everything's connected to something, which, in turn, is connected to something else, until it ultimately comes back to the original thing. I wondered if there was anything that wasn't connected to everything else.

"You know, guys, it was right around here that the old Honeymoon Bridge collapsed that Ol' Gordy told us about, and showed us that picture of" I said.

"Yeah, that's right, and then Ol' Gordy built the Rainbow Bridge!" Wayne replied.

"Gee! You think it might fall on us, too?" Billy asked.

"Don't hold your breath, Billy. That bridge ain't coming down in our lifetime," I assured him.

"How much farther is it?" Billy's whining knew no limits.

"Not far," I said. "With all these ins and outs we're taking, it's hard to tell how far we've come, but we know the Falls is just a little ways from the Rainbow Bridge, right? It sure sounds close, doesn't it?"

"How come we don't see it?" Lenny asked.

"Can't see anything over all this ice. Just be careful until we know exactly where we are."

"How do we know we can get out of this ice? How do we know it doesn't end all blocked in somewhere?"

"We don't," I answered. We should have walked over to the Falls yesterday as I had wanted to, so we could see how much ice there was and seen what this looked like, but under the challenge from Chuck yesterday, that hadn't been an option.

"Geez, what'll we do then?" Billy was troubled by that thought.

"Turn around and go back, that's what," I said. *And that wouldn't bother me one bit,* I thought.

The sound of the cataracts increased as we forged ahead. Navigating through the ice maze, we came to a large overhang that stretched across and down from the columns of ice around it, joining with the wall of ice growing out and over from the gorge side. It effectively formed a complete enclosure, leaving only a crawl space, like a tunnel, open on the bottom.

I knelt down and peered into the tunnel. It looked to be about twenty feet long and was open on the other side. It was large enough for us to crawl through. Bright light glared on the other side, and a brisk wind blew through the opening, carrying a distinct promise with it. We looked at each other, excitement bursting on our faces.

"What do you think?" Chuck asked.

"Can't see what's on the other side with all that glare, but I don't see any water," I replied. Excited—scared—the Comet was clicking and clacking up the wooden track again. I looked around at their faces. "Smells like water on the other side to me. I think this is it. You guys ready for this?"

Wayne wasted no time. "Heck yes, it's what we came for!"

"I'm ready. Let's do it," Lenny added.

"I'm not going first this time," Billy whimpered.

"I'll go first." I said. "Follow slowly, in case there's water on the other side."

The roller coaster made the turn at the top, beginning its fast descent—as I crawled into the tunnel.

Chapter 22

Crawling through the ice tunnel, the freshness and moisture carried on the breeze, was invigorating and stimulating. Emerging on the other side, the View-Master lever was cranked once again, and I entered yet another new and mysterious world.

Immediately, the gorge warden turned the volume control to full blast, assaulting me with an overpowering, deafening thunder. While it had been loud inside the maze, I hadn't realized how much the ice had absorbed and deadened the sound. But now, there were no barriers to absorb any noise, and my ears were assaulted by a constant roar. Never had I heard anything so loud.

The sun, no longer obstructed by columns and overhangs of ice, flooded over me, breaking the cold, dead grip in which the tunnel and ice maze had cloaked over me. The air had a crispness and taste to it, unfiltered by the maze; it was saturated with moisture and wet on my face, more water than air.

The columns, overhangs, and pillars of ice were behind us now. Ahead was an open area, larger than a football field, contoured by low, rolling hills and knolls of pure white snow interspersed with ridges and deep troughs. At the far end of the open area, was a row of enormous, jagged, protruding ice sculptures, all topsy-turvy and tumbled on top of one another, looking beautiful and forbidding at the same time, like a pile of collapsed skyscrapers. Directly behind this wall, an enormous mountain towered over the frozen landscape. This wasn't a picture hanging on a wall; this was real. This mountain thundered and roared, howling its name in loud proclamation: *N-I-A-G-A-R-A!*

We were here—*Niagara Falls!*

We stood on the ice bridge of Niagara Falls.

My heart pounded uncontrollably, adrenaline shooting through me like lightning bolts. The roller coaster had left the tracks and was flying off into space.

"I—am—here !" I shouted at the top of my lungs, unable to hear my own words. I felt an exultation I'd never felt in my life. This was true adventure. I was doing something. I was an explorer stepping onto a new continent; I was Columbus and Lewis and Clark rolled into one. No, this was stepping forth onto a new world; I was Alan Sheppard in space.

"*I am Kevin!*" I shouted to the world. "Look at me! I'm Kevin, and I'm here, standing on the ice bridge of Niagara Falls! Hey, Pa, look at me now. I'm not a 'nobody'. I'm a somebody—I am!"

I looked for the others. Each was in his own world of jubilation. Billy was running around, waving his hands in celebration. Wayne was jumping up and down with arms flailing and flying as he did jumping jacks. Lenny was on his knees, praying. Chuck was stomping out some kind of Indian war dance in a figure eight. Soon Billy joined him, followed by Wayne. Without knowing how or when, Lenny and I found ourselves there too, dancing like Indians, arms pounding each other's backs, shouting fierce war whoops of glee, while Niagara roared its outrage at us.

We were united. There were no differences between us at this moment; race, status, background, all meant nothing. We were five specks of human flesh, jumping around like lunatics, on a frozen river at the base of Niagara Falls.

It was one of the purest moments of joy I'd ever experience in my life.

Chapter 23

Billy grabbed Wayne by the arm and yelled something into his ear. Wayne nodded his head and stooped down while Billy fumbled in the knapsack until he pulled out his old man's camera case. He waved us over, and we got in a huddle, trying to hear.

"We gotta take our picture for the wall!" Billy shouted. We all nodded and started grooming ourselves for the picture, brushing off snow and plucking chunks of ice from our pants.

I grabbed Billy by the arm, shouting at him, "We can't all get in it! Someone will have to take the picture!"

Billy shook his head. "No, there's a timer on the camera, so we just set it and then we can all get in the picture." I watched as Billy got the camera out of the case. It was a rugged looking black metal box that had "ROLLEIFLEX" written across the top in bold silver letters. There were knobs and buttons all over it. I wasn't up much on cameras, but this one looked pretty neat, especially when compared to the little Kodak Instamatic my mom had gotten with the S&H Green Stamps she saved at Loblaw's.

Billy removed the cover on the lens, and the top had this nifty lid that, when pushed down, popped up, revealing the viewfinder. You'd look down into the camera from above to take your picture in front of you. It was really cool. Billy touched a small silver lever on the side and shouted that this was the timer control.

He picked out a knoll that was the right height, cleaned off a spot, and set the camera on top of it, facing Niagara, while he knelt behind it. He motioned for us to move in front of him, with our backs to the Falls. Looking down through the viewfinder, he motioned us back. We shuffled a couple of feet backwards until he waved at us to stop. Then, squeezing his hands together like an accordion, he motioned us to jam in tighter together. We did, and after a couple more squashes, we were how he wanted us. I figured we looked like a human bug, having a long, frosted body, eight legs, four heads, and an arm at each end. Billy wiped off the lens with a dry cloth from inside the case, looked into the viewfinder one last time, gave the camera one last tweak, stood up, and walked around in front. Glancing back at us, he put out his left leg for a head start, pushed the timer lever down, and ran like the blazes to join us.

Halfway to us, he tripped, burying his face in the snow, quickly scrambled up, and dove into the end of our bug line. There was no way we could hear the timer click or know if the camera worked, but it didn't matter, because we were all laughing so hard and pointing at Billy's white face that no one was posing anymore, anyway.

After we settled down and Billy wiped off his face, we were ready to try again.

"How long is the timer for?" I yelled at him.

"I don't know. You just push the lever and wait until it done." He shouted and ran back to the camera while we waited. The picture must have taken, because he wound the film to the next frame, wiped the lens again, and repositioned the camera back on the knoll. After a repeat of the squeezing routine, he got himself back into a starting position, pushed the timer lever down, and ran like the blazes again.

This time, he didn't trip and got into the bug line without any mishap. We stood, stiff and frozen by the cold, but also stiff and frozen by the camera, afraid to move as we waited for the picture to take. We probably waited a million times longer than was needed, with crappy grins frozen on our faces. Billy finally broke away and ran to check. He gave us the thumbs up, indicating it had taken and then began laughing, holding his stomach. We ran up, as if expecting to see the picture, but of course, there wasn't one. My dad had one of those new Polaroid cameras that actually did make pictures on the spot, but there was no way I dared bring that. He'd kill me if he ever knew I'd taken it. Besides, I didn't know where he hid it.

"What's so funny, heh?" Lenny shouted.

"You are, that's what!" Billy laughed, pointing. "We all are! Look at us! We look like a bunch of hobo penguins at a family reunion at the North Pole."

It was true—we were indeed a pathetic-looking group. Five young, wannabe explorers wearing mismatched coats, pants, hats, gloves, and oversized boots. We had pink frosted faces (except for Lenny, whose face was a shiny shade of reddish brown) all plastered over with mist, frost, and ice, and our squinted slits for eyes were set in scrunched-up frozen faces. A pathetic-looking group of explorers, for sure, but we were here, standing on the ice bridge of Niagara Falls. No matter how we looked, that picture would look terrific hanging on Ol' Gordy's wall. Soon, we were all laughing and pointing at one another.

Chapter 24

I was in a complete state of disbelief that it was me who was standing, on the river, directly in front of Niagara Falls. It had to be someone else, not me. I couldn't be doing this. My life was too dull, too nothing, for this to be me. I had to be dreaming, and I expected to wake up, at any moment, still in my bed wishing I could do something exceptional. This was an extraordinary thing we were doing, and I wasn't great. I was only Kevin, and Kevin didn't do extraordinary things, he only dreamed about them.

Years later, I realized it was at that moment in my life, standing on the Niagara River on that cold February morning in 1962, in front of the mightiest waterfall in the world that I began to understand that great things usually don't happen to great people. Things happen to regular people, and great people emerge from them. I learned that what made people great wasn't what happened to them, but what they did about it. I also learned that truly great people are usually great in other people's minds—seldom in their own, and that most people who think they're great—usually aren't.

Without anyone taking the lead, or even saying anything, we all began walking towards the mighty Niagara, which beckoned us like a king into its presence.

I realized something was wrong with this picture, and it took me a while to know what it was. The image I had in my mind was from the picture hanging on Ol' Gordy's wall that we had examined. But the real world is not always like we conditioned ourselves to see it. To the left, was the side of the gorge, covered in layers of glacial sentinels lined up like guards. Next was Niagara itself, immortal, never changing. Both looked just like they had in that ancient picture from seventy-two years earlier. What was different was the massive hill in that old picture reminding me of Chestnut Ridge, was missing from this ice bridge. Here, there was the open area, and ahead of us was the towering pile of jagged ice sculptures that formed a gigantic wall at the base of the Falls, just like in the picture from fifty years ago—but there wasn't any high hill. I was glad there wasn't a hill; if there had been, Wayne or Chuck would have wanted to climb it. I didn't.

As we drew nearer to the "mountain", it grew in intensity and grandeur. We halted at the point where we dared not approach any closer and stood together, forming a line, watching this spectacular wonder of creation as freezing rains swirled around us like mini tornados. We were the only things in sight that weren't entombed in layers of ice. In every direction around us, there were no boulders, no trees, no ground—only ice. Everything was enclosed in a frozen crypt, subservient to the mountain king. Only the king lived and moved, surging and thundering, spewing out its freezing breath, encasing the immobile inhabitants of its kingdom in ever thicker tombs and icy mausoleums.

"Holy crap!" Billy screamed over the deafening roar that violated and pained our ears. No one heard him.

Although Niagara was no more than a hundred feet in front of us, I felt like I could reach out and put my hand into its fury, and it beckoned for me to do so. We were the only things it hadn't conquered, and it wanted to claim us as special trophies in its frozen empire. Niagara was its own life, throbbing and pulsating, a living mountain towering above us. We were insufficient to its power and immortality. It proclaimed its sovereignty with authority, enslaving all into its kingdom of ice, as prisms of color danced around its base, anointing its altar in a rainbow of glory. I recalled the reflecting lights and colors we had touched at the wall, and the peace that had come over me there. I knew that peace was connected here with the wonder and magnificence of Niagara. Watching Niagara like this, made me appreciate the true wonder of the world God had created for us, and I felt a reverence that I had never felt in the Revival Temple. Was this what God was really about? Something inside of me told me this was closer to the answer than those judgments and damnations so freely given by them who claimed to be chosen above all others.

I thought of the many times I had stood on the shore above, watching, transfixed as the river poured over the brink, plunging into the chaos below, roiling and churning in turbulent swirls and furious whirlpools that opened and closed from unknown depths underneath. I'd always been mesmerized by this unending dance of beauty and chaos.

Then it hit me like a wild pitch striking me right between the eyes, I was standing in the same spot where I'd seen all those furious whirlpools opening! I was not standing on solid ground. I was not *on* but *in* the middle of the Niagara River as it sped away from the brink of the largest waterfalls in the world. In its grip were trees, logs, everything that ever went into the river, churning and spinning and being sucked down into secret depths, to be spewed back up like lava from a volcano. There was no ground beneath me except at the very bottom of the river, maybe hundreds of feet below.

It rolled over me like an avalanche thundering down the side of a mountain. What in the world was I doing? Was I mad? I felt weak—the muscles in my arms and legs began a violent trembling, and my breath came in short, quick gasps. My heart pounded so loud I could hear it above the roar of the Falls. My knees wobbled and shook. I became scared like I'd never been scared before. How thick was this ice? How strong was it? Would it break up? Was there a giant whirlpool coming up right this minute to break the ice apart and pull me down into its icy depths as I stood here? Was I going to die out here? In my mind, all I could see was that picture of those people stranded on the ice, waiting to be swallowed by the river. What had Ol' Gordy said? *"Only a fool would go out on that ice."* I was that fool. I wanted to run away as fast as I could. My old man was right. Who did I think I was, anyway?

Turning in a panic, I slipped on the smooth ridge and stumbled over Wayne's oversized boots. Looking up, I saw him staring ahead as if in a trance. His lips were moving, but I heard no sound. The roar was everywhere. It was the sound of a hundred freight trains coming right at you, never ceasing, never fading, only swelling and becoming more deafening, more staggering every second, vibrating into the very marrow of my bones. It shook my joints apart and set my insides to quivering uncontrollably.

As if floating above the frozen river, Wayne began drifting forward to the beckoning call of the mountain king. Slowly, smoothly, with a grace not inherent in him, he moved from the relative calm of the ice bridge toward the forbidden chaos of the jumbled ice wall.

"Wayne! Stop! Come back!" I screamed at him, but to no avail, my words swallowed by the freight trains. "Wayne, don't go closer! It's too dangerous! Stop!"

I knew he couldn't hear me, but it didn't matter; he wasn't listening anyway. Wayne's sudden desire to go and meet the mountain king broke the wave of terror that had come over me, and I started running toward him. But my legs hadn't recovered their strength yet, my muscles still quivering, went out from under me, sprawling me on the ice, digging my face into the hard crust of the permafrost.

I saw droplets of my blood on the ice—bright red, foreign looking, out of place in this world of snow and ice. As if insulted by color, the droplets were immediately covered over by the mist and quickly blurred—claimed by the mountain king as an offering, my second of the morning. Removing my glove, I felt my face, my nose, my chin for damage. While my fingers came away red, I felt no pain and couldn't tell what was bleeding. My face was too cold to know it was injured.

"What the heck is he doing?" Lenny shouted as he and Chuck began running after Wayne. I felt something shaking my arm, and looked up into the frightened face of Billy. He was shouting something in a great panic. And he wasn't looking at Wayne, so it wasn't obvious why he was worked up. Waving his arms, he pointed toward the uppermost edge of the gorge.

I looked up, past the ice sentries that stood guard, past the dark, rippled columns of ice lining the gorge, past the torrent of water pouring down the mountain, until my head was bent straight back, looking up at the top edge of the gorge. What I saw there, added another level of fear to my already panic drenched spirit. There, moving around in animation, were people, and they were pointing and gesturing down into the gorge. Although they looked tiny from where I stood, it was obvious they were pointing at us.

"Come on, guys, we gotta get outta here!" Billy screamed, and although I couldn't hear him, I knew he was whining my song this time.

Chuck and Lenny had gotten Wayne turned around and were bringing him back from the sacrificial altar of the mountain king. Pulling myself to my feet, I clumsily ran forward, grabbing Wayne by the arm.

"Wayne, are you all right? What the heck were you doing?" I shouted into his face. Wayne didn't respond but only stared ahead, his eyes unfocused. I began shaking him, trying to break the hypnotic spell the mountain king had put on him. "Wayne! C'mon, buddy, snap out of it!" I shouted. "Darn it, Wayne! C'mon! We don't have time for this!"

His eyes focused on me, and he came back from wherever the monster had taken him. "Stop shaking me" he said.

"Wayne, you okay, buddy?"

"I said stop shaking me. Let go of me!" he snapped. Whatever spell he'd been under had passed. I stared into his face, trying to understand what had just happened, but it was beyond my comprehension.

"Okay, fine!" I shouted, releasing his arms. "Then look up there!" I pointed to the top of the gorge. Everyone followed my outstretched arm, looking up.

"Oh, crap, they're pointing at us!" Chuck yelled. "They see us down here! We gotta haul ass!" Even though we couldn't hear Chuck, it was the general sentiment. With that, everything changed. In a mad rush, we all began running back to the ice maze, slipping and stumbling over the ice and each other.

Chapter 25

Reaching the crawlspace from where we had emerged onto the bridge, we crouched behind the ice columns, hiding from the probing eyes above.

"Kevin, can you see up there?" Chuck shouted. Moving around, I strained to get a clear view to the top of the gorge. There, gathered along the edge of the Falls was a large crowd gesturing and pointing down. From this distance, I couldn't see if they were pointing at us or just pointing into the gorge. There was no doubt they had seen us and had obviously watched us run this way. I doubted if they could see us now, hidden as we were, behind the pillars and under the overhangs, but what I saw next sent chills, colder than the ice on which I knelt, up and down my spine. To the left of that large group of tourists, a scene unfolded from the worse nightmare I could imagine. There, directly in line with a small opening in the frozen sentinels lining the gorge's wall was a second, smaller group of people. This group was distinguished by the bright yellow slickers and long black hats they wore. I knew those uniforms all too well. They were the Niagara Falls Fire Department, and they were throwing something over the edge of the gorge.

"Yeah, I can and holy crap, there's a rescue team up there, and I think they're coming down over the side!"

Chuck worked his way to my side in order to see for himself. As he stared at the scene above, fear didn't hide behind his eyes in the back room any longer—it was all over his face. He was scared. "Oh, crap, they are. They're going to rope down from there. Man, that's dangerous, coming down that close to the Falls, they must think we're trapped down here to be doing something like that. There's gonna be hell to pay for certain now!"

"Oh, crap, what're we gonna do now?" Billy's shrieking voice was shrill, and his cheeks were wet, and not only from the swirling mist around him. "We're gonna go to jail! I knew we shouldn't have come! My mother's gonna kill me now!"

"Shut up, Billy, and quit your jabbering!" Chuck snapped at him. "Let's get outta here. Come on, we gotta get back."

"What if they're coming down in the tunnel too?" Lenny asked. "We'll run right into them. Do you think they know about that way?"

"What do you think?" Chuck answered, without malice or sarcasm. "You remember that barricade in place at the entrance?" Lenny nodded his head. "Well, who do you think put it there? Besides, sooner or later, they'll see our tracks in the snow up there and figure out that's how we got down here."

Chuck paused, looking at us carefully. He seemed to be sizing us up, as if to see if we were ready to hear the truth. He must have decided we were, or it was too late to matter if we weren't. "It doesn't matter." He stared at us, "We can't go back up that way anyway."

"What do ya mean; we can't go up that way? Why not? We gotta get out of here before they put us in jail! That's the way out. That's the way we came." Billy shrieked.

"Yeah, why not?" Lenny added. "How else are we gonna get back up?"

Even in this desperate situation, Chuck couldn't stop himself from smirking, if only a little. "You remember that ice ledge we had so much fun getting off of in the tunnel? The one you guys roped down and I 'Geronimo'd' down?"

"Yeah, sure we do, so what?" Lenny said.

"Did you ever wonder how we'd get back up it?" Chuck let the thought sink in.

Oh, my God—Chuck was right! How could I have been so stupid? I never thought about that. We couldn't get back up that pillar, even if we had spikes on our feet. Holy crap, what had I been thinking? How *were* we going to get out of here?

As the realization sunk in, that there was, in fact, no way we could scale that sheer, smooth pillar of ice, a wave of panic swept over me, engulfing me in fear and desperation. I was feeling utterly stupid that I hadn't seen it.

"Well, I'll tell you how." Chuck answered his own question, speaking what we all feared. "We *ain't*, that's how. Besides, now that they know we're down here, there's going to be cops all over up there. We couldn't just walk out with all those cops around and say, 'Howdy, guys! What's going on?' Now, can we?" He paused. "Not unless you want to be on the six o'clock news tonight, that is."

"Oh, crap! We're going to jail. My mother's gonna kill me," Billy whined.

"Don't feel alone man," Wayne had his own concerns. "There's a beating coming my way for sure, too. But how are we gonna get out of here? We're trapped. We gotta let them rescue us. There's no other way." Seems like whatever had driven Wayne to come down here, in the first place, had dissipated, along with his strange encounter with the mountain king.

"Being on the six o'clock news ain't gonna make my dad any too happy. That's the last thing he wants right now, having me splashed all over the news as the *bad colored boy*. My folks ain't gonna like this at all." Lenny's fears were for a different reason. He was afraid because of his color and what that would mean. There'd be a special backlash against him. He feared not only the punishment he'd get personally but more so for what his parents would suffer, because their colored son had gotten himself stranded in the gorge and had to be rescued and then arrested for breaking the law. No matter what the crime or who else was involved, there would be an outstanding stigma attached to him because of his skin color. Coming to America as a colored man and just getting settled in his new role and all, this was not the publicity his father sought.

Me? Yeah, I was afraid, too, in the same way every person is afraid of what he doesn't understand. I feared what I didn't understand about my old man and how he would use this as an excuse to beat me. My sense of justice told me that punishment was probably in order for breaking the law and coming down here, but what I also knew was that the punishment I'd get would far outweigh the crime committed. I knew that I would not only be punished for the crime but that the crime would serve as an excuse for further punishment. Especially, since the fire department was involved, and he'd see his name being held up for ridicule.

I looked over at Chuck and realized that, under his boasting and bravado, he was afraid, too. But I think Chuck was afraid of *not* being punished, that no one, except his mom, would care one way or another that he had gone out onto the ice bridge, or even if he came back or not. I didn't know how I knew this, but somehow, like earlier, I did, and I now realized that the fear I had seen living behind his eyes yesterday, was the fear that no one cared.

It was probably the worst fear of all.

"Did you know we couldn't get back up when we came down that ledge?" I asked.

"No, of course not. If I had, I'd have tied off ropes to climb back up. I didn't think about going back up until we were walking through the maze, and that's when it hit me."

"So, what are we gonna do?" Lenny asked. "How are we gonna out of here?"

"We're trapped down here! We're gonna die down here!" Billy was on the verge of a full-blown panic attack.

Chapter 26

"We have to go down to the Whirlpool, and go up that path." I said.

Chuck nodded. "Yeah, that's what I figured, too."

"The Whirlpool! Oh, crap! That's a long way! I don't know if I can make it to the Whirlpool." Billy wasn't happy about the opportunity to walk the gorge under these conditions—or any conditions for that matter. "Oh, crap! I'm gonna die for sure."

"You got any better ideas?" Chuck asked. "And you're not gonna die, Billy. You can make it to the Whirlpool; it ain't that far."

"What if they see us from the top and follow us up there?" Lenny asked. "What if they're already at the Whirlpool, waiting for us there, too?"

"They won't be able to see us from up there," I said. "Unless you're standing at the edge of the gorge, you can't see straight down. Once we get away from the Falls, if we stay close to the side, with all this ice, we'll be under the overhangs, and nobody will be able see us."

"No one's going to think we walked over to the Whirlpool when they saw us up here. That's why they're roping down the side of the gorge here; they think we're trapped right here." Chuck's reasoning was sound.

"What if those overhangs fall on us?" Billy asked.

Chuck sighed, his patience wearing thin. "They're not going to fall, Billy. Why would they just happen to come down right when your skinny butt is walking under them? Come on, let's get going, we're wasting time here, and they're gonna come down soon."

"How far is it to the Whirlpool from here, Kevin? Is it hard to walk?" Lenny asked.

"It's a couple of miles, and it's not an easy walk in summer, with all the rocks and everything. There's not a lot of shoreline to walk on most of the way, especially at the rapids themselves. Walking by them in the summer scares me. I don't know what it's like in winter. I guess it's gonna depend on how much ice there is on the shore."

"We don't have to walk by the rapids, do we?" Wayne asked. "I thought they were on the other side of the Whirlpool, past the trail going back up."

"There are rapids on both sides," I answered, not wanting to tell him the worst were on this side of the Whirlpool and we'd have to pass right by them.

Billy whined, "Let's just wait here for them to come and get us, and take our medicine. It's too cold to walk all that way to the Whirlpool." Billy's fear of getting rescued, getting a beating from his mother or of going to jail had all now receded, having been replaced by his fear of making the trip downriver to the Whirlpool. "They wouldn't really put us in jail, would they?"

"The walk will warm you up. If not, then your mother will when she gets her hands on you. There's no other choice." Chuck insisted.

I could see the swirling mists working to claim our small group, as it had claimed everything else down here. Each of us had turned a pallid white, with frost building on our clothes and faces. It occurred to me that if we stood still long enough, we would become part of the gorge—frozen, turned into ice sentinels that waited and guarded the

Falls until the spring thaw. We'd be claimed by the mountain king as part of his kingdom. My hand already had turned white like the ice—*my hand? Where's my glove?* Checking my pockets, I remembered I'd taken off my glove when I'd fallen out on the ice. I had left it out there during all the turmoil of Wayne's diversion and then when we ran back. I was glad I brought an extra pair.

The trip downriver with the rapids scared me, and I looked for a reason not to go. Maybe it *would* just be best to stay here and let them rescue us and take whatever came, as Billy said. *They wouldn't actually put us in jail, would they?*

"Talking about it ain't going to get us anywhere," Wayne said. "If people are coming down to look for us, we'd better get moving back to the Schoellkopf in a hurry, 'cause we got to go that way no matter what."

"Wayne's right," Chuck said. "Let's beat feet and on the double. We got to get back there before anyone comes down." With that, Chuck abruptly turned and started crawling back under the overhang into the maze. Wayne, Lenny, and Billy, reluctantly crawled after him.

After taking one last look at the mountain king, I turned and followed.

Volume Three

the Feather

Chapter 27

Following our path back through the maze was easier than when we had forged it. Knowing what was behind each pillar and around each turn made the trip almost routine. With the trail clearly defined and our destination fixed in our heads, as well as having a major dose of motivational fear spurring us on, we traveled back in a third of the time it'd taken us earlier. Behind, we left a clear trail having tracks going in both directions. Following us would be a simple matter.

Once again approaching the Rainbow Bridge, we kept to the shadows as much as possible to prevent anyone from seeing us. Fortunately, being a cold, Sunday morning, there weren't any pedestrians walking across and the traffic was light. Most people driving over the bridge looked out at the Falls, not immediately below. If anyone did glance over, it'd be hard to see us from up there since we were camouflaged with a thick coating of white frost and ice. Should someone happen to see us, the most they could do would be to advise the customs agent after crossing over. By then, we'd be gone.

Our concern was if someone were on the bridge looking for us. Hopefully, the excitement over at the Falls, with the rescue team and all, would keep the spotlight there, before they looked around.

Once under the bridge we were hidden from any searching eyes above. Reaching the opposite side, we hung back in the shadows, staring up to see if any faces stared back. None did, so we quickly emerged and proceeded downriver at a fast pace, staying in the shadows as much as possible. Glancing back, I didn't see anyone on the bridge.

We reached the ice ledge at the bottom of the Schoellkopf tunnel and paused. Looking at it with a deep yearning, I sure would like to get up that ledge and climb the tunnel out of here. I wasn't eager to walk to the Whirlpool. But, of course, Chuck was right; there was no way we were going to go up that thirty-five-foot ice slide. There was nothing on top to throw a rope around or lasso. All was smooth, solid, unassailable ice. How could I have been so stupid? And, where was Superman when you needed him?

"We should go up there." Billy didn't have to shout any longer, but the fear he nourished caused him to anyway.

"Got any ideas how?" I asked.

Chuck dismissed it. "We'd only be wasting our time. Even if we could get up it, they'll be coming down this way sooner or later, and for sure, they're up there right now wandering around. There's no way we'd be able to avoid them."

Billy continued to shout his whining, "So what, why avoid them? It'd be better than dying down here!"

"For crying out loud, Billy, we're not going to die down here. We're gonna walk to the Whirlpool; and then climb out there, that's all," Chuck said. "And stop shouting; we can hear you."

"I say we should just wait here and let them come and get us," Billy shouted. "What if we can't climb out at the Whirlpool? What'll we do then, huh? Stay down here til it's dark? Then what'll we do, huh? We'll freeze to death for sure. Oh, crap! We're gonna die down here! I knew

I shouldn't have come. Why'd you guys make me?" Billy wasn't even attempting to hold it together any longer.

"Maybe we should just wait here for them to find us," Lenny said. I didn't know if he wanted to stay, or if he was only trying to calm Billy down. Whatever his reason, it was all the encouragement Billy needed.

"Yeah, that's right, Lenny! Come on, guys, let's just wait here. Lenny's right. We'll wait for them to come and get us. We can't walk to the Whirlpool—it's too far. We don't have to die down here. Who knows? Maybe we'll be heroes."

"It's not that far to the Whirlpool. We walk more than that to go to Ol' Gordy's every day," Chuck said. "It's either that, or face 'the man' up there, and you won't be any kind of a hero neither. You're just a punk to them that's caused a lot of trouble, and they'll throw the book at you."

"Maybe we should wait here, Chuck," I said. "Passing by those rapids isn't easy in the summertime. I don't know if they're passable in wint . . ."

"There's no other way, Kevin," Chuck cut me off. "They catch us, there's gonna be hell to pay. Be plastered all over TV? You ready for that, having your old man to deal with? And who knows, he might even be part of that rescue team coming down out there right now. You want to face him down here—or back home? He ain't gonna like his little boy causing him so much embarrassment now, is he? Then there are the cops and a court with a judge. I'm not going there; you can bet your ass on that!" He looked directly at me, and I could see a fierce determination on his face. "Let me make it real clear. I *can't* go there. I got a belly full of dealing with *the man* already, and I can't have any more crap with them right now! All I need is something like this, and I could be visiting my ol' man in Attica. And not just to say howdy, neither."

Looking at him, I saw a different Chuck than I'd seen before. This one had secrets our group knew nothing about. Apparently, there were some people who might care that he was down here—the wrong people, for the wrong reasons.

"We've already beat this horse to death," Chuck snapped. "We're wasting time. We know we can't get up this ledge, no matter what, so that leaves two choices: sit here and wait, or go to the Whirlpool. Well, I'm not about to just sit here and wait for all hell to break loose. Now quit crying like a bunch of girls, and let's get going."

"Let's vote on it." Billy tried one last hope.

"I'm not voting!" Chuck said. "I'm going, period. You do what you want, but I'm not going to sit on my ass, waiting to get 'rescued'. I'm going to the Whirlpool. It's not that far, and no one will be looking for us down there. Now, who's going with me?" Once again, Chuck brought it down to simple terms—and a decision.

The four of us stood there, unsure of what to do. None of us wanted to be rescued and get into trouble, but none of us wanted to walk to the Whirlpool either. Time moves slowly when everyone is waiting for someone else to make the first move.

"Fine, suit yourselves," Chuck finally said. "I'm going. Just get one thing straight—when you get caught, no one better mention my name, you hear? Anyone mentions me, and you're dead meat. I was never here; you got that?" Chuck turned his back on us and started walking toward the pillars on the opposite side.

We stood, watching him as he felt his way among the columns, looking for the best way around. "Geez, what'll we do, Kevin?" Lenny asked.

I knew I couldn't stay here waiting for a rescue team knowing that Chuck was out there, walking the gorge, alone. I looked at Wayne who was watching Chuck also. He turned to look at me and nodded, and we both knew what we had to do.

"We can't leave Chuck alone," I said. "I don't know what's going to happen, but we're in this together. We came here together, and we leave here together. C'mon, let's go."

Wayne and I followed after Chuck. Behind me, I could hear Billy whimpering, "Oh, crap."

Chapter 28

Reaching Chuck, I looked back and saw Lenny and Billy coming up behind us. Large tears cut trails through the frost on Billy's face, like the sad clown at the circus. Chuck looked at us and nodded. He didn't say anything, but I could tell he was relieved. He hadn't relished the idea of going to the Whirlpool alone.

"Look, we can go under this overhang here. It's out of view of anyone who comes down, and if we cover our tracks, no one will know we went this way, so they won't follow us and there won't be anyone at the Whirlpool waiting for us. They'll see our footprints at the Falls and be out there looking for us, while we'll be climbing out of here at the Whirlpool."

"Won't they see our tracks coming back here?" I asked.

"The path is beat down with tracks going in both directions, and we'll make some more now, so they'll think after we got back here and couldn't get up the ledge, we went back, looking for a way out. When they can't find us, someone may come back to look this way, but by then, we'll have hauled butts and be long gone. What'd ya think?"

"Yeah, okay, sounds like a plan" Wayne answered for all of us.

"Okay then," Chuck said. "Wayne and I will walk back down the trail a ways and then backtrack here. You guys walk around, so it looks as if we were milling around all over."

Chuck and Wayne walked back towards the Falls until they were out of sight and then returned, walking backwards. Meanwhile, Lenny and I walked around randomly, tramping everything down. Billy stood and watched.

"Good," Chuck said after we reassembled at the far-side overhang. "Now let's walk out of here. C'mon, Wayne, you go first with those big boots." Chuck guided him under the overhang. "Step careful and try not to mess up much snow until you're around the back side." Wayne carefully stepped under the huge overhang until we couldn't see him any longer.

"Okay, Lenny, step in the middle of Wayne's tracks." Lenny carefully followed Wayne, stepping into each of Wayne's tracks. It looked like only one person had gone there. After Billy and I went through, Chuck took off his gloves and, holding them by the cuffs, he stepped backwards into the single set of tracks. Using his gloves like a broom, he swept over and covered each track with fresh snow as he followed us around. The snow here was about four inches deep, so the tracks filled in easily without a lot of disturbance in the surrounding area, leaving no furrows. After Chuck had joined us, we looked back to see his handiwork.

"Cool," Wayne said. "They'll never know we came this way."

Chuck nodded, proud of his handiwork "Not bad, if I have to say so myself. Must be my Indian blood, and the wind will blend it in even more. Okay, let's beat feet."

Chapter 29

Staying as close to the wall of the gorge as we could, we began the journey to the Whirlpool. The columns, ledges, and massive overhangs of layered ice became less pronounced the farther away we got from the swirling sprays and winds of the Falls, allowing more sunlight in.

The result was spellbinding, and welcome, as the sun flooded the gorge with warmth and brightness. We were blinded by the brilliance as it sparkled and spread out a welcome heat that soaked into our outer clothing. Especially gratifying was the warmth on our faces. After being inside the enclosed stairway at Schoellkopf and then out on the ice bridge, where the sun had shone brightly but had been filtered by the mist and spray from the Falls, the unfiltered rays felt good on our skin and surprisingly, raised our spirits.

My eyelids squeezed into tight slits as the sharp needles of light pierced inward and, even with my eyes closed, light penetrated inside my head. Where the sun's rays encountered the arctic overhangs and suspended icicles, rainbows and refracted color beams shot out in all directions. The bottom of the gorge looked like an immense treasure chest, full of sparkling jewels.

I'd periodically scan upwards to the top of the gorge, searching for people who were searching for us. I couldn't see the top. It was too steep, with protrusions of thick ice and outcroppings blocking the view, and if I couldn't see the top, then no one could see the bottom.

Although snow-covered, more of the features of the gorge began revealing themselves. Boulders, ledges, and rock overhangs became more pronounced; protruding outwards through the layers of snow. Brushing snow away from boulders and rocks, as we traveled, genuine rock was exposed underneath. It was still encased in ice, so there was no bare rock to touch, but the layers of ice were less thick and were clear enough in spots to see Mother Earth below. It was the first ground we'd seen since leaving the world above.

With each step we took, the tremor of the Falls receded, while the low rumble of the river grew louder, and then I realized: *we hadn't seen the river.* We had walked and stood on it; yet other than where it plummeted over the crest, we had not seen the river. Being in the gorge, without the river providing a reference or a landmark, made me disoriented and left a sick feeling in my stomach.

Normally, the river dominates the gorge with its power and grandeur. It's beautiful. Huge rocks and boulders line the shore, protruding outwards and causing the green, racing water to surge and swirl in a constant onslaught of gurgling foam. It was dangerous; one mistake and you'd be swept away, smashed against the rocks, ripped apart by the inventory of submerged debris that traveled with it, or sucked down into unknown depths by the numerous whirlpools that opened and closed constantly. The river was the force on which everything was centered in the gorge, and you knew where it was.

Now, there was no river. It was under the ice. I could hear it rumbling—murmuring. I could feel it surging and pulsing. But it didn't dominate the area—the ice did. The river was secondary and other than a vibration, invisible. Where was it? I didn't know, and not knowing scared me. It was close. I knew that.

But, the ice is also the river, so in a way, I was seeing the river. The same river, only different. I wondered how the same thing could be so totally different. It was like my dad, taking me to Crystal Beach and having a swell time one day, and then beating the crap out of me for no reason the next. It was a lesson I was to learn well over the years and hold dear as one of the few truths of life. People have said there are no black or whites, and that everything is a variation of gray. But, it seems to me there are no grays and neither is everything black or white. Rather, everything is black *and* white. It's a matter of when and where a person is at any particular time. What's black today can be white tomorrow, and what's white for one is black for another. I think folks want things to be gray, so they can cope with it all, and not have to take sides. I wondered if there were any absolutes.

The travel was better than I expected, with the ice and snow helping, not hindering, our footing. The shore, along the gorge, is scored with boulders, large and small, interlaced with a thick tangle of foliage and vines all knotted together. This makes traveling in the summer difficult, with crevices and tripping hazards everywhere and seldom a flat surface to step on. Now, the snow and ice had packed into the crevices, providing a crusty surface that compressed under our feet, covered the tripping tangle and making for flatter surfaces to walk on.

We traveled along the side of the gorge with relative ease for some distance. Coming from behind an exceptionally large, ice-encased boulder, we found ourselves on a low, flat ledge. And, like some magician's trick, there it was, rolling, surging, lapping at the very ledge we stood upon, mere feet from our boots—the river.

And it was every bit as beautiful as I remembered it to be. Rising and falling like a giant green snake. It undulated, rippling up and down as it rushed through the gorge, on its journey to Lake Ontario. In this frozen, immobile gorge, it was even more dominant than during the warmer months. Sunlight reflected off its surface like flashing green mirrors, and chunks of ice spun and swirled along its surface, smashing full speed into one another, before crashing and grinding against the boulders and shore ice.

Upon seeing the river, a peace came over me, and I felt tension easing from my body. I'd been disoriented, in a foreign land without familiar surroundings, unsettling to my mind and soul. Now, it was like meeting an old friend, and it quelled my uneasiness, raising my level of confidence that we would get out of this okay. I knew where I was. I knew where the river was. And knowing those things, made all the difference.

The river is quite wide here and deep, so although it's swift moving; it's not turbulent and wild. Knowing where the edge of the river cut into the shore helped us to pick our way around the boulders and obstacles jutting out of the snow and ice. We continued with a heightened sense of optimism and awareness.

Chapter 30

We came upon a large group of boulders, where an expansive canopy of ice had formed across the top, creating a natural shelter. Figuring we had traveled far enough away from the excitement at the Falls, we decided to rest and eat something.

Lenny removed the pack from Wayne's back and reaching in, he pulled out his big paper bag and distributed a shiny aluminum package to each of us. Unwrapping these silver gifts, we discovered treasures inside: two PB&J sandwiches and a few chocolate chip cookies in each.

"Holy cow!" Wayne exclaimed. "How in the world did you sneak all this out without your mom knowing? Man, that's a whole jar of peanut butter for all these. My mom would have killed me."

"I didn't sneak them, my mom made them. I told her we were going hiking and we were each bringing something, and I was gonna bring sandwiches, heh? I was hoping she'd make one for each of us, but instead, she made two and threw in a thermos of cocoa and a hand full of her chocolate chip cookies, too."

"You got some mom, man," Wayne said woofing down a PB&J. I noticed Chuck was listening close and not saying anything. I also noticed that Chuck hadn't brought anything of his own, other than a candy bar I saw him eat earlier. He seemed to be enjoying his PB&J sandwich

"Oh, man, it's crunchy too, that's my favorite. Right on, Lenny!" Wayne exclaimed.

We all devoured the sandwiches. I never knew a PB&J could taste so delicious. The thermos of hot cocoa was passed around. It had cooled off some, and there was only enough for a couple of swallows each, but it was like manna from heaven. Apparently, Chuck had lost his contemptuous opinion of this "girl's" drink, as he gulped down his share without hesitation.

After finishing off the sandwiches and chocolate chip cookies, we started in on a half full package of Oreos that Billy had brought. We polished them off in short order, along with one of Wayne's Dr. Peppers and a Coke. It was amazing how hungry a little thing like visiting the ice bridge of Niagara Falls could make a fella. While we ate, our conversation was on things other than where we were. No one wanted to talk about that as we tried to put a sense of normalcy back into our lives, if only for a little while.

Wayne noticed a snow-covered rock formation off to the side. "Man, look at that statue over there. It looks just like Marilyn Monroe!"

"Marilyn Monroe?" I replied. "Where do you see Marilyn Monroe?"

"What, you can't see her? It's just like in that movie with her white dress blowing up," he said, pointing at a certain mound of snow, as we stared, mystified. "Look," he said in exasperation, "that's her head right on top there and below is that gorgeous body of hers. See it? Right there in front of you, for crying out loud?" The snow sculpture that Wayne referred to did have a head-type top and had some protrusions below it, but it took a whole lot of imagination to create Marilyn Monroe out of it.

Chuck shook his head in a mixture of amusement and disbelief. "Your problem is you need to see the real thing spaz, so you can tell the difference between a woman and snow."

"I've seen plenty, don't you worry about that." Wayne defended himself lamely.

"Yeah, right. Who'd you ever see?" Chuck pushed. I wanted to know, too.

"None of your business, that's who. That's for me to know, and you to dream about!"

I couldn't tell if Wayne was bluffing or not.

"Shoot man, I'll bet you've never seen anything," Chuck taunted him. "Not even that Judy who you've been hanging out with forever now."

"Like crap. What do you know? I get my share; don't you worry about it."

"Share? Only 'share' you get is when you cop a feel in the hall at school," Chuck said. "*Oh, I'm so sorry, Betty Sue! I didn't mean to trip and grab you with both my hands like this!*" Chuck mimicked while pantomiming mashing two good handfuls. We busted a gut, knowing each of us was guilty of using the same ploy at one time or another.

"Hey guys listen—do you hear that?" Lenny broke in, who hadn't been laughing.

"What? Hear what?" Wayne said eager to change the subject.

"Be quiet! Listen!" Lenny ordered. "There, that! Hear that?" The laughter stopped, and everyone strained to hear what Lenny was talking about.

"I don't hear anything," I said. "What do you hear?"

"Nothing now," Lenny replied. "I thought I heard a rumble."

"What kind of 'rumble'?" Chuck asked.

"I don't know—a rumble. I don't hear it now." All we could hear was the rush of the river as it continued racing by.

"Only rumble you heard was the rumble in Wayne's head, thinking about that statue of Marilyn Monroe over there!" Chuck said, and everyone, except Lenny and Wayne, broke out laughing again.

Chapter 31

We pooled the remainder of our food together. There were a total of four Hostess cupcakes, three packages of Twinkies (guess I wasn't the only one who had swiped them), five candy bars, one box of Milk Duds, and four bottles of soda pop. Even being inside of Wayne's knapsack, things had gotten damp. We used the leftover aluminum foil, wrapping everything and crimping the ends tight, before storing them in the knapsack. There was enough foil remaining to wrap around the camera case, just to be sure no moisture could ruin our prized picture. Cleaning up the wrappers and stuffing them into Wayne's knapsack, it occurred to me that no one had thrown any wrappers or garbage away. None of us could bring ourselves to pollute the gorge with a candy wrapper.

"How much farther is it, Kevin?" Lenny asked.

"Well, I know we're more than halfway."

"Hey, that's cool. We'll get there before you know it then, heh?" Lenny said.

I didn't want to throw a damper on Lenny's optimism or to set Billy off, so I didn't say anything about what was ahead. The distance didn't concern me—the rapids did. Billy had calmed down considerably since leaving the tunnel, which for him, was spooky. We were used to his whining and whimpering, and his silence scared me.

"Do you think anyone is following?" Wayne wondered.

"Nah, they'll be poking around at the other end, probably going nuts, trying to figure out where we disappeared to." Chuck said. "C'mon, let's haul ass."

The sides of the canyon became steeper the farther we traveled downriver. Every now and then I was able to catch a glimpse of the top edge, but I couldn't see if anyone up there would be able to see around all the growth and obstructions. The road that ran along the top edge of the gorge didn't have many places where people could stop and look over the edge, so I wasn't particularly concerned about being seen, but I couldn't stop looking all the same.

The river was our constant companion, not an adversary or a threat, but a comfort. The gurgling tempo of the water was soothing. There were a number of tight spots where the gorge and the river came close together, which took time and care to move past, but we were able to past through them without incident.

Coming out from around a large boulder, and looking like a picture on a postcard, the railroad and the Whirlpool bridges loomed directly ahead of us. Straddling the width of the river, they looked like a pair of giant safety pins holding the United States and Canada together. The bridges were a familiar sight to me, signaling we had made considerable progress, but while the others rejoiced openly, a chill traveled the length of my spine. I knew what those bridges signaled lay ahead, and it scared the daylights out of me.

The river began necking down, like a large funnel lying on its side. The closer the shores got to one another the faster the current became, rushing into the funnel. A change occurred, not only to the river's width, but also to its depth as the bottom rose up. The result was one of utter chaos, as all the surging energy of the racing river attempted to occupy the same space at the same time. The river turned into a white, foaming monster spewing its vengeance into the air with fury and abandonment, crashing down on the boulders and icebergs. The sight stopped us dead. It was exciting and beautiful to see, from a distance. Up close, it was the most terrifying thing I'd ever seen in my life.

Overhead, the motionless eminence of the bridges, contrasted with the wild turbulence of the river. They were imposing and majestic, calmly spanning the wild violence below, connecting two different worlds together.

"Man, imagine jumping off those bridges into this monster!" Wayne said. Looking at his enraptured face, the jingle of an ice cream truck played in the recesses of my mind.

"You know, it was right here that my people came over, heh?" Lenny said.

"Your people? Came over?" Wayne asked, breaking away from his fascination with jumping off the bridges. "What are you talking about?"

"When they came up from the South."

"The South? I didn't know you came from the South. I thought you came from Canada," Wayne said.

"Not me, my *people* Wayne, when they came over from Africa." Lenny said.

"Africa? Your parents came from Africa?" Wayne seemed surprised.

"You mean they came over here as slaves, don't you, Lenny?" I asked.

"Is that right, your parents were slaves?" Wayne had never made the connection between history and real people. He didn't have much sensitivity about it either.

"My parents weren't slaves!" Lenny flared up. "I told you, not me or my parents, I'm talking about my ancestors." He paused, and then said, "And yeah, they were slaves."

"What do you mean saying 'this is where they came over'?" I asked, trying to soothe his anger, plus I wanted to know.

"I mean this is where they escaped from slavery into Canada" Lenny explained.

"They escaped? Here? How do you know that?" I asked.

"My mom and dad brought me and my sister here when we moved from Canada this summer. Of course, we were up there, on top, not down here. My mom wanted to show us the bridge and tell us the story. It was my great-great-great grandma, when she was only a girl. She escaped on the Underground Railroad to Canada, right here across the old railroad bridge that was here before this one."

"Man, that's cool! So you were American before you became Canadian?" Wayne continued, unruffled by Lenny's anger.

"Not me, Wayne! I'm Canadian and always have been. My ancestor granny and *she* wasn't an American either; she was a slave." Lenny was miffed by the question, his voice taking on a tone I hadn't heard before. "You're not a citizen when you're a slave, Wayne. You're not even a person! You're a thing. She escaped like a criminal and only became a free person when she got to Canada." Lenny had some pent up feelings locked away inside him. "Ask the owner if a slave is a citizen and his answer is 'No, they're my property!' Is a chair a citizen? Well, a slave is no different."

"That was really bull crap back then, people thinking they owned people," I said. "Thank God that's all behind us now and slavery's a thing of the past."

"What makes you think it's all in the past?" Lenny spat back. "People here still think they're better than others because their skin's a different color."

"Yeah, some people are always gonna think that, Lenny, but the Civil War ended slavery. That was over a hundred years ago. This is 1962, not 1862—there's no slavery now."

"Yeah? Well, you go tell that to your old man. See what he thinks about it. He won't even let me in your house because I'm *a colored boy.*'"

"My old man can be a real jerk sometimes" was all I could manage to say.

"Well, there's a lot of jerks around then, ain't there?" Lenny replied. "Slavery may be against the law, but racism isn't over by a long stretch. Ain't much difference in some areas than it was a hundred years ago. Black folks still live like slaves down South. And that's not just some people thinking that way, neither, Kevin, that's the law. Can't ride the bus; can't drink the water; can't eat in the restaurant; can't get a decent job. 'Yes sir, masta . . . no sir, masta'. Lenny looked at me sharply but without malice. "Don't tell me slavery's over. Not by a long shot it isn't."

We had never talked about race before. It had never come up as anything between us, but now I realized, just like the river behind him, there was a lot going on under the surface I didn't know anything about.

"From where down South did your people come, Lenny?" Chuck asked.

"I don't know. I asked my mom that too and she didn't know. The story's been passed down from generation to generation, and some of it's been lost, but they probably didn't even know. They were slaves in a foreign land, with a language they couldn't understand; shuffled around from plantation to plantation. Didn't know anything about different States or even what continent it was. Amazing they were able to find their way North. Without the Underground Railroad working for them, they never could have."

"I remember reading something about an Underground Railroad in school, but I didn't know it was around here," Wayne said. "Are those the same tracks the train ran on then?"

"There weren't any tracks, Wayne, it wasn't a real train." Looking at Wayne, then back at Lenny, I realized although they lived a few blocks apart, their worlds were as different from one another as the ice bridge was from the city of Niagara Falls.

I looked up at the railroad bridge with a different feeling and sense of awareness than I had just ten minutes earlier. I'd seen this bridge many times, but had never made a connection to slavery with it before. I glanced over at Lenny, and he was staring at the bridge, as well. I tried to imagine what was going through his mind. Maybe he was wondering about his ancestors, fugitives on the run, who escaped from slavery right here on this spot, to a life of freedom, giving Lenny a future. I wondered how they did it. How did they know where to go or what to do in a country they knew nothing about and where they clearly stood out? Coming North from down South somewhere, the journey must have been hard and scary. Who were the people who helped them escape? The Underground Railroad was something I knew about but never thought much about. In my mind, slavery was down South, in places I'd never been to, and in history books about people I didn't know. But now, standing next to Lenny and feeling its impact upon his life, it held a whole new meaning for me, and I wondered greatly about it . . .

Chapter 32

Lizzie's Story

The Niagara Escarpment
1859

Squatting on the ground, the dampness seeping in through her coarse cotton dress, Lizzie wished she had more clothes. It was a lot colder in this place than it had been back on Massa Johnson's plantation. Her stomach made noises, but she was used to it talking to her and to having those empty feelings in her belly.

It surprised her that the others stayed so quiet, no shuffling or coughing. They made no sound, save their breathing, which was lost on the brisk night air. In the blackness, Lizzie couldn't see her mammy next to her, but she knew she was there by the warmth of the hand that tightly held hers.

Hiding in the bushes, waiting for the lantern to flash three times, as Mother had said, Lizzie's thoughts went back to when the journey had begun.

The trouble started when Massa Johnson wanted Latisha, who was Lizzie's mammy, to stay in the big house at night. Latisha, who everyone said was a most beautiful mulatto, refused. Lizzie didn't know why her mammy said no. It was a real nice house and warmer than the slave quarters they lived in. She guessed Mammy worried about leaving Pappy and her alone at night, but Lizzie wouldn't have minded if her mammy stayed in the big house at night and came back in the day.

Tomas, Lizzie's pappy, minded a lot. He was terribly angry and paced about, saying bad things about Massa Johnson.

The next day, Massa Johnson changed Tomas's work from working the blacksmit'n he was good at to working in the 'bacca fields. This made Tomas even more angry, not 'cause of the work, but 'cause he wouldn't be around the house during the day and he worried about Latisha being alone.

But Lizzie thought Pappy needn't have worried, 'cause Mammy's work got changed too, from working with the cows and goats to working in the big house, where she would be safe. Though this was better work and Latisha was given a new white dress of nice, soft cotton, not the common sacks the other slaves wore, this made Tomas even angrier and he ranted louder than before. The other slaves kept telling him to hush up and not be making such a scene, but he wouldn't listen. Lizzie didn't know why her Pappy was getting so worked up and angry just 'cause things were getting better for her mammy.

Then one day, Latisha came back from the big house crying, and her new dress was torn down the front. Tomas was beyond himself, ranting and screaming dangerous things about Massa Johnson. Latisha kept pleading for him to stop and come inside, but he wouldn't listen.

Lizzie cried because she never seen her pappy so crazy before. Gosh, it was only a dress, she thought, I could fix it for Mammy.

Before long, Big Steven, the overseer came out and with him was Jer'macus and three other colored men followed behind. Lizzie got real scared when she saw Jer'macus with Big Steven, 'cause Jer'macus lived in the 'Judas House'. Living in the 'Judas House' meant not having to work in the 'bacca fields or doing any chores and getting more food and clothes too. There were always lots of women friends visiting the 'Judas House'. The slaves called it the 'Judas House' 'cause whoever lived there did the things Massa Johnson wanted done to the other slaves and decided who worked what jobs, how much food you'd get and who got what punishments. The women friends who visited the 'Judas House' never went to the 'bacca fields to work or got any punishments, no matter what they did.

Jer'macus carried the whip o' bedience with him.

All the slaves were forced to come out to watch, and they looked away out of shame for Tomas when those men pulled off his shirt and pants and chained him to the tree o' woe. The whip o' bedience was an ugly thing, having long strips of leather bundled together at the handle. The strips had once been soft and pliable but over time had become hard and stiff lashes from the brine and blood. The end of each lash was tied into a tight, mean knot. It made a strange rasping sound as Jer'macus shook out the lashes before dipping them into the barrel of brine kept at the tree o' woe.

Big Steven stood to the side, his arms crossed with his revolver in his hand. They waited a long time for Massa Johnson to come out of the big house.

Massa Johnson shoved Latisha to her knees in front, so close that when the lashes swished through the air, ripping into Tomas's flesh, she felt the wind brush past her face and drops of brine and her husband's blood splattered her. Lizzie didn't know how many times the whip o' bedience hit her pappy. She could count to ten, one for each finger, but she didn't know how to count more after that—and when she ran out of fingers, the whip o' bedience didn't stop. Latisha's new, torn dress got soiled by Tomas's blood.

"That's enough," Massa Johnson finally said. "Leave him chained here 'til morning and don't no one minister to him, y'all hear? Anyone goes near him will get what he got!" he shouted. "Let this be a lesson to y'all. I won't be tolerating no kind of mutiny talk on my plantation." He took Latisha's blood and tear-streaked face in his hand, forcing her to look up at him. "There's a new dress for ya up at the house, when ya change your mind." He turned and walked away.

That night, Latisha and Lizzie, sat outside their quarters, crying and watching over Tomas from a distance to scare off any dogs or animals that would go after him as he hung on the tree o' woe. Tomas's back and thighs looked real vile and ugly, and by sun-up, when Big Steven finally motioned for him to be unshackled from the tree, they were crawling with creatures.

Latisha was allowed to stay back from doing work that day to minister to Tomas. She knew that Massa Johnson didn't want Tomas to die 'cause a "good nigger be worth lot of money," but she worried greatly that Massa Johnson would sell Tomas to another plantation soon as he was healed and better.

That evening, Jer'macus burst into their hut. Over his arm, a new white dress was draped. He thrust it out toward Latisha. She looked at him in contempt and shook her head—no. Jer'macus left, laughing, taking the new dress with him.

Latisha was sent to the 'bacca fields the next day, and Lizzie stayed with her pappy. That evening, when Latisha went for their food, Ol' Ke'na'hi gave her only half their share. Latisha protested, "Ah's gots a young'un ta feed, an my man be hurt!" But Ol' Ke'na'hi wouldn't look at Latisha and just shook her head under the watchful eye of Big Steven.

While eating their meager portions of food, Jer'macus burst into the hut once again carrying the white dress over his arm. He stared at Latisha for a long moment before thrusting it out to her. Latisha shook her head—no.

During the night, there was a tap on the side of their hut. Inspecting, they found food placed at the doorstep.

This happened four more days, and when Jer'macus left their hut on the fourth day, it was Saturday evening. The next day, being the Sabbath, no work in the fields was allowed. Massa Johnson was strict 'bout the Sabbath observance. Every Sunday he took the missus to town for their worship, where they gave thanks for all their good fortunes and blessings. Then they would be in the big house entertaining all day or out visiting other plantation owners.

Working in the 'bacca fields now, Latisha didn't have Sabbath chores to do, and she knew Jer'macus wouldn't come on the Sabbath evening either 'cause Massa Johnson would be with the missus at night.

As soon as Jer'macus left their hut that evening, Tomas rose from his bed. Latisha and Tomas had been whispering together a lot the past couple of nights and two evenings ago Latisha had disappeared all night, coming back just in time to go to the 'bacca fields. They talked a long time that night, in excited voices Lizzie couldn't hear.

Tomas's backside was still hideous with dark scabs and welts, but there weren't any open cuts or sores, and Latisha had kept the infection away with an ointment medicine mammy Sheila had gotten for her. Lizzie watched as her mammy stuffed their things into a cloth traveling sack she'd gotten from somewhere. Their things weren't many: a comb, some ragged pieces of clothing, a threadbare blanket, scraps of braid and ribbon, one bread knife, three tin bowls, cups, and spoons.

Latisha had one treasure she greatly prized—a feather. It wasn't a regular feather, like from a crow or blackbird, being bigger than Tomas's two hands put together, tip to tip. Large at one end, with light wisps of fluff that fluttered with the slightest breath, it was radiant, having the colors of the rainbow; blue and turquoise, orange and yellow, red and green, all mixed together. It was the most beautiful thing Lizzie had ever seen.

Latisha told Lizzie that her own mammy had brought it from the home country when she had been captured and made into a slave. Latisha's mammy had been raped by the boss man of the slavers. Lizzie wasn't sure what raped' meant, but Latisha told her that was how Latisha came to be born. Granmammy was with child', and Latisha was born on the boat crossing the big water, bringing them to this strange land. Gran mammy gave Latisha the feather just before she died, when Latisha was a young girl like Lizzie is now, and Latisha treasured it dearly. She'd sit at night, stroking it, dreaming of the home she had never seen. She kept it under their cot, wrapped in a special waxy paper that she then wrapped in a scrap of oilcloth, tied carefully with a yellow string. Sometimes, Latisha would let Lizzie hold it for a few minutes.

Latisha had been saving food the others had been leaving at their hut, and after Jer'macus closed the door to his quarters Saturday evening, many of the slaves quietly came, bringing more food, hugging, crying, and wishing God's blessings on them. Forming a circle around the small family, the slaves joined hands and, led by mammy Shelia, they prayed that God would watch over the family and guide them on their journey to safety and freedom. Lizzie didn't understand why they were doing this until her mammy grabbed her hand and said, "Come, chil', we go now."

"But Mammy, where we g'wan?"

"We goes ta meet Mutter Moses."

Staying on the road, they traveled all night. There wasn't much traffic, and only two times did they have to jump into the bushes when carriages rattled by. Tomas kept looking back for riders and listening for hounds. None came.

With the first rays of the sun, streaking across the treetops and igniting them in a golden glow, they moved into the woods to eat and rest for a short time until Latisha made them get up and move again. Traveling in the woods, but keeping the road in sight, Latisha said they needed to get far away during the Sabbath day, before someone know'd they were gone and come after them. Lizzie was scared 'cause Massa Johnson and Big Steven had horses, dogs, and guns, but her mammy said it be all right.

"The Lawd be wid us, chil'. He wil take care o us. Now hurry, we need ta git ta de ron-day-voos afore she leave."

With the coming of dawn, road traffic increased, and they had to hide behind bushes often, whenever carriages and horsemen passed by on the road. Latisha and Tomas watched the travelers closely to notice any urgency or alarms raised. None were, and the rests were favorable for Tomas. Red blotches bled through his shirt where scabs had opened, but he never complained. During the morning, they saw Massa Johnson and the missus pass by in a carriage, going to give thanks.

Latisha kept count of the crossroads carefully. They had crossed four roads by the time the final glimmer of radiance extinguished in the sky, allowing them to leave the woods and go back on the road, where traveling was easier and faster.

"How much farder, Mammy? Ah's tired."

"Ah knows chil'. It no be long now. We 'bout dere."

Upon crossing the seventh crossroad, Latisha walked slower, saying she looked for the mark. After a short ways, they came to a large rock taller than Tomas, alongside of the road. In the misty moonlight, Latisha found the 'X' carved into it.

"Tis be wher we go in." She said, and turning, she led them back into the woods, this time moving directly away from the road. The part of the moon that was shinning, lit the forest with a hazy glow, helping them see their way, but the going was still hard, and Lizzie tripped several times. Thorns tore her legs and arms, and branches whipped her face. Latisha never let go of her hand and never scolded her, no matter how many times she fell.

They traveled like this for a time until Latisha abruptly stopped. Ahead in the murky shadows was an enormous tree. It was as wide around as seven men touching hands and rose high into the night sky, covering the area of a 'bacca field. No trees grew around it as no sunlight filtered through its thick canopy.

"Dat be de tree," she said. "We waits here."

Crouching in the bushes, they heard things moving in the woods. A loud screech made Lizzie start causing her to shake, and she squeezed her mammy's hand hard. Mammy squeezed back, and the screech went away. An owl hooted, and Latisha tightened her grip on Lizzie's hand. The owl hooted again, then once more. Immediately, Latisha pulled Lizzie to her feet, saying, "Come, chil'," and they made their way toward the owl. Lizzie jumped when her pappy made an owl-hoot noise, too. A light flickered in the woods ahead, then disappeared. They stared at where it had been, and the light flashed again. Lizzie was about to ask her mammy what the light was when it flickered one more time.

"Dat be de signal," Latisha said, rising and pulling Lizzie forward.

"Careful, Latisha, dat et no be a trap," Tomas whispered, holding her back. "Yous an Lizzie wait here. Ah goes ahead ta see. Ef'n Ah don' comes back, yous runs away fast." He hugged them both and headed to where the lights had flashed. The woods were deathly silent as Lizzie and her mammy huddled in the dark, shivering . . . waiting.

Lizzie had begun to worry her pappy had gotten caught when she heard a rustling in the woods. Crouching lower, she strained to see in the dim moonlight. A figure moved through the brush, and Lizzie's heart jumped in her throat . . . Jer'macus!

"Latisha?" came a whisper. "Latisha? Ar yous der? Et be me, Tomas, yer husband." Latisha pulled Lizzie to her feet and together they ran to Tomas. "Et be okay, Latisha. Mutter Moses be here."

He led them to a thick tangle of bushes, and as they walked around the foliage a woman stepped out from the darkness. She was small, not much taller than Lizzie, with high cheekbones and a wide, flat nose. A kerchief was folded on her head, covering her hair. Over this, she wore a funny-looking hat that had a flat top with a wide brim. Her mouth was set in a firm, straight line.

"Gawd be wid yous, Latisha." She said, her voice low and husky.

"Yes, Mutter, an ta yous too. Ah's so happy ta sees yous again,"

Mother Moses took Latisha's hands and held them tight. "Bless yous, chil', yous g'wan be free now."

Latisha collapsed against Mother Moses, crying, burying her head in Mother's coarse dress. "Oh, Mutter, t'ank yous, t'ank yous!"

"No, chil', yous no t'ank me. Yous t'ank de good Lawd above. Ah jes' do His biddin', s'all." She pulled Latisha into her arms, holding her close and then looking at Lizzie, she said. "An dis mus be yer li'l girl, Lizzie, yous told me about."

Her eyes burned with a deep passion radiating from within her as she held out her free arm to Lizzie. "Come, chil', come ta Mutter." Lizzie moved to her, and Mother folded her arms around her, pulling her to her bosom. Lizzie felt Mother's strong heart beating and could feel the force burning in her like a bed of coals. A calmness engulfed Lizzie that she had not felt since leaving Massa Johnson's.

"Don' be frighten', chil'. Gawd will watch ober us an guide us on our jeurney."

"Wher we g'wan, Mutter?" Lizzie asked.

"We goes ta Can'da chil', de land o' promise, where de colored folk be fre." Then, letting go, she stepped back and looked hard at Latisha and Tomas while, from deep in the furrows of her dress, she pulled out a revolver and pointed it at them. "Dere be no turnin' back once yous start dis jeurney. Yous wan ta turn back, yous do's so now. If'n yous wan ta turns back later, yous be dead."

"We nebber be g'wan back, Mutter, no matter what be ahead o' us," Latisha said.

"Nebber Mutter," Tomas added, "Ah's dies afore Ah's g'wan back."

"Den faller me. We mus' git ta de cave afore de suns gits up." Mother turned, and they followed, putting their lives into her hands from that time forward.

Mother led them through the dark forest. The ease and agility with which she moved through the dense foliage surprised Lizzie and her parents. Never stumbling or tripping, never slowing, she moved making no noise. The family struggled to stay with her, but no matter how hard they tried, they could not stop from tripping and falling, sounding like a herd of goats tromping in the woods. Numerous times, Mother waited for them to catch up and as soon as they'd get to her, she'd turn and start again, giving them no time to rest.

Coming to a steep ravine, they followed Mother down the bank, where a creek flowed at the bottom. The creek was as wide as a man and fast-flowing, making a musical gurgling sound.

"Walk in de midder o' de creek," Mother said. "Dat'll cover yous smell from any h'unds." The water, though only a foot deep, was freezing. They stayed in the creek until another smaller creek merged with it, and Mother turned to follow that creek. After a time, their feet having no feelings except as numb lumps, they came upon a large outcropping of rock along the side of the ravine. The sun was just beginning to convey a deep purple cloak across the horizon, crowning the treetops with a radiant, golden hue.

Mother stepped out of the water and made the owl-hoot noise three times again. Immediately, an owl hooted back from the outcropping and Mother started forward with the exhausted family trailing closely behind. On the backside, a large rock stuck out from the face of the ravine. Under it, in front of a small, dark opening, a colored man crouched nervously. He nodded when seeing Mother and then looked at the newcomers before moving back into the opening. Mother followed the man, and the three fugitives followed Mother into the black hole.

The opening widened into a cave, where three more colored men sat huddled around a small fire that flickered in the middle of the floor, casting devil shadows against the cave walls.

"Shut dat fire off!" Mother yelled at them, angrily kicking at the fire, spreading it around. "Did Ah no tell yous, no fire an no noise?" Some of the burning twigs hit the men's pants, who jumped up and down, patting them out. "Dat smell be travelin' all over dese woods, yous fools!" Mother spat.

"We no t'ought dat li'l fire would hurt," one of the men whined, stomping the fire off his pant leg. As the final flames extinguished, total darkness descended, and, if not for Latisha holding her hand, Lizzie wouldn't have known she was there.

"Yous do what Ah says, an no what yous t'ink," Mother hissed back. "We wait 'til de suns go down. One o' yous git outside, list'nin' fer h'unds. If'n dey come, yous all run fas' in different ways an pray." She turned to where Lizzie stood in the darkness, "Now, you res', chil'."

No hounds came, and the family slept soundly. When the sun set, that evening, they moved out from the cover of the cave and followed Mother, staying in creeks where possible. Mother constantly watched the sky, saying she followed the North Star and the "drinkin' gourd." During one rest stop, Lizzie asked Mother what was the 'drinkin gourd.'

Mother pointed to the sky and traced some bright stars, forming the shape of a ladle, like Ol' Ke'na'hi had used on the plantation. "Dat be de drinkin' gourd, chil'." And then she softly sang:

"De ribberbank mak's a very good ro'd,
De dead tres show yous de way,
Left foot, peg foot, travelin on,
Foller de drinkin gourd.
When de sun comes back an de first Quail cals,
Foller de drinkin gourd
Fer de Ol' man es waiting ta carry Yous ta freedom,
Ef yous foller de drinkin gourd."

As daylight approached, Mother led them to the middle of a swampy island, surrounded by waist-deep water that they had to wade through to get to, in which to hide during the day. Lizzie saw a large snake swimming in a big "S" across the surface of the water. She didn't sleep much that day.

They continued traveling at night in the darkness; hiding during the day in the light. They stayed at what Mother called "stations." Sometimes these were secret places in the woods, like at the cave, and sometimes these were houses, where people hid and fed them. Mother called those stations "safe houses."

Mother had a station lined up for each day along the journey, where they could rest and sometimes get food. Lizzie had no idea where they were or where they were going, other than she knew they had come from Massa Johnson's plantation and were going to someplace called Canada. One of the other men was fearful of what they would find in Canada. He said he'd been told it was so cold men's ears and noses fell off, and that there were enormous mountains of ice that never melted with howling winds that never stopped. He said that fierce, giant monsters hunted colored folks down to devour their bones.

"Dat ain't no talk but ta scare yous off," Mother told them. "Ah's been ta Can'da, an et be de lan' o' promise, flowin' wid milk an honey. Yous be free dere."

On the fifth day after leaving the cave, the posse came. The fugitives had reached a safe house at the home of a white farm family, and were in the barn, feasting on cornbread and chicken, and drinking milk from the cow. It was the best meal Lizzie had ever had, when suddenly, the farmer's son galloped up to the barn, yelling, "Patterollers coming up the road, and they got slave hounds with 'em!"

Latisha's heart jumped in her throat, knowing the reputation and cruelty of the patterollers in hunting down runaway slaves.

Like lightning, the farm family went into action. The farmer grabbed Tomas, pulling him to his feet. "Come, this way. Bring your family. Hurry!"

Latisha grabbed Lizzie's hand as they ran out of the barn. The farmer's daughter was quickly picking up all the food and utensils and rushed them into the house, while his son led the other fugitives in an opposite direction. Mother stood calmly watching, ensuring that all traces of their having been here were erased.

They hurried out to the pasture, where the farmer told them to walk in the cow manure and squish their feet in it real good, before leading them to the tall haystacks that stood in the middle of the cut pasture. Lizzie figured they were going to hide behind them. She hoped no one would come out there to look, or they'd find them. Following them out, another daughter rode a manure wagon, dropping clumps of cow manure on the ground where they'd been.

Approaching a high haystack in the middle of the field, the farmer went around to the opposite side and pulled on the hay. A small section came away, revealing a false center inside. "Quick, get inside, sit in the middle, don't move, and don't make any sound until we come to get you. Understand?"

The family nodded their heads as they crawled into the hollowed out haystack and sat down in the center. The farmer came back with an armload of fresh hay and threw it on top of them before closing up the secret door, making sure it was secure and that it blended in, before hurrying back to the farmhouse. Inside the haystack, covered in fresh hay, they could hear the manure wagon rolling by and smelled the pungent odor as it spread its ripe cargo around the haystack, before heading back to the barn.

Shortly, they heard the howling of the hounds and the horses galloping up to the house. Lizzie was so scared her chest hurt as she tried to breathe. Latisha poked a tiny hole in the side of the haystack allowing her to see as the posse rode up to the farmhouse.

"Hello!" the farmer shouted to the men on horseback, "And who might you be, and what business do you have on my farm with those noisy mongrels of yours?"

"Good day, to you, sir. We're agents of the court, come seeking runaway slaves. We have reason to believe they are being led by that renegade niggra bitch, Harriet Tubman and that they may be, in fact, hiding, here on this farm." The unmistakable voice of Massa Johnson boomed out and then paused as he looked down at the mud-splattered hounds. "And these 'mongrels,' as you call them sir, are the finest purebred bloodhounds this side of the Shenandoah Valley."

"There are no slaves on my land, so you might as well turn around and take your leave," the farmer replied firmly. "And you can take your purebred mongrels with you."

"As you may or may not know, sir, there is a reward of forty thousand dollars for the capture of the black bitch, and I will personally see to it that you receive that reward, should you assist us in arresting her."

"That would be the devil's money, earning a place in hell's eternal fire!" the farmer replied. "I'd have none to do with it, even if I could and as I have already stated, there are no slaves on my land, so I again ask that you leave."

"Be advised, sir, that according to the Fugitive Slave Law of the United States of America, you are not only forbidden to aid and hide fugitive slaves but are also compelled to assist us in any way we deem necessary in capturing these criminals and returning such property to their rightful owners."

"I am fully aware of that barbaric and idiotic law, and I suspect that it shall soon be repealed," the farmer retorted. "No law shall stand in this country that enslaves another man."

"Be it barbaric and idiotic, as you wish, sir, it still remains the law of the land, and I can have you taken in chains yourself, should you choose to defy it or me in exercising my rights."

"How dare you come to my house and threaten me!" the farmer fired back. "As there are no slaves here, I am defying no law, and I demand you take your gang of ruffians away from here and leave us in peace."

"If, as you claim, there are no slaves on your land, then I am sure you would not object to our looking around for ourselves."

"I most assuredly do object to such a rude intrusion. You have no authority here to invade the privacy of my land."

"The high court of the United States has vested me with the authority to do whatever I deem necessary to recover my property, and if you continue to resist me, I shall place this entire household under arrest and search your property at will. As you can see for yourself, these men will be more than pleased to oblige me." He motioned toward his posse of thugs, most of whom held rifles or pistols menacingly, with evil smirks on their rough, unshaven faces.

The farmer, knowing he had pushed it as far as he dared, and knowing that the fugitives were as secure as they were going to be, capitulated. "Very well then; under protest do I grant you permission to search my land, but do so quickly, as you are disturbing my family, and I have cows that need tending to." After a pause, he added, "But you have no right to and shall not search my house."

Massa Johnson waved the others off, as he focused on the farmer's objections to entering his house. They continued to argue back and forth while the posse dispersed across the property. Three men went into the barn, a group of four went to the north fields and another group of three went off to the south fields. Each group carried guns and had a pair of large hounds on long leather tethers, barking loudly, straining to get loose.

"Dey coming!" Latisha whispered, sealing the tiny peephole back up tight with fresh hay. They could hear the hounds moving across the pasture, barking and howling as they worked to pick up slave scent. Pappy grabbed one of Lizzie's hands, and Mammy clutched the other, and they formed a circle of silence—and fear.

"Pray Lizzie. Pray dat de Lawd protect us an dat we'd be strong. Pray, an don't t'ink 'bout dem. T'ink only 'bout heaven." Breathing the sweet aroma of fresh hay, mingled with ripe cow manure, they prayed for the mingling odors to hide them from the hounds. Their fate was now in the hands of God and cow manure. Lizzie's body shook with terror. Mammy and Pappy squeezed her hands tightly, but she felt the tremor in them, as well. Lizzie closed her eyes tight and visualized walking on the streets of gold.

Before long, the slavers were directly outside their haystack. They could hear the dogs slobbering and breathing they were so close. The three of them held their breaths but were certain the posse would hear their hearts pounding. They silently prayed together, waiting any second for the haystack to be torn apart.

"Come on, Jeb, there's nothing out here but hay and cow shit. That farmer's got 'em hid in that house of his. That's why he won't let us in. Let's get back and break the stinking door down on that niggra-loving bastard." Gradually, the howling receded as the slave-chasers headed back to the house. Slowly, Lizzie's heart returned to normal as Latisha carefully reopened the peephole. The other search teams had also returned empty handed, with everyone focused on the house.

"... and I assure you, there are no slaves in my house," the farmer argued with Massa Johnson as he watched, out of the corner of his eyes, each of the search groups return.

"By the power of the United States government, I demand to determine that myself!" Massa Johnson shouted back when the posse had fully reassembled behind him.

The farmer, seeing that all the searchers had returned, without discovering anyone, changed his tactic. "Very well, to comply with the law, and under protest, which shall be duly recorded with the magistrate, you may enter my house. But I will not allow that rag-tag gang of thugs with you or those filthy mongrels of yours to tramp through my house, bringing discomfort and distress to my wife."

"I thank you for your hospitality, sir. It shall only be my overseer, my man Jer'macus and myself who shall enter your house, and we won't require the services of the bloodhounds." Glancing at Jer'macus, he added, "I assume you do not mind having a niggra enter your house, sir?"

"No more than I mind you entering my house."

Massa Johnson dismounted and turned to his posse. "Couple of you boys go 'round the backside, in case they try to run out that way. Rest of you keep your guns ready, but don't shoot either of them bitches. I want that old crone alive to watch her hang, and I got plans for that other one." Crude laughter rippled through the posse. He motioned three men over and spoke to them in a low voice. "You boys stay alert and keep your irons ready, and arrest this white-trash family as soon as the first niggra runs out." He snarled, "Then y'all can do what you will."

The mistress of the house stood in the threshold of the front door. Massa Johnson tipped his hat to her. "Madam, I apologize for any discomfort to you, and I assure you, we will be quick and shall not disturb your household."

"That would be greatly appreciated sir, as I have not been feeling well of late and my daughters and I do all things ourselves."

"I am truly sorry for that, madam. Perhaps you should consider having a house slave or two of your own, to ease your burden. I could arrange for an attractive price for you."

"That, sir shall never happen in my household!" She said and reluctantly stepped aside, allowing them to pass.

"As you will, madam, as you will." He chuckled and entered the house with Big Steven and Jer'macus, followed closely by the farmer and his wife. The farmer's sons and daughters stood close together across the top of the porch steps, not allowing anyone from the posse below to go up. The three men Massa Johnson had spoken to separately, spread out across the bottom of the porch, their hands on their pistols, itching to pull them at the first sign of a fugitive on the run. One, having an ugly scar running across his face, leeringly stared at the farmer's youngest daughter in some unspoken anticipation.

They searched the house thoroughly, looking under beds, inside closets and pantries. They opened every door and checked every conceivable space. They tapped all the walls for hiding places and examined all the floors for hidden trapdoors. They pulled and pushed against bookcases and cupboards, looking for secret entrances. They checked the basement, the food cellar and the attic and crawled out onto the roof. They found nothing.

After a long and frustrating search, they came out. Massa Johnson was highly agitated as he stood on the porch, next to the stacked pile of firewood. Picking up a small log off the top of the stack and smacking his open palm with it, he reluctantly addressed the farmer and his wife.

"Sir—madam, my apologies for disturbing your day and intruding on your home. It appears we've been provided false information."

"As I told you, there are no slaves on my land."

With a loud crack, Massa Johnson slammed the log back onto the woodpile. "Good day to you, sir," he said, striding off the porch. Mounting his horse, he snarled at the disgruntled posse, "Let's go; there's no one here."

The family watched the posse ride away. As the dust settled in the distance, they continued to stare down the road, scanning the fields and trees for any signs of movement until they were satisfied that the slave-chasing posse had indeed left and weren't doubling back.

Moving to the pile of stacked firewood on the porch, the farmer unhooked a hidden latch, and with the help of his sons, he raised the entire top of the woodpile as if it were the lid on a chest. Reaching into the opening, his hand was grabbed by a small, bony, black hand. He pulled upwards and Mother Moses rose out of the woodpile as if rising from a grave. On her face, she wore a wide, toothy smile.

"Oh, Mrs. Tubman, I am so sorry for such an inconvenience," the farmer's wife said, helping her out of the hiding place as the farmer told his sons to go fetch the other fugitives.

"Dat's all right, missus. If de Lawd wan' me den, Ah's be ready." She brushed herself off, fluffing down her stained dress. "Gawd bless yous both so much." Then she turned directly to the farmer, a taunting twinkle in her eyes. "Dat be a right nice rewards yous turned down fer me, Jon'than."

"There's no money that's worth destroying God's children, Mother. We both know that."

"Yes, we do, Jon'than, an yer reward in heaven will be great fer et, too." She nodded her head in a knowing way, "An I'll pray, fer yous

Jon'than, dat de Lawd forgive yous fer dat fib yous tell 'bout dere no slaves being on yous land."

"But Mother, that was no fib, there are no slaves on my land."

Four days later, they reached a station Mother had been talking about. There, they hid and waited, while Mother went to make arrangements. She was gone for three days, and they were getting worried she'd been captured and hauled away when, like a spirit, she appeared. She looked tired, having to avoid slave chasers everywhere, but said all the arrangements been made, and they'd be leaving that night.

One of the other men had been spooked and nervous ever since the incident at Jonathan's farm and with Mother being gone so long, had worked himself up into a frenzy. Tomas and the other men had to restrain him from leaving, and when Mother returned, the man told her that he wanted to turn himself in.

"Untie him," Mother directed the others. They removed the ropes, and he stood in front of Mother. "Now, yous free. What yous gonna do now? Dere ain't no g'wan back. Ah's tol' yous dat afore we started," Mother said sternly.

"But Mutter, dey catch me, dey's g'wan whup me an maybe kilt me. Ah turns myse'f in an go on auction, den Ah's no longer be a runaway, an Ah's be safe."

"An' yous be a slave, too!" Mother spat at him, pulling out her pistol and pointing it squarely in his face. "Ain't no g'wan back, et be too late fer dat. Yous knows too much ta leave now, dem patderrollers beat et otta yous. Dead Negros tell no tales. Yous e'ter goes on er yous dies here an now, a slave," she said, cocking the hammer back.

"No, Mutter—no! Ah's no wanna die." He fell to the ground, clutching her legs, burying his face in the folds of her dress. "Ah's sorry, Mutter. Ah's g'wan wid yous. Ah's jes' so skeered Ah's g'wan die."

"Yous ain't g'wan ta die, chil'. Yous g'wan ta be free." Uncocking her pistol, she cradled his head in her hands, and softly sang to him:

"Dark an thorny es de pathway,
Where de pilgrim make 'is way;
But beyond dis vale o' sorrow,
Lie de fields o' endless days."

Pulling him to his feet, Mother held his hands in hers. "We goes ta de lan' o' promise, chil', where yous be slave ta no man, no mo', an when yous dies dere, yous dies a free man."

Shortly after sunset, they heard wagons approaching. Mother motioned for the others to wait while she went to meet them. Soon, they heard the familiar owl hoots, and they went to join her. Mother stood talking to the wagon masters of three, deep-bed, peddler wagons piled high with boxes and bundles of goods. Ropes were stretched across the beds from side to side and front to back, holding everything securely in place.

After, untying the ropes from one side of the wagons, the wagon masters unhooked hidden latches, and the whole side of each wagon dropped down. Removing the front row of boxes, behind them was . . . nothing.

"This'll be yer home fer the next few days," one of them said to the fugitives. "Attend to yer personal needs, before y'all get in. Y'all gonna be in there fer a bit." Tomas helped Latisha and Lizzie crawl into the space of one wagon and then crawled in after them. The wagon master replaced the boxes, closing them in, secured the sideboard back in place and retied the ropes.

They lay in darkness, getting as comfortable as possible. Some empty sacks had been thrown into the space and Latisha positioned them as pillows and cushions, as best she could. Cracks, between the headboards, allowed fresh air in, as well as slivers of light.

When the wagons were all secure they began moving. At first, it felt better traveling without having to walk, but it wasn't long before it became clear this was going to be a hard and painful journey. The road was poor, having numerous ruts and bumps that jarred their bodies and bruised their flesh in all quarters. Being able to lie on their sides for only a short period before their bones and joints would scream with pain and they'd have to turn over, repeating the cycle.

They were four days in the wagons, traveling night and day. They'd travel three to four hours at a time, before stopping for a couple of hours in secluded areas off the road. These rests were needed for the wagon masters to get some sleep, and for the passengers to stretch, take care of personal business, and soothe their aches and pains.

Lizzie felt bad for her pappy, knowing it hurt his backside something awful. Latisha ministered to him during the rest times, putting on salve that Mother had gotten at one of the safe houses and washing the dirty dressings before putting them back on the scabs, which kept breaking open during the jarring trip. Tomas wouldn't cry for himself, so Lizzie cried for him.

When stopped by slave chasers, they'd hear the wagon masters talking to them as they poked around above. It was a good thing they didn't have slave hounds—for sure they'd have been smelled out. During one stop, they heard a slave-chaser yell in a gruff voice, "Unload that wagon, Ol' geezer!"

"Would if I could, young fella," the wagon master answered. "But, ain't no way with this here bum back of mine. Can hardly sit all day, riding this wagon, as it is. Y'all want this wagon unloaded, y'all welcome to do so fer yourself. I'll jes' go over there and rest a bit while you do it. But y'all best put everything back in right order, and tie it all back up right, proper too. Ain't gonna be my ass if things gets busted up, ya know."

"All right already!" the gruff voice barked. "Jes' move on and get those wagons outta here."

When they finally emerged from the wagons for the last time, Mother thanked the wagon masters, bestowing God's blessing on them. The wagon masters left to deliver their goods, wishing the fugitives safe passage to Canada.

Mother told them that they had covered considerable distances while in the wagons, and they were close to Canada. The weather had changed significantly during the journey. What started out as warm days and frosty nights had become cold days and colder nights. It rained freezing needles, stinging their faces. Their thread bare clothing did little to protect them and became heavy as the coarse cotton absorbed the cold rain. Food was scarce, and Lizzie was cold, wet, hungry and had no idea where she was or where she was going.

Crouching now in the wet foliage, waiting for Mother's signal, thinking of all that had happened, shivers shook her thin body, and the frigid night air stung her throat. Lizzie wondered if she would ever see Canada and what it would be like. She wondered how big the beasts were that the man said would try to devour them, and she wondered if the master of that plantation would beat her pappy, as Massa Johnson had done. Mother said they would be free in Canada, but Lizzie didn't know what that meant, she'd never been free. Her mammy said, when she was free it meant there'd be nobody to make her do things she didn't want to do. That was okay with Lizzie. She'd never done anything she wanted to do. She didn't know what to want; she'd never had occasion to think about such a thing. Being free meant thinking about things she never had to think about before.

Mother said this was the last safe house before they entered Canada. She said they were in a place called Lewiston, which was in a place called New York. Lizzie didn't understand how one place could be in another place. Mother also said they were near the largest waterfall in the world. Lizzie didn't understand that either. The only waterfall Lizzie had ever seen was in the creek they walked through in the woods, and that was as tall as her head. She wondered how large the world's largest waterfall was. There was so many things Lizzie didn't understand.

Ahead, a light flashed three times, and holding hands together, the family emerged from the bushes and walked towards the light.

Approaching where the light had flashed, they made out the shape of a large building that looked like the big house on Massa Johnson's plantation. It was white, with big columns in front and a long porch on the side. Mother met them at the edge of the trees and told them to be quiet—there had been people here asking about colored folks. They weren't looking for them in particular, she said, but slave-chasers were everywhere, looking for self-emancipated Negro people for whom they could get a reward from the owners or sell to the slavers for a trip to the auction block.

A recessed side door opened, and they were ushered into a lower level, where a wave of sweet-smelling warmth engulfed them. Glowing gas lamps revealed sacks of flour, rows of food in glass jars, and bushels of apples, peaches, and grapes. Lizzie stared at the food, and her belly talked loudly.

"Come now, this way. Let's get you settled in, and then you'll have all the food you want," said a portly white woman with rosy cheeks. Her hair was piled high on her head, and two long golden curls twirled down each side of her plump face. She wore a full, green dress that had large yellow flowers on it. Lizzie thought she looked like a giant daisy.

The woman led them to the back of the room, to a wall with shelves stacked with linens. She pushed on the end of one shelf, and the whole wall swung in, revealing another set of steps that led down to a second cellar. She gave Mother the lantern and left to secure the outside door. Mother led them into the darkness below, and when she placed the lantern on a table, it flooded the cellar with light. The table was piled high with food. In the middle sat a large platter overflowing with an enormous roast, the robust flavor of which overcame the mustiness of the cellar. The rich aroma made Lizzie's stomach explode into gurgling growls and bellows. Surrounding the huge roast were bowls of baked potatoes, sweet potatoes, turnips, and steaming corn, piled high. One end of the table had baskets of breads and rolls, and the other end had baskets of apples, peaches, and grapes. Was this the promised land? Were they in Canada? Or was this Heaven?

The cellar door opened, and the portly white lady came down. She smiled at them and said they should call her Miss Jacquie. She told them that they were welcome in her house and that they'd be here a few days while Mrs. Tubman made arrangements for their escape into Canada. Miss Jacquie said it was extremely dangerous outside, that there'd been an unusual number of slave chasers in the area, watching the bridges and the river crossings, looking for fugitives to sell to the auction dealers. Some of them were even staying in Miss Jacquie's rooms above, so they must be very quiet, and no one should leave the cellar without her. They would stay here until it was safe to cross into Canada.

Mother prayed, "T'ank yous Lawd, fer bringin' us here safely; an bless dese pe'ple who care fer yer chillens, an tak care o' dem dat dey see no harm an dat yer blessin's be wid dem. An we ask dat yous guide us, Lawd, through de troubled waters ahed, an prepare us ta enter inta de freedom lan'. No matter what lie ahed der Lawd, we T'ank thee fer all Yer goodness an love fer us. Amen." Finishing her prayer, she looked at Lizzie, smiled, and said, "Now eat, chillens, an den res' . . . soon we enter de lan' o' promise."

Lizzie ate.

They stayed at Miss Jacquie's for several days waiting for Mother to make her arrangements on both sides of the border. Latisha cleaned and braided Lizzie's hair and Miss Jacquie gave her bright, yellow ribbons that she tied into each braid. Miss Jacquie gave Latisha one of her dresses and a pair of shoes. She gave Lizzie a beautiful blue dress made of heavy, woven cotton, she had from when she was younger, to replace the tattered sack Lizzie wore. Latisha gave Lizzie a hot bath and Miss Jacquie gave Lizzie some under-things and socks. Lizzie had never worn any socks before, and she thought they felt real nice when walking. Other than her mammy, no one had ever done anything nice for Lizzie and she wondered if this is what it was like to be free.

During the daytimes, they heard many boots walking on the floors above, but no one ever came down to their cellar. They waited and rested, while Tomas's wounds healed and Lizzie's stomach stopped talking to her.

After five days hiding in the basement, Miss Jacquie came in and motioned for Mother. They huddled for a few minutes and then Mother said, "All de 'rangements be made. Dis night, we leaves. Everyone be gone from upstairs now, so Miz Jacquie will sneaks yous out, one et a time, ta attend ta yer private bizness afore we go."

The men allowed Latisha to go first. Taking Lizzie by the hand, she followed Miss Jacquie out of the building, into the cold evening air. Miss Jacquie stood watch while they snuck under the long porch to the privy out back. The sun was setting, and when they were coming back, Lizzie saw an enormous ditch to her left. It was so deep and wide she couldn't see the bottom of it, and the other side was a long way across. Back in the cellar, she asked Mother what it was she'd seen.

"Dat be de gorge, chil'. On de bottom, o' dat gorge, be de ribber. We cross dat ribber tonight on de bridge ta freedom. Dat lan' on de udder side yous seed be de lan' o' promise—Can'da."

The land of promise had not looked harsh or forbidden to Lizzie. It looked the same as the land on this side of the big ditch. Why was it the land of promise? What made that land free? Lizzie's mind was full of things she couldn't understand. She understood leaving Massa Johnson's plantation to save her pappy, but being told that the land on this side of the great ditch was slavery and on the other side of the great ditch was freedom, made her mind all confused . . . but her heart beat faster all the same.

She couldn't rest, while she waited; her stomach churned and her hands trembled thinking about Canada and freedom, and of crossing the great ditch. She didn't know what waited for them on the other side, but whatever it was, it would be better than what was back on Massa Johnson's plantation.

The others did not rest either. They sat huddled together, softly singing songs and rocking. Lizzie couldn't get the words out of her head: "I'm going home, on mornin' train." Tomas and Latisha sat huddled together, their arms around one another. At times, they laughed; at other times, they wept. Lizzie hadn't ever seen her pappy weep, no matter what pain or hardship he endured, but—he wept now.

Latisha motioned Lizzie to them; and they all sat hugging, crying and laughing together. Lizzie would never forget her pappy crying that night.

The cellar door opened, and Miss Jacquie came in again, waving to Mother. After a brief discussion, they left together. Shortly, Mother came back in carrying blankets, which she handed to each of them. "Miz Jacquie wan's yous ta hab dese blankets ta keep yous warm." Wrapping a blanket around her shoulders, she motioned for them to follow her. "Come, chillens. Et be time."

Emerging from the house, Lizzie was amazed to see the cold night sky filled with large white flakes, falling and covering everything. Lizzie jumped back under the protection of the overhead porch. "Mammy, what ar dose?"

"Dat be snow, chil', from de angels in hebben. Et means Gawd givin' us His blessin's t'night." Lizzie looked afraid. "Touch 'em, Lizzie; don' be skeered. Dey won' harm yous. Dey be from de angels."

Lizzie stretched out her hand into the falling flakes. They felt cold and quickly disappeared, leaving behind tiny drops of water. The sky was a beautiful sight as the flakes twirled down from above. So many there were! More than the stars on Massa Johnson's plantation. On the railing, the flakes had gathered together and running her finger through them, it came away with a small pile of white cold. Touching it to her lips, she tasted the gift from the angels. Lizzie looked at her mammy and smiled. Mammy smiled back.

Mother hugged Miss Jacquie good-bye and motioned for the others to follow. When Latisha and Lizzie went to Miss Jacquie, tears were running down Miss Jacquie's rosy cheeks as she pulled Latisha and Lizzie to her ample bosom.

"You will not be far from me when you get to Canada," she said. "Remember me and my house. It's called the Barton House. Someday, this horror will be over, and it'll be safe for you here. Come back and see me then. Go with God now, my friends, and be free." She looked down at Lizzie and smiled. "Little Lizzie, you'll be a free woman now. Grow well, my dear, and with love. Make your children strong and teach them of God's love for all. Come back and tell me; I want to know."

"I will, Miz Jacquie." Lizzie said, squeezing her tightly.

"T'ank yous fer all yous has done fer us, an we will no fergit yous," Latisha told her, with tears in her voice and on her face. From her sack, she pulled out her most valued treasure—her beautiful plume of rainbow colors, brought from the home country and wrapped carefully in the waxy paper and oilcloth, tied with a yellow ribbon. She handed it to Miss Jacquie. "Take dis, an keep et in yer family. Et wil bring happiness an peace fer yer pe'ples."

"Thank you so much, my dear. My family will hold it to our hearts forever as a remembrance of you and your family. Go now, and God go with you."

Lizzie had never cried for a white lady before.

They followed Mother into the woods along the edge of the great ditch. As dark as it was, and with the white flakes filling the sky, Lizzie couldn't see far ahead. When she caught glimpses of the great ditch, it scared her—like looking into the bowels of the world.

The path through the woods was easy to follow. They didn't stop to rest but moved at a comfortable, steady pace. Once, hearing movement in the woods ahead, they halted and stood in the darkness, waiting and fearing that men would step out with guns. Instead, two deer walked out and were as startled at seeing them as they were of the deer. The deer bolted back into the woods and the group quietly laughed at their fears, although Lizzie's knees continued shaking.

Coming to an opening in the woods, Mother stopped, squatted low, staring ahead for long minutes. She motioned them up to her, pointing into the darkness. Slowly, they could make out the shape of a massive rock rising out of the ground. The clouds moved in the sky, uncovering the moon, and from out of the vapors, the ghostly rock became a giant pillar looming in front of them. Huge ropes were strung off the top, looping into the giant ditch before disappearing in the snowy night darkness. Lizzie had never seen such a thing.

As the clouds cleared, she saw there was a second giant pillar behind the first one, and there was a road between the two pillars. Then it came to her that this was a bridge—a bridge that went across the giant ditch. She couldn't see the other side as it vanished in the snow and darkness. Mother had told her the land she had seen on the other side was Canada, the land of promise. This was the bridge to Canada. They'd made it!

Mother huddled them together. "Dat be de bridge ta freedom. Yous cross dat, yous be free. But we gots ta be carefol. Look fer anyone. Sometime dey puts men dere looking fer runaways." She gave an encouraging smile. "We almost home, chillen. Der be pe'ple waitin' fer yous on de udder side who will take yous ta yer new life. This night, yous wil be free."

They crept slowly towards the freedom bridge, looking for anyone; they saw no one. The moon played hide-and-seek, poking out from behind the clouds to bring light and show more of the bridge as they got closer, then ducking back, throwing them back into darkness. The massive pillars grew larger and larger until they filled most of their vision. Lizzie noticed there were actually two roads on the bridge, a big one on top and a small one on the bottom. Why two? she wondered. Then she understood: the big road on top was for white people, and the small road on the bottom was for colored folks. White people went to the land of promise, too? she wondered. Why? Weren't they already free?

The men wanted to rush to the bridge to cross it, but Mother held them back, waiting and watching. After long minutes, she pointed and said, "Der! Sees dem?" Latisha stared in the direction she pointed, but saw nothing.

"Ah sees dem," one of the men said. "Dere be two o' dem."

"Dere be t'ree," Mother said.

"Where? Ah don' sees dem.," Latisha said.

"Look on de bottom, no on de top," Mother replied. Lizzie had been looking at the upper road, too, thinking that was the white man's road. Shifting her eyes to the bottom road, she saw them. Through the openings between the bridge supports, three people moved back and forth. By their hats and postures, they appeared to be men, and they were flapping their arms around trying to keep warm. Why were they on the colored folks' road? Lizzie wondered. Of course! They were there to catch colored folks going to the land of promise.

"Who dey be, Mutter?" Tomas asked.

"Don' know. Could be nobodys. Most likely, dey be slavers."

"What we g'wan do, Mutter?" one of the men asked.

"We wait," Mother said.

As they waited, Lizzie became stiff and cold, and she was wondering how they were going to cross the bridge with those men there, when three other men came up the road on horseback and rode right out onto the bridge. Dismounting, they talked with the men on the bridge for a little while. Then the three men who were on the bridge got onto the other men's horses and rode away.

Tomas said they were changing guard and would be keeping watch all night. "What we do, Mutter? We can't cross de bridge wid dose men der."

"Wait, chil', Gawd will provide."

During intervals of darkness, when the moon was hidden behind the clouds, the fugitives slowly worked themselves up to alongside a high mound of dirt and stone that looked like a long ridge that ran all the way to the pillars. The top of the mound went to the upper road that crossed the bridge, and the bottom of the mound went to lower road.

Crouching behind the large rocks piled along the mound, hiding in the shadows, they waited. The men on the bridge were tossing something against the side of the bridge. Sometimes, their voices carried with the wind, and it became apparent that they were absorbed in playing some kind of dice game. The fugitives wondered how they would cover the distance to the bridge without being detected.

The night continued to pass. It wouldn't be long before daylight would dawn, and they'd be exposed to the men on the bridge. They were wondering if Mother didn't know what to do, but before they could question her, they heard a low rumbling sound coming from the other side of the great ditch.

Lizzie strained to see in the pre-dawn darkness but saw nothing. The snow continued to fall, filling the air, the bridge still looked like the bridge to nowhere, and the rumble grew louder, when the mound started vibrating under her. She clutched her mammy's hand in fear and was about to ask what was happening when the air shattered with the loudest, shrillest scream she'd ever heard. Her question became her own scream of fright, swallowed by the other scream. A light moved in the darkness from across the great ditch.

The ground was shaking hard now, and Lizzie trembled uncontrollably as the rumble grew into a roar, filling the cold air with its intensity. The light grew bigger and brighter and was coming directly at them. A long, black body was behind the light coming out of the air. Again, it screamed. Lizzie screamed back, and then she realized what it was. It was one of the giant monsters those men had said were in Canada . . . coming to devour them!

"Mammy, I'm scared!" Lizzie screamed.

"Hush, chil'," Mother said sternly.

"Mammy, et's coming ta git us! Et's de mon'ter!" Lizzie screamed.

"Et be de train chil'. Now hush an be ready ta run when Ah tells yous ta."

Latisha pulled Lizzie to her and covered her mouth with her hand, as the snake train got nearer. It was enormous and powerful, with thick black and white smoke billowing out of its head, leaving a long tail behind. It was coming at them on the upper road, and it was coming to devour them. Lizzie screamed again when it roared right over them, throwing stones and cinders at them. The ground shook hard, and they crouched down covering their heads against the onslaught of flying shrapnel, while black, stinging smoke from the snake train swirled around them.

Mother jumped up, shouting for them to run along the side of the train to the bridge. "Run! Git on de top when de train go by, an run hard yous can! Run! Do no stop! Run ta yous freedom chillens! Run!"

They stumbled up, running opposite the snake train as it thundered by. Lizzie held on to her mammy's hand, stumbling and kicking, trying to get her cramped legs moving right, her breath coming in gasps while Latisha dragged and pulled her on. The blanket Miss Jacquie had given her flew off, snatched by the snake train. Tomas ran behind, keeping his family in front of him. Mother and the other men, all ran ahead.

Running alongside the snake train was the most terrifying thing Lizzie had ever done. It was so powerful and loud it roared by her in a blast of wind that didn't end, spitting stones, stinging her body, showering her with dirt. She trembled, her bones shaking, and her head wanted to explode from the shattering scream. She was certain that, at any second, it would leap at her and devour her in one bite.

As they ran, the last of the snake train roared past, leaving them in a swirling, choking cloud of dirt, smoke and snow. The others had reached the top of the large mound and were running onto the bridge of freedom to the land of promise.

Tomas helped Latisha and Lizzie climb the mound. On the top, large timbers were lined up in a long row, going out onto the bridge as far as Lizzie could see. Two metal rods ran across the timbers, disappearing into the great ditch. Tomas yelled to run on top of the metal rods, but when Lizzie did, the rods were alive—moving under her feet. Jumping off in fear, she fell to the ground, tearing her new dress. Her pappy pulled her up, yelling that it was okay and to just keep running.

Once on the bridge, Lizzie could see to the bottom of the great ditch. Her eyes bulged out—she couldn't believe what she saw. Far below, was water that, even in the dim light, she could see was wild and violent, with massive white waves jumping high into the air.

"Mammy, look!" she yelled, stopping and pointing, "Down dere!"

"Don' stops, chil', jes' run. Don' look, run!" She pulled Lizzie forward, and as Lizzie looked away from the water she saw the men on the lower road, running to the end, so they could get on the upper road. They had revolvers in their hands and were yelling.

Then Lizzie saw another sight that took her breath away and made her stop. "Mammy! Look!" Turning to look at where Lizzie was pointing, Mammy stopped and stared too. In the distance were lights that shone and flickered, lighting up an entire wall of moving water that was coming down from out of the sky.

Tomas shouted at them from behind. "Don' stop! Keep runnin'! Go! Go!" Ahead of them, Mother and the other men disappeared into the nothingness that the bridge became. Lizzie couldn't get her feet to move—she felt paralyzed by the sights below and beyond.

A shot rang out, ricocheting over her head.

"Stop! Stop in the name of the law ya son-of-a-bitch!" Harsh voices came from behind. Another shot rang out, zinging off the bridge.

"Run! Run!" Tomas yelled. Latisha clutched Lizzie's hand, yanking her hard out of her trance, half pulling, half dragging her to get her moving again. Her feet got caught in between the timbers, and Tomas bent down to get them out; then they were all running again. The men with the guns had moved rapidly and were on the top road, closing the distance between them.

"Stop, you stinking run-away! Get back here, you hear me boy? Stop! I'm a-warning you! Next one be in your black ass!" The family ran as fast and as hard as they could. Lizzie knew her pappy could outrun them easily, but he stayed behind, pushing them forward, keeping himself between them and the slave-chasers. Then Lizzie saw more men coming out of the darkness ahead, appearing like ghosts from where the bridge disappeared—they were running toward them. The men in back were now so close that she heard their feet hitting the timbers. Men were in back, and men were in front, they were trapped between them. We not g'wan make it, she thought.

"Run, Latisha! Run, Lizzie! Run hard yous can! Don' stop; don' lok back!" Tomas yelled. They ran, and didn't know he had turned to face the men until they heard his mighty shout. "Aayyyiieee!" Tomas threw himself at the two men in the lead, knocking them both down, giving his family time to escape.

"Tomas!" Latisha screamed, turning around to go back to him. The third man raced around the two men wrestling with Tomas on the deck of the bridge and jumped in front of Latisha. He held out his hand to her.

"That's right, sugar, you just come to Daddy now. It's all over. We're gonna take good care of you."

Before the man could reach Latisha, one of the men running toward them from the other side grabbed her from behind and pulled her back. Latisha started fighting with him, while another man swooped Lizzie up into his arms and started backing away from the man holding his hand out to Latisha. He yelled at Latisha, "Stop it! Stop fighting us! We're from Canada. We're here to help you. Stop fighting us! We're not going to hurt you."

Latisha finally understood and quit struggling and the man pushed her behind him, shielding her from the slave-chasers. The man holding Lizzie took Latisha's arm, and slowly began walking them backwards on the bridge.

"You boys leave that there man alone, and go on your way now, heh?" The man from Canada shouted at the two men who held Tomas.

The man in the front raised his revolver and yelled back, "Who the hell are you? This here ain't no man; it's a runaway slave, and this ain't none o' your business, mister. Now, you let loose o' them there bitches and let us go about our business."

"You don't have any business here, mister. Now turn that man loose and leave him be, so he and his family can go on their way."

"Family? These ain't no family. These are slaves, and runaway slaves at that! They ain't got no way 'cept'n going back from where they run from. And the law says you gotta stand aside while we do our job here."

"Not here, it don't, mister. No laws like that here, you're on Canadian soil now, and that man is a free man. Now you release him, 'cause I know you don't want any trouble, heh?"

The slave-chaser pointed his revolver at the man shielding Latisha. "Heh, your ass, fella! This here buck ain't going nowhere 'cept'n ta the auction block, y'all hear? Now, let them bitches go, and no one's gonna get hurt!"

The man from Canada continued backing up, taking Lizzie and her mammy further onto the bridge, further towards freedom—further away from pappy.

"You pull that trigger, you got yourself a heap of trouble, mister. Look back there," he motioned over his shoulder. "Those are Mounties coming up behind us. You gonna shoot a Canadian citizen on Canadian soil, with Mounties coming, heh? You sure you want to tangle with them? Not real smart, if you ask me. Something like that'd be enough to start a war, wouldn't you think? And, seems like you folks are about to start your own war, amongst yourselves already. You boys ready for two wars? That is if you don't get yourself killed first. Those Mounties shoot first and ask questions later, heh?"

The man with the gun looked beyond the man who was holding Latisha and Lizzie and could see people running on the bridge towards them.

"Forget them bitches, Jessie, we got this one here. He'll bring us a pretty penny. Let's get outta of here before those Mounties get here," one of the other men urged.

The man holding the revolver looked back and forth between Tomas and the Canadian men, deciding how far he was willing to go. He looked at Latisha lustfully. "Yeah, the bitch ain't worth it." He began backing up but kept his revolver pointed at the man in front of Latisha. "Get that buck up, and let's go," he said to his two partners.

As they relaxed their grip on Tomas, so he could get to his feet, in a powerful surge he broke away from them and ran towards his family.

"Stop!" The man with the gun yelled. "Stop, damn you, boy!"

The shot sounded like a cannon as it echoed off the walls of the bridge. Tomas jerked forward, stumbling against the side railing of the bridge. He pulled himself up on the rail.

"Come on now, boy. You get yourself down from there, and we'll take care of you."

Tomas looked at Latisha and Lizzie, then down at the river below.

"You come down from there, boy, or I'll put another one in you! Get down off that railing, you hear?" One of the men reached out to grab him, and Tomas jerked his arm back, revealing a dark red stain on his left side. He looked at Latisha and Lizzie and smiled before shouting, "Ah dies a free man!" He pitched backward into the open dimness of the great ditch to the raging river below.

"Tomas! No!" Latisha screamed.

"Pappy!" Lizzie screamed.

"No, Tomas! No! No!" Latisha collapsed into the arms of the Canadian men, who carried her and Lizzie into the land of promise where the colored man is free.

Latisha and Lizzie settled in a town called St. Catherine's, where there was a large community of colored folks, many being former slaves like them. Mother Moses lived there for a while, until the war broke out between the States, and she went back to do spy work for the Union army.

Latisha never went back to visit Miss Jacquie, or to the United States.

Years later, Lizzie buried her mammy in the Negro burial ground at a place called Niagara-on-the-Lake, alongside a marker that held an empty pine box for her pappy. At their graves, she put up a plaque that read:

Bless the Lord!
Tomas and Latisha—Pappy and Mammy
They ain't slave—to no man—no more.
They were free on earth before they died
Now they're free with their Lord above

Lizzie went back to America when she heard Miss Jacquie was sick, and she thanked her for giving her pappy his freedom, and for giving mammy and herself their lives.

She was there when Miss Jacquie passed on to her reward, and Lizzie knew that the angels, along with her pappy and mammy, were there to welcome Miss Jacquie home. Miss Jacquie cherished mammy's feather of rainbow colors from Africa and had it mounted, along with the yellow ribbon, in a glass case, which she'd kept on her hutch on display. The plume was handed down to her children and to their children.

It wouldn't be until many generations later—when Latisha's great-great-grandson was chosen as the head electrical engineer for the new power generation station being built at Lewiston, New York— that any of Latisha's people would move back to America. Of course, when Lizzie's great-grandson moved to America, he brought his son, Leonard, with him.

Chapter 33

City of Niagara Falls
February 18, 1962

Ken sat at the table, using a penknife and a pair of needle-nosed pliers to gently pry open the back of the frame, careful not to disturb the delicate objects inside. Holding the pieces together, he slowly turned it over, placed it on the table, and lifted the frame away from the glass. He carefully removed the broken pieces of glass and painstakingly rearranged the heirloom so as to expose the handwriting on the fragile backing underneath. He positioned the new special plate glass he had ordered and then replaced the frame, holding everything together.

After carefully securing the back to the frame, he turned it over to inspect his work and was pleased that everything looked okay and was in its original spot. The large feather under the glass was still intact, and although it was dulled and had lost much of its luster and brightness over the decades, it still was colorful and striking. The yellow ribbon had lost most of its color and was frayed and worn thin.

The heirloom had been handed down in his family for generations, going back to the Civil War era, when his ancestors owned land along the escarpment. Ken cherished the feather, proud of the history and heritage of his family. In the frame under the feather, faded handwritten words could still be read:

To my family: Keep this forever in love of freedom and of God, for in the love of both was it given.
Jacquie Barton
November 1859

Ken worried about how he could maintain the family tradition and hand it down to his son, Kevin, when Kevin seemed so willing to let *those* people handle such a cherished and priceless family treasure. Kevin didn't understand or appreciate the sacrifices his family had undergone to preserve their heritage. It was time for him to step up and become a member of the family, and to set aside some of his silly notions, to include this so called friend of his.

Ken's thoughts were interrupted by the loud wailing siren of the fire station, summoning him to an emergency at the Falls. *Now what?* he wondered. *Always some crazy fool doing some crazy thing down there.*

Chapter 34

The Niagara Gorge

The shore shrunk where it passed under the Whirlpool and Railroad bridges and as if, in conspiracy with the narrowing river, it pushed us closer to the edge of the water.

But this wasn't just water.

The river, that only a few yards back, had given us comfort and assurance, had turned into a raging lunatic. Green, roiling waves threw themselves high into the air, in foaming rebellion against the sides of the gorge. They were close, so close we could touch them—if we had the nerve to. They roared with vehemence, smashing and crashing in furious conflict with tons of stationary rock and ancient boulders that had been deposited in chaotic style, thousands of years ago, as the cataracts cut their way south.

The shoreline was indistinguishable from the river. Megaton boulders crossed the invisible line between river and shore as the swells came and went, back and forth at will. One minute shore, the next minute—river. There was little pathway to follow on the shore—there was little shore.

The walls of the gorge had become steep, at spots pushing within feet of the raging river. What shore remained, was riddled with broken boulders layered in ice and snow.

"Oh, man!" cried Lenny. "Look at those waves! They're bigger than we are!"

"Yeah, one slip in there, and it's all over for sure," Wayne observed.

Billy was terrified. "We can't get by this! We gotta go back!"

"There's no going back. We've come too far for any of that now," Chuck said as he strained to look downriver as far as he could see. "How much farther is it to the Whirlpool, Kevin?"

"Half-mile, I guess, but it's like this the whole way."

"Can we get by this?" Wayne asked.

"There's a couple of spots that were scary in the summer. I don't know what they're like in winter. I guess it's gonna depend on the ice."

"Spots? This whole thing scares me. We should go back and wait for them to come and get us," Billy whined.

"We'll tie ourselves together with the ropes, so no one can fall in." Chuck said. "We can get by this. We just gotta be careful that's all, right Kevin? We can do it together. Come on guys, we're too close; the path is just around the bend. We can't quit now." Chuck turned to Billy but not with any malice or derision. "If you want to go back, Billy, then go ahead. You can't get lost. Just follow our route in the snow back to the ruins and wait for someone there. No one is making you go on; it's your choice." Chuck looked at me. "What do you say, Kev?"

Going back wasn't an option any longer. "Being tied together will be good, as long as we can get pass these rapids." I agreed with Chuck; we'd come too far to turn back now. I looked at the others. "But no one should go if he doesn't want to. If you can't do this, now's the time to go back.

Once past these rapids, you won't be able to go back to the tunnel. At the bottom of the tunnel, just stay there and wait, and someone will come sooner or later. When we're out of here, we'll make an anonymous call to the firemen that you're down there." The idea of being tied together gave some sense of confidence; looking at those rapids took it away.

"Well, I'm going on," Wayne said. "I don't see a choice. Ain't no going back."

"What'd you say, Billy?" Lenny tugged on Billy's coat. "C'mon, let's get this over with. There's nothing back there. Stick with me, man, it'll be okay, we'll get you home."

Billy was defeated. "I'm not walking back there by myself. If you're all going ahead, then I have to, too. But I don't want to, and that water scares me."

"Yeah, me too, makes me want to wet my pants." Lenny said.

"I already wet mine, but I'm so wet I can't tell the difference," Wayne added.

"Well, let's get those ropes outta your pack before they turn yellow." Chuck said.

"I guess I'll lead," I said. "I know the way the best."

After tying the rope securely around my waist, I passed it to Wayne. Our mood had taken on a whole new dimension of seriousness, with no ribbing or small talk. We were tired and cold, and we all knew we were dealing with a situation that carried a dire outcome if not done right, one that literally was life or death, something we'd never knowingly been confronted with before.

"I'll be last, as anchor," Chuck said. "C'mon, Billy, you go after Wayne. It'll be most secure in the middle."

As Chuck tied the rope around Billy's waist, I gave some impromptu instructions. "I'll keep to the side of the gorge, away from the river, as much as I can. We have to work together, or we'll be jerking each

214

other around. Make sure you got solid footing all the time and don't take big steps when moving. Don't jerk on the rope and use the tug as a signal for moving. If anyone slips, then everyone else stay where you are and hold fast 'til he gets his footing again, okay?" I didn't have a clue what I was talking about, but it sounded right. There was a chorus of "Yeahs" and "Okays," echoing that they didn't have a clue what I was talking about, either.

When Chuck finished tying the end of Lenny's rope around Billy, he tied Wayne's rope around Billy, too. Using both ropes gave us more slack between one another. Once Lenny was tied on, Chuck secured himself to the end. I wondered if we had even the slightest idea of what we were getting into.

"It'll be slow going, so don't get in a hurry, okay?"

After everyone was ready, I started off, hugging the inside of the boulder, which was under a vicious assault by the rabid river on its outside. Pushing the toes of my boot hard into the icy crust, I formed steps that they could follow in, and I worked my way forward until I felt the rope go taut. Holding firm, I waited while Wayne followed in my footsteps. Once he had worked his way to me and was secured, I moved ahead until I felt the rope go tight once again. Wayne moved up again and then it was Billy's turn.

In this manner, segment by segment, one man at a time, we worked our way around the boulder to the other side. The massive swell of the river was only feet away, licking at our faces as it challenged and harassed us. It was harrowing, having those humongous, powerful waves slamming into the boulder, coating us with their cold spray as we progressed slowly around it. Each crashing wave cut a tiny nitch into the fabric of our nerves, leaving us more and more frazzled.

Once pass the monolith, I angled into the side of the gorge, away from the river. It didn't gain a lot, only a few feet, but not having those massive waves crashing directly over us was like removing Boris Karloff from *Frankenstein*.

We fell into a weary cadence and despite some erratic jerking and tugging along the line, were moving forward at a consistent pace, making steady progress. Until we came to a sudden and complete halt. The side of the gorge had forced us back to the edge of the river once again, begrudgingly providing a mere eight-foot space between the steep wall of the canyon, rising two hundred feet above us on the one side and a seething wall of water on the other. This would have been plenty of room to pass through, if not for the boulder that towered twenty feet over our heads and sat squarely on the waterline, half in the river—half on the shore, taking up more than six feet of that opening. The remaining narrow, tight gap between the side of the boulder and the gorge would have been just large enough for us to crawl through, if it hadn't been packed tight from bottom to top with ice, sealed up like mortar in bricks.

Standing there, wet, cold and tired, staring at the solid wall that sealed us off from the world on the other side, my spirit, soul and mind all abandoned ship together.

The part of the boulder situated in the water was under a violent assault. The river smashed into the boulder with the wrath of a hurricane, throwing white-capped waves furiously over its top above our heads. Frothy water broke and sprayed across the top like a mini Niagara Falls. Each shattering eruption of icy water shriveled my heart. I felt weak, my stomach heaved, my chest constricted, and I couldn't breathe. We stood before a foaming monster with no way around it.

"I wanna go home!" Billy cried. No one answered.

"How do we get around it? It's a solid wall," Lenny said.

"We're trapped," Wayne said, defeated.

"I wanna go home! Oh, crap, we're gonna die here!" Billy continued whining and crying, and I began wondering if he wasn't right.

I was cold, my clothes, frozen like boards, crackled when I moved. My body ached, and my feet throbbed. My stomach was too numb to be sick. Looking at the others, I saw my hopelessness and despair reflected back on their faces. Rage swelled inside of me. I wanted to scream; to kick the boulder 'til my feet bled. How could this be happening? How could my world have been totally destroyed in a single day? Why was I here? Why was I so weak? Why hadn't I the guts to say no when I should have? Why didn't I fight harder? Now we were all in real danger because of my weakness. My dad was right—I was a nothing—a nobody.

We stood helpless, completely trapped by the river, the gorge, and the wall. Mice in a maze, having no exit, while the river mocked its disdain of us without letup.

The boulder had a thick layer of ice from the constant assault of the river. I touched the ice; it was glassy and hard.

"Please God, I wanna go home," Billy whined.

God didn't answer, and Billy wasn't whisked away into the cold air, transported home. Remembering my hatchet, I removed it and tapped the ice to see how hard it was. It was. Moving to where the ice was packed like mortar, in the space between the boulder and the gorge, small pieces chipped off. I hit it harder, and a chunk, about two inches long, broke off.

Billy continued whining, "Please, please Mom, get me out of here. Please." Apparently, he'd given up on God.

We stood together, staring at the imposing blockage. On one side—a vertical wall of rock two hundred feet straight up, thickly layered in ice; on the other side—the seething river, relentlessly hammering, without letup. Between the two, a wall of stone and ice. We couldn't go ahead. We couldn't go around. We couldn't go back.

We were as Wayne had said—trapped.

Chapter 35

I continued chopping at the ice, breaking it off in chunks and pieces. It appeared the ice covering the crevice was an outer shell around an inch or two thick. Behind, this shell, was a dense packing of coarse, granular ice.

"I never should have let you guys talk me into coming down here." Billy had moved away from us and sat in the snow, facing back from where we had come. "We're never gonna get out of here. We're gonna die down here. I knew we shouldn't have come. I knew it, but you guys made me come."

I had chopped out a hole about ten inches square and scraped it out about six inches deep. Chuck inspected the hole, "What do you think Kev? Can we can dig our way through?"

"No. We don't know how wide this boulder is. If it's like some of those other ones we crawled around, it could be ten or fifteen feet across."

"Man, how would we tunnel through that?" Wayne asked.

"We chop a tunnel out, just like Kevin did with that hole there, and then we crawl through to the other side, that's how," Chuck said, sounding desperate for the first time. "It'll be hard, but we can do that, don't ya think, Kevin? You made that hole pretty quick."

"No, we can't. I told you it's not large enough to tunnel through," I answered, annoyed. "If there was nothing in the crevice, there'd barely be enough room to wiggle through sideways. There's no way we can with it packed full of ice like this. How do we even know it doesn't become narrower or fully closed off? We can't go through . . ." I stepped back, scanning the wall to the top. "But I wonder . . ."

The boulder slanted out toward the river, making the gap between the gorge and the boulder wider at the top. It looked solid all the way up, and there weren't any overhangs or ridges of ice on top.

"I wonder if we could make steps in this gap area, like that hole I chopped out and then climb over?"

"You think you can do that?" Chuck asked.

"If it chops like that hole did, I can," I answered. "And if the steps hold."

"We're gonna climb over this thing?" Wayne said. "With those waves breaking over the top like that? Are you crazy?"

"We'll stay away from the water side, Wayne, and hug the gorge side."

"What if it's too hard up there to chop or what if those steps crumble? We'd fall into the river, Kevin." Wayne continued. "What if we get up there and can't get back down the other side? What if—"

In a rage, I turned on him, venting the misery pent up inside me. "*What if? What if?* Get off the *what ifs*, for crying out loud, will ya?" I slammed the ice with my hatchet, more out of my own frustration than at him. Anger boiled up inside of me and exploded. Without thinking, and not able to stop myself, words spewed out like lava gushing from a volcano. "Don't you get it yet, Wayne? Everything about this whole stinking thing has been a *what if. What if* we'd never went on this stupid dare to begin with?" I turned on him with a sneer, "*What if* the Russians drop the A-bomb? You remember that, Wayne? That's what you said back at Ol' Gordy's when I said we shouldn't rush into this thing, remember? But no, you had to drag our dumb asses down here to take Billy's stupid picture!" I turned on Billy, "Oh, yeah, Billy, we're gonna be famous! Gonna be up on *the wall*—as if we're somebody, sure we are! And all you've done is whine and bitch the whole time. What *are* we doing here anyway? Who do we think we are? We're just a bunch of nobodies!" Inside of me a voice was saying *Stop! Shut up!* but I couldn't. Someone else was in me now, and he had the floor and wasn't giving it up. My words attacked my friends, but in my mind, I saw my dad. "*What if* you kept on walking into the Falls back there, huh, Wayne? What was that all about, anyway? I think that stupid ice-cream truck squashed your brains! We've *what if*'d this thing to death all day, and we can keep doing it all night, and guess what? It ain't gonna make a bit of difference! And it doesn't change a thing, either. What were we thinking?" The words, vile and nasty, continued to flow as my frustrations broke and overflowed. I took out my anger for my own shortcomings on my best friends.

They stood in stunned silence, not knowing what to say, their fallen faces looking pale and lifeless. I was ashamed. After all, it was me who had started with the *what ifs* in the beginning. I didn't recall ever letting loose like this before. Even Billy had stopped his whining and just stared at me. I felt worse than I'd ever felt in my life.

"Look," I began again, "lets *what if* this from a different way, okay? What if we don't try, and what if this is the only way out of here? Where would that leave us? We sit here because we didn't try the only way out? Everything down here is a what-if, so we might as well pick the what-ifs that have a chance of working. What if we don't get around this boulder? Then how do we get out of here? There's no going back, so we have to find a way around it. Anyone know of another way around this thing; or how to get out of this gorge? If you do, let's hear it, I'm all ears."

In the silence that followed, I started chopping a second hole. My tirade had vented my frustration and fear; but at a high cost. Wayne stood alone with his head down and wouldn't look up. Billy sat in the snow, trembling, looking like a ghost, openly crying for his mother. Chuck stood silent looking at me with a blank expression. I had a hole inside of me that hurt more than any beating my Ol' man ever gave me. I looked at Lenny, who hadn't said anything through my tirade

"It'll be okay, Kevin." Lenny said, "The steps will work, and we'll climb over it."

"Oh yeah?" Wayne demanded, turning on Lenny. "And how do you know that? What makes you the expert all of a sudden? They hold rock climbing lessons in Canada?"

"No, Wayne, I don't know anything about climbing boulders, but . . ." Lenny hesitated as if not sure of continuing, before going on, "but God is with Kevin and He won't let him fall." Lenny replied calmly.

I stopped chopping and looked at Lenny. The others turned to look at Lenny too, as if he were an alien who had just stepped out of a spaceship.

"God?" Wayne bellowed. "Is with Kevin? Are you nuts? I think you got your directions wrong coming from Canada. God ain't down here, Lenny! Look around, show me where you see God. Is He in the ice or maybe He's in the snow? Maybe He's in this stone that's blocking our path?" Now it was Wayne's turn to vent and all his pent up anger and fear was directed at Lenny—or at God? "Maybe God's in the river out there, roaring and raging at us. Oh, look, Lenny, there He is; He's in the rapids. Why, He's water skiing! Wow! Look at Him jump those waves! He should go out for the Olympics." He turned to Lenny, his face flushed with anger, "God ain't down here, Lenny, no more than he was there when my brother drank that booze and died. Even that priest couldn't bring God then, so what makes you think He's here now? God ain't nowhere. And you know why? Because there is no God, that's why, Lenny! We're on our own—here and everywhere else in this lousy world."

"He's here Wayne, you just have to open your eyes, and you'll see Him. Look around at creation and you see God is everywhere." Lenny said.

"I only see ice." Wayne said. He opened his mouth to say something else, but Chuck cut him off.

"All right Wayne, you made your point. Let's just drop it. If you don't believe God is here, that's fine, but if Lenny does, so what? What does it hurt? I for one will take all the help we can get, right about now, to get out of here."

Chuck put his hand on my shoulder "You want me to do it?"

"I got it!" I snapped at Chuck while looking back and forth between Lenny and Wayne. I didn't like being in the middle of this God talk. I'd already heard enough of that at my old man's Revival Temple. Shrugging off Chuck's hand, I resumed chopping. "I'm gonna chop steps all the way up this stinking rock, and we're gonna walk our butts out of here, if it's the last thing I do."

"My butt is so frozen you could slide it across the gorge like an ice cube," Chuck said, trying to break the black spell this rock had put on everyone.

"Man, that's a picture I don't wanna see—your white rear end sliding down the gorge." Lenny said, seemingly oblivious to Wayne's outburst.

Only Chuck laughed. Wayne stared at the river, and Billy continued crying for his mother. Above Billy's whimpering, the only sounds were my hatchet chopping at one end of the wall and the river hammering at the other end.

Chapter 36

I didn't need to cut holes as large as the first one I'd made, needing only enough room for our feet to fit, and before long, I had six steps, staggered apart, going up as far as I could reach, with enough snow crystals scraped out for footholds. Putting my foot into the lowest one, I stepped up, followed by my other foot into the next hole. Standing in the steps, they felt solid and didn't crumble or break off.

"They feel solid," I said. "I think we can get to the top this way, if we're careful."

"We don't know what it's like on the other side," Chuck said, looking at the top.

"Well, we'll know when we get there, won't we?" I snapped back.

"But *Kevie*," Chuck taunted in a whining, girlish voice, "*what if* there isn't another side? What are we gonna do then, Kevie, huh? What then, Kevie? *What if* this boulder doesn't end, Kevie? *What if* it just goes all the way to the Whirlpool, huh, Kevie? What then, Kevie?"

I stopped chopping and looked down at him. His face was contorted in a look of mock terror as he stared back up at me. Was he deliberately taunting me, looking for a fight? For the briefest of seconds, there was a stillness in the air and time stood suspended. Then Chuck's face broke into a wide grin along with laughter in his eyes, and I burst out laughing, realizing just how stupid I had sounded. Chuck had opened the door for my redemption with my friends and the dam burst open as everyone began laughing.

Everyone, except Billy.

I resumed chopping staggered sets of holes, working my way up the side of the wall, one step at a time. A few feet from the top, I paused to rest my arm, and I looked down at my friends. Three frosted faces stared back. Billy, still sitting off by himself, stared into nothingness.

Reaching the top, I chopped two handholds on the top edge of the gap to pull myself up. This was the tricky part—if the ice broke in my hands when I pulled, or under my feet when I pushed, I'd fall, possibly into the river.

"Okay, here goes." Securing a deep grip, trying not to pull on the outer ice layer of the hole, I made my move. It didn't break, and I didn't fall, and I got over the edge onto the top. "I made it, I'm on top." I called down to the jubilant shouts below.

The crevice on top was depressed slightly, as it ran across the length of the wall, like a small trench. The boulder was a full fifteen feet wide and the chaos on the river side of the boulder constantly splashed over the top, keeping everything wet and slick. I carefully crawled on all fours to the opposite side to see what obstacles lay over there.

"Kev, you okay? How's it looking up there?" Chuck called.

"It's okay, come on up. Don't push too hard in the steps and stay in the gap when you come over the top."

Instead of Chuck, Wayne climbed up the side of the boulder. "C'mon, buddy. I got ya. Dig your hands in deep, and don't pull on the outer shell itself," I said, grabbing his coat to help him over. I heard Chuck giving instructions below: "Billy, you and Lenny, go on up next, and I'll bring up the rear." That was smart, making sure Billy wasn't last.

I sat on top of the boulder and looked out across the river. It was a spectacular sight. The river churned powerfully across its entire width, sending towering waves of freezing chaos high into the air. They smashed against the house-sized boulders protruding up from the depths and whipped back around to beat against themselves. Looking at this scene, it was hard to believe I was in America, and that it was 1962. Just two hundred feet above us, the civilized City of Niagara Falls went about its daily business and routines, going to church, watching TV, reading comics at Ol' Gordy's, while down here, nature continued this primitive dance that had begun thousands of years ago.

It looked as if there were a lot more ice in the river than there had been a little while ago. I figured it was an illusion created by the rapids and the narrowing of the river. I watched as one unusually large iceberg, caught in the turbulent waters, smashed into a rock that was every bit as big as the iceberg itself was, except that it was solidly anchored to the river's bottom. It was astonishing to watch these two goliaths clash and see the iceberg shatter into several pieces, each of which was still larger than the boulder I sat on.

"Wild, ain't it?" Wayne had moved alongside of me, watching the ice-car demolition derby.

"Yeah, it's wild, all right," I turned to him "like I was a while ago. You know, Wayne, I didn't mean all that crap I said down there. I was mad at myself, not you."

"Yeah, I know. I'm cool. Don't sweat it."

"I'm just an A-one jerk" I said. "I'm no different than my old man."

Wayne grabbed my coat sleeve and stared into my face. "Don't ever say that, Kevin, you're nothing like your old man and don't ever think you are."

I looked at Wayne and saw desperation in his face I didn't understand. Something was inside of him that was causing him pain, and he needed me to be an anchor for him. I didn't know if I could be; I had my own pain.

"You came down on Lenny pretty hard, back there Wayne. I never heard you say you didn't believe in God before."

"Do you? I know you go to that church with your old man, but I didn't think you actually liked it."

"I don't like it. I go because I have to. You know I don't even think about God when I'm there. I think about Him at other times, when I'm alone, and I wonder about things."

"But do you believe there's a God?"

"Yeah, I guess I do. Doesn't everyone? I don't know. Do you really believe there's no God, Wayne?"

He paused before answering. "He wasn't there when Clarence died," he said.

"Wayne, we don't always understand why some things happen, but I don't think we can blame God for them."

"You don't understand, Kevin. I prayed; I prayed hard. When that priest was kneeling over Clarence and praying, that was the first time in my life I prayed. I prayed hard that God would bring Clarence back— and He didn't, and it's all my fault. If there's a God, why wouldn't He have brought him back?"

"You can't blame yourself for that, Wayne. It was an accident; there was nothing you could've done."

He didn't answer right away, and I felt he was struggling with something. Then he turned and looked at me, and I saw the pain on his face.

"I showed Clarence where the old man kept his liquor and how to get into it." He looked away, out across the river, "It's all my fault that Clarence died."

Chapter 37

There was plenty of room on top of the boulder for all of us, without anyone having to move out of the trench, which no one was eager to do, as the waves crashing over the top edge reminded us.

"How's it look down the other side, Kev?" Chuck asked, moving to look over the edge.

"Not good. The river cuts in tight to the gorge, so there's not much shore, and there're rocks all over. It's pretty ugly."

"Can we get down?" Chuck asked.

"We have to, unless we want to stay up here until spring." My emotions hadn't settled down yet. "There's a rock we can stand on part way down, and then we'll go from there."

"Yeah, I see it, but how do we get to it?" Chuck asked, leaning over.

"I'll have to chop steps going down, like I did coming up."

"How you gonna do that going down?" Chuck asked.

"I'll have to hang on the rope while you guys hold me."

"Bull crap, your arms will never last, or you'll rip your shoulders out."

"I can do it."

"What if we lowered you down with the rope first, and you make steps coming back up, as you did on the other side?" Lenny suggested.

"Hey, good idea, Lenny," Chuck said, nodding his head.

"Why don't we just lower everyone down to the rock with the rope and not worry about making anything?" Wayne asked.

"And then who lowers the last guy down, Wayne?" Chuck asked. "Didn't we go through that already? I ain't going to 'Geronimo' this time. Not on those rocks down there." Chuck said with a laugh then turned to me. "You want me to chop this time?"

"No," I said. I started it, and I'll finish it. For some reason, that was important to me.

I chopped two handholds on top again, this time for going down over the edge. The others held the rope securely; and, lying on my belly, I slowly let my feet over the edge. Hanging there, like a dead man, I realized Chuck had been right—there was no way I could have chopped hanging like this. "Okay, I'm ready. Lower me down."

They lowered me down foot by foot, until my feet touched something hard. Looking down, I was on the edge of the rock I had seen from above. As expected, it was slippery. "Keep the rope tight while I clear this ice away," I called to them. Using the flat side of the hatchet, I bent over and broke off the ice on top of the rock, making for firm footing.

Standing back up and looking around, I was about five feet from the bottom—that was good; there was no level ground anywhere below—that was bad.

The river cut sharply in towards the gorge, and the water had created a slick ice-slide from the boulder up the side of the gorge. The small amount of shoreline remaining was full of jagged, slippery rocks. There were no rocks high enough to act like steps, and it would be impossible to jump down without twisting ankles, breaking legs, or worse—sliding into the river. The only unobstructed area was a flat rock on the river side which was underwater. It was shallow, with the water racing fast across the surface. The river dropped off on the outside edge of the rock, and it looked deep. If we could get to that spot, we could step around the ice slide and move onto the small piece of shore—*if* we could get to that spot. Well, one thing at a time.

I turned back to the boulder and began chopping steps going back up. The ice on this side was thinner than it had been on the other side, probably due to its being on the opposite side of the waves, so it took less effort and time to cut out these holes. But the boulder leaned outward a little, making it harder to stand than it had been on the other side. On that side, gravity had pushed me into the boulder; here, it pushed me slightly away.

"Keep the rope tight!" I called up. If I fell, I'd end up in the river.

"We got it, Kev," Chuck called back.

Determination, or desperation, finally paid off, and I chopped my way back to the top. I stood there, catching my breath, allowing the involuntary quivering and muscle spasms in my arms and legs to settle.

"How you doing?" Chuck asked. "You okay?"

"Yeah, just need to stop shaking is all."

"When am I going to get off of here?" Billy whined. "I'm cold, and I'm sick of seeing those waves wash over."

"We hear you, Billy." I felt different about Billy than I had at this time yesterday, but then, I guess we all felt differently about each other. "You're getting down now." While talking to everyone, I looked directly at Billy. "When you climb down, you'll be on that rock I was standing on. From there, it's just a five-foot jump to the bottom."

"That's no big deal, we can jump five feet," Lenny said. Billy just stared at me.

"You can't jump to the right; we're cut off that way. It's an ice-slide into the river," I said, looking at Billy.

"What does that mean?" Lenny eyes showed confusion while his mouth formed the words. Billy continued to stare at me.

"There's one flat rock we can jump to," I answered, staring into Billy's eyes.

"Okay, that sounds good," Lenny said.

"It's in the river."

"Are you crazy?" Billy exploded. "I ain't jumping in that river! We're gonna die. I knew it! You're out of your mind. You want me to die that's what."

I'd expected the outburst and was ready for it. "No one wants to die down here, Billy. You'll be tied to the rope, with everyone holding it."

"Piss on your rope!" Billy answered. "Piss on you too! No way! Oh, crap! I'm not doing this! Oh, God! Why did you guys make come down here? You're crazy! That's what you are. You're all crazy!"

"I'll go first and show you that it's okay." I turned from Billy and looked at the others. "You guys hold the rope tight. Give me enough slack to jump and when I land, keep it tight so if I fall you pull me back right away, okay?"

"Yeah, we got it. Don't worry, you'll be okay. We got the rope," Chuck said. Wayne and Lenny nodded behind him. I gave Billy, who hadn't stopped his rant, one last look and climbed back down. Standing on the rock, with muscles quivering again (although this time not from fatigue or cold), I faced the river, looking it over carefully. The rock, or landing zone, was a generous size, about three feet wide, and the water flowing over its surface was only a couple of inches deep. It looked flat and smooth under the rippling water. After centuries of being washed by the river, it was polished smooth. I assumed it would be slick as butter. The far side of the submerged opening frightened me; the flat rock abruptly ended about three or four feet out and the bottom dropped off. The current was supercharged as it surged around the boulder. The water color changed to a darker, sinister green where the rock ended as it disappeared into the deep, strong current. If I slid off, I'd be swept away into the river.

I looked back up at the group. Chuck was leaning over the edge, watching me carefully. He had the rope around his waist and held it tightly in his hands. Wayne and Lenny were behind him, holding his back to keep him from being pulled down. I didn't see Billy, but I could hear his whimpering. I checked the knot around my waist and moved it to my back. "How much slack is there?" I called, my voice cracking. Chuck held up the rope, showing about six feet in it. "Is that okay?" I nodded my head, as words wouldn't come out if I tried to speak.

"We're ready on this end, Kev. Don't worry, we got ya."

I took a deep breath and managed to say, "Okay, here goes."

How many times in one day can someone's heart pound through his ribcage? How many times do you ride the roller coaster? Well, this wasn't the Comet, this was for real. The river was spellbinding as I watched the swirling current. I forced myself to look away from the mesmerizing water and to focus on the landing zone and tried to pretend the river wasn't there. Right—good luck. Like pretending, there was no hair on Michael Landon's face in *I Was a Teenage Werewolf*.

I picked out the exact spot I wanted to land and crouched down, positioning my feet for a clean dismount. I told myself to keep my feet firmly on the ground when I landed, and with every fiber of strength and courage I had within me, I jumped into the raging rapids of the Niagara River.

I hit the spot perfectly—and my feet flew out from under me like greased pigs.

The submerged rock was a sheet of butter, and I would have disappeared into the river's embrace, if not for the sudden jerk of the rope yanking me backwards, hard onto my butt. The current grabbed at my legs, trying to pull me in. Kicking, scrambling, and clawing, along with the guys pulling the rope, I managed to turn myself around, stand upright, and stepped out of the water onto the narrow shore.

Through the uncontrollable shaking of my whole body, I could hear cheers and yahoos in the recesses of my consciousness. I held up my hand toward them. "It's okay, just give me a moment."

"We're sending Billy next!" Chuck called down.

Billy went into full-blown panic. "No way! Not me! You see what happened to Kevin? I'll go into the river! You guys won't pull me out. I'm not going! Let Lenny go!"

I knew Billy would never be able to make the jump in that condition. "Hold up, Chuck. That rock is real slippery. Keep the rope tight on me while I clean it up." Carefully, I stepped back into the fast current of the landing zone and used my hatchet to scrape away at the slippery moss and greasy slime. I cleaned it up pretty decent, and when rubbing it with my foot, there was a lot more traction than when I had jumped on it. I continued scraping as far out as I dared reach. I wanted, not only to remove the slickness on the stone, but also to build confidence in Billy, by having him see me standing there. "Okay, that's better now." Stepping out, I untied the rope from around my waist, and Chuck hauled it up.

"Chuck, I think you should come down next. We'll be able to hold the rope better from down here without worrying about getting pulled off, and we're gonna have to do that for the last guy anyway. Let Wayne and Lenny hold the rope up there now, and I'll grab you from here."

Chuck stared down at me for a long minute, thinking it over. Finally, he said, "Okay."

I watched Chuck tie the rope around his waist and climb down. When he was standing on the rock, he checked the amount of slack in the rope and made sure the guys above had the rope secured well. I positioned myself at the edge of the landing zone, just outside of where Chuck would hit. It was small and tight, without much room to stand, but I was able to plant my feet firmly and still have enough room to pull Chuck out.

"I'll grab you and pull you back. Try to land in close, and keep your feet back, so they don't fly out from under you, as mine did."

"Got it, kemosabe."

"Wayne, Lenny, you guys ready up there?" I called to the faces staring down.

"Yeah, we're ready. We got it; he ain't going nowhere."

"Okay, hold tight and pull the slack in after he hits."

"Got it," Wayne confirmed.

"Okay, whenever you're ready, Chuck."

"On three." Chuck's voice was shaky. He checked the slack to make sure it wouldn't trip him, crouched down into a jumping position, focused on the landing zone, and counted. "One . . . two . . . three!" He leaped into the air and came down, hitting the landing zone dead center. I grabbed his coat and arm with both my hands as he hit. Wayne pulled the rope; I pulled his coat, and he was out of the landing zone, standing on the shore in a flash.

"Geronimo!" Chuck shouted.

Chapter 38

After untying the rope, he called up, "Billy? You next? You see how easy it is now?"

"Let Lenny go," Billy whined "I'll go after him."

"I'll go. You watch, Billy and see how easy it is," Lenny said to Billy and then turned to Chuck. "I'll tie this end here, and you hold that end down there." After tying the rope around his waist, Lenny climbed down to the rock and stood looking at the river.

"Okay, Lenny," I said, "Chuck's anchoring the rope, and I'll grab you, just like I did Chuck." Lenny stared at the river, and a look of absolute horror came over his face. "Lenny, you ready?" He continued staring into the river. "Lenny! Stop looking at the river. Look at the place you're going to land on. You can't go in; we got you. Don't look at the river."

Lenny broke his stare away from the river and looked at me with determination. "Okay, you guys ready, heh?"

"We're ready when you are."

"Okay, here goes—on three."

Lenny crouched, and Chuck braced himself with the rope. Lenny counted to three, leaped into the air, and landed on the spot. Chuck pulled back with the rope. I grabbed Lenny's coat and he was out of the landing zone, barely making a splash.

Billy needed to go next. He couldn't be the last one left on top—if he froze, how would we get him off? "Okay, Billy, just like Lenny did," I called up, wondering how difficult this was going to be.

Surprisingly, Billy climbed over the side and was standing on the rock within seconds. He seemed almost eager. Watching Lenny had given him confidence. Lenny tossed him the rope, and we watched as Billy tied it around his waist.

"Move the knot around to your back, Billy," I said. Chuck took up the slack, and I positioned myself to grab him. "Okay, Billy, whenever you're ready, on three. Just remember—don't throw your feet way out." Billy stood there staring at the river, not moving. "We're ready when you are, Billy." Billy didn't answer. "Billy, you ready?" He stood there, not talking. "Billy, stop looking at the river. Look at the landing zone. Come on, we're ready." Billy didn't respond; he only stared into the tendons of water that surged and foamed across the river.

"Billy, let's go!" Chuck shouted at him. Billy stared. "Billy, look at me!" Chuck screamed. Billy didn't look. "We ain't got all day, Billy!" Chuck started violently flicking the rope up and down, making it jerk and snap on Billy. "Look at me, Billy. You don't look at me right this minute; I swear I'll jerk your butt right off that rock. You hear me? I mean it! I'll pull your whining ass down on top of that water; and then haul you in like a snagged fish, I will." Billy turned slowly and looked at Chuck. "Good. Now don't look at the river again. Keep your head down and stare at your feet. That's it. Now move your eyes out and raise your head only enough to look at where you're going to jump. Look at it. See it? Right there, just a few feet in front of you. Yeah, that's it, that flat rock right there. It's a piece of cake, man. Look at the spot you want to land on. Just a little jump and you're outta here. Don't look at anything else, just that piece of rock. Don't worry about anything, we got you. You can't go anywhere with this rope on you, and Kevin's gonna grab you, just like he did Lenny. All you have to do is jump. We'll do all the rest."

Billy stayed focused on the landing spot. "That's right," Chuck encouraged him. "You got it, on three. Just keep looking at where you want to land. Keep your feet straight down, and we'll do the rest. You saw how easy it was with Lenny. Just a little hop. One . . . two . . ." Before Chuck could say three; Billy jumped. His feet hit the landing spot. I grabbed his coat and Chuck jerked back on the rope, pulling him back. Billy was out of the opening and lying on his back in the snow and ice before he realized he had even jumped.

"All right, nice going! You did fantastic, Billy! No sweat, man," Lenny cheered.

Billy sat in a swoon, and I thought he was going to faint, but he suddenly burst out in uncontrolled crying as the tension released from his body. Tension flowed from mine, too, as now, with Billy down, the hard part was over.

"Okay, Wayne," I called to him, "you're cleanup batter." Wayne was already standing on the rock and had made short order of tying the rope on. "Whoa, Wayne! Take it easy, man. It's slippery on that rock. Keep your fee—" Wayne jumped, and we weren't ready. He landed on the furthest part of the submerged rock, and his feet caught some of the moss I hadn't scraped away. His oversized boots couldn't get a grip, and they shot out in front of him like those toboggans at Chestnut Ridge, spilling Wayne on his side. The river grabbed him, pulling him into its cold embrace. Chuck almost lost the rope before he was able to get a grip on it.

"Lenny, help me!" Chuck yelled. Lenny grabbed the rope and together they began pulling backwards, dragging Wayne against the strong current that wanted him just as badly.

Jumping into the landing area, I grabbed Wayne by the arm, and pulled him back as he kicked and splashed in the cold grip of the water. Together, we clawed our way off of the flat rock and collapsed in a heap on the shore, winning the tug-of-war.

Chapter 39

After long minutes of catching my breath and shaking off the shock of what just happened, I looked at Wayne. He lay exhausted on the ice, his pants and coat clung to him like a second layer of ice skin. One of his gloves was missing, apparently claimed as a souvenir by the river, but by some miracle, he had managed to keep both boots on his feet. I was lucky in that my boots were laced tight around my calves, which didn't allow much water in during my short struggle with the river. Wayne wasn't so lucky.

"You okay?" I asked.

He looked at me, and I saw his fear. "That was close. I thought I was gone."

"Big goofball, you just couldn't wait, could you? We weren't ready, and those stupid boots of yours . . ."

"Skis, that's what they are!" Lenny added, "Almost took you for a ride down the river, man!"

"Yeah, the river of no return!" I jeered. "There goes Wayne, off to Lake Ontario, bouncing from wave to wave, like Wild Bill on a bucking bronco!"

Lenny held up his hand and intoned solemnly, "I hereby consecrate this ground 'Hallowed Be Thy Wayne,' and christen this rock as 'Wild

Wayne' for all generations to come in honor of Sir Wayne of Niagara, the Holy Knight of the River."

While Chuck and I enjoyed this, Wayne seemed annoyed, giving Lenny a look of displeasure.

"Come on, Wayne, we got to get that water out of your boots before you freeze to death." I said, sensing he was going to open up on Lenny, for some unintended slight.

"Well, I could just stay here as a statue to decorate Lenny's 'holy' monument," he spat out.

"What do you say we eat something? I'm hungry," Chuck said. I agreed—hunger had moved into the void left by the release of our pent-up fears and frustrations.

"Yeah, that sounds good, if it's not all ruined," even Wayne agreed.

"Let's move around this bend a little and get away from this monster." I said, helping Wayne to his feet.

Moving away from the ice-slide, the shore straightened out, widening a little. Stepping further away from the river, and those nerve shattering waves, proved to be cause for the dark cloud to lift from our spirits.

"Here, Wayne, let's get that knapsack off your back and see what got wet," Chuck said.

"Yeah, and let's try to get that water out of your coat and boots, too," I said, helping him out of the heavy, wet coat. Pulling his boots off; water and gobs of soggy newspaper flushed out. I was right; Wayne had stuffed the toes with yesterday's news. He wrung out three pairs of socks, and we gave him gloves to stuff in the toes of his boots to replace the newspaper.

Lenny sat down in the snow and began removing his own boots.

"What are you doing, Lenny? Did you get water in your boots, too?" I was surprised because Lenny had made the cleanest jump of all of us and had barely touched the water.

Pulling off a pair of socks, Lenny said, "Here Wayne, I wore two pairs. Put these on. They may be a little tight, but you can stretch them out and they're dry."

Wayne was taken by surprise, and he looked at Lenny in disbelief. He didn't know what to say. "Are you sure? You'd give me your socks?"

"Why not, you'd do the same for me."

A long moment passed, during which time, Wayne didn't move, and we stood there watching Lenny lacing his boots back up.

"Here, Wayne, I got two pairs on too. Let me take these boots off and get a pair for you, too." I said.

"Yeah, so do I." Chuck added, pulling off his boots.

"Thanks Lenny. Thanks guys, thanks a lot." Wayne's voice broke while putting on Lenny's socks, followed by two more pairs.

We wrung out Wayne's coat as best we were able. It was a military jacket his old man had gotten at the surplus store on Lockport Avenue and being wool, most of the water drained out, but it still was wet. Wayne had extra gloves to replace the one he lost, and I gave Wayne a sweater I was wearing under my coat before he put the wet jacket back on.

Meanwhile, Chuck had opened the backpack and tipped it upside down. Not much water had gotten in. Landing on his side, Wayne's back hadn't gone down into the water, which was lucky. Not only would we have lost the food, but the camera would have been ruined, as well. That wouldn't have gone over too good with Billy's mom, but then, looking at Billy, I figured she was going to have a few more problems than just a wet camera.

Chuck took out the bottles of Dr. Pepper and the aluminum foil packages. We opened a Dr. Pepper and passed it around before unwrapping the foil packages. God must have been smiling down upon us when we decided to wrap our remaining food supply in the aluminum foil, for that alone saved it. The six Twinkies were crushed, but semi-dry and edible, and we quickly made them disappear. Then we passed around the Good 'n' Plenty and Milk Duds, and they were delicious. The Hostess cupcakes were a total loss. They were crushed, and the foil had broken open, so they were a soggy goo, looking like something Wayne's little sister left in her diaper. The candy bars came through in pretty fair shape, and we divided them up.

"How much farther is it, Kevin?" Lenny asked.

"Not far. We're almost there. The beginning of the Whirlpool is just around that bend ahead. The river widens out there and takes a big turn to the right, and the path is right in that area. The worst part is behind us. We're almost outta here, guys!"

No one doubted what I said. How could it be any worse than 'Wild Wayne' had been? The Whirlpool and Railroad bridges loomed behind us now, spanning across the gorge like two imposing sentinels, connecting countries and generations together. I glanced at Lenny. He also was staring at the bridges. He turned and looked at me and nodded. I nodded back.

"Back there, at 'Wild Wayne', Lenny, why did you say that God was with me?" I asked.

"Because He is," Lenny said. "It's pretty obvious, isn't it?"

"What makes you think so?"

"Would we have gotten out of there without your hatchet?"

It didn't take long to reply, "No, without the hatchet we'd still be there, for sure."

"Well then, why did you bring it?"

"I don't know, just felt neat, I guess."

He put his hand on my shoulder, "That's all? You brought a hatchet with nothing down here but snow and ice, because it felt neat?"

"What? You think it was some kind of divine intervention? Come on, Lenny. You think I got a guardian angel?" I laughed.

"Why not? You think a God that created the entire universe, couldn't do something as small as send an angel to watch over you? Is that really so far fetched?"

I only stood there, not willing to tell him about the urges that had pushed me to bring it along. Instead, I changed the subject.

"Well, I guess you have your own story about these bridges now, *heh*?"

Lenny laughed. "Yeah, for sure, but I don't think I'll be telling it to my mom any time soon." It was true; this was the most exciting thing any of us had ever done, and we couldn't tell anyone about it. I wondered how long that would last. Not long I figured. With Billy in the condition he was in, she'd put him under the swinging light, and when he spilled the beans, she'd be on a warpath. And, then with that rescue team involved, I didn't think this adventure was going to be kept secret for long. Man, I hoped my dad wasn't involved.

It was time to get moving again. We put everything back in the knapsack, and Chuck offered to carry it, but Wayne said it helped to keep his back warm. With a sense of loathing, we reconnected ourselves to the ropes and steeled our nerves for what lay ahead.

Chapter 40

Turning our backs to the bridges, we resumed our journey, trying to stay as close to the gorge and as far away from the river as possible. The shoreline was narrow, butting up against the side of the gorge in several places, and the river was always just a misstep away. The rapids never stopped or died down but were a turbulent mixture of water, foam, and spray in a constant battle with the boulders. Huge, frothing waves leaped across the river, like liquid demons dancing on the surface, assaulting our minds until we wanted to scream. They never stopped, never rested, never paused, just kept slamming and smashing into the stone monuments in the never-ending marathon to the lake.

We encountered two more spots where boulders blocked our path, but neither one was the total blockage that 'Wild Wayne' had been and we were able to squeeze around each without mishap.

I wondered how long my chopped-out steps at Wild Wayne would endure before they were filled in and lost to the river. It saddened me, knowing that the hour of my greatest achievement would be lost to future generations, erased from history by ice and then the sun. I wanted them to stay there forever, so one day I could come back with my Ol' man and say, "See? I did that."

Was this how Sir Edmund Hillary felt after conquering Mt. Everest and watching his footprints get filled in by the blowing snow? Or Columbus, watching his footprints wash away in the sand of the New World? The earth is forever, and we're just visitors—and only for a short time at that. By the time we begin to understand enough about the world to ask the right questions, our visit is over, and someone else is asking the same questions.

Coming around a massive boulder, there was a noticeable change in the river. It widened and opened into an enormous lagoon area. The violence of the rapids dissipated and calmed. The sharp bend to the right that I had been looking for was there, and the river flowed into a giant green pool, swirling in circles, reminding me of the water draining from my bathtub on Saturday nights.

We had made it—we'd reached the Whirlpool.

We stood watching the swirling waters, hypnotized by the slow, spinning action. I found it to be soothing and calming after having endured the chaos of the rapids. Enormous blocks of ice rode the current, some bypassing the whirlpool, some getting caught in the powerful suction of the water. I visualized these blocks being sucked down into the depths below, spinning and grinding against one another as they swirled downward. Eventually, they'd be spit back to the surface, to follow the river or be recaptured, repeating the cycle all again. There are stories of decomposing bodies that stayed in the Whirlpool for weeks, waiting to be released and recovered.

We moved along the shore, looking for the path that would take us up and out of our nightmare. The ground had a greater slope here, and the ice and snow were deeper.

"Where's the trail at, Kevin?" Lenny asked.

"It's right around here somewhere."

"What does it look like?"

"It's easy to see in the summertime. It's open and cut through all the foliage real clear, although now it'll be under this snow. Look for a pile of stones marking it."

As we moved around, looking for the trail, the rope kept us from branching out too far, and we kept pulling and jerking each other as everyone tried to go in different directions. Soon, I noticed the rope wasn't jerking any longer on Chuck's side. Looking over, he was standing immobile, looking downriver, which seemed odd.

"Chuck, what's up? What's wrong?"

"There's no trail up," he said.

"What do you mean, *there's no trail?*" Billy shouted, "Kevin said there was a trail." Lenny and Wayne kept moving along the gorge, searching for the trail.

"You guys can stop looking; it's right here," said Chuck, pointing, "but we ain't going up it." We gathered where Chuck was standing and looked at the area where he pointed. It was clearly the path, cut wide and open through the frozen brush, with stones and rocks piled on both sides marking it. The stones and brush were covered in a thick layer of ice—ice that grew to at least a foot thick in the shallowest parts and more than three feet deep in spots. The ice ran the height of the gorge, as high as we could see. On each side of the trail, ice-covered rocks, frozen branches, bushes, and a tangle of vines, all encased in solid ice spread out. It was an excellent trail in the summertime. Now, it was impassable.

"I knew it—I knew we weren't going to get out of here," Billy whined quietly—not shouting any longer. "I'm gonna die down here."

"What do we do now?" Wayne asked.

"We go to Devil's Hole," Chuck said calmly.

"But that's miles away, ain't it, Kevin?" asked Wayne.

"It's a ways," I replied, defeated.

"No more of this! I can't take any more," Billy whimpered.

"Wayne, how are you holding up? How's your feet?" Chuck asked as he began untying the rope from around his waist.

"They're cold, but as long as I keep moving, I'm okay."

"Well, then, let's keep moving. We gotta go to Devil's Hole."

"And what if that's blocked off, too?" Billy cried, but we had all turned away and began walking downriver toward Devil's Hole.

"Oh, crap." Billy rose to his feet; and followed us.

Volume Four

the Drum

Chapter 41

Leaving the vortex behind, the shore widened, which made a major improvement to the passage. There wasn't any path to follow, but with the wall of the gorge moved back, and the river staying more within its boundaries, it quieted considerably, losing its intense turbulence.

But it didn't last long.

Rounding the Whirlpool bend, the river once again necked down, and we encountered the second set of rapids. While not as extensive as the first set, they were every bit as brutal. Despite the intimidating tempest, I felt some degree of comfort, knowing these were the Devil's Hole rapids, which put us on the final leg of our journey—I hoped.

I worried about the trail at the Hole. The gorge was steep in that area, and if the stairway was impassable, I didn't know what we'd do. The next stop after the Hole is Lewiston Landing. In addition to being a long ways down the river, in-between the Hole and the Landing was the large power station that Lenny's dad worked at. It was still under construction, although part of it was in operation and the discharge plumes went into the river where the shore used to be. I didn't know how we could get by it, and even if we could, the wall of the gorge was straight up and down and came directly to the river's edge from there to Lewiston. I didn't think it was passable, even in the summer. *Well, one roller coaster at a time*, I thought. *First—let's get to 'Devil's Hole'.*

The shore became treacherous again, being a depository for tons upon tons of rock dislodged from the ancient gorge. The snow hadn't built up here and wasn't as deep as it had been previously, providing us that cushion to walk on. Branches and roots protruded everywhere, coated in layers of ice, straining to be free from the bondage of winter. Stepping on them, the ice broke away like peanut shells, freeing them to spring up, grabbing at our boots and legs. The constant spray from the rapids provided a fresh layer of freezing water, keeping it all extremely slippery and making progress costly. With the uneven surfaces and the protruding rocks and branches, my feet turned in and out so many times that I forgot what it was to walk on even ground, and my ankles burned hot in my boots. It was amazing none of us sprained an ankle.

The perilous shoreline, coupled with the unrelenting rapids, forced us to use the ropes again. Tying ourselves together like railcars on a train cast a pall over us, as fresh memories and the dread of encountering another Wild Wayne overshadowed any confidence our progress had instilled in us. Numerous times, the icy wall built out to within inches of the river, forcing us to shuffle between them, with the constant danger of slipping into the turbulence looming over us. On a high note, we encountered no more Wild Waynes.

We were tied together, strung out like a string of Christmas tree lights. I feared if anyone slipped into the river; we'd all slide in. I visualized being hauled out of the lake at Fort Niagara by a couple of Blue pike fishermen snagging a stringer of five dead wannabe explorers. We'd make the six o'clock news for sure then.

We carefully picked our way past the powerful rapids, openly being brave but secretly clinging to each other in fear, and by doing so, we got by them.

I lost all concept of time, not only in the immediate knowledge of hours and minutes on this February day in 1962 but also in the greater sense of existence. Was it really 1962? A scattering of seagulls flew haphazardly across the opening of the gorge, swooping down crazily toward the river before banking sharply upwards into the open sky, the same way they'd done for centuries. *How I wish I could fly like that and leave this place behind me.* High above them, in the heavens, a plane's trail streaked across the sky. Time seemed to have lost all meaning; 1962 AD or—BC? Was there a difference? Maybe, up on top, there was; down here there wasn't.

The sun had disappeared over the top edge of the gorge, casting brilliant hues of colors against the canyon walls bringing them alive with dazzling orange, yellow and purple radiance. Looking at the side of the canyon made me think of the rescue team back at the Falls. I wondered what they thought when they found no one on the ice bridge. They'd probably think we were inside the Schoellkopf stairway, on our way up. No, too much time had gone by, and they'd be beyond that point by now. Had they found our hidden trail we'd made at the base of the ruins tunnel yet? Could they think we had slipped into the river and been swept away? No, there were too many of us for them to think we all went into the river. Then again, I'd just thought that myself, a few minutes ago. Down here, there was no logic, anything was possible.

How long would they look for us? At what point would they give up? They'd be in contact with teams on top, telling them where our trail was leading, providing they had found it. Would they follow along the escarpment? They would know we had headed to the Whirlpool. I wondered how far that ice blockage went up the side of the gorge on the Whirlpool trail. Was the upper part of the trail passable? If it were, they might start coming down it, until they'd run into the ice blockage from their side and had to turn back. I didn't think they'd

251

give up without being sure of what had happened to us. It wouldn't go good for them if they stop searching, and then our bodies were found in the spring all lined up in a row, like a shish kebab, our bones picked cleaned by seagulls. But there wasn't any point in wondering what they thought; there was nothing I could do about it anyway. All I could do was keep moving.

My thoughts continually came back to what we'd find at Devil's Hole. Was it passable? Was there another way out after the Hole? Lewiston was a long hike down the river; and even if it was passable, we'd never make it in our present condition. Billy was a train wreck; Wayne was suffering severely from the cold, and all of our hands and feet were blocks of ice. We were exhausted beyond anything we'd ever experienced. It'd be getting dark by then, too. Navigating this shoreline in the daylight was difficult enough; in the dark, it would be suicide—impossible. We had no way of making a fire, and even if we did, what would we burn? Ice? *Lenny thinks it was divine intervention that caused me to bring the hatchet, does he?* I thought *Well, where was the little nudge to bring a bundle of firewood and matches along, too?*

It was too far to the top of the gorge for anyone to hear us, even if there was someone up there listening. Bottom line is the Hole was our last hope. If we couldn't get out there, I didn't think we'd see another sunrise. It was the first time in my life that I actually thought I could die—it wouldn't be my last.

I wanted to express my concerns to the others, but I didn't dare. Billy was a nut case already and Wayne needed encouragement just to keep moving. I worried about his feet getting frostbitten, if they hadn't already. I didn't know how Lenny would handle my concerns and fears, although, his calmness and steadfastness had been a surprising strength for us. There was no point in talking. We had to move and pray to God the way was clear when we got there. It seemed ironic; I was praying to God for salvation at the Devil's Hole.

I wondered what Chuck was thinking and if he worried too. Glancing back at him, I was startled to see he was looking straight at me. Again, our eyes locked, and I knew we shared the same fears. Was he somehow reading my mind?

Chapter 42

The going remained difficult and slow. The abundance of rocks created a virtual gauntlet for us to traverse. Instead of being pummeled by tomahawks and clubs on our backs and shoulders, we were assaulted by rocks and ice on our feet and legs. And, of course there was the river, always there, calling to us, taunting us, waiting for one misstep to welcome our bodies into its cold caress, and carry us into its hidden secrets beneath the surface.

We traveled without stopping, driven to reach the Hole. Our clothes, stiff, frozen and heavy with layered ice, protested loudly with each step. Chuck had been right; the walk kept our feet and hands semi-thawed. Billy's frozen tears gave his face a constant whiny look, although he wasn't whining anymore, moving mechanically and not saying anything. I never thought I'd miss his whining, but not hearing it for so long worried me. The patch of hair sticking out from the good side of Wayne's head had long icicles hanging that clinked against the ones clustered on his eyebrows. I didn't hear the ice-cream truck jingle. I tried to recall it—I couldn't.

Struggling forward, scared of what might not be at the Hole, I came around a bend in the river—and the river changed again, from frothing rapids to deep tendons of translucent green water rippling along the surface. Surging past towering, white-tipped boulders, they flowed into a pool where the water was almost calm. Inside the pool, water flowed against the current, backwards, toward the Falls. Due to this strange shifting of current flow, ice was contoured in unusual designs where the shore met the waters of the river. I knew this place. It was one of my favorite places in the gorge.

"We're here, guys! This is it, Devil's Hole." I exclaimed.

"Where's the stairway?" Billy spoke for the first time since leaving the Whirlpool, not whining, but demanding. "You said there'd be a stairway!"

"There's a stairway, Billy. It doesn't come all the way to the edge of the river but starts up there a little ways. There's a path here that leads to it."

"Where? I don't see it. Where is it?"

"Take it easy, Billy," Chuck said firmly, while giving me a look revealing his concern. "It's under the snow and ice, we'll find it."

We crawled over the icy boulders to where the wall of the gorge became slightly more horizontal, with me leading the way to where I thought the path was. It wasn't hard to find it. The bushes and branches, pushed back and broken off from the past summer, exposed what was clearly a path underneath the blanket of snow and ice.

"This is it," I said, recalling what it had looked like last summer. "If I'm right, the stairway should be up ahead a little ways."

Following the trail a short distance, we arrived at the bottom of the stairway. And stairway it was. Consisting of hundreds of wide, stone steps zigzagging across the face of the gorge, it climbed all the way to the top of the escarpment. The steps were uneven and irregular, with odd spacing and varying widths that made them tiring to travel, even in summertime. But they were steps and . . . they went to the top. There was snow on them, but—they were unobstructed.

"Hey, this looks great, we can climb these, heh? It's a stairway to heaven!" Lenny said, expressing our thoughts. "These are cool! How'd they get here like this, Kev?"

The stairway at Devil's Hole had always been a wonder to me. My dad told me about it when he brought me here, years ago. I remembered I'd run up and down with the agility and quickness of a panther. The grass and foliage was green and lush then, with trees and bushes everywhere. Birds sang, and the river had a crisp, clean smell coming off it. My dad had yelled at me to be careful, not to slip and fall. I wondered what he'd think if he saw me now. How I wished it were green and warm today and that I could run up and down the steps now as I had then.

"My dad said it was built during the 1930s by these guys working in something called the CCCs. It was some kind of thing that they did during the Great Depression. I'm not sure what it was all about, but it had something to do with making work for people. This was when there weren't any jobs, and people were jumping off of skyscrapers."

"Why?" Wayne asked.

"So people could walk down to the bottom of the gorge," I snorted. "Why do ya think?"

"No, I mean, why'd they jump off of skyscrapers?" Wayne said.

I was starting to worry about Wayne. He seemed to have this fascination with jumping off of skyscrapers and bridges or walking into Niagara Falls. I refused to allow the jingle of the ice cream truck to play in my head.

"It looks passable," Chuck stated with relief as he checked out the steps. He looked up the side of the gorge as far as he could see. "Only a few of the steps have ice on them. We can pick our way around them easy enough. We're gonna walk out of here, Billy, you hear me?"

Billy didn't answer and looking at him, he looked empty, defeated, completely devoid of emotion of any type. Billy had not said anything and it was clear there was something really wrong inside of him.

"Thank you, Jesus!" Lenny said, and he meant it. "How high is it to the top?"

"Couple of hundred feet, I guess, but it zigzags back and forth, making it seem longer, and it's steep, too." I answered. "But as long as it's open like this, we'll just take it easy and walk out." I was elated by the clear and open condition that the steps were in. As high as I could see, they were open.

"Well, we don't need this stupid rope anymore," Wayne said, speaking for all of us as he worked on the knots. "Let's get this thing off." The ropes were frozen, layered in ice, and we fumbled with cold, uncooperative fingers working the stubborn knots loose. It took us a while before we were free of the lassos.

We had lost our individuality as defined by colors, types, and makes of clothing. Except for height, we looked the same with white, frozen clothing being our trademark. Color was gone, and even the shapes and materials we wore tended to blend together; the gorge had equalized us. With the ropes removed, each of us had a ring around our middle that stood out as a dark streak against our frozen coats, making us look like members of a gang—the "Niagara Gorge Ice Gang." We had earned the title.

Chapter 43

Huddling together in celebration of reaching Devil's Hole and seeing it was open going up the side of the canyon, we passed around the last bottles of Dr. Pepper and shared what candy remained before starting the climb.

"Why is this called Devil's Hole, Kev?" Lenny asked.

Before I could answer, Wayne jumped in, "It's that lagoon out there in the river, where the water goes backwards. There's a hole in the bottom of the river, right out there that's Devil's Hole. And there's a creek that flows acid, the devil's blood, and it empties into the lagoon. It'll make your hands bleed if you touch it, so it's called Bloody Run." He seemed pleased to offer this information, and he continued in a matter-of-fact tone, "The acid keeps making the hole deeper and deeper, and fish that swim through it turn into skeletons."

I stared at Wayne, amazed. Did he have frostbite of the brain? The ice-cream truck was playing a fully orchestrated crescendo inside my head.

"Tell me you're making that up just to humor us!" Chuck blurted in disbelief.

"What'd you mean? That's the truth." Wayne glared at Chuck, and I realized Wayne did believe it. "My dad told me about it."

"The *devil's blood is acid?* And *it makes a hole in the bottom of the river?* You got to be kidding me! You don't honestly believe that crap." Chuck's voice was different, not his usual sarcastic, wise-cracking tone but was serious and intense. Wayne had touched a nerve with Chuck.

While it was a relief to have something to laugh about and break the tension, I felt bad for Wayne hanging himself out like that, and as a good buddy, it was time to save his butt, once again. "That's a good one, Wayne—*the devil's blood is acid.* You got us good on that one!" I said, taking a swig of soda pop, "Man, this Dr. Pepper certainly hits the spot, doesn't it? Good thing you brought extras." I passed the bottle to Lenny. "What do ya say, ready to climb out of here?"

"So why is it called Devil's Hole?" Lenny asked again.

Before Wayne dug himself a deeper hole, I spoke up. "It's a hole, just like Wayne joked about, and of course, it's not in the river. It's in the ground; it's a cave". Then to divert attention away from Wayne I added, "and it's supposed to be haunted."

"Hey cool, a haunted cave. Are there ghosts in it?" Lenny asked.

"I don't know, maybe. Ol' Gordy called it the Cave of the Evil Spirit."

"Well, that sounds like a ghost to me." Lenny said.

"Yeah, I guess it doe . . . ."

"It's not a ghost." Chuck cut in. "It's a snake. It's an old Iroquois legend about the demon snake, called 'the evil one'. He's the cousin of 'Heno' the snake who made the Horseshoe Falls, and he lives down here, inside the cave, and anyone who goes inside is cursed and will die."

"Man, that's cool, heh. A cave haunted by a snake with a curse. Do you think it's true, heh?"

"Heck yeah, it's true!" Chuck proclaimed with a grin. "I've been in the cave, and I'm cursed being here with you morons, ain't I?" Despite the exhaustion and cold, everyone laughed. Everyone, except Billy, who turned and stared at Chuck in a strange way.

"You've been in this devil's cave?" Billy asked, and I perked up, Billy's voice had an edge to it that hadn't been there before.

"Yeah, more than once, ain't no big deal." Chuck hadn't picked it up.

"You've been in the devil's cave? And it's cursed by the devil, so you'll die?" Billy asked. "You defied the devil? So you have the curse on you?" He jumped up, as a surge of adrenaline pumped through him and he began shaking his finger at Chuck. "That's why all this has happened to us, because of you! Because of your curse! And now you brought the curse on us! We're all gonna die here—because of you! You did this to us."

Silence fell over us. We were too stunned by Billy's outburst to know what to say. He had to be putting us on, but I couldn't see Billy joking about anything down here.

"Where is the cave, Chuck?" Lenny asked, ignoring Billy's outburst.

"Up towards the top, off the stairway a little," Chuck muttered, keeping his eyes on Billy, who was backing away from Chuck but staring at him with loathing. *This can't be for real!* I thought.

"That's where we're gonna die, up at the cave," Billy went on, "the Devil's cave, because of him!" He pointed his finger at Chuck in horror. Billy wasn't joking. He couldn't understand how this had happened to him, and he was grabbing at this in his attempt to find an answer and a reason, along with someone to blame. "Don't you guys see it? This was all to get us here, so we could die down here at this Devil's Hole. That's why he knew the secret way down, and he knew all along we couldn't get back up that ice ledge. This was his plan from the beginning to get us here. We're gonna die here with the devil, and it's his fault!"

"We're not going to die, Billy," I told him. "We're gonna climb these stairs, and walk out of here. It's over, and your joke isn't funny." Billy had backed away from Chuck as far as he could, while continuing to stare at him as if he had snakes all over his face.

"Oh, there's no joke, Kevin, the devil is here all right, and we're all gonna die. That's what his plan was all along. That's why he talked us into coming down here. He made a deal with the devil to take us instead of him. That's what he was doing back at that ledge, talking to the devil. Remember Kevin? Remember Wayne? When he put his hand on that ice and stayed there staring into those lights? I thought something was wrong, and I was right. He was sealing his pact. He traded us to save his own ass, lifting the curse off of him. He brought us here to die in his place!" Billy screamed.

"You're nuts, Billy, that's the stupidest thing I've ever heard of." I shouted back, "He didn't make any pact with the devil! I was there too, Billy, what in blazes are you talking about? Why don't you just shut up?" I had moved in front of Billy my fists clenched, and he could tell by my face that I'd had enough. A long silence followed, with everyone not knowing what to say or what to do, until I couldn't believe what I heard Lenny ask Chuck, as if nothing had occurred.

"What about Bloody Run, Chuck? Is that real, too?"

"Yeah, it's real," Chuck answered cautiously, "but it's nothing more than an underground creek coming out on the side of the gorge."

"Why's it called Bloody Run?" Lenny asked, and I wished he'd drop it, for crying out loud.

"Because there was a massacre here, and they said the creek ran red with blood."

"A massacre? Who was massacred?" Lenny persisted. *Was there no end to his questions?*

"British soldiers were ambushed and slaughtered by the Iroquois." Chuck answered, watching Billy carefully.

"When was that?" Lenny asked. "I didn't know there was any fighting around here."

"It was during the Revolutionary War," I said, trying to end this. "Come on, let's get outta here."

"No, it wasn't," Chuck corrected me. "It was before the Revolutionary War, after the white man's war, during the Prophet's War—Pontiac's War." He looked at Lenny, "There's been a lot of fighting around here, Lenny. Indians wars go way back."

"Whoa!" Lenny said. "Revolutionary War? Pontiac's War? Indian wars? How many wars were there? And what's—*the white man's war?*"

"Your history books call it the 'French and Indian War', but it wasn't an Indian war. It was a war between European invaders fighting over Indian land—Iroquois land," Chuck explained.

"The Iroquois were the Indians who were here, right?" Lenny asked.

"The Iroquois are the 'people,' the keepers of the land, who lived here long before the white man came." He looked at Lenny, forgetting about Billy, who had sat back down in the snow, "And it's not *were,* Lenny, it's *are.* We're still here; I'm Iroquois. My father is a full-blooded Seneca." Chuck's tone had clearly changed now, as Lenny's had when he was talking about his *people,* earlier.

"The Revolutionary War was about white men revolting against their own homeland in England to be free in the land they called the 'New World'. But, the land never belonged to them to begin with. Their 'New World' was the Iroquois's world until white men stole it from them."

Lenny shook his head, still baffled. "Iroquois? Seneca? Pontiac? Man, it's all kind of confusing, heh? Who's who around here?"

"The devil, that's who!" Billy shouted. "This is the devil's place, and he's killed all those people, and now he's gonna kill us!" He wagged his finger at Chuck again, "Because of him and his Indian curses."

"The devil can only hurt you if you let him Billy. You're in control of what the devil does to you, not Chuck." Lenny spoke of the devil as if he was real too, yet he didn't sound like he believed all that nonsense Billy was spouting.

"There's no devil here, Lenny, that's all nonsense." I said.

"There's a devil, Kevin. He may not be a snake or live in a cave, and he didn't put a curse on Chuck, but he's real enough, don't ever doubt that." Lenny said.

"It's not that confusing, Lenny." Chuck ignored this exchange and continued, while still watching Billy, not sure of what he was going to do. "The Iroquois are a confederation of six Indian tribes with the Seneca being the largest. Think of it like the States making up America. You can be a New Yorker, from New York, and you're also an American too."

"Yeah, I got it, that's like our Providences in Canada."

Chuck nodded and continued, "Well, when the white men came from Europe and England, they fought each other over the land, Indian land, and they pitted the Indians against each other. Pontiac was a great Indian medicine man, called 'the prophet', who had seen a vision to unite all the Indian tribes together and drive the white man from the land forever."

Chuck shifted his gaze from Billy to Lenny before continuing. "Your people came over as slaves and became free; my people were here free and became slaves."

Looking back at Billy, he sneered, "The Prophet had a good vision; too bad it failed."

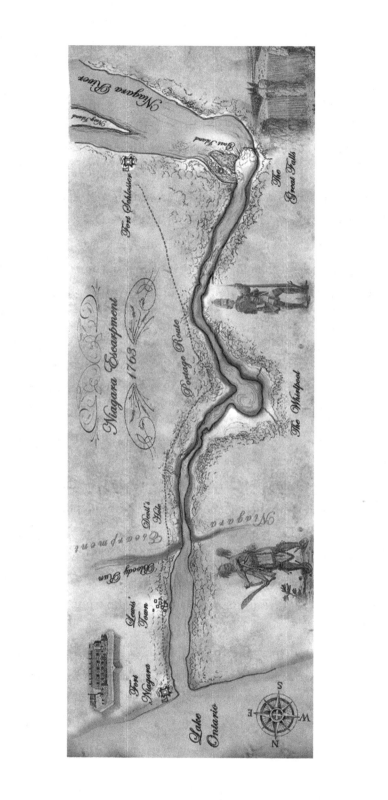

Chapter 44

The Drummer Boy's Story

The Niagara Escarpment

September 14, 1763

The English

The drummer boy marched—proud and excited—scared and trembling.

The sound of his drum, beating out a steady cadence for the strutting regiment, was an arousing sound, giving him comfort in this strange and dreadful land. He didn't know what he feared more—that deep chasm to his left housing that rabid river below, or the deep forest to his right housing those savage Indians above. They were on a fast march north, quick-stepping through the dense forest of the Niagara escarpment from Fort Schlosser to Fort Niagara.

He had arrived in the New World six weeks earlier, coming across the ocean that he'd never dreamed was so vast and where he had gotten the sickest he'd ever been. The ship had finally docked in a place called Philadelphia. After recovering from the ocean voyage, he was assigned to the 80th Regiment of the Light Armed Foot Infantry. Quickly equipped and oriented, the replacements were immediately dispatched west across the Ohio Territory to Fort Schlosser, situated on a river called Niagara, which they said, had the largest waterfall in the whole world on it.

During orientation, he'd learned that a fort, called Fort Little Niagara, had been built by the French on the shores of the Niagara River, just above this great falls. Captured, early in the war, by the English, the fort had been rebuilt and renamed Fort Schlosser. This was followed by the capture of the larger Fort Niagara, which was located on the same river but below the great falls, at the far northern end, where it emptied into Lake Ontario. With Fort Schlosser on the southern end and Fort Niagara on the northern end, the English controlled all the shipping from the Old World to the New World to supply the Ohio Valley. Between the two forts, the mighty cataracts roared and thundered.

Arriving at Fort Schlosser, he could see the giant plume in the distance, which they told him marked the thundering falls where it plummeted over the precipice. He had not yet had the opportunity to go and see the thundering falls, and he looked forward to doing so during his first three-day pass with high anticipation.

Fort Niagara guarded the entrance to the river from Lake Ontario, with massive cannons and armaments, daring ships to sneak around to attack the settlements along the river. It was the focal point of all trade between the western colonies and the eastern seaboard. Supplies and munitions from the great seaports of Boston, Philadelphia and New York, were unloaded at Fort Niagara, where they were then portaged around the great falls to Fort Schlosser for distribution to the forts, colonies, and garrisons scattered throughout the territories along the Ohio Valley. In turn, the lucrative bounties of tobacco, spices, and beaver pelts were shipped back for transport to the hungry markets in England and Europe.

Between these two forts, deep ravines and high ridges of rich, dark forests lay, covering the entire length of the escarpment, bordering the treacherous canyon that the great falls had cut into the earth. It was vital for England to maintain a secure supply route for its continued survival in the New World. The portage around Niagara was the key to that success.

The 80th Regiment's job was—to keep that portage safe.

The replacements were assigned to their respective quarters, and the drummer boy was just getting acquainted with the members of his regiment when they were ordered to proceed directly to Fort Niagara to reinforce that garrison, as there was growing concern of an attack by Chief Pontiac.

The boy didn't know who Chief Pontiac was, or why there was any fighting still going on, for that matter. After all, wasn't the war over? He'd come over as part of the reinforcements in the war against the French, but upon landing, they'd learned that a treaty had been signed in Paris, ending the war. The French had conceded the colonies to England. The war was over, and—they had won.

The drummer boy was thrilled. He had no desire to be in a war—he had no desire to be in the army. His father had conscripted him against his wishes, three years back when he was thirteen, and they made him into a drummer boy. Carrying no weapons, he was a spectator. Granted, being a spectator was preferable to being a combatant, but being a spectator in the middle of the battlefield was not an enviable place to be. He didn't think his drum would provide much protection against flying bullets, nor would his drumsticks be formidable weapons against slashing swords, especially in this uncivilized world with their barbaric ideas of warfare.

In Europe, battles were fought in a civilized fashion, with serried ranks facing off against one another. No one aimed at drummer boys. Even in close combat, they were ignored, not deemed a threat, and many times, deliberately spared to capture for ransom. But here, in this God-forsaken land, with those cursed French dogs, who held no regard for proper battlefield etiquette, along with those heathen savages, who cowardly attacked from behind trees, there seemed to be no such rules for civilized engagement. The soldiers told of horrific tortures—burning men alive and of their custom of cutting the scalps from the soldier's heads while they yet lived. They told him the savages skinned drummer boys and made tobacco pouches out of their skins. He didn't know if that were true or if the soldiers were only having fun with him; but it didn't matter, the idea was planted and took root. With such tales living in his mind, he feared and dreaded this terrible land.

One of the soldiers said it was the English officers who paid the Indians to bring in scalps. The boy dismissed this as disgruntled soldier talk. It wasn't possible that civilized English gentlemen would condone such barbaric atrocities.

Upon hearing the war was over, his fears had subsided, and his outlook changed. He had no need to fear the battlefield and could truly appreciate all that this land had to show him. He looked forward to exploring this wild and beautiful country. It was so different from his home in Yorkshire—it was alive and vigorous, teeming with forests and lakes. The settlements they passed through were small, and the people all knew one another and worked together toward the greater good—independent minded, yet united in spirit.

Philadelphia was nothing like London, which was dirty and had an air of staleness and decay about it. Stinging smoke and greasy soot coated everything in a layer of dirty, oily grime, and most of the city had the pungent smell of people and waste about it. This city was clean; the air being fresh and exciting. It was surrounded by deep woods, rolling hills, streams, lakes, and waterfalls everywhere. People didn't fear their neighbors—unlike England, where one had to be on constant lookout for the street ruffian, and there was danger on every corner.

Then, just as things were settling down, everything turned upside down. Unrest erupted on the frontier, threatened by a new war. Savages, led by this Chief Pontiac, had attacked and destroyed the small forts and outposts in the Ohio Valley, killing the inhabitants. They terrorized settlers and traders and laid siege to the larger Fort Detroit and Fort Pitt.

This confused the boy, as he understood that these were the same savages that had been their allies during the war against the French. He didn't understand why the savages were waging war against the very people who had been sent by divine providence to save them from their heathen and barbaric ways and turn them into God-fearing, decent people. Why would any people rebel against such an endowment?

During the war, the natives had chosen sides. The six tribes of the Iroquois nation had sided with the English against the French and their long time rivals, the Huron. The boy silently commended the Indians for having the wisdom to make the right choice, as not only did England win the war, but who better to lead them out from the darkness of their heathen ways?

Following the war, the government issued the Royal Proclamation of 1763, restricting white settlers from Indian land. What more did these heathens want? They were under the protection of the King and reaping the benefits of English civilization and technology, while being assured of keeping their own lands and being brought into eternal salvation. The English were being exceedingly generous and honorable—such blessings to bestow upon a primitive people who had once trafficked with the lowly French and existed outside the salvation of the cross.

And things were going well, until this Chief came along, claiming to be a prophet, and stirred the heathens up to revolt against the English and actually foretold of the demise of the white man. What betrayal to the King! What a foolish, ignorant people to turn on the hand, God had sent to save them.

Now, on the march to Fort Niagara, the regiment reached a spot by the edge of the deep canyon where the Lieutenant signaled to halt and rest. Looking down at the river, the drummer boy was amazed by the violent rapids below, leading to a widening of the river that flowed into a sharp bend where the water circled in a giant pool. His stomach turned along with the slowly churning water. Such an unpleasant sight it was, those sickening, green waters swirling around. He found it unsettling, and it created a great uneasiness in him. Upon leaving the odd whirlpool, the river narrowed once again and resumed its meanness and turbulence. Even from this great height, he could see the waves spewing high into the air to crash down on the numerous rocks and boulders lining the shore. Down there is no place to be, he thought.

Resuming the march, they crossed a deep depression that rose steeply up the escarpment on either side. Ruts in the trail told of the difficulty of passage for the heavy supply wagons that followed this trail making the portage trip.

By late morning, they had reached the settlement of Lewis Town and Lieutenant Campbell gave the order to bivouac and set a perimeter guard. The lieutenant would dine with the town leaders, and the regiment would finish the march to Fort Niagara on the morrow.

The drummer boy had finished setting his quarters and was exploring the settlement when the stockade guard sounded the alert. Gunfire was heard not far to the south, the same area the regiment had passed through this morning. Scouts were dispatched to investigate, and the camp went on high alert, with everyone scrambling in preparation for whatever might unfold.

The boy hustled to get into his red musick, pulling it back on over his blouse and trousers, then aligned and buttoned. His hands trembled so that his fingers had trouble fitting the brass buttons into their openings. Once properly attired, he hefted his large drum, drawing the thick, heavy, black strap over his right shoulder, positioning the drum in front. He fastened his feathered hat securely on his head and fell in formation with the soldiers.

There was shuffling and fidgeting up and down the line, as everyone got into his proper position. When the sergeant major called the regiment to attention, a sharp edge of excitement filled the air.

The drummer boy was just scared.

"Fall in!" The sergeant major ordered in a gruff, gravelly voice that carried a thick Scottish accent. The sergeant major embodied everything the boy visualized a career soldier in the King's service would be. Tall, strong, and rough, he sported a large white handlebar mustache that curled above his lips like the horns of a ram. A veteran of innumerable wars and conflicts throughout His Majesty's empire, the sergeant major knew everything about the army. The soldiers warned the boy not to cross the sergeant major, or the penalty would be severe. The boy heeded this advice well; he wanted no trouble.

"Check yer powder, soldiers. Wet powder only get ye kilt," the sergeant major shouted to the men as he walked up and down the line, inspecting them with a sharp, knowing eye, missing nothing.

"Mr. Webster, yer hat, sir."

"Yes, sir, Sergeant Major!" Webster replied, straightening it.

"Mr. Coleman, set yer pack proper."

"Yes, sir, Sergeant Major!"

He stopped in front of William Perry, a replacement who had come across the ocean with the boy. William was the youngest soldier in the regiment, and although a combat veteran against the French, he had not seen Indian combat. During the voyage, he confided to the boy his fear of the New World. He believed he would die here, killed by savages in an uncivilized manner. He had a wife and son waiting for him back in England. He said he would never see them again.

"Well now, Mr. Perry, have ye forgotten something?"

William looked bewildered by the question. "I don't think so, Sergeant Major."

"Ye 'don't think so, Sergeant Major'! Is that so, now, Mr. Perry? Well, yer not in the King's army ta think now, are ye, Mr. Perry? Yer here ta die! And yer duty ta King and country is ta not die until ye've kilt ten of the bloody heathens first! Only then are ye allowed ta take yer worthless ass and give it for the King! Do ye understand, Mr. Perry?"

"Yes, sir, Sergeant Major!"

"Well, that's good, Mr. Perry! I'm glad ye do, and that we have that cleared up between us. Now then, ta do that, one must fight, mustn't he, Mr. Perry?"

"Yes, sir, Sergeant Major!"

"What's that? I can't hear ye, Mr. Perry!"

"Yes, sir, Sergeant Major!" William shouted.

"And ta fight, Mr. Perry, one needs ta have a weapon, does he not?"

"Yes, sir, Sergeant Major!" William looked confused, glancing at the musket in his hand.

"Where might yer bayonet be, Mr. Perry? Or do ye plan on fighting the savages with yer johnson? Now, I know ye think ye have the world's greatest johnson, Mr. Perry, but can ye kilt the bloody savage with it now? Maybe some old squaw will swoon over it, Mr. Perry, you give her enough beads and needles, but it'd make a small trophy hanging on some buck's lodge pole, now won't it, Mr. Perry?"

"Yes sir, Sergeant Major! I mean, no sir, Sergeant Major!" William broke ranks and ran to get his bayonet from his tent.

"Scouts approaching!" the sentry called out. The wooden gates were opened wide enough to allow them through.

"Report, scout!" Lieutenant Campbell ordered.

"Fighting south of here, sir. Not far away. Something big happening, sir."

"Indians?"

"Yes sir, sounds like lots of 'em, too."

"Rider approaching!" The sentry called out a second time. "It's a civilian, sir!"

"Let him in!" the lieutenant ordered.

The rider galloped into the camp in a panic. It was Mr. Stedman, the portage master, screaming that his supply train had been attacked while making its portage back to Fort Niagara.

The drummer boy had seen Mr. Stedman, with his wagons, at Fort Schlosser. He'd been intrigued by them. They called them Conestoga wagons, and they were covered in large sheets of white canvass. They were recently installed to replace the Indians, who had previously been employed to carry the supplies on their backs on the portage around the great falls. Mr. Stedman thought the Indians were too inefficient, and he'd had to pay them with rum and goods. With these wagons, he didn't need the Indians anymore. The boy thought this was fair, as it saved the heathens doing all that hard work. He thought the heathens should be thankful they didn't have to make that journey any longer. More and more, he thought they were an ungrateful people.

The lieutenant peppered the rider with questions. "What tribe are they? How many are there? How far away?"

"Senecas what they are! A mile out and there are hundreds of the bloody heathens, too!"

"Very well, then, you can escort us to the scene, Mr. Stedman."

"Not on your life, Lieutenant. I'm heading to the fort for reinforcements." Stedman wanted to put as much distance between the Indians and his scalp as possible.

"Sir, we are the reinforcements. We're here now and are fully able to rescue your men, and we can use your assistance," the lieutenant reasoned with him.

"You do what you gotta do, Lieutenant, and I'll do what I gotta do." With that, Stedman spun his horse around and galloped out the gates, heading north.

"Sergeant Major, is the regiment ready to move?" the lieutenant asked.

"Yes, sir! All present and accounted fer, sir!"

"Very well, then. Move the men out. Columns of two; double time march. We have a job to do."

"Yes, sir!" Turning to the formation, he called out, "Attennnnnnn-hut!" The men snapped in strict precision at the sergeant major's sharp command.

"Charge muskets!" Somberness fell upon the men as they efficiently charged their muskets with powder and then rammed and seated a patch and ball down the barrels. In seconds, all muskets were charged, and the troops were back at attention.

"Ready Primer!" The men adjusted their primer flasks to the front of their 'possibles' pouches, which held the patches and balls for their muskets.

"Port arms!" The sergeant major's deep voice drew out the command in a long, extended shout that sent shivers up and down the boy's spine. The air echoed with the sharp slap of hands on polished wood and cold steel as eighty muskets sprang up and snapped into position.

"Columns of two!" A second row of forty soldiers lined up behind the first row.

"In double time!" Anticipation filled the air, so thick it could be bottled.

"Forwaaaard . . ." Electricity crackled through the formation.

"Maaarch!"

The drummer boy beat the fast, double-time cadence on his drum, and 176 boots began quick-stepping in-place as one. With muskets held at port-arms and peeling off two at a time, the regiment fast marched through the open gates of the settlement.

The citizens of Lewis Town watched with pride and a feeling of safety as the regiment moved out into the Niagara escarpment.

Unlike the British Regulars, who were loaded down with heavy gear and who fought in serried ranks, the Light Foot Armed Infantry was a tactical guerrilla unit. The regiment consisted of eighty-eight members, including eighty infantrymen, the sergeant major, two junior, noncommissioned officers, two junior officers, Lieutenant Coleman, the drummer boy, and Mr. Wilson with his fife.

The British army had established this elite corps of skirmishers to adapt to the warfare of the New World. They were handpicked and groomed for combat techniques gained during the French and Indian war, adapting Indian techniques of combat. Equipped and trained to react quickly and cover ground fast, these tactical units discarded the ornate frills and fluff of the British Regulars. The high-plumed caps; heavy, bright-red wool coats with tails and facings; multiple arrangements of polished silver, brass and pewter insignias and buttons; stiff duck breeches; tight stockings; heavy canvas spatter dashes; and bulky knapsacks, were discarded. Instead, the Light Foot Armed Infantry wore short, dark-red coats of lighter wool over considerably less bulky and cumbersome clothing. Their uniforms included plain, unpolished pewter buttons and brimless hats, and they carried light backpacks, all in an effort to achieve stealth and quickness in deployment and battle. The officers wore only two gold fronts on their coats to distinguish them.

On the march, they traveled at quick-step in double or single file, with an officer in the lead. The regiment would quietly follow the officer's hand signals without sounding commands. These men were chosen for their muscular builds and athletic stature, coupled with a high degree of marksmanship and bayonet hand-to-hand combat expertise. They were the elite, hardened veterans of combat conditioned for guerrilla warfare in the New World.

The Iroquois

Hata'kaw'wa stood among the bodies, head hung low. This day, he would not earn his manhood. He had not counted coup, had never gotten close to any of the enemy to have been in on a kill. There were too many warriors to battle the white wagons, accompanied by so few red-jackets.

Shay'wah'ki will be greatly saddened, he thought.

They were in love, wanting to raise their lodge poles together. His mother, a leader in the Wolf clan, had to speak to her mother, a leader in the Turtle clan, to seek permission for Hata'kaw'wa to pursue Shay'wah'ki.

But before she could ask such permission, Hata'kaw'wa must have warrior standing within the tribe.

Earlier, out of sight of prying eyes and the gossiping tongues of the longhouse, she had prayed for the Great Spirit to be with Hata'kaw'wa and for him to count coup that day. She gave Hata'kaw'wa two wampum strings of the white and purple shells that were the favorite of the Great Spirit, to wear into battle, so the Great Spirit would smile upon him.

Shay'wah'ki was most beautiful, of gentle heart and spirit, and when she walked through the camp, it was as if the goddess Le'lawa had come down from the Thundering Waters herself to walk among the people. Her silken black hair, set in long braids down each side of her fair face and tied off in bright yellow ribbons, framed her slender, fluid body. Many Mohawk braves looked with longing after her. Hata'kaw'wa knew he needed to move soon, or he would lose her. He had given many pelts to the white trader for beads and gifts of the hard metal as tokens of his feelings, but until he gained his scalplock and wore his hair in the proud manner of a warrior, he was forbidden from giving them to her.

Many coup had been counted by the Mohawk during the white man's war, but Hata'kaw'wa had not counted coup—he was too young and not yet worthy to join the war parties. When his sixteenth summer came, the chiefs called Hata'kaw'wa to their council. He was of age and had shown great skill and courage with the beasts of the forest. He would join the war parties. Hata'kaw'wa and Shay'wah'ki were elated, he would go into battle, earn his scalplock, and they would marry.

Before the next war party left the longhouses, the war had ended. The English had won, and the Fren'che had been driven out. There would be no war party. He would not count coup. The Great Spirit had deserted him.

Hata'kaw'wa knew the anger of his people. The white men had brought wondrous things with them, the likes of which the people had never before seen—tomahawks and knifes made of the hard metal that did not shatter or chip and pots that did not break when dropped. His mother thrilled with the hard metal needles that made her sewing so much easier than using the bone splinters. Most of all, the white men brought the mighty thundersticks that took away the spirit from deer and man, at great distances.

These were extraordinary gifts, much cherished by the Mohawk, but they came with great sorrow. The white man also brought the sickness that caused so many of the old and young to leave the body, moving on to the Great Beyond before their time. They brought the firewater that made the mighty warrior act like the crazy woman and lose standing in the tribe. And they brought their holy men, who carried the cross, forcing it on them, and causing the Mohawk to lose favor with the Great Spirit.

Hata'kaw'wa did not know why the white men would war against each other over the land of the Mohawk—land the white man did not own. No man owned the land. The Mohawk were put here by the Great Spirit to watch over and protect the land. The white men held no love for the land. They used it and destroyed it; cutting down the sacred forest, dirtying the sacred waters and destroying the ways of the creature brothers who shared the land with the Mohawk.

The ugliness that came along with the gifts of the white man was changing the way of life for the Mohawk, from one of honor and reverence to one of dishonor. The people had lived many moons without the white man's gifts; and were in favor with the Great Spirit. With these gifts, the people were losing their way, and the Great Spirit frowned upon them.

In their war against the Fren'che, the English fathers had promised many thundersticks and gifts, if the Iroquois would fight with them against the Fren'che. They promised cooking pots, needles, scissors, amulets, and beads of colors like the rainbow. They promised axes, knives, and tomahawks made of the hard metal, and they promised many thundersticks with the black dirt that burned and the grey balls that killed.

Most important of all, they promised when the Fren'che were driven from the land, no white man would settle in the sacred lands.

The people listened to the English and believed the words. So the six tribes of the Iroquois—the Seneca, Oneida, Cayuga, Onondaga, Tuscarora, and Mohawk—had fought alongside the red-jackets against the Fren'che, the Algonquian, the Ojibwa and their mortal enemy, the Huron. Many warriors had fallen, gone on to the Great Beyond, for the English.

When the Iroquois went to the white fathers to receive their promises, the white fathers did not believe they had killed the Fren'che. They said to bring them the scalplocks of the dead; only then would they give the promised gifts to the Iroquois.

These words offended the Iroquois greatly, as no warrior would count coup falsely and go to the Great Beyond in falsehood. His spirit would wander forever, never to enter the Great Spirit's hunting grounds. And to lose one's scalplock was a great dishonor, an act not to be done to an honorable warrior killed in combat. The Fren'che were foreigners, who invaded the scared lands and showed dishonor to the Great Spirit, and so did not deserve honor in battle. The Huron fought with the Fren'che, and they took the scalplock of the Iroquois. They showed no honor to the Iroquois, so if the taking of the scalplock was what the white fathers wanted, then it shall be so. The Iroquois took many scalplocks.

With the war being over and the Fren'che expelled from Iroquois land, it was time for the English to make good on their promises.

Council was held at Fort Unghiara, on the big water, with the English fathers and the chiefs of the Iroquois. The English showed the chiefs a paper from the Great White Father across the water, banning white men from settling on Iroquois lands. They restated their promises to give tools made of the hard metal, gifts for the women, thundersticks, and the burning dirt.

The chiefs left the council with a paper and promises—but no gifts.

During the following days, the Iroquois learned that issuing a paper from the Great Father had no strength, as white men descended on Iroquois land in great numbers. They desecrated the sacred places, dishonored their women, displaced the Iroquois from their lodges and killed them without cause. When the chiefs protested to the white fathers, they did nothing and only laughed at them. No justice was offered for the grievances done against the people.

In council, the English words had spoken of honor and respect. Outside of council, their manners spoke of scorn and falsehoods. The English words were empty, holding no truth or honor.

Hata'kaw'wa had feared for Shay'wah'ki and was glad her mother kept her away from the English settlements, where the red-jackets were always looking for Iroquois maidens. Hata'kaw'wa knew of young maidens lured away from the people with shiny gifts and of those who were forcibly abused and defiled by the red-jackets.

The great medicine prophet, Pontiac was visited by the Master of Life in a vision, who berated Pontiac and all his Indian brothers for their weakness and dependence on the white man's gifts. He told Pontiac to gather the tribes together, to bury their differences and unite as one to drive the white man from the land of the Great Spirit for all times.

The prophet sent out wampum belts to all the tribes, including the Shawnee, the Delaware, the Miami, the Ottawa, the Ojibwa, the six nations of the Iroquois, and even the Huron. He called for all the tribes to unite together against the English and drive them from the land.

The response was immediate and complete. Within weeks, thousands of warriors, who had fought among themselves, rallied together and attacked and burned forts up and down the land of the Great Spirit. The prophet wanted the red-jackets to know they weren't safe in the large forts either, so he laid siege to Fort Detroit and Fort Pitt.

He knew Fort Unghiara was where the white man's goods came by the big canoes across the great water; if he could stop that supply, he could isolate them and defeat them one at a time. But Fort Unghiara was too strong and could not be captured by warriors alone. Giant thundersticks, carrying great death, fired from the walls, sending warriors to the Spirit world before they could get close to the fort. The English could bring the big canoes from across the great water carrying more of the giant thundersticks that fired from the water. Attacking Fort Unghiara was not possible but stopping the flow of supplies from the fort was crucial to the prophet's success.

The Mohawks had planned to ambush the English white wagons that carried the supplies from Fort Unghiara. These wagons had taken the work away from the Mohawks, who were cast aside like worn moccasins. Now, they had no work and could not obtain the things made of hard metal, the blankets, or the beads.

Sixty warriors would attack the white wagons, and Hata'kaw'wa would join the war party and would earn warrior status. He knew the Great Spirit was pleased with him by allowing Hata'kaw'wa this second chance for Shay'wah'ki's mother's approval.

Then the prophet was told of the Mohawk's plan to attack the supply route, and he liked the plan. It was a good plan and would make the English fearful of moving supplies from Fort Unghiara around the Thundering Waters. He said, to put fear into the hearts of the English, the attack must be overwhelming. The supply lines for the English must be broken for good, and so a resounding victory was needed. So Pontiac ordered the Seneca and Ojibwa to join with the Mohawk in great numbers. This was a good thing for the People—but not a good thing for Hata'kaw'wa. Instead, of sixty warriors attacking the supply wagons, there would be four hundred warriors, and there would be no chance for Hata'kaw'wa to count coup among so many seasoned warriors. The Great Spirit had indeed deserted him.

Scouts watching Fort Unghiara reported the travel in and out, while the Mohawks waited for the Seneca and Ojibwa warriors to arrive. Two suns ago, the scouts had reported the white wagons had left Fort Unghiara, headed to the fort above the Thundering Waters. Many warriors had wanted to attack then and capture the supplies, as well. The chiefs would not allow it. They had given their word to the prophet to wait for the Seneca and Ojibwa, and so they would wait.

There had been great excitement in the longhouses, as warriors prepared for the attack. Scalplocks were braided and tied off with beads and the shells of the Great Spirit. Roaches were groomed; the narrow strips of hair greased stiff and tall down the middle of their shaved heads and were colored with the bright red of the berry and the yellow of the river clay. Faces were blackened and then painted with the marks of their clans; breechcloths, leggings, and head dresses were repaired and worn with pride. Turkey, eagle, and hawk feathers, representing past acts of valor and bravery were ceremoniously attached to scalplocks, roaches, and war belts. Thundersticks were cleaned and decorated. Tomahawks, knifes, and arrows were honed and blessed by the shaman to bring honor in battle.

Hata'kaw'wa had tested the pull of his bow and the spine of his arrows. He fitted the flint heads, so sharp they could cut the hair on his arm, to the shafts and then checked them for balance and tightness. Not having earned a scalplock, Shay'wah'ki had tied his hair in a single braid that ran down his back and fastened the wampum strings to the end. He blackened his face with the ash of the fire, and ran stripes of yellow across his forehead and down each side to honor Shay'wah'ki and the yellow ribbons she wore in her hair. He wore amulets on his arms and decorated his leggings with drawings of the wolf, his clan's protector. He put on his newest breechcloth, made by his mother, with colored beads sewn into the flap.

He was sleek, strong, and quick—ready to earn his status as a warrior and Shay'wah'ki as his bride. He welcomed the battle—his fear overshadowed by his longing for Shay'wah'ki.

The chiefs arrived with their warriors. Hata'kaw'wa was amazed by the number and types of thundersticks they owned. Many had been claimed from the Fren'che over the years, in trade or battle. The newest ones, taken from the slain English red-jackets.

Warriors were adorned with medals, buttons, and insignias stripped from the Fren'che and the English. They had seen much battle, counted much coup, and taken many scalplocks. While Hata'kaw'wa had felt pride at watching these mighty warriors of the people, his heart had fallen, knowing his chance of success in combat fell with their vast numbers.

Council had been held that evening. There was much talk of attacking the white wagons when they returned to Fort Unghiara or of waiting until they were filled with supplies again. Capturing the supplies would be good, but it was risky to keep so many warriors here. How would they lodge and feed such large numbers for the days of waiting? How would they restrain them from striking out at red-jackets, giving away their presence? The chiefs decided. They would attack now—the message to the white fathers more powerful than the supplies in the wagons.

The Mohawk knew the perfect place for the ambush—the Longhouse of the Evil Spirit. A steep ravine cut into the Great Divide where a waterfall had once spilled over the edge, until the Evil Spirit came and pushed the waterfall into the ground. The white wagons followed a path that crossed this ravine where there would be no escape for them—except into the Great Divide.

Scouts reported the white wagons had left the fort above the Thundering Waters and were returning to Fort Unghiara. Hundreds of warriors had quickly departed for the Longhouse of the Evil Spirit.

Joining his Mohawk brothers, Hata'kaw'wa had looked back to where Shay'wah'ki stood. Their eyes locked; his with anticipation, hers with fear—both with love.

Hunkered low in the brush, Hata'kaw'wa had smelled them approaching—the scent of the oxen reaching his nose before he'd heard the rumble of the wheels. He smelled sweet tobacco and heard a harsh shout at the oxen. Hata'kaw'wa had wondered what the man would think if he knew this was his last smoke. Before the wagons came into view, Hata'kaw'wa smelled the men themselves. Did white men ever bathe? How unclean they were. These ones will never bathe again, he thought.

Six red-jackets had come first. They walked bored, fatigued. He wondered why the red-jackets wore such foolish clothes—coats, leggings, headpieces, boots, and carrying their heavy packs and thundersticks. How can they fight with so much on? He wondered, and why do they wear such red coats that can be seen so easily?

Behind the red-jackets, the white wagons had followed. He counted on six fingers the number of wagons. Two men rode in each wagon; one carried a thunderstick. The wagons moved noisily along the trail; some pulled by horses, some by oxen, the heavy wheels bouncing through the many ruts and holes. Men on horseback rode alongside the white wagons. They too carried thundersticks. Six more red-jackets followed the white wagons, also not alert, looking weary and without thought of danger.

When the middle wagons were crossing the bottom of the ravine, the ambushers had fired. Scores of muskets and bows released, filling the air with hundreds of hot, heavy balls and fast, sharp arrows. All the red-jackets were killed instantly, most hit many times with both, ball and arrow. Many of the men on horseback were killed, as were some of the men driving the wagons. In the ensuing smoke, the warriors attacked, charging the survivors. Horses panicked and reared high into the air, flailing their feet at the sudden explosions and the burning smoke. They turned in the only direction not filled with screaming warriors—the Great Divide—and pulled their wagons into space, tumbling down the side of the canyon, crashing onto the boulders below. One driver, realizing his predicament too late, his wagon already over the edge, leaped from his wagon—into nothingness. The outside wheel of another wagon went off the side of the Great Divide, tilting the wagon dangerously. The sudden drop of the wagon jolted the horses backwards and off balance. They kicked at the air and stones, trying to regain their footing. The driver desperately whipped them as the wagon slipped farther over the edge, until the outside horse stepped into the air. In a collage of snapping wood, neighing horses, and screaming men, they vanished over the side of the canyon. A driver was pulled down between his terrified horses and dragged over the cliff with them.

It was over in minutes. A handful of teamsters were no contest against hundreds of warriors, intent on revenge. One man escaped on horseback, fleeing in the confusion and dense smoke. Tomahawks and scalping knifes slashed, and warriors counted coup. Others stared with envy into the Great Divide, at the smashed and broken bodies below that had taken their hair and thundersticks with them, many already swept away by the river, depriving the warriors of their trophies.

The remaining bodies were stripped of hair, clothing, belts, boots, rings, necklaces—anything of value before being unceremoniously hurled over the side to be reunited with their comrades below. Thundersticks, knifes, axes, and pouches were prized possessions for the few who gathered them. Wagons were unhitched and pushed over the edge. Horses were led away for sale and oxen taken to the villages for slaughter and victory feasting.

Only one warrior was injured, a self-inflicted wound to his thigh, when his knife slipped while scalping a struggling teamster.

Defeating the white wagons was not a mighty victory. There was no resistance, no battle, and no honorable foe. Hata'kaw'wa's defeat was shared by many in the war party. Many warriors had not counted coup. Gloom hung over what should have been a celebration of victory.

At the beginning of the attack, Hata'kaw'wa had released a single arrow, but in the smoke and ensuing flurry, did not know if it had struck its mark. From that moment on, Hata'kaw'wa had been a witness only. Hundreds of warriors swarmed past him like a flood. He'd never got close to a white man to count coup.

He stood now amid the carnage; his head hung low—defeated. The Great Spirit had deserted him.

A murmur of excitement rippled through the war party. Scouts reported that a large force of red-jackets was hurrying to the scene from the white man's village. They would be here soon.

Rather than run, the war party would wait and ambush them, as well.

Quickly throwing the remnants of the supply train over the edge, the warriors faded into the forest. Those warriors who had gained trophies during the attack on the supply train would hold back, allowing others to share in the victory. Hata'kaw'wa's spirits rose again. He had learned much from the attack on the supply train. This time, he would not shoot an arrow but would rush forward quickly to attack the red-jackets. He would count coup this day. The Great Spirit had not deserted him.

The red-jackets were coming from the opposite direction of where the white wagons had come from. The warriors lined the woods from the south edge of the Great Divide, in a circle, leaving the trail open on the north side, allowing the red-jackets to enter the ravine. Once in, warriors would close the trail, springing the trap. Those most skilled with thundersticks were placed to kill the red-jackets who wore the gold cloth. Without their chiefs, the remaining red-jackets would not know what to do. That opening volley would signal the others to attack.

English

Quick-marching at port-arms, the men moved through the thick terrain with ease, following the path through the densely wooded forest. At times, they were along the very edge of the giant canyon, which was both thrilling and frightening to the drummer boy. Viewing the turbulence of the foaming river at the bottom of the canyon was breathtaking and spectacular; quick-marching so close to the edge, scared the daylights out of him.

The forest was dense, having a heavy ground cover of vines, ferns, and other flora. It had to be difficult for the supply wagons to get through with the overhanging tree limbs and vines grabbing at the wagon tops. A short distance out, the lieutenant ordered the drummer boy to stow his drum, and the column proceeded in relative quiet. The discipline and coordination of the elite soldiers as they moved effortlessly through the forest renewed the boy's faith, making him feel secure despite the unknown danger ahead. These men were the best in the King's service; he couldn't be any safer.

The sharp odor of burnt gunpowder and sulfur drifted on the breeze. There were no sounds, no movements, no birds chirping or critters stirring in the bushes. The stillness was unnerving.

The junior officer in the lead raised his hand and stopped. Immediately, the column came to a halt. The lieutenant signaled for the two point men to advance as scouts and had the sergeant major pass the signal for the men to prepare for battle. As the scouts quietly disappeared into the dense foliage, along the ranks, muskets were primed, flints were stroked, and bayonets were fixed. Steel slid on steel as the long, pointed knifes were fastened to the working end of the muskets. The air was charged with tension; everyone was on alert, straining to hear, see, or smell anything that indicated a threat.

There was nothing, only the thunder of the silence while they waited.

Hata'kaw'wa strained to hear. He marveled at the quietness of so many warriors, no noise, no rustlings, no stirring in the bushes. The birds and their creature brothers of the forest knew the men were there, and sensed the tension in the air. The creatures were still—the forest and death waited.

Movement in the trees caught Hata'kaw'wa's eye. One . . . no two red-jackets moved in the woods at the edge of the opening. They knelt, scanned the area, and then advanced carefully into the crossing. After making a brief reconnaissance, they faded back into the trees. Hata'kaw'wa wondered if the red-jackets had detected the trap and if they were reporting it to their chiefs.

Like mirages, the scouts materialized from the thick foliage. Positioned next to the lieutenant, the drummer boy was privy to the report. "Supply train was ambushed in that steep ravine we came through earlier today, sir," the scout reported softly. "Looks like they were right in the middle when they were attacked."

"Survivors?" the lieutenant asked.

"No one, sir."

"Wagons?"

"No wagons, horses, or anything, sir."

"How do you know they were ambushed there?"

"Ground's all torn up—blood everywhere, wagon tracks disappearing into the gorge, sir."

"Did you look?"

"Yes, sir, wagons on the bottom, smashed. Pretty obvious what happened. Looks like there were a bloody lot of them, too, bushes tramped down everywhere," he paused and in a lower, more subdued tone, added, "then there are the bodies, sir."

"Where, soldier?"

"In the canyon sir. Horses, oxen and men; stripped—mutilated."

"Very well." The Lieutenant turned to the column. "Sergeant Major!"

"Sir!"

"It appears we're too late. We'll advance at normal pace. I doubt if we'll encounter any of the hostiles, as they've obviously vacated the scene. Probably back in their wigwams bragging to their squaws what mighty warriors they are. Bloody savages." He shook his head. "Defenseless civilians. Sound the fife and drum sergeant, if there're any stragglers out there, let them know we're coming. We'll see if they wish to tangle with the king's elite."

"Yes, sir!" The sergeant major passed the word down the ranks and the column resumed its march forward, two by two, with muskets and bayonets held high, at normal walking pace, to the beat of the drummer boy's drum, while Mr. Wilson played the marching song on his fife.

In the distance . . . a drum. Was it possible the English would announce their coming to their enemy? What fools were these warriors? Did they think the Iroquois would tremble and run hearing their drum? Or was this the English trap? To make the Iroquois think they come from one way and then attack from behind? Hata'kaw'wa wanted to jump up and warn the others that the drum was a trap. The red-jackets knew they were here. Couldn't they see the deception?

Before he could shout out the warning, he saw flashes of red through the trees. The red-jackets were entering from the north, moving down the steep ravine. Were they walking into a trap or setting their own trap? He didn't know. He didn't dare move and give away their position. He couldn't raise the alarm, but he would remain vigilant to his backside, as well.

True to the scouts' word, the ground was torn up everywhere as soon as they cleared the trees. The drummer boy saw the wagon tracks made in the earth and where they disappeared over the edge. He thought it was a perfect ambush spot, the middle of a ravine, with steep climbs in front and behind, bordered by a forest filled with savages to one side and the sheer drop of the canyon to the other. He not only saw but smelled the pungent odor of the blood in the grass and mud.

He was relieved the lieutenant was secure in his knowledge that the savages had left, and although he felt sadness at the fate of the supply train, he also felt a sense of ease, knowing they were not going to confront these savages.

The warriors remained silent, hundreds of hidden eyes watching the red-jackets march into the ravine. Excitement surged through Hata'kaw'wa at seeing such a large number of red-jackets—surely he would count coup. The red-jacket chiefs stood out by the gold stripes on their coats. Listening to the rousing beat of the drum, Hata'kaw'wa picked out the drummer, marching close to one of the chiefs. He is young, like me, Hata'kaw'wa thought. He felt pity for the drummer. The boy was a decoration only, not belonging on the battlefield, as he carried no weapons. He would die with no honor, unable to defend himself in a warrior's death.

The roar of thundersticks startled Hata'kaw'wa out of his musing as the red-jacket chief flew backwards, twisting in erratic jerks, as several musket balls tore into his body. The young drummer went down, probably struck down by a missed shot at the white chief. He is lucky to have died so quickly, Hata'kaw'wa thought. Instantly, the air shook with a second explosion of many more thundersticks. Through the thick smoke, a volley of bullets and arrows descended on the column of red-jackets. Hata'kaw'wa did not shoot, charging forward, tomahawk held high.

The roar of many muskets firing together made the drummer boy's heart stop, his bladder release and a scream tear from his throat. Around him, men screamed in pain and anguish, jerking in ghoulish pantomimes as the hot lead balls ripped their bodies apart, tearing through clothing and flesh alike. Many were struck two, three, and more times, being literally torn to pieces. He spun hard to his side as a heavy lead ball smashed into his drum, spinning it around his body, throwing him to the ground. Muskets fell to the ground, unfired as soldiers collapsed with arrows protruding randomly from their bodies. The lucky ones were dead before touching the ground. Half of the regiment was killed by the initial volley that descended upon them.

The lieutenant died instantly—lead balls ripped into his chest, legs, and arms. A shot tore through his face, taking out the back of his skull.

Through the stinging smoke came the war cries of hundreds of savages as they swooped from the surrounding forest into the ravine.

Those soldiers who remained could not see through the billowing smoke and fired blindly. Before they could reload, the savages stormed out from the smoke, like demons rising from the mists, with war clubs smashing and tomahawks slashing. The soldiers tried to fight back, but their bayonets, on the ends of the long muskets, were unwieldy and clumsy in such close quarters. The short swing of the war club and the quick chop of the tomahawk were efficient and brutal. The surge of so many warriors from all directions pushed the remaining soldiers to the brink of the canyon.

Hata'kaw'wa raced forward, screaming his war cry, charging through the acrid smoke. The surge of warriors pushed the red-jackets against the Great Divide, firing their muskets blindly at the onrush of warriors. For each warrior that fell, four more took his place. The heavy thundersticks with their long, sharp knifes were no match for the short war club. Hata'kaw'wa ran straight at the red-jackets, his tomahawk eager to taste English blood.

The drummer boy lay frozen in fear at the carnage around him. A blur to his side was followed by the dull thud and massive weight of the sergeant major falling across his legs. The sergeant's eyes, stared in bewilderment, before exploding out of their sockets as a war club smashed into the side of his skull. The bloody head was yanked up by a screaming savage. The Indian sliced a circular cut around the misshapen head and, in one mighty pull, ripped the sergeant major's scalp completely off. Holding the scalp high, the Indian let out a chilling war cry and ran into the melee, waving his trophy.

The boy stared at the pile of gore that, just seconds before, had been the strong, masculine features of the sergeant major. He kicked in horror at it, pushing the bloody body off his own, stumbled to his feet, and backed up as soldiers were pulled down and butchered all around him.

He didn't know what to do. The savages were everywhere, screaming and killing in a frenzy. There was no escape. The regiment had been taken totally by surprise, was disoriented and in total panic. The boy saw Mr. Wilson raising his arms to surrender and heard him scream as he was pulled to the ground by slashing savages. A soldier thrust his bayonet into the chest of a savage an instant before the chiseled flint end of a heavy war club slammed deep into the soldier's neck. His head flopped to the side like the trap on a gallows.

The boy's feet touched the edge of the canyon, and he looked down at the raging river far below. There was death below him and death around him. There was no escape—he would die.

"Yeee-ahhhh!" The cry was loud and close. Jerking his head up, he saw the ecstatic, paint-smeared face of a screaming savage rushing at him, tomahawk raised and swinging a death blow to his head. He spun to the side, attempting to evade the descending weapon. Sharp flint caught the flesh of his face, slicing deep into his cheek. The rushing motion of the savage, not being halted by a solid hit with his tomahawk, hurled him forward into the open air over the edge of the canyon. He plummeted down the side, bounced off the boulders, and was claimed by the river.

As the drummer boy jerked backwards, feeling the intense pain in his face, his foot went over the edge. He teetered on the brink for a moment and flailing at the open air, he too tumbled over the edge.

Through the cloud of thick smoke, Hata'kaw'wa saw a warrior charging a red-jacket, tomahawk swinging. The red-jacket swerved, and the warrior vanished over the edge of the canyon. The red-jacket wavered on the brink briefly before following the warrior into the canyon.

Crashing into a thick tree, growing out from the canyon wall, the drummer boy broke through the branches, until suddenly he was jerked upwards, suspended. Looking up, he saw the large, thick strap of his drum securely caught on a stout branch. He hadn't fallen far, less than thirty feet. Hearing the madness above him, he dared not move for fear of being discovered or dislodging himself. His life had come to an end; the only question remaining was whether he would die by the savages or the river.

Hata'kaw'wa looked down. The red-jacket had not fallen far, caught in a tree, and was still alive. Hata'kaw'wa raised his bow with arrow nocked and aimed directly at the red-jacket's chest. It would be an easy kill—with a short climb down to take his scalp, count his coup and join with Shay'wah'ki.

He noticed the drum in the tree and realized this was the drummer he thought had been killed. The drummer turned his head and looked up at Hata'kaw'wa.

He looked straight into the eyes of a savage staring down at him with bow raised and an arrow pointed at his chest. The savage's face was blackened, with yellow stripes down his cheeks. The boy shuddered. At this short distance, he couldn't miss. Eyes bulging with fear, he looked into the face of death, waiting for the moment when he would feel its final sting.

Hata'kaw'wa drew his bow back for the deadly release. Pausing briefly at full draw, he remembered the sound of the drum and recalled the pity he'd felt for the defenseless drummer. He wondered if the Great Spirit smiled upon the boy. He had been saved from the lead balls when Hata'kaw'wa thought he had been killed; he had been protected when the warrior attacked him, costing the warrior his own life; and now, the Great Spirit had put this tree here to save the boy from the Great Divide. Three deaths the Great Spirit had spared him. The Great Spirit did not want the drummer boy to die. Killing this boy would put Hata'kaw'wa in disfavor with the Great Spirit. Hata'kaw'wa lowered his bow, without sending the arrow into the boy's chest. He knew now; he had been sent here by the Great Spirit to protect the boy . . . not to kill him.

The boy was easy prey exposed on the tree. If he were to survive, he had to look dead and not show his hair to attract other warriors. Hata'kaw'wa pointed to the battle behind him, then down at the drummer boy and shook his head. He touched his own hair, and shook his head again as he pulled his hair, pushing it back out of view.

The savage again pointed at the drummer boy and held his arm over his head. The drummer boy stared at the savage, not knowing if this was a form of heathen ritual before the kill. The savage covered his head with his arm. Did he want him to hide his hair? Why? He didn't want to kill him with his hair showing? Then understanding burst upon him—the savage wasn't going to kill him, and he wanted him to hide his head. Why wasn't this savage killing him? He reached back over his head and pulling his wide collar forward, he tucked his head down into his coat as far as he was able. Glancing up one last time and saw the savage nodding.

Hata'kaw'wa gave the drummer boy one last look; he appeared to be dead and showed no hair to entice a warrior. Hata'kaw'wa had done all he could to save the boy, now it was for the Great Spirit to watch over the boy.

Turning to rejoin the battle and count his coup for Shay'wah'ki, the bayonet pierced into his chest, ripping through his lungs and coming out his spine.

"Bloody savage!" The red-jacket's face was distorted in hatred and pain as dark red blood spurted out of his chest from a massive, ugly hole. The soldier collapsed in a heap on the stock of his musket, wedging the bayonet in Hata'kaw'wa's chest, pinning him upright.

Hata'kaw'wa stared ahead. Bubbling, reddish-pink blood foamed from his mouth, ran down his chin, soaking the breechcloth his mother had made for him. His last thought was of Shay'wah'ki and of how sad she would be.

A warrior pulled the dead red-jacket off the musket and jerked the bayonet out from Hata'kaw'wa's chest. He watched Hata'kaw'wa sway back and forth on his feet as his life force left him to join the Great Spirit, while his body silently fell backwards into the Great Divide.

A body crashed in the tree above the drummer boy, settling right on top of him. An outstretched arm dangled across his covered head. The arm was bare—brown—with an amulet on the bicep. The boy feared the extra weight would break him loose from the tree, sending him to his death below. But the tree and the strap held firm, and he did not fall. He had been spared once again. How many lives did he have left?

After, removing the red-jacket's scalp, the warrior cut it into two equal parts. Holding one part high in the air, he sang a death song asking the Great Spirit to receive this Mohawk brother home. Then he tossed the scalp onto the body of the brave warrior tangled in the tree below.

Hata'kaw'wa, the warrior—counted coup.

The boy heard an Indian chanting above him. Would he die now? Was an arrow aimed at his back? The boy hung suspended under the dead Indian, feigning death, waiting for the fatal cut of the arrow. But the body of Hata'kaw'wa, the warrior, covered the boy, protecting him even in his death.

Time moved slowly hanging in the tree, listening to the butchery above. A rock stuck his leg hard and bounced down the side of the canyon. He willed his body to be still, to be dead. Bodies were thrown into the canyon on both sides of him, but none landed in his tree again. After a long while, as daylight sunk away, the noise above diminished and then stopped, no war cries, no jubilation, no movement . . . just quiet.

Still the boy hung there, not moving—waiting—praying.

The sun set. He watched its rays slowly inch their way down the face of the canyon. It was radiant and glorious, reflecting gold and orange mingling with the lush green of the dense foliage throughout the canyon. The river below sparkled green capped with shimmering whitecaps. If he hadn't been hanging here, amid all this death and carnage, fearful of dying, he would have thought it beautiful.

But he was hanging here, and he was fearful of dying—and things weren't beautiful.

Darkness descended in the canyon. The moon was out in a clear sky, shedding ghostly illumination on the gorge. His joints and muscles were stiff and numb, beyond pain. Not having heard any sound from above for a long time, he gathered all his remaining courage and slowly pulled his coat back to look upwards, fearful of seeing the face of a savage staring down at him. No face stared down.

Slowly and carefully, he began to move his arms and legs, feeling the joints crack and muscles creak. He was careful not to move too fast or too much at any one time, so as not to break loose and fall. He managed to wrap his arm around a stout branch and slowly shifted his body onto the wall of the canyon, taking his weight off of the drum strap and moving out from under the dead savage who sprawled above him. Every slight movement was accompanied by screaming pain as his muscles revolted. He gradually found he was able to obtain a solid purchase with his feet on a small ledge. Shifting his weight, he was able to support himself by holding on to the branch.

A loud crack broke the silence of the night as the body of the dead savage slowly slid to the side, snapping branches and breaking free of the tree, falling to the rocks below.

During the hours, he had hung suspended in the tree; he had examined the canyon wall carefully noting the brush and rock as to how he could climb down. Although it was dangerous, he felt better about climbing down—than he did about climbing up to the top, just feet above him. Going up would be easier, but he was too fearful of running into savages in the dark, they were out there somewhere, hundreds of them. He felt certain he'd not be able to avoid them. He was sure they weren't below by that raging river. He had watched the canyon's bottom until the sky turned so dark he couldn't see anymore and nothing had moved down there except the river and the seagulls, which delighted in fighting over the gore. Maybe with tomorrow's light, they would climb down to claim treasures from those who fell and weren't claimed by the river, but not tonight, not in the dark and not with so much celebration in the villages. If he could climb down safely, he could follow the river to Lewis Town, where he knew the river flowed, being there earlier.

He carefully eased the drum strap off his shoulder until he was free of it. He wanted to take it with him, as it had saved his life in more ways than one, but he couldn't climb down with the drum. If he threw it down, it would be broken from bouncing down the side of the canyon, and he didn't want the noise to alert any savages.

Watching his footing and his handholds, he began the dangerous climb down. The wall was steep, but there were many supports, allowing him to work his way down.

Along the way, he encountered mutilated bodies caught in trees and bushes, stripped of everything, including their hair. Multiple cuts had been made until every patch of hair had been removed from the heads, beards and, in some cases, even their chests. It hadn't been just about counting coup against an enemy—it was pent up rage against the destruction of their world. He pictured some savage warrior proudly sporting the large white handlebars that had been attached to the upper lip of the sergeant major, as a trophy.

Moving around a body sprawled face up in a thick bush growing out from the side of the gorge, he looked into the lifeless eyes and hairless head of William Perry who had feared he would never see England or his family again. Neither his bayonet nor his Johnson had served him well in fulfilling his prophecy.

When he was almost to the bottom, the boy heard his drum beating above him. Snapping his head up, he saw it hurtling down the side of the canyon, from branch to rock. He flinched as it bounced by, and slammed into a large boulder, careening off into the river. From his vantage point on the canyon's wall, he watched it begin its journey downriver to Fort Niagara, riding high on the tips of the surging waves.

As he continued his descent, the river became increasingly louder and threatening as he drew closer. It was monstrous, sending massive waves crashing into boulders, declaring a constant, steady roar of power and domination.

Finally, he stepped onto the bottom of the canyon. He was sickened by the bodies of the soldiers, teamsters, and animals scattered about like rag dolls dropped from the clouds. Across a large flat boulder, the body of a savage, laid face-up. It was the only savage among the dead, and the boy studied him carefully. The hair was set in a long braid, and the face had a yellow stripe drawn down each cheek and across the forehead. Under the paint and blackened face, the drummer boy could see that the savage was a boy, like himself. A large, ugly hole had ripped open his chest.

The drummer boy stared into the face of the savage for a long time.

He untied the rawhide strip that held white and purple shells fastened to the braid of his hair, and clutched them tight in his hand as a remembrance of the Indian who had saved his life.

Slowly and carefully, the drummer boy followed the river to Lewis Town, all the while wondering why he alone was alive. He thought much about the young Indian who had given his life in exchange for his own. As the boy climbed carefully around and over the boulders lining the shore, the spray from the raging river mixed with the tears that ran across the deep gash in his cheek.

Chapter 45

"Come on, what do you say? Let's get outta here," Chuck said, looking away from Billy and advancing on the stairs.

In single file, we began the long climb to the top and out of the gorge. At any other time, this trek would have been a piece of cake. But now, wet, cold, exhausted—we might as well have been climbing Mount Everest. What normally would have been a walk in the park for us was a substantial chore as we hauled our frozen butts up those steps. But with each step, we knew we were one step closer to getting out—to freedom—to the world we knew. Slowly, steadily—we climbed.

A number of times, we had to detour and move off the stairs due to buildups of ice covering one or two steps at a time. Sometimes, this was easy, sometimes not, depending on the terrain and the condition of the gorge at those places. We'd push the toes of our boots into the snow base around the ice; and grabbing whatever we could for support, we'd work our way around these spots, back to the stairs.

Despite knowing we were on the final leg of the journey and were headed out of the gorge, our spirits weren't high. There was little chatter, no joking or ribbing. Mentally, as well as physically, we were utterly and totally exhausted. Our brains were saturated, overloaded with the events, sights, and experiences we had endured. No one had the strength, or the desire, for any further adventures. And no one wanted any additional insights about each other, neither. Too many had already surfaced during this single day already; not all were good, and we needed time to digest them and allow ourselves to become friends again, with each other and ourselves.

It would be a long time before I'd come back here again.

We had traveled about two-thirds of the way up the side of the gorge, when we came to where a pathway detoured off the main stairway. Resting for a minute, Lenny asked Chuck if this was the path leading to the cave.

"Yeah," Chuck mumbled, hoping Billy wouldn't pick up on it.

"The devil's cave." Billy said immediately. He hadn't said anything since his rant at the bottom of the stairway with his prophecy of doom and death, keeping as far away from Chuck as possible. I had hoped that climbing these stairs to safety would have taken away his conviction of doom, but I was wrong. "The haunted cave, where *he* cursed us." Billy's voice dripped with venom as he pointed at Chuck.

"Knock it off, will you Billy? Don't start that crap again; I don't want to hear it." I said. "No one believes all those old Indian legends." I didn't want to inflame Billy's distorted thinking any further by admitting that I'd been in the cave too, more than once. "Hundreds of people have been in that cave, and nothing's happened to them. Let's just get out of here, ok?"

"We ain't never gonna get out of here," Billy yelled. "We're gonna die here. You'll see."

"What's the matter with you?" I asked. "All this stupid talk, about curses and dying! We're here, aren't we, on our way out, walking up a stairway, for heaven's sake? There's no such thing as a haunted cave!"

"You think not, huh?" Wayne cut in, surprisingly. "Well, what about that train wreck? How do you explain that?"

"Train wreck, what train wreck?" Lenny asked.

"There used to be a train that ran around the side of the gorge, a long time ago and it crashed right here and smashed all the way to the bottom, with tons of people thrown all over the place, killing a bunch of them," Wayne threw out.

"Is that true, Kevin?" Lenny asked.

"I don't know. Ol' Gordy might of said something about a train once, but I don't know if it's true or not." I looked at Wayne in disbelief, mixed with an underlying feeling of anger at his selective memory. I didn't know why, of all things and all times for him to remember anything, it had to be that and now.

"Well, I know," Wayne insisted, "and that wasn't just old Indian legends, neither. And you said yourself Kevin, Ol' Gordy's never lies. We'll ask him about it when we see him."

"That ain't going to happen," Billy said. "'cause we ain't never getting out of here." I couldn't understand what was happening. I didn't know who was losing their minds faster, Billy or Wayne—or me! Wayne had this obsession with staring death in the face, and Billy was convinced Chuck consorted with the devil, to get us all killed.

It was obvious that Billy's mind wasn't able to handle the things we had confronted. So many fears and emotions were swirling in his head; fear of getting caught, of being stranded, of facing death by the river or of freezing, and worse of all was the fear of his mother. They had mixed together in just a few, hard hours—and it was all just too much for Billy to comprehend. While my world had been turned upside down and shaken to pieces, Billy's sheltered, mother-protected world had been shattered and destroyed. He needed somehow to explain it all to himself, no matter how loony or ridiculous it was. And with the explanation, he needed someone to blame.

"We're getting out of here right now, Billy, that's what we're doing," Chuck said, walking up the steps. "I don't know anything about any train wreck, but if there was a train that was stupid enough to run on the side of this gorge, then it deserved to crash! Let's go."

Chapter 46

The stairway took a winding route across the face of the gorge. If I looked down on it from above, it would look like a giant snake wrapped across the side of the gorge. Chuck had said the Devil's Hole was named after a giant snake. *Were we walking on the snake?* I wondered. *Does that mean the trail itself is evil?* I quickly dismissed that notion. Now Billy had me thinking crazy like him, as well.

Following the stairway, we had climbed high up the side of the gorge. I knew we were getting close to the top because, not only was the river was far below, but we were starting to feel a breeze on our faces. My spirits had climbed along with the stairway. Then, coming around a bend in the stairway, we were stopped dead in our tracks.

By a rock—again, and, this time, not even a large one.

It sat directly in the middle of the stairway on a step. It was rectangular and was only about three feet wide, four feet high, and three feet deep. This rock had been parked on the stairway for years, and hundreds of people had walked around it. Seeing it now, I remembered climbing on it during my summer visits with my dad.

No one was going climbing on it this time—or walk around it.

The rock had become the centerpiece of a large ice formation. Through the course of the winter, ice had formed on it early, growing thicker and higher as the winter progressed. It was an ice magnet. It had expanded up and outwards, encompassing more than two dozen steps above it and merging with the ice on the wall of the gorge, forming one massive block of ice, ending in a large, overhanging lip. On the other side of the stairway, the thick ice spread out thirty feet along the side of the gorge before tapering off along the steep wall.

It was a complete stoppage.

"Oh God, what're we gonna do now?" Wayne gasped, voicing the despair each of us felt. No one had an answer. We stared at the barrier, as the misery that had receded with each step we had climbed on the stairway, now swept over us like a hurricane flood. We were lost for words and only Billy seemed satisfied now, although he was smart enough to keep his mouth shut.

Finally, it was Chuck who spoke, "Well, we either go over it or around it." Feeling the smoothness of the ice, he added, "It looks hard, not like 'Wild Wayne'. I don't see any places to make steps. What do you think, Kevin?"

Not saying anything, I removed my hatchet once again and tried chopping at the ice. It was like hitting stone. It didn't break off in chunks as it had at Wild Wayne, and it wasn't a shell with packed granular ice behind it, but was solid all the way through. "This stuff is hard as concrete. Gonna take forever to make steps in this and even if we could, how would we get over that lip hanging out up there?"

Chuck looked above the blockage. "I don't see anything we can throw a rope around. Everything's in ice."

"We have to get around it!" Wayne lamented, pointing up. "We're almost out! Look, that's the top of the gorge right there." Wayne was right; the top of the gorge was less than fifty feet above us. We were so close!

"We can't walk around it. It's too steep and icy out there," Lenny said.

"There are branches and rocks to hold onto," Chuck replied.

"They're all coated in ice. It looks really scary to me," Wayne said.

I agreed with Wayne; it looked really scary out there. The side of the gorge was steep here, consisting of a frightening mixture of ice, rock, and protrusions, all the way down to the bottom. Falling here would be disastrous.

"Anyone got any ideas?" I asked.

Billy sat on the steps; staring vacantly down the gorge, mumbling, "Say your prayers, it's like I told you . . . we're gonna die here."

The wind swirled along the side of the gorge, and the river below was a faint murmur. Other than that there was only silence. It hung in the air like a low, dark cloud. Defeated in body and mind, no one spoke. This long journey, starting as a simple dare, had become one life-threatening hurdle after another in a strange and unforgiving world. It had sapped our strength, distorted our thoughts and dissolved our wills. Never had I been so fatigued and sore—my legs and arms screamed in agony with each step. My hands and feet were frozen and numb. Never, in my life, have I been so miserable. I had no feeling in my face—and no desire in my heart. Like Billy, I yearned to sit down and let whatever was going to happen—happen.

What had we been thinking to challenge Niagara? Niagara is eternal; who were we to defy its power and dominion? It's a gigantic mouth with a voracious appetite, chomping its way through thousands of tons of granite and stone, leaving this deep scar in its wake. You don't challenge Niagara. It tolerates you for a time, allowing you the illusion you're winning—until it tires of you and embraces you, swallowing you whole, leaving no trace you'd ever even been there.

Every truth and untruth we'd ever known in our lives had been wiped away in this one day. The world we were comfortable with—home, school, girls, Marty's Market, my old man—had been annihilated and replaced by this hard, cold, unforgiving, primitive world. Those things that had always been so familiar to me, the Falls, the gorge, the river were now foreign and strange. Those things I knew so well, I didn't know at all, and the things I'd never known at all were now burned deeply into my mind. The immortality and invincibility of my youth was forever crushed and shattered by this single day.

Lenny had said that God was with me. I couldn't get that out of my mind, and I needed time to digest it. I had never felt God was a real being, but considered God to be, at best, some mystical concept to explain those things I couldn't understand or at worse, nothing more than a self-serving crutch to excuse bad social behavior like my old man did. It was clear that Lenny believed God was, not only real and wasn't just a theory, but that He was a knowing and a personal being that cared about what happens to us. Lenny had a source of strength and assurance inside of him that I'd hadn't seen before. When things got bad for Lenny he had something to fall back on, and it seemed to be a real something. The rest of us had nothing to fall back on except ourselves; and from the looks of Billy and Wayne and even Chuck and myself, that wasn't anything to get excited about when all was said and done.

What could we do? There were no options. We couldn't go back—the route was impassable. Even if we could, where would we go? We couldn't climb over this blockage, but we couldn't sit here either. Night was coming. No one would be looking for us here, and we wouldn't be found for months, and by then we'd be dead, just like Billy said.

"I'll climb around it on the gorge side and then back to the stairway above it." Chuck said. "Once there, I'll drop a rope down to you guys."

"You fall out there; you'll die, if not from the fall, then from exposure," I said.

"Thanks for the encouragement, Kev." Chuck laughed. "That's the chance I'll have to take. I don't see any other way. There are enough rocks and trees I can grab onto. I think I can make it okay."

"Maybe you can, but what if you don't?" I said, feeling the cold grow denser. "It's no good, too dangerous out there by yourself. Too easy to slip, or for something to break and for you to fall."

"And you will fall," Billy quietly predicted. "You will die and meet your devil out there."

"I'll tie the rope on, and you guys can hold me," Chuck offered, ignoring Billy.

"That ain't gonna work either," I said. "Dragging a rope across all that crap out there while you're going up and down will only get all tangled and caught up. Rope itself will probably get snagged and pull you down."

"Well, crap Kevin! We can't just sit around! You have any other ideas?" Chuck yelled.

I nodded slowly. "Yeah, I do. We all go."

"And you all die," Billy added.

"We tie ourselves together again, and we all climb around it." I said. "The rope goes with us, so it won't get tangled and if one person slips, the rest are there to keep him from falling and get him back up."

"Or we all go down with him!" Wayne complained.

"Not if we're all holding on to something. One person moves at a time while the others hold tight. That's the only way we can do it. It's

312

too dangerous for one or even two people out there. We have to do it as a team."

"Kevin's right, that's the way we have to go," Chuck said as he opened the knapsack on Wayne's back. He took out the dreaded rope. "Let's tie up."

"And then what?" Wayne asked.

"Do what Kevin said. I'll go first and make a path for you to follow," Chuck continued as he worked to unravel the frozen coil of rope that crinkled and cracked with each twist.

I expected an outburst from Billy, but he surprised me by just sitting there and in a quiet, calm voice said, "Go ahead; do what you want. I ain't going. I've had enough of this crazy crap. I'm done with it. I'm gonna stay right here and wait for them to come and get me out of here. You can all go and die, I don't care, I'm not."

"No one is coming to get us, Billy," I said, "it's about time you realized that."

"Yes, they are, they know we're down here. It's just taking longer cause of that stupid trick *he* did, hiding our tracks back there. We just have to wait for them, that's all. Let *him* go out there, if he wants to! *He's* the one the devil wants anyway!"

It was obvious we couldn't depend on Billy tied to a rope out there. "All right, Billy," I said evenly. "You don't go. You're right; you stay here. We'll go, and once we're back on the stairs above, we'll drop a rope down for you."

Billy shook his head firmly. "I don't want any rope. I'll just sit here and wait for them to come for me."

"Billy, when they come to rescue you, what are they gonna do? They can't go down this ice thing no more than we can, so they're gonna lower you a rope and pull you up, right?" Billy didn't answer.

"Okay, you just sit here, Billy, and relax. Don't worry about it." I turned to the others. "Wayne, Lenny, you guys okay with this?"

Wayne nodded but didn't look enthused about it.

"I don't see any other way," Lenny said. "But, I think we should pray before we do it."

"Pray?" Wayne blurted out, "I don't believe in that crap. That's for girls and old priests. Bunch of sissy stuff. What the heck for anyway?"

"No one's making you to if you don't want to, Wayne." Lenny looked at me, "What do you say Kev, are you willing to pray with me before we do this?"

I wanted to wilt and hide. I'd never prayed with anyone before, much less with my friends, and especially standing on the side of the gorge, with Chuck being here. I felt foolish and was embarrassed by his asking. I was waiting for Chuck to start laughing and let loose on Lenny.

"I don't know Lenny. What are we praying for? What's it gonna do?" I didn't like being under this spotlight.

"We're praying that God protects us out there and gets us back home safe. Seems like a pretty compelling reason to me." He said.

I didn't say anything. In truth, I would not have minded Lenny's prayers, going out there scared me, but I was squirming inside, too embarrassed to open my mouth.

"I'll pray with you Lenny." Chuck said without any ridicule or mockery. "I'm not ashamed to ask God to help us get out of this mess anymore."

I couldn't believe what he had just said. I looked at Chuck to see if he was joking as he had been with me back at 'Wild Wayne'. He wasn't.

"Okay, Lenny, let's pray." I said.

Billy sat on the steps, staring at the bottom of the gorge. Wayne stood to the side with a sour look on his face.

We prayed.

Chapter 47

Chuck wrapped the frozen rope around himself and began tying a knot. "Last leg, guys! After this, we're home. We're practically pros at this by now." Chuck tugged on the knot while continuing to speak in a slow, easy tone, speaking to himself as much as to anyone else. "Look how far, we've come. The top's right there, just like Wayne said. We're getting out of here now. Okay, who's next?"

"This is becoming a bad habit," I said, taking the rope from Chuck.

"Let's move back down the steps a little to get below this ice," Chuck said, "and we'll move one at a time, just like Kevin said, holding the rocks and branches for support."

I wrapped the rope around Lenny, and I felt the quivering under his coat. I didn't think it was all from the cold. As I finished tying Lenny on, Chuck reminded us, "Make sure you always have a good grip on something before anyone else moves, okay?" He took a deep breath. "C'mon, Wayne, you're last. We go just like we did before, taking turns moving, okay?" Heads nodded, ever so slightly, too afraid to speak.

"Maybe we should call out when we're moving and when we're stopping so there are no screw-up's," I added. "There can't be any mistakes out there."

"Yeah, good idea Kevin," Chuck agreed. "Everyone good with that?"

Again, silent nods.

Chuck looked at Billy and said with genuine concern, "It's gonna be okay, Billy. We'll be dropping a rope down to you before you know it." Billy remained sitting, not responding, just staring down the gorge. "We're gonna get you out of here, Billy." Then turning to the gorge, "Okay, here I go."

Chuck started out onto the gorge under the ice blockage. He made footrests in the hard crust on top of rocks or branches, and he grabbed at others, breaking off the layers of ice to make solid handholds. Before long, the rope tightened and tugged on me.

"Okay, I'm set." Chuck called out. I swallowed hard, trying to steel my nerves. My foot wouldn't move. A jerk on the rope made me look up. Chuck was staring at me. He nodded for me to follow. I looked down at the frozen rocks jutting out from the snow, forty feet below, and then to where they continued to drop another hundred feet along the steep wall of the gorge. I tried to speak, but nothing came out from my lips. I was frozen in place. My heart hammered against my ribcage, trying to escape, and my pulse pounded the sides of my head like a bass drum. Sucking in, gulps of air to absorb the dizziness threatening to sweep over me, I looked at Chuck, who was watching and waiting. Again he jerked his head for me to follow.

"Moving!" I called as best I could, which wasn't exceptionally strong.

Placing my boots in the steps Chuck had made and desperately gripping the same branches and rocks he had gripped, I forced my body to move off the stone steps, out onto the face of the gorge and began moving across it.

Reaching Chuck, with both feet firmly planted and hands holding on tight, I called out, "Okay".

"Moving!" Chuck called and carefully stepped sideways, taking up the slack my new position had given him. After he was anchored again and gave the 'okay' signal, I called out a second time and had only moved a couple of feet when I felt the rope to Lenny tighten.

Securing a solid hold, I called out. "Okay," and nodded to Lenny to follow.

"Moving!" Lenny yelled at the top of his lungs, startling me with the enormity of his blast.

We continued in this fashion, alternating moves, and it was surprising how everyone fell into the rhythm of the movement. It wasn't long, before all four of us were off the steps, hanging onto the face of the gorge like a bunch of tied up spiders. We were only feet away from the top, and safety and 150 feet above the river, which patiently waited below for us to make a mistake. There were a couple of times when someone's foot slipped, and our hearts stood still while they scampered back into place. Thank God we were tied up spiders.

Chuck reached the end of the ice blockage, and he began climbing up to get above it. No one talked, except for the quivering calls of *"Moving,"* and *"Okay"* from one parched throat after another.

Finally, Chuck's feet were above the blockage and he began making his way back toward the stairs. He had traveled a short distance back, and we were spread out in the shape of a backwards C, with Chuck at the upper left point, me in the upper corner, Lenny in the lower corner, and Wayne moving along the bottom—when there was a loud crack. The branch Lenny had been holding onto broke away clean, and Lenny fell off the face of the gorge.

Lenny's scream shattered the stillness, and a loud cry of pain escaped my lips as the sudden yank of the rope around my waist cut deeply into my stomach. I desperately gripped the gorge as Lenny's weight pulled on me like an anchor. I must not know how to make knots very well because the more Lenny kicked and struggled, the tighter the rope squeezed in on my waist. My insides were being squished together.

"*Help!*" Lenny thrashed and kicked, while I wished I could melt into the wall. I prayed that nothing else would break, or we'd have a chain reaction peeling us off the wall like the skin off a banana.

Wayne was shouting, at Lenny, to stop kicking. With the rope cutting into my guts and hanging on with a white-knuckled death grip, it took all I had just to breathe. Dizziness and nausea swept over me and if not for the bitter bile in my throat, I would have passed out.

"Stop, Lenny! Hold still! Quit kicking!" Wayne yelled, repeating it over and over until it finally registered in his brain, and Lenny hung limp. "That's it, take it easy! Don't move—you're okay!" Wayne called to Lenny. He looked up at us and yelled, "You guys hold on tight! I have to raise my foot off, okay?"

"Okay, I'm good!" Chuck shouted in reply.

I couldn't speak but nodded my head, holding on tight, gasping for air as the rope continued squeezing, cutting off my air. Wayne lifted his right foot, stretching it out to a limb encased in ice. He placed his foot on it and pushed the limb over toward Lenny. I heard cracking as the layer of ice broke off, and the limb reluctantly bent, but it didn't break. My face, pressing flat against the gorge, looked straight at Billy, who continued to sit on the stairway, just staring ahead, not paying any attention to us.

"Grab that branch, Lenny!" Wayne yelled. Lenny reached for the branch but came up short. "Come on! Grab it! You can get it."

Lenny grabbed for the branch, and my guts screamed again. On the third lunge, he caught it and pulled it toward himself. Pushing it down, he was able to get his knee on it, and after wiggling his body around, he got both knees supported on the branch. Searching for something to grasp he saw the broken branch was just out of his grasp. Putting his full weight on his knees and stretching up as far as he could, he grasped the branch below where it had broken and pulled on it. It held fast, and he pulled himself up a bit more to get both hands on the branch and raised himself enough to get his feet up under him. He was able to stand once again.

As Lenny stood, the constricting weight on my middle relaxed, and I was able to breathe, if ever so slightly. Lenny buried his face into the side of the gorge, breathing deeply—and probably praying.

"You okay, Lenny?" Wayne called.

There was a nasty gash on his ear, and blood ran down the side of his neck, but other than that, and missing a few years of his life, he seemed to be intact.

"I'm okay," he said, his voice breaking.

"Okay, everyone just relax for a minute. Lenny, you got a solid grip again?" Chuck asked.

"Yeah, I'm solid," he said.

"Kev, you okay?" Chuck asked.

"Can't breathe—can't loosen the . . ."

"Hang on, I'm coming over!" Chuck called. "You guys hold tight and don't move. I'm going over to help Kev." Chuck carefully moved over to me, and hanging on to the gorge with one hand, he began working the rope loose around my waist with the other. The knot was tight, and it took a lot of tugging and pulling to loosen it up. After what seemed forever, I was able to take in a full breath of air. My legs began shaking uncontrollably, and my feet beat out a crescendo on the branch I stood on.

"You okay?" Chuck asked. I nodded.

"Lenny, you okay? Can you move all right?" Chuck called.

"Yeah, I'm okay."

"All right, then, I'm moving back, everyone hang on," Chuck said.

Following that, we each tested our footing and handholds even more carefully as we resumed the crawl across the face of the gorge. Finally, Chuck stepped onto the stone steps. "I made it, I'm on the steps!" he called.

One by one, we each continued to work our way back to the stairway, above the blockage. Once back on the steps, I removed the rope and opened my coat and shirt. A dark ring of abrasions ran around my middle, with spots of blood scattered along its length. It had already turned an ugly maroon and dark blue color.

"That don't look good, Kevin. How do you feel?" Wayne said, looking at the injury.

"Not good, it hurts bad inside."

Lenny's ear was badly cut where it had caught on something during his thrashing around, and the blood had left a red smear, now frozen, down the side of his neck. His gloves were torn, and the underarm of his jacket had ripped out.

But we were otherwise in one piece—and twenty-five feet from freedom.

Chapter 48

We looked down at Billy. He was sitting exactly as we had left him, not moving. We lowered the rope to him, and Chuck called, "Okay, Billy, there's the rope. Go ahead and tie yourself on, and we'll pull you up." Billy didn't move.

I motioned to Chuck not to speak, and I called out, "Billy! Hey, Billy! There's the rope. We're gonna pull you up now and get out of here." Billy still didn't move.

"Aw, crap," Chuck said quietly. "What's the matter with him?"

"I think he's in some kind of shock or something," I said.

"What are we gonna do?" Wayne asked.

"Well, one of us is going to have to go down and get him." I said.

"All right!" Chuck said, "I'll go."

"You can't go." I said. "He blames you for everything that's happened. He'll freak out if you go down. I'll go."

"You can't go either," Lenny cut in. "Look at your stomach. You're not hanging on any more ropes. I'll go."

We ran the upper end of the rope around a small tree, and Lenny tied it under his armpits. He sprawled on his belly on the top of the ice blockage, and we lowered him down to the steps below.

He sat down next to Billy and talked to him in a low voice. I couldn't hear what he was saying, but Billy didn't flip out, and after a few minutes, he stood up with Lenny, who tied the rope around him. Lenny pointed up to us, while continuing to talk to Billy, who slowly nodded his head. Lenny placed both his hands on Billy's shoulders and spoke to him again. Billy nodded, faced the ice, and held onto the rope.

"Okay, Billy's ready! Pull him up!" Lenny called.

Chuck and Wayne pulled the rope, and I took up the slack from around the tree. Billy was dead weight, not even attempting to climb, but being on the ice, he slid up fairly easy.

"Gotcha, Billy. Come on—get your feet up here. That's it!" Wayne said, grabbing him by the coat and dragging him over the overhanging lip. It was more like handling a sack of corn than a person. Billy had lost his will, along with his whining; for Billy, the two went together. I never thought I'd see the day when I wished he'd whine about something. Once untied, we lowered the rope down to Lenny, and soon he was back with us too.

"What did you tell him down there?" I asked.

"Not much—just that God didn't want him to stay down here, but wanted him to go home and see his mother who was waiting for him."

Chapter 49

At last, we climbed over the top—and out of the gorge.

It seemed anticlimactic, just walking up those last few stairs, after everything we'd been through. There were no bells and whistles, no fanfare, and no celebration. When we moved, the sound of breaking glass, the ice, followed us. Not the ice under our boots but the ice that we had become. We were more ice than human. Chunks of it stuck to our pants and coats, fused together from the spray, and forming solid layers on it. Wayne's pants were hard planks from where he had gone into the river, and I felt he almost certainly had some frostbite. Lenny's ear looked awful, and his clothes were trashed. Billy wasn't anyone I knew anymore. Physically tattered and worn; his whiney expression was gone, replaced by—nothing. His eyes were vacant, empty. Billy had some serious injuries—inside his mind. For my part, I knew something wasn't right inside my middle.

Other than being physically and mentally exhausted, Chuck appeared to be okay.

We stood together, looking down at the gorge. It was different now; in fact, a lot of things were different now. It would take a long time to sort it all out—if we ever would. For each of us, the person stepping out of the gorge was a different person from the one who had stepped through that magical snow door at the Schoellkopf ruin, so few hours and so many lifetimes ago.

The river continued its eternal course, as if we had never been there. It was the sole constant in the gorge, dominating and controlling its ancient kingdom, as it had done for thousands of years. Despite my pain and bruises, I felt warmth spread across me that wasn't generated from the last rays of the sun, which were disappearing over the horizon, or from the efforts of our travels. Niagara wasn't just a river to me anymore, a name on a map, or even an address where I lived. It was something special, something living, and I was now a part of it, and would be for the rest of my life. We had done something. We had walked on the ice bridge, and we had touched the river.

No one talked. Fatigued from the struggles, drained of thought, and confused with emotions of what we had seen and done, each of us hearing too many voices, to share spoken words with one another. One day of our life—one day that had changed us forever.

We turned our backs on the river and began walking home.

Chapter 50

A chain holding a large sign, laden with ice, was padlocked across two trees:

NO ENTRANCE—STAIRWAY CLOSED
DANGEROUS ICE CONDITIONS
KEEP OUT

"No kidding, Dick Tracy," Chuck murmured. No one laughed.

"How are we gonna get home?" Lenny asked. "It's too far to walk."

Home—where we would hear the story about some people being stranded down at the Falls, and of a failed rescue attempt that didn't find them with everyone wondering who they were and what had happened to them.

Home—where we'd be indifferently asked, "What did you do today?" And we'd indifferently reply, "Nothing." But not this time, not in the condition we were in. I knew better than that. Billy's mom was not going to be indifferent on this day. Neither would Lenny's mother, when she saw his ear and coat. There would be lots of questions. Wayne would have some explaining to do and could be headed to the emergency room, if he were frostbitten. My mom was gonna want to know what happened to my mid section. I'm sure my dad was gonna have something to say about it too, especially if he had been involved with that rescue attempt. *Please, don't let him be.*

"Let's hitchhike a ride back," Wayne suggested.

"Who's gonna pick up five guys, especially the way we look? Besides, it's too cold up here to walk." Lenny's reasoning was right.

"Let's just find a phone, and I'll make a call," Chuck said.

We looked at each other, shrugged, and walked down the road. After a while, we came to a gas station that had a phone booth out front. Chuck closed the folding door, dialed, and talked to someone for a couple of minutes before coming back out.

"Okay, it's all set. She'll be here in a few minutes," he said. We wondered who "she" was, but no one asked.

The gas station had a cooler of soda pop inside. The proprietor stared hard at us and, without inviting us in, passed two bottles of Coke through the doorway after we chipped in together for them. Although the cold liquid burned our parched throats something awful, it tasted terrific.

"You fellas look pretty rough," the proprietor said. "Where you coming from?"

"Hiking," I answered for us all.

"Hmph, to hell and back, ya ask me." He went back inside his warm office, closing the door behind him. He still didn't ask us in.

We milled around, not talking much, trying to keep warm as the shopkeeper watched us from inside. With the sun down and without the protection of the gorge, the wind was brutal, and after a short time of just standing around, we were freezing when a red Chevy Impala pulled up, with Marilyn Monroe sitting behind the wheel—and this Marilyn wasn't made of snow.

"Our ride's here," Chuck said, opening the passenger door. "Guys, this is Molly."

"Hi guys, how are you doing?" She said as we all squeezed and shivered into the car. "My gosh, you guys look like horrible! Looks like you've been up to the North Pole and back!"

Not up, I thought, *down—and not at the North Pole. There was no Santa Claus where we've been.*

We sat bunched up, with the heater on full blast, wanting to feel the heat. But what should have been a pleasant feeling of warmth was one of pain and anguish as the heat slowly worked on my frozen flesh, sending needles of agony throughout my body. I couldn't imagine what Wayne must have been experiencing. During the ride back to Niagara Falls, none of us talked, while Molly kept up a steady monologue that meant nothing to us. To this day, I can't get into a car with a heater on without seeing the back of Molly's blonde head and hearing her monotonous voice, while feeling flaming needles stabbing up and down my legs.

Chapter 51

Following Chuck's directions, Molly dropped Billy off first. "Okay, Billy, you're home. See ya," we said.

Billy walked away without saying anything. He hadn't said a word since we'd left him on the stairs in the Hole. He moved like a zombie. There was going to be hell to pay, for sure. As he approached his house, he stopped and turned back to look at us. His shoulders shook; he was sobbing. I started to get out of the car, to go to him, when the front door of his house opened, and his mother rushed out. She stared at him—and then at us, as we drove off. I hoped Billy was going to be all right. I didn't think he would be.

The rest of us got dropped off together because we lived within a block of one another. We all said good-bye to Molly and painfully exited the car. Although Chuck was going with her, he got out with us.

"Well—see ya around, Chuck," I said. After everything that had happened, it felt awkward.

Chuck nodded. "Yeah, see ya around Kev." He turned to go back into the car and then stopped, turning back, "It was a heck of a ride, huh?"

"Yeah, it was, but . . ." I raised my head and for the final time that day, our eyes locked. "We did it, didn't we?"

"Yeah—we sure did kemosabe. Take care, Kev. See ya around." He got into the car, and Molly drove away.

Wayne headed over to his house, and Lenny and I turned to walk to the next street, where we lived.

"See ya, Wayne," I said. "Take care of your feet, man."

"Yeah, you too, Kev. See ya, Lenny."

"See ya, Wayne."

Wayne moved slowly, shuffling more than walking. I felt his pain with each step. The car's heater had thawed the outer layers of ice but hadn't come close to taking the cold out of our bodies—or Wayne's feet. The tire tracks protruded prominently across his frozen head. I knew he was hurting.

No jingle played. There was no music.

As Lenny and I approached his house, the door flew open and his mother came running out. It was obvious she was distraught. "Oh, thank God!" she cried. "Where have you been? Everyone's been looking all over for you boys!" She looked at Lenny in shock. "Good Lord, child! What's happened to you? Look at your clothes—you're soaking wet and you're coat is ripped!" She grabbed his arm, pulling him around. "What's that on your neck?" She asked, pushing his head to the side. "There's blood all over your neck! Good Lord, Leonard, what's happened to your ear? It's all torn! What in the world have you been doing?" Before Lenny could answer, she spun on me. "Kevin, you gotta go home right away! Your mother's at the hospital, and she's worried sick about you."

"My mom! At the hospital? What happened? Is she all right?"

"It's not your mom, Kevin, it's your father. Something happened at the Falls today. Some people were stranded down there. Something about an ice buildup, of some kind. I don't know—I don't understand it. Anyway, your father was part of a rescue team that went down to get them out."

Oh God, no! "Wha—what happened?" I stuttered. My whole body began shaking and trembling again, definitely, not from the cold this time.

"I'm not sure. They said on the news that whatever this ice thing was, it broke up, and your father was caught in it somehow and got crushed. They said it was a miracle they were able to get him out. They think the people who were down there probably got caught in it, too. Your father would have been lost, if not for Thomas Harris saving him. It's been on the radio all day. Your mother's been calling all over, looking for you, and said your father was hurt bad, and if I saw you, to have you come to the hospital right away."

My world was spinning around while she talked, the pieces all coming together. The rescue team we'd seen—the rumble Lenny had heard—the large amount of ice in the river all of a sudden. The ice bridge had broken up, just like Ol' Gordy had said. And my dad had been on it, trying to save me, and now he was hurt, because of me. My insides hurt with a throbbing, cutting pain where the rope had squeezed things together that weren't meant to be squeezed together but even without that, I felt sick, nauseated, and lost.

"I'll call ahead and tell them that you're on your way," Lenny's mother said, "and then I'll drive you to the hospital. They'll have to look at Leonard's ear there, too."

Chapter 52

The year following our walk on the ice bridge, they began installing an ice boom every winter at the mouth of the Niagara River at Buffalo. The boom held the ice in Lake Erie, controlling the amount that flowed into the river but not allowing it to clog up at the outlet and thereby limiting the ice that went over the Falls. They'd remove the boom in the spring, letting all the ice out when it was too warm to freeze over. The official reason given for the ice boom was to protect property along the shorelines, such as the Maid of the Mist docks. Unofficially, it was to keep anyone from ever going out on an ice bridge again. It effectively signaled the demise of the solid ice bridges of Niagara Falls.

So, in the end, our desire to be a part of something—destroyed it.

We didn't see much of Billy once the dust settled. There was a barrage of phone calls, reporters, interrogations and accusations that seemed to go on forever, but eventually died down, finding its place as just one more footnote in that deep reservoir of Niagara lore. Whenever I'd see his mother after that, at the store or what have you, she'd give me a hateful look and quickly move off in the opposite direction. One day, a moving van, pulled up in front of their house and the whole family left to destinations unknown.

I never heard from Billy again after leaving the gorge on that cold February day in 1962. I miss his whining and many times wonder how he is and if he's ever confronted his devils.

Wayne did, in fact, have frostbite and ended up having two toes amputated on one foot and one on the other. Actually, Wayne, Lenny, and I all ended up in the hospital before that night was over. Billy's mother took him to the hospital too, but other than having some hypothermia, his problems weren't physical. She was on the TV news afterwards, complaining about the "gang of punks" who'd had abused her son, forcibly dragging him down into the gorge against his will.

Wayne moved to San Francisco in the early seventy's. He said he needed to 'find' himself, and that was where it was warmer, and people didn't ask questions about 'ice-bridges' or anything for that matter, at someplace called Haight and Ashbury. We never lost touch with one another, and when I got discharged from the Army at the Presidio in San Francisco, I visited with him for a while. He hadn't looked well.

A few years ago, we started getting together every February 18. I don't know if it was for remembrance or remorse, but either way, it provided us some sense of closure, if not outright acceptance.

We'd meet at Marty's Market, which was now the 'Niagara's Flaming Hearth'. When Chuck and I returned from Vietnam, Ol' Gordy was seriously sick and couldn't work the store any longer, and everyone was going to the large supermarkets by then anyway. The store had been vacant for a couple of years. We bought it from Ol' Gordy and tore it down to build the restaurant, but we preserved his wall of pictures, and it's become a main attraction for locals and tourists alike. Always, there is a waiting list of reservations requesting tables in 'Ol' Gordy's Room'.

After exchanging greetings with one another and catching up on our lives, we'd share a prayer of thanks and then head into Ol' Gordy's Room. There, standing under 'the picture' (still hanging on the wall) we'd share a toast of 'bootlegger whiskey' to the memory of Ol' Gordy and to Niagara. We figured wine would work just as well and didn't think Ol' Gordy would've minded. Then we'd head over to the Falls and watch the ice spilling over the top, crashing and churning down below.

After a while, we'd drive down to the Whirlpool to watch the swirling waters with each of us silently recalling our own vivid memories of the rapids and 'Wild Wayne'. Then, onto Devil's Hole, where we'd stare at the rapids and the river continuing its same ancient dance, far below.

No matter how bad things turned out for us back in 1962, there's always a tear in my eye, and my heart beats a little faster on the eighteenth day of February.

*   *   *

Of course, Billy never attended our get-togethers, but the four of us would meet without fail. Chuck and I, being partners in the restaurant, and Chuck being the pastor of the church on the Tuscarora Reservation, still lived in Niagara Falls. Lenny would fly in from Washington, where he's been our congressman for some years now, as well as a prominent national figure in the civil rights movement. Wayne would fly in from Frisco.

*   *   *

This year, the three of us stood at the iced-over railing and stared into the swirling mist at the base of the Falls. There was still a lot of ice built up down there, but there wasn't an ice bridge, of course—that was all in the "old days" now. The ice that went over the brink and built up on the bottom was able to find its way out to the Whirlpool without many problems these days.

The Falls roared its thunder and anger at us, challenging us to come down and visit again. We had taken away its ice bridge, denying its wintry kingdom. It remembered us and had something it wanted to say to us.

I leaned against the icy railing, with the mist slowly freezing my face into a mask of shimmering frost, the same as it had those many years earlier, and stared into the turbulence, listening to the thunder—hearing the voice.

"It's calling us," Chuck said.

"I know," I replied.

"Does it remember us?" Lenny asked.

"It wants us," I answered.

"Why?" Lenny asked.

"Revenge," Chuck said.

"It's taken its revenge," Lenny said.

"Some. It wants it all—it wants us," Chuck answered.

"Why?" Lenny asked again.

"We stole a piece of it," Chuck said.

"It's immortal on this earth . . . we're not," I said.

While I spent many days now standing at the top, watching the endless plunge, I hadn't gone back down into the gorge since that February, twenty-five years ago. The tunnel at the ruins had long ago been torn down, and while I had started down the Devil's Hole stairway more than once, each time I had turned back without going too far—not past the "rock".

There's a bridge there that I can't bring myself to cross.

334

EPILOGUE

Wayne didn't come to our gathering this year—and he won't be coming in any other year, for that matter. Three days ago, he jumped off the Golden Gate Bridge.

Our prized picture of us standing on the ice-bridge of Niagara, never did hang on Ol' Gordy's wall. We have it, and who knows— maybe someday it'll find its way into a thin black frame at the end of a row.

Then again—maybe not.

I don't know whether it was an angel Chuck and I touched that day in the ice, or whether it was God touching us through Lenny.

As time passed, I wondered if there was a difference.

ACKNOWLEDGEMENT

Knowing that no man is an island, the work he produces is not his alone, but is the culmination of all parts of his life from the first word to the last letter of the final word. To that end there are many who directly or indirectly, had a part in the writing of this book and my heartfelt thanks to them all. A special thanks goes to those who have directly contributed to the work. I want to thank all those who have invested so much effort and energy into exploring and documenting the fascinating history and lore of Niagara and in giving it to us. Their work has been of incalculable value to me. Included in this group are Pierre Berton's two exceptional books, "Niagara—a History of the Falls" and "Niagara Falls—a Picture Book". I would also like to thank Ralph Greenhill and Thomas D. MaHoney for their insightful book, "Niagara" as well as "Echoes in the Mist" by Michael N. Vogel. Each of these works, in different ways has captured the majesty and spell of Niagara down through time.

This book is dedicated to all those who have witnessed the beauty and glory of Niagara, especially those courageous and hardy souls who have journeyed into the great gorge itself and have felt the power— tasted the wonder—and breathed in the mystery of the Niagara River as it continues its eternal journey across the Niagara escarpment.

Most importantly, I want to thank the Good Lord for creating the Niagara Gorge and for His direction, guidance and inspiration in producing this work through me for His edification and affirmation of His purpose in our lives.

Raised as a 'river-rat' on the Upper Niagara River, I grew up, not in awe, but in fear of the mighty Cataracts, viewing them as a threat to my Upper river escapades. More than once, I found myself and my fellow 'rats' barely escaping the swift current while tubing down the river or fishing off of Navy Island in a rubber raft. Niagara Falls was not to be marveled at or held in great esteem but was held in great fear—to be avoided at all costs.

That changed the first time I went into the gorge and "discovered" a new river. There, I was in wonder of the great canyon and consumed by the mystery of it. I saw there were two rivers, the "Upper" and the "Lower" Niagara; as different as night from day. One an open spigot, empting out the 'Great Lakes' in a roar and thunder, the other a life-force, craving across the earth, leaving a trail of beauty and attitude. Much has been written about Niagara, most about the mighty cataracts; little about the Gorge. Truly amazing, when one considers the extensive and exciting history that engulfs the lower river. My heart remains in the gorge, watching—listening to the "water".

I spent some time in the military, serving in Southeast Asia and then earned my college degrees from New York State University while raising a family in Western New York. Always enjoying a good read and with a love for writing, this story is for you and to honor our Lord's promise to protect those who put their trust in Him.as David stated in Psalms 23. It is my fervent wish that you found something of value in it. I would like very much to hear from you.

This story, I give to you and hope you enjoy reading it as much as I did in writing it. I invite you to visit my site where you'll find pictures and information about the historical stories you'll find enlightening and engaging.

Connect with DK LeVick On-Line:
Wordpress: http://dklevick.wordpress.com/
Twitter: http://twitter.com/#!/dk_levick
Email: duanelevick2011@gmail.com
Face book: http://www.facebook.com/pages/Bridges-DK-Levick/157243617667780